THERE MAY BE HEAVEN

THERE
MAY
BE
HEAVEN

Elisabeth Ogilvie

McGraw-Hill Book Company
New York · Toronto · London

ABOUT THE AUTHOR

Elisabeth Ogilvie's striking evocation of the atmosphere of the Maine seacoast that is the background of *There May Be Heaven* is no accident, for she has lived in just such an area for many years, and her love for its people and their way of life has influenced all her novels.

Her activities on Gay's Island, where she spends most of the year, include writing, gardening, and "trying not to suspect that a bear is at the door, a moose lurking in among the alders, or a horned owl hovering overhead about to bear away the cat."

She has done considerable writing of magazine fiction and children's books, and is the author of several novels, including *Call Home the Heart, The Witch Door, Rowan Head, The Dawning of the Day, Storm Tide*, and one book of nonfiction, *My World Is an Island*.

Library of Congress Catalog Card Number: 63-23461

SECOND PRINTING
47619   OCT 2 '64

THERE MAY BE HEAVEN

· I ·

The brothers were having one of those meetings Rafe was always calling when he could think of nothing better to do; at least that was what Finn thought was the reason behind the summons to the fishhouse. It was too rough to haul, Rafe had run out of traps to build and buoys to paint, and he didn't want to go home for a cup of coffee and listen to Hester, who was either yammering at him that his mother was a disgrace or that the Curtis young ones were likely to set the woods on fire. But, being Rafe, he couldn't simply visit in somebody's fishhouse and make the restful, desultory conversation of men with their work caught up and time to spare. No, he had to do some yammering of his own. Good thing he and Hester never had kids, Finn thought; poor tykes would have both ears talked right down to nubbins.... Finn yawned and leaned on the workbench and gazed through watering eyes at the pale-blue water. Snow still lay in patches on the yellow fields and in the woods on the island across the harbor, but there was a soft milky brightness in the air that was new. Damned if it doesn't *look* like April, Finn thought in pleased surprise at the discovery. Not a scrap of green grass anywhere, and the wind was cold, but it looked like April. You couldn't mistake it. He realized that he had probably noticed the phenomenon all his life but had never put it into words. And the funny thing was that if you put it into words you saw more and more, and the whole thing got sharper until the fact that it was April became so important it turned Rafe's words into just a noise going on and on. He settled his elbows more comfortably on the workbench, yawned again, and studied the luminous end of winter.

"Not keeping you up, am I?" Rafe's voice was cold. "Hate like hell to do that. Mama's infant needs his sleep."

Finn smiled at him. "Oh, don't worry about me. I get my sleep."

"Here and there," said Roy, the oldest brother, and burst into ribald laughter, joined by Finn. Finn was the biggest of the lot, rangy, big-nosed, hollow-cheeked with the leanness the others had lost, his black hair crew-cut. When Judsons laughed their eyes went into slits between cheekbones and brow. Rafe's mouth was thin with disgust; his silence a menacing caricature of patience. Cleon heaved his bulk off a nail keg and went over to stoke the oil-drum stove. He said, leisurely, "While I think of it, Finn you'd better drop that little tart before she gives you a dose."

"Or before her old man shows up down here with a shotgun and claims you're one of the ten fathers of her kid," said Rafe. "You'd be just fool enough to marry her, and then we'd have another screeching slut to add to the ones we've got already on the Point."

Roy said, "If you hauled me away from my work to listen to you lecture Finn, I'm leaving." He started to get up and Cleon waved him back, rumbling amiably, "Sit down, sit down, we got things on the agenda." He moved with a deliberate stoop and slowness as if, Finn thought, he had this picture of himself as the Wise Old Man of the Tribe. "Come on, Rafe, get to the point."

Rafe stood by the stove, trim and dandified in his L. L. Bean winter clothes. He had a naturally soft, light voice, and like it or not you had to give him all your attention if you wanted to know what he was saying. "The Abbott place has been sold," he said.

They were all instantly silent and attentive, as if a warning sound had united them in a common wariness.

"I found out this morning when I was uptown seeing Stark about my income tax," Rafe said. "I had to wait, and I could hear all the congratulations going on in there, and who should come out but old Mag and her niece and the gent who'd just handed over the check."

Finn hoisted himself up on the bench. "Summer guy?"

Rafe's small smile was deadly. "A lobsterman. No mistaking that. And you should have seen Mag's face when she saw me. She was all grins with the sweet talk he was giving her, and then her face flapped down like an old pair of pants. She hurried him out some fast. Made out she didn't know me."

"Likely afraid of what you might say," said Cleon.

"Yeah, she got the message all right. Afterwards I asked Stark who he was—didn't let on anything. He's Paul Gardner from Ballard's Island. Try laughing at that one, Sunny Jim," he said to Finn. "Another lobsterman moving in here, and one that's used to running four or five hundred traps."

"What's he moving into this gunkhole for?" Roy demanded. "I thought those fellas out there had the Promised Land. About twenty lobsterman and all God's ocean between 'em."

Rafe shook his head with slow drama. "I found out some more by asking in the right places. If he hasn't been run off Ballard's he's getting out just in time. He took on the Fergusson clan out there single-handed and like to ruined 'em before they finally got together and gave him the word."

"Talented, isn't he?" said Finn.

"Got the kind of talent we could do without," Roy said. "Let alone plastering the place with pots when they're thick as spatter now. Goddammit, there's always something."

"Wait a minute, now!" Cleon was grinning and rubbing his hands. "Go on, Rafe."

"He's coming over here from Port George tomorrow to get the lay of the land. We tell him he's not wanted, and then we make him an offer for the place and buy it. All of us."

Roy's head jerked up. "That can work both ways. If he sees we want to get rid of him so bad, he can put on a price that'll knock your eyeballs out."

"Not if he's smart, and I hear he is." Just by the new lightness and softness in Rafe's voice, one could tell how good he felt, how powerful. "Look, we don't make any threats he can take to law. But he'll know the story the minute we meet him at the wharf and ask him to step aside. He'll have to make what he can out of the deal, and believe me, he'll be glad to." Rafe lit a cigarette and smiled at his thoughts. Roy stared at the floor, Cleon watched Rafe with admiration, and Finn observed them all. Having no money to be involved, he felt pleasantly detached.

"So we buy," Roy said at last. "It's all right for you guys, with nothing to do but make money and spend it. But I can't make up my mind in a minute to put out a couple of thousand."

"We know that, we know that," Cleon said soothingly. "We know you got plenty on your back. We'll put in your share for ye, and you can pay up when you can."

"Well, you can scratch me off," said Finn. "I can't raise any money unless I get Dolly to mortgage the island."

A dark flush went quickly over Rafe's face. "She's got no right to mortgage the island! You been at her? That the only way you can figure to get yourself a decent rig? When are you going to start making and saving money like a grown man?"

"Oh, for God's sake, shut up." Finn slid down off the bench. "Nobody's mortgaging the island. You're the one who's been buttering up Mag Abbott for years, why don't you buy the place from Gardner yourself? What's with this family deal?" He grinned. "Hey, you going to start a business in it? Judson Brothers, Modern Motel and Whorehouse."

Roy laughed and Cleon's mouth twitched. Rafe said coldly, "I just happen to think it's time four brothers began working as a team to turn this all into Judson territory. We can start with this Gardner. Right now. Today. We get the place, then if any one of us wants it, he buys the others out." He shrugged. "I just happen to have a lot of family feeling, that's all."

Drained of laughter, Roy's angular face became harsh and too old for his years. He was watching Rafe through cigarette smoke, his eyes glittering under dropped lids. "That a fact? Seems like whenever you work up to family feeling it's pretty goddam expensive for the rest of us."

Rafe turned his back and stared out the window.

"You take Mag's place," Cleon explained pacifically. "If none of us wants it we can sell to some summer complaint for a damned good price. If we get a few summer people down here we can work up a business on the side, taking out fishing parties, supplying their lobsters, tending their boats in the winter. Roy, you could plow up that front field of yours and put in a big garden; you'd sell all you could raise—"

"Of course," Rafe said, silky again, as if Cleon's enthusiasm had supplied him with something the others had tried to drain from him, "nobody with any class is going to buy here once he gets a look at the Johnsons and the Curtises."

There was a thoughtful pause. Finn leaned on the bench and looked out again into the pale soft light along the wharves and fishhouses to the small huddled one Larry Johnson and Elmer Curtis shared. Elmer appeared on the wharf, lugging another new trap to add to the double row. Working, not talking, Finn thought. They can't afford to yarn around in somebody's fishhouse thinking up ways to spend money. They're knocking themselves out getting ready for the spring crawl because maybe this'll be the year they get the bathroom in, or the kid's teeth straightened, and a backlog of traps built so they'll have some decent ones on the bank if they lose half the others in a storm.

He realized then that he knew all the time what Rafe was getting at, and he was angry with the others because their silence reflected his guilt at his own. Then Roy said, "Look, I don't think we need any new fishermen here. I'll stand with you on that. But running out men that have their own property here and got their kids in school—I can't see that."

"Haven't you got vision, for God's sake?" Rafe demanded. "Can't you see this Point all Judson property the way it used to be all Salisbury land? Ever think how our father was poor white trash here once, and now we've got most of it?"

"We've got enough," said Roy. "The way taxes are, I feel like I'm personally supporting the school. Go buy out Larry Johnson if you got so much money you can afford paying the price all his relatives'll tell him to stick on his place. Larry'll be rich for once in his life and you'll have Hester out of your hair."

Rafe's skin flushed dark. "You leave my wife out of this. You know damn well that bunch is a disgrace to the Point with their rimrack old tubs in the harbor and their rotten traps on the bank, and their screeching kids. They'll never be self-supporting lobstermen, and in the meantime they make us look like Poverty Hollow down here."

Finn said amusedly, "That new string of traps Larry and

Elmer built this winter doesn't look much like Poverty Hollow to me. They're going to fix the wharf too. I hear Gil's lending them the cash."

"*That* bastard. We ought to buy him out and run our own business. Put our own man on the car and do the buying. Sweeten up the price now and then and toll them in from Pruitt's Harbor and Port George—" His eyes took on a blue shine, his soft voice was weaving spells. Roy shattered them like a booted foot coming down through a spider web.

"I got no more time for this goddam foolishness," he said. "Sure, our father was one of those who came here like Larry and Elmer, with nothing. Now we each got a decent place, a good boat, and you with a new one abuilding. We own most of the shorefront, and there's the island over there worth fifteen or twenty thousand or more to some rich summer guy. Now why in hell can't you leave things be?"

"Mebbe this is the wrong time to talk about money," Cleon said quickly. "End of a bad winter and all, and Roy's got extra expenses this year." He cleared his throat. "But hell, it's no harm dreaming a little, is it?"

"I'm not dreaming," Rafe snapped. "We've got to look out for ourselves."

"And we will, we will," Cleon soothed, wagging his head, making calming gestures with his big hands. "Roy knows what you're getting at. We got to operate as a clan. If we stick together—and I'm not talking about money now, I'm talking about the *moral* side of it—four brothers, and your boy's growing up all the time Roy, so that makes another one of us—why, hell, there ain't nothing we can't accomplish! Of course, that means each of us has a duty to the rest."

Cleon looked at Finn, who grinned. "What I do now?"

"I can't name it offhand," said Cleon, "but mind your failings anyhow. Every Saturday night I wonder if you're getting some little tramp in trouble. Why in hell can't you start sparking a *good* girl, and marry her, and start acting like a solid citizen?"

"I don't know," said Finn. "I guess I got naturally low tastes."

"That's the trouble with you guys!" Rafe erupted. "Roy's scared of spending an extra dollar, and you're this big clown—everything's funny, you got no feeling for anything *real*. If we

· 8 ·

ever did decide to pull together and get rid of Elmer and Larry, you'd be playing cards with 'em that night and telling 'em to watch their gear."

"I guess I feel at home with the poor white trash," said Finn, "on account of our father being that when he came here."

"And he was when he left," said Rafe. "It's no thanks to him that we've got what we've got."

Roy straightened up from the workbench and started toward the door. "Ah, you turn my stomach," he said. "If there's a war on when you're fifty-five, you won't have the guts to go and enlist. No, you'll be organizing a goddam black market and getting fat, while my kids and Larry's are getting killed."

"Pa only went to get out of here!"

"How do you know?" Finn asked. "Might be he felt patriotic. You wouldn't, but maybe he did." He started to follow Roy.

"Stop making him a hero!" Rafe yelled at them, his voice was congested. "Stop—"

"Simmer down," Cleon advised him. "Don't get fighting over the old man. My God, this is what happens every time. Can't we ever get together on anything?"

"But he wasn't a hero," Rafe protested. "He skinned out of here and left a wife and four kids, and he didn't have to. Maybe she was cutting up, but there was *us*—"

"He sent home more money than he ever made lobstering," Cleon said. "We got to be fair."

"Then stop making some kind of saint out of him. He went off to have a damned good time and he did till the minesweeper blew up. I'll bet he was laughing when it happened."

"I hope he was," said Finn. "I hope to God he was." He went out behind Roy into the cold sweet air and the pale gilt light over the yellow slopes to the shore, the chatter of chickadees in the spruces. "Rafe always gets so chewed up about Pa," he said. "Chewed up about everything. Why can't he relax and enjoy life?"

"Could you, married to Hester?" said Roy. "She's told him so many times what a favor she did him by marrying him he almost believes it himself. He was her last chance, if you ask me, but tell him that and he'd slit your gullet." He sighed heavily. "Well, I got to get up to the house and clean up. I'm going to Augusta this afternoon."

"How is she?" Finn didn't want to ask about Roy's wife, but he had to; if you didn't ask it was like deserting her somehow.

"Better," Roy said. It was what he always said.

"Well, give her my love. Hey, wait a minute. Come on down to Gil's and I'll get her some candy and cigarettes."

· 2 ·

It wasn't until after Claire Carradine got into the store on the wharf, and Gil Murray invited her to take a chair by the stove, that the reaction hit her, and for a moment she was panicky for fear the tears would show in her eyes and the trembling in her hands. Now don't, now don't, she told herself as if she were calming her child. One vicious woman when the rest were so nice, even the ones who couldn't give. Is she so important...

Gil was rumbling on. "Calendar says April but the wind's still got teeth in it. Freezing overhead and mud underfoot.... Dunno why they have all these drives this time of year, everybody's feeling poor."

"I know it," she said, "and I feel apologetic asking. But people are so decent. That blond girl who lives next to you said she didn't have a dime, but she wanted me to have some coffee."

"Ayuh, Josie's good-natured. Friendly as a speckled pup." He gave her a dollar and she said, "Oh, *thank* you," and began to fill out a receipt for him. Her hand felt shaky and she said with an unsteady laugh, "I hope you can read this."

"I don't have to. I know I gave ye the money." He went back to his desk in the corner where two windows gave him separate views of the harbor. It was quiet in the store except for the spruce chunks snapping in the stove and a faint sound of water underneath the floor, rippling around the cribwork. The sun slanted across the floor in narrow rectangles. She wished she could sit here indefinitely, listening to the hush and letting it soak into her. She felt fragile and bruised, the encounter with the woman at the turn of the road had left a physical soreness in her flesh. I was never like this before David died, she thought; it's as if that wound turned me into one huge scar that always wants to ache.

The lobster buyer sucked on his pipe and his ancient swivel chair creaked as he settled back in it and studied the papers. He was a pudgy middle-aged man with pale reddish hair and eyebrows and quick light-blue eyes. Claire liked him because he was too busy to talk at her or to fidget because she still sat there. She began to feel calmer. Her mind skimmed over peaceful things, the blue harbor beyond the windows, the mist rising above the island woods. It went on to touch lightly over the schoolroom where her child was, and to her great-aunt's house where the strong ticking of the clock marked off more than the seconds of an earthly measure of time, had powerful intimations of eternity. She hoped the man who bought the place would take the grandfather clock too, and keep it there in the same place.

The swivel chair creaked, papers rustled, an empty pipe was sucked. She looked dreamily at a Linen Thread calendar and thought how long it had been since she had simply sat like this and how peculiar it was that she had chosen this place and this moment to do it in. She was a pale young woman with a faint pink flush on her cheekbones from the heat of the woodstove, her tweed coat pushed back from her shoulders, her hands lying idle on the manila envelope in her lap. Her dark hair was combed back casually, curling around her ears and falling lightly over a wide forehead; she looked too thin, which made her aquiline features seem more aquiline and yet there was a gentleness about them, a mildness in the width across the eyes, and a general air of almost-timidity.

Suddenly she heard heavy feet on the planks outside, the sliding door was thrust open, and two men in rubber boots and heavy clothes came in. She got up quickly, catching awkwardly at her sliding material, feeling the heat deepen in her cheeks.

"Don't hurry," Gil said. "Here's two you ought to nab while you can."

The older man gave her a preoccupied nod, the other grinned. There was a strong resemblance between them, as if they were father and son. "My gosh," said the young one. "Those Jehovah's Witnesses get better-looking all the time."

"I'm afraid I'm nothing so exciting," she said. "I've got Saltberry Point for the cancer drive."

"Wouldn't you know it?" he groaned. "Good-looking girl shows up and she's after money."

"She didn't just show up," said Gil, tilting back in his chair. "If you weren't so busy sky-hooting all over town you'd know who she is—Mag Abbott's niece. Mrs. Carradine, Roy Judson's the hard-bitten one with the cold eye, and Finn Judson's the other. Playboy of Saltberry Point."

The playboy's smile was uncomplicated; he liked the world, and she was part of it, no separate thing to be appraised and speculated upon. She felt at ease now, and said, "Well, that's a sort of distinction, isn't it?"

"Depends on what you call distinction," said Roy Judson. He brought out a wallet and began picking over the bills in it.

"I'm not asking anybody for anything. I know it's a poor time of year. But they wanted someone to go around the Point and Aunt Mag volunteered me."

"Ayuh, I can hear her." Finn began to laugh. "Told you the fresh air'd do you good, and you'd get to meet folks."

"Well, I guess the fresh air part was right, but I haven't found many people home this morning except two awfully nice girls with about ten children between them, and"—she stopped short, remembering what she's almost forgotten, and looked down quickly, feeling heat in her face—"one Mrs. Judson."

"Mrs. Rafe," said Finn. She glanced at him sidewise and he gave her a small smile, as one gives to reassure a child. It made him older for an instant.

"I know you never got any money from her," said Finn. "She thinks it's all a bunch of rackets. And Roy's wife's away, and Onni's probably on the road somewhere. That's Mrs. Cleon. Look, I'll give you a dollar each for Rafe and Cleon. Got a dollar of my own here somewhere, too."

"Gorry, he's well-heeled," Gil said. "Somebody better grab him."

They all laughed. "So you're Mag's niece, huh?" said the older brother. His glance of absent appraisal didn't bother her; he had other things on his mind beside curiosity.

"Step-grandniece, really. I'm helping her get ready to move."

"We just heard she'd sold the place," said Roy. "You looking for a lot of new business, Gil?"

Gil sucked tranquilly on the empty pipe. "If you mean did I make up Mag's mind for her, I didn't."

"Oh, nothing's the matter with Mag's mind. Just wondered why she settled on this one, that's all."

Finn hunched his big shoulders over the candy case. "I'll take that box of Bolster Bars. Helen always liked them. And that carton of Tareytons. How much I owe ye, Gil?"

Gil figured. Claire wrote out receipts for all the Judsons and gave them to Finn, who said solemnly, "I'll see that Rafe and Cleon get theirs. They'd hate awful to lose a chance to take something off their income tax."

"In that case maybe they'd like to contribute more," Claire said, and felt the pleasure of accomplishment when he laughed. Roy nodded at her, said "Glad to meet you," and went out and down the wharf. She gathered her materials firmly and said, "Well, I guess it's time to start for home."

"You know the short cut, to save you going around by the road?" said Finn. "Come on, I'll show it to you. I'll lug your stuff."

"Won't do any good to say you know the way," said Gil. "He'll show it to you anyway." She found herself laughing again, easily and youthfully, as if she had no cares. She felt years older than the boy and thus at ease with him. The fact that he knew nothing about her meant that he wasn't sorry for her, and that gave her a sense of airiness and freedom. Nothing could minimize David's death; but not to see it, framed by pity, in the eyes of this young man who tramped through the rotting snow beside the path gave her a curious relief.

"I hope Mag isn't going to clear out right off," he was saying. "I'd like you to see the Point when spring really busts out. You never saw so many birds. You have thrushes where you come from? Over on the island they come and stay all summer. Sound some pretty at dusk and early in the morning. You ever see woodcock courting? They've already started over there. I could row you over some evening."

"I'd love that," she said. "No, I don't think Aunt Mag will hurry away. There's the accumulation of ages in that house. . . . He's coming over from Port George late tomorrow afternoon to take a look around, but he told her she wasn't to hurry herself. . . . I would like to see spring here," she added. "I wouldn't even mind winter." She meant it. The silence and space were like balm.

"Well, now," said Finn. "You'd ought to marry you a fisherman. Oh, I forgot, you're married already. What's your husband do?"

She kept her eyes on the luminous harbor and said, "He was an accountant. He died last year." She turned and started along the path again.

"Hey, I'm sorry," said Finn. "I guess everybody's got their troubles, huh? My father got himself blown up in the war. And Roy, there, his wife's up in the state hospital at Augusta. Mag told you that, most likely."

"Aunt Mag hasn't told me much about anybody," she said truthfully. "She's been in such a flutter about selling the place. She's talked more about the past and Uncle Ralph."

"Hi, Finn!" a small child's voice called and they looked up. Two of them tumbled in the snow like small shapeless gnomes in their heavy clothes, and Nell Johnson was hanging diapers on the lines strung between the spruces in her back yard. "My God, Finn, you're a fast worker!" she shrieked.

His cheekbones rose when he laughed, his eyes went into shining slits. "You just found that out?" he called back. A small skinny young man, with a bright-eyed lantern-jawed face, came out of the fishhouse on the other side of the path and said, "I'll thank ye not to carry on in public with my wife."

"You know Larry Johnson yet?" Finn asked Claire.

"No, but I've had coffee with his wife and Mrs. Curtis." Another young man came out, moon-faced and smiling, high-colored, so that with his corncob pipe he had an irresistably comic jack-o-lantern effect. The two were introduced and spoke with the soft-voiced politeness she'd come to expect here. "No trouble getting my boy up schooldays now," Elmer Curtis told her. "Always hated school but now he says 'I got to hurry for the bus so I can sit beside Nancy.'"

"If he ain't just like his old man," said Larry.

"Starting even younger than me," said Elmer with modest pride. "I swear, these kids scare the devil out of me. If I liked a girl I never told anybody. Not in the first grade anyway. But now they *brag*."

"It's this atomic age," said Larry. "And this here Finn's influence, if you ask me. Kids all want to be like him." He waved an arm and shouted warningly at the children. "You young ones keep that sled up there in the yard. What I tell ye about coming toward the shore? . . . No wonder I'm going gray young."

"This is a wonderful place," said Claire. "I could stand in the sun all day and talk, but Aunt Mag will be calling up everybody to find out if I'm swamped in a mudhole. It's been nice meeting you," she said to the men.

"Be neighborly now," said Larry.

"Ayuh, us parents ought to get together," said Elmer, "seeing as our kids are going steady on the school bus."

Claire laughed. She called up across the slope to Nell and started along the path. Finn came behind her. As soon as a ledgy rise separated them from the fishhouse, and the short second growth hid the houses behind them, he said, "I didn't know you had children."

"One," she said. "She's six. . . . Tell me about your brother's wife."

"Sometimes she's good, sometimes she's bad. They had a boy drowned last year, hauling traps from a dory, and it seemed as if something went in her all at once. Maybe it'd been coming on, with her age and all. It's hell—hard on Roy. They've got this other boy, and they won't let him be a fisherman. They want him to go to college and get out of here."

"I can understand that," she said. "You were getting the candy and cigarettes for her, weren't you?"

"Helen and I always got along good. When I was a kid I'd board there when my mother was away working. Our place is over on the island." They stopped and looked out across the old Abbott wharf and the narrow channel of blue water. She saw the white house on the high part of the island, facing out to sea, the winter-black spruces climbing a hill beyond it. Behind the house bare alders were like a bank of purple smoke pierced here and there with the white intricacies of birches.

"There in the alders," he said. "That's where the woodcock are."

"And where are the thrushes?" she asked.

"They'll be in the deep woods when they come," he said. Suddenly she thought of thrushes singing in the deep woods, with a wild longing like pain, and she was frightened by the rush of feeling. She said quickly, "I see the old road. I guess I can find my way to the house from here. Thank you for showing me the footpath."

He didn't say anything as she turned away, and she felt she'd been clumsy and schoolgirlish, and she turned back and saw him standing there on the ledge, young and long-legged, his hands hanging by his sides, watching her with an absent and rather kindly expression. "It was nice meeting you," she said. "My first encounter with the Judsons wasn't very successful." She smiled. "You and your brother saved the day."

"When can I row you over to the island?" he said. "You can bring young Elmer's girl friend if you want."

The awkward moment had gone, and she felt a positive gratitude; since David's illness and death she had felt inept and untalented with people, as if an essential part of her were missing. She said, "When would be the best time for you?"

"Tomorrow after she gets home from school?" Then something crossed his face and he said, "No, not tomorrow. How about next day, after I get in from hauling? I'll walk up to the house and fetch ye."

"I'll be looking forward to it," she said. "Good-by now. Or Aunt Mag will be calling the Coast Guard."

Saltberry Point had once been called Salisbury Point, for its first white owners; it had not been named, as Hester Judson maintained when she was proving that the Salisburys had come late as squatters driven out of someone else's grant down the coast, simply for a variety of wild berry, once growing where the tide could reach it.

For a long period that bridged the time between the historical past and the first world war, the Point was reached only by water. At first one traveled from there to another community by pink or wherry, then by mail packet, and eventually aboard the small steamer that worked up and down the coast between Rockland and Boothbay. Even after the wagon road was cut through the woods, the steamer still did a good business. When the road became macadam and summer places began to appear in town, the Point still maintained its insular integrity. In the present day a Pointer might drive to Limerock in the morning, shop at the new supermarket, or deposit his money at the drive-in window of the First National Bank; but when he drove home in the afternoon, entered the woods, and came out to a view that had not changed for the white man since Richard Salisbury took possession of his grant in 1628, he became consciously or unconsciously an islander.

Saltberry Point was a part of the town of St. Andrew, and often contributed a selectman, an assessor, or a member of the school board; but every so many years the Point sensibilities would be bruised at a town meeting, and a movement would arise like a third wave among a few who wanted to secede and make the Point a town by itself. The wave was always spent before it reached shore, but at the same time it managed to be always there, like the woodlots that old Hattie Salisbury Murray and Mag Salisbury Abbott would never sell; they walled off the Point like a private forest.

The Salisburys had persisted with remarkable vigor for several hundred years. Richard and his sons maintained such good relations with the Indians of the region that the Point and the island across from it were left untouched by the wars that devastated the rest of the coast. Local Indians helped Captain Walter Salisbury man his fort against red and white invaders from Canada. Baron Castin found the place insignificant anyway, and after a brief look passed it by for more blood and scalps to the westward.

Salisburys and their septs fought in the Revolution, and the survivors came back to commence what they hoped was an eternity of peace. According to their various notions of what was fitting, they built square stately houses or the lowposted story-and-a-half sort, all with oaks and elms around the doors and orchards behind, the wind broken by the spruce wall to the north, and the salt air giving a milder winter than could be found ten miles inland.

Most of the houses along the road to the Point were built by these men, and on the Point proper there remained Mag Abbott's square house with its big carriage house across the road. Only the ghosts of horses were nostalgically evident on the hot summer day; now old Abbott's two pet dories filled the main floor. The Murray homestead on a rocky rise as one came down the hill to the Point was one of the old ones; the low house above the inlet, where Rafe Judson now lived, was another. It had been built by a Clark who'd married a Salisbury and started a boatyard on the shore of the inlet, sending ships into the West Indies trade. He and his sons made a small fortune in salt cod, barrels, and shakes cut from the family woodlot, and the two sons built the twin houses halfway down the harbor now owned by Cleon and Roy Judson. These had started modestly enough, but later generations added wings and gables and gingerbread until, whenever the houses were freshly painted, they glittered with spurious splendor against the woods, looking as giddily artificial as wedding cakes beyond the weatherbeaten reality of fishhouses, wharves, and piles of lobster traps.

The last good crop of sons had appeared in time for the Civil War. Three had survived, but had fathered daughters as plentifully as their fathers and grandfathers had brought forth sons. Gil Murray was the last direct male survivor of the Salisburys, through his mother; and there was Mag Abbott left alone and apparently as indestructible as old oak since her cousin Hattie had died two years ago. The twin heirs to the island farm died in Libby Prison at the age of seventeen. With its sheep and its carefully tended woodlots, its fields cleared by long, patient endeavor, the island went through a succession of owners who lived there only to fish, and let the bay and alders and junipers steal the fields. It was inherited at last by someone on the West Coast who never came to look at it, and was finally bought at a tax sale by a veteran Grand Banks fisherman from Jonesport. He had married late and wanted to raise his family away from the corrupting influences of moving pictures, automobiles, and the Turkey Trot.

Naturally, not one of the boys became a fisherman. They all left home as soon as they could. There was a young daughter, a gay and amiable creature who sighed at the dullness of the Point during the first world war with all the young men gone. One of her brothers came home on leave from the Navy with a gangling, grinning, black-haired boy from Aroostook. It was summer, Jud was an authentic hero, and in spite of his big hands and feet and bashful smile, he was a romantic; suddenly Dolly found the island unbearably beautiful, and in no time at all Roy was on the way. Dolly's father happily rushed the two into marriage. He had been fearing something like this for a long time and was glad to meet it head-on. Besides, Jud was a decent boy, and he liked the island so well there seemed no possibility of his taking Dolly and departing by the steamer for high life in Limerock.

Jud, the romantic, sometimes spoke of the dead twins as if their spirits still roamed the island, hunting squirrels, digging for arrowheads, and fishing from an old dory. "Seems like there was meant to be boys here one way or another," he said. "Because why do we keep shucking 'em out?" He was indulgent when his boys were late for meals or chores. "It's their kingdom. They should know every inch of it."

Lobstering was poor between the wars, and Jud was never

a very good lobsterman anyway, even though he was enthusiastic about it, and went out in all weathers in his little decked-in dory with its one-cylinder Palmer. Dolly was still gay and amiable but made restless by the lack of money. Eventually she began taking jobs around town. She was a good practical nurse and found all the work she could handle, as far away as Limerock. She was always good-tempered with Jud and his unworldliness, but she was even better-natured when she began making money of her own. She spent it generously on Jud and the boys; on her days off she hurried home to bake, clean house, wash and iron and mend, and enthrall them with her experiences.

Jud seemed not to resent her absences. He cooked for the boys with enjoyment and some skill, and always got them off the island in time for school in the morning. He enjoyed their company but didn't fret when they were away from him on their own affairs, which happened more and more as the older boys found out they could earn money by making themselves useful over on the Point. The summer Roy was twelve he went lobstering with Old Abbott, baiting pots and plugging lobsters. Cleon was nine and tending out on Gil Murray's mother, who took summer boarders. He carried food and water to the chickens, gathered eggs, learned how to kill a hen, picked strawberries.

Rafe was too young to hire out, though he rowed his old skiff from one end of the harbor to the other asking for jobs.

"I'll take you on as my hired man, Rafe," his father told him. "A quarter a week. But you'll have to earn it, mind ye."

"I'll earn it," said Rafe. He scrubbed the old dory every day when they came in from hauling, and fussed about painting her until Jud bought paint he couldn't afford and gave Rafe a free hand with it. The older boys were shocked to see half the paint slopped on the beach rocks, but Jud said mildly, "Only way for the boy to learn. Besides, he's ambitious."

"He can't be Jud's, then," someone said on the Point, and everybody laughed, but not maliciously. It was impossible not to like Jud all the more because he could be looked down upon for letting his wife go off to live her own life, and for showing more excitement about an Indian ax the kids found or the size of the cabbages he raised, than driving himself to make every cent he could. His sons heard and half-understood the cryptic remarks about Jud.

That summer Dolly was working in a nursing home in Limerock. She came home all at once in July, to stay. The boys were delighted at first. Then, late one night when they should have been asleep, for the first time in their lives they heard their father speak to their mother in a strange voice choked with passion as if by tears; a terrifying voice, all the more so for speaking incomprehensible words.

"*It's not mine,*" he said. "But you want me to claim it, is that it? Good God in heaven, haven't you rubbed my nose in it enough already?"

There was nothing more after that outburst. The three boys lay tensely listening under the steep-pitched chamber roof, and fell asleep after a long while. In the morning everything was so much the same that they might have dreamed the outcry, except that each saw it in the others' half-guilty glances. What was it, they wondered, that Ma had rubbed Pa's nose in? They couldn't figure it out.

There was a baby born that fall, a girl, and the boys jealously expected that Pa would be foolish with happiness over it, he always made such a fuss about other people's girl babies. But the baby died. The night he came home from the hospital and told them about it his eyes were sunk deep in his head, and the skin stretched tight and shiny over suddenly sharpened bones. He looked old; the boys watched him with awe. Roy and Cleon had known their mother was carrying, but in some odd way the baby hadn't seemed to be an actual fact. Roy felt he should be sorry, but this was all mixed up with shame, revulsion, and curiosity.

"It's too bad," Jud kept saying, shaking his head. "Poor little thing. Through no fault of her own. Almost feel like it's my fault. God does strange things to punish us. . . . Your mother's all right, though," he assured the boys. But they could not imagine Dolly being otherwise than all right.

Dolly had less than her usual bounce when she came home, and her eyes looked strange. She blamed it on eyestrain and wore dark glasses for a time. She didn't go back to work, and the boys settled down. The next disruption in their lives was the fantastic offer made by a rich yachtsman who spent a weekend in the harbor and fell in love with the island. The boys could not imagine anyone wanting to give so much money for it, but they were eager to take it even though they considered the man unbalanced.

But Jud turned down the offer in a grandly offhand manner. The sons looked at him in despair and went to their mother. "Here's his chance to pay all his bills," Roy pleaded, "and start off with everything brand-new, not had the guts kicked out of it by everybody and his brother before it gets handed down to us. And he says no to this feller as if we had oil wells."

"It's not your father's fault he wasn't born with a silver spoon in his mouth," Dolly said. "He's certainly got the manner for it. And as long as we have the island he feels like landed gentry."

"And we feel like trash," said Cleon.

"Ayuh, pure trash," young Rafe echoed, and his mother laughed and pulled him to her bosom.

"You're too young to feel like trash. You don't know what it's like. You're my blue-eyed baby and you're supposed to be happy. You've got a nice home and your ma and pa love you."

"Ayuh, but why can't Pa have a decent string of traps?" he argued. "And that weeny little old boat! *I'm* going to have one that'll dig up the harbor when I go through, like Gil Murray's, and everybody'll have to look out! I won't even slow down for anybody like Gil does!"

"You do that, honey," Dolly told him. "You just do that. All of you do big things, but don't keep after your pa because he's not that kind. He had to get away from home because they was always carting it to him that he was a no-good, and it's kind of hard lines to have his own kids acting the same way."

"Oh, gorry, we *like* Pa!" Roy was shocked. "He's the finest kind when it comes to some things."

"Yep, Pa knows an awful lot for somebody that never had much schooling," Cleon said. Even at ten he could sound tolerant and elderly.

"Well, you just remember those things he's finest at, and all the stuff he's got in his head, and figger that if he was one of those go-getters like his brother Rafe, he wouldn't be half the father he is to you. He wouldn't have the time. Your Uncle Rafe's boy ran away from home because he thought his father wouldn't even miss him."

Rafe said importantly, "Anyway, I tell all the kids my uncle I'm named for has a lot of money."

Dolly's robust guffaw blossomed warmly around them. "Don't be too sure of that, darlin'. It's likely to be all tied up in hay."

Dolly sometimes worked by the day around the Point, helping out when somebody came home from the hospital, papering and painting, even cooking for Mrs. Murray's summer boarders. But she never took a job that kept her away from home at night. Three years after the birth and death of the baby girl, Finn was born.

Jud and Dolly were like a young couple with their firstborn; the others found it hard to believe that their arrivals had occasioned the same excitement. Besides, it was shameful for people that old to be doing such things. Roy and Cleon went off to school with long Judson jaws thrust out hard, their ears strained for jibes. Rafe claimed that he was too sick to go to school and stayed home for a week, watching his mother and the baby. "You never fed me like that," he accused her.

"Of course I did! You can't remember, naturally."

But he was sure she was lying. After a period of brooding, he asked Jud, "Does my Uncle Rafe live in the same place?"

"I guess so, boy. Why?"

"Did his boy ever come back?"

Jud burst out laughing. "You figger on going up and being his boy?"

Rafe walked out without answering. The next day he was ready to go back to school, and after that he tried to live as if the baby weren't there. "Why couldn't it have died, like the other one?" he asked Cleon.

"I dunno," said Cleon. "We damn sure don't need him. Pa acts like this is the crown prince and we're this bunch of numbheads he's had to put up with till now."

"Oh, shut up," Roy snapped at them. He was trying to study, and he hated going to high school in Williston. He begrudged every hour spent away from the Point, and lived only for the day when he could go lobstering full time. "It's only because they're so old that they're so foolish about him. They'll likely make a proper fool of him and spend money on him that should be spent on gear. But he's here and he's our brother."

"I heard some snickering on the lobster car yesterday," said Cleon. "Bart Collins said he knew now what Pa was doing when he was so late getting out to haul."

"So that's what you're doing, standing around with your ears flapping when you're supposed to be getting my bait."

"I don't care, I hate that brat," said Rafe.

"Hey, Roy, I bet if *he* wants Pa to sell the island, Pa'll do it faster than you could spit through a knothole," said Cleon.

"Hey, Roy," said Rafe, "do you know if Uncle Rafe's boy ever came back?" When Roy ignored him, scowling at his books, he asked Cleon the same question and Cleon said, "Oh, Jesus, you're another one we could've done without."

·4·

Finn remembered his father very well, though not as a well-known face or clearly defined form. *Pa* was a word that meant many things: shrieks of laughter as you went up to the ceiling and the joyous certainty of being caught by hands like steel; it meant knees you stood between while you tried to get your fingers curved around the oar handles. It meant the queer way a voice rumbled under a clean-smelling flannel shirt if you leaned your head against it. In a perfectly natural way *Pa* signified coming suddenly upon a place in the woods that was blue with long-stemmed violets; and being stopped in another place and held hard by the shoulder to let a disobedient partridge chick run across the path. *Pa* stood for the importance of counting the crabs that went into one basket and the lobsters into another, and the almost explosive happiness of being allowed to steer. *Pa* was a word that conveyed the exact atmosphere of waking in the night, the pad of heavy bare feet in the dark, the beam of the flashlight turning the room strange, the mug of water held to your lips, the pat that you needed to tip you back into sleep again.

He thought of his father when he told the girl about the thrushes in the deep spruce woods. On the winter afternoon before his father went away they had taken a walk over the ridge of the island to the heaviest woods, and had sat on a log in a sunny cutting. The young spruces were bright green in the sunshine and the highland cranberry vines covering the ground had a rich and shiny look. Finn was five. "No thrushes this afternoon," he said.

"No, not till next spring," Pa said. "If I'm not here, you listen to 'em for me, son. Listen hard. Thrushes and white-throats make the finest music in the world."

"I like gulls in the morning," said Finn. "And the mackerel gulls, when they come. And the medricks hollering."

"Ayuh, they're fine too," said Pa, putting his arm lightly around the boy, not enough to hold him fast.

It was a long time before he could get used to Jud's being gone. Going to the first grade helped; it was as if he had already lived one life and now was beginnig another in which he went out from the house every morning like a man and crossed the Gut with Cleon and Rafe to board the school bus over on the Point. Roy went away that year, and since Roy liked him better than either Cleon or Rafe did—at least, he thought dryly in adulthood, Roy was better able to tolerate him—he missed Roy.

Then Roy came home on leave, a severe and impressive stranger in his Marine greens, and Dolly cried when she saw him. This in itself was an astonishing event, and shook Finn without his knowing why. To see Dolly, the strong and gay, clinging to Roy and making great gulping noisy sobs was like having the island vanish from under his feet. He went down to the big cove that opened on the ocean side of the island to meet Rafe and Cleon when they came in from hauling.

"Roy's here," Finn said, "and Ma's crying."

Rafe sat on the gunnel of the old dory, scoop in hand, and regarded him with a curious expression, almost smiling, though his lips were turned into a thin line. "Want to know why?" he asked.

Cleon, carrying a bucket of baitbags up the beach, stopped and looked back.

"Why?" said Finn.

"Because Pa's dead," said Rafe, keeping his blue eyes fixed on Finn. "He's deader'n a mackeral. He's all blown to pieces."

Finn stared at him. "*Jesus,*" Cleon gasped. "You wasn't supposed to tell him."

"I didn't hear you stopping me." Rafe didn't look away from Finn. "Well, what do you think of that, Little Lord Fauntleroy? You're no better'n the rest of us now."

Finn still gazed, motionless, and Cleon said nervously, "Hey, Finn, are you all right? You having a fit or something?" He glanced up at the house.

"Oh, he's all right," said Rafe, tossing a dead crab out into the sunlit water. "Kids don't take in anything anyway."

Finn got up without speaking and went away from them, going around the shore over the rocks, climbing, jumping across chasms, sliding down the familiar places. He went around the fishhouse beach over the wet rockweed. He crawled up a steep slippery slant of dark-red rock, reached the lichened ledges among the bay bushes, and went into the woods. He walked a long way until he came to the cutting, all bright now with new leaves on the young hardwoods, and noisy with birds. It was a great surprise to find that the thrushes had come back even if Pa wasn't there.

On this April morning seventeen years later Finn reviewed the scene without anger. Rafe was a son of a bitch even then, he thought dispassionately. But what the hell, I lived through it. . . . The recollection had taken him back along the footpath by the fishhouses, but nobody hailed him now; it was dinnertime and in the sunny silence the sparrows chirped loudly as they hopped in and out of the new traps. The children's sleds lay askew on heaps of melting snow. Gil came out of his store, hooked the padlock through the hasp, and left it hanging there open as a sign he'd gone home to dinner. He trudged up the muddy slope toward his house. It was a comfortable solid building of no particular period or style, built where the dirt road curved in from the black one. His cat came off the back steps to meet him, Gil spoke to her, and together they went inside.

Rafe and Cleon stood in the open doorway of Rafe's fishhouse. They were watching Finn approach, and he grinned. They'd seen him with the girl, of course, and Rafe must have guessed who she was. It was a good thing Finn hadn't let her go to the fishhouse. Rafe could be honey-tongued with women when he chose, but today he wouldn't have chosen, and you could tell this was a girl who couldn't look out for herself. She had a kind of gentle way with her, and a trick of glancing up as if she weren't sure what was going to happen next. Losing her husband must have knocked all the gimp out of her, if she'd had any to begin with.

He swung an arm at his brothers and turned down onto Gil's wharf. When he appeared beyond the store Cleon shouted at him. "Come here a minute!"

"Can't stop!" He waved again and ran down the ramp and onto the float. He rowed his skiff down the harbor with short quick strokes. In the hush he heard the door of Rafe's fishhouse slam, and he smiled, then looked over his left shoulder to where the chimneys of Mag's house showed between the tops of spruces and birches. He imagined the girl going in among all the ancient things, her quick half-smiling, half-shy glance touching them, the mild voice answering Mag. He wondered what Mag would say to her about him. That was all right, he assured himself; Mag liked him. He took her a mess of clams now and then, or a bag of shore greens, and she'd say, "Now you don't have to do that. You know you're like your father? Many's the hod of clams he's brought us when Raph's back got so bad. And the nice fish. Never went handlining without remembering us."

Sure, that was all right. If she didn't change her mind after tomorrow afternoon when Gardner showed up. Well, she's got her money, he argued, it's no skin off her nose unless he tries to get it back, claims the place was misrepresented. But she never wanted Rafe to have it. What'd she have against him anyway, old honey-tongue sweet-talking Rafe? What was the difference between him and anyone else, what did it matter to her, now that she was so old, like a dry leaf you could crush to powder in your hand? There was something halfway frightening about so much passion in a thing so fragile, only a breath away from dying....
Cold touched Finn's back under his shirt, delicately like a small prying draft of winter, and he rowed harder. He saw the girl's

face turning chill and pale, gazing through him. Goddam, he thought angrily, there's one thing we don't need around here and that's a thieving lobsterman, never mind all the rest of Rafe's bull. . . . His oars shattered the calm of the water, and he reached his own wharf with a thump against the spilings.

Well, I'll try, he thought. Maybe I can get the girl over here before she hears about it.

This time of the year there was no point in going to haul every day. Lobstering wasn't good, and sometimes a day's gas outbalanced a day's haul. But if the traps were heavily baited and allowed to lie over, a man with a decent string of gear set far enough out could bring in enough lobsters to make a few dollars.

On the morning of the day Gardner was expected, Finn rose early and brought his boat in alongside the island wharf and began to put his bait aboard. He lowered each bucket of stuffed and juicy bags to the stern of his boat by the hoist on the corner of the wharf, then went down the ladder and unhooked the rope, went up the ladder and hauled back the rope and hooked on the next bucket. The sun wasn't up yet and the air was still and cold, but there was a gold wash over the sky beyond the black rise of the eastern woods; the gulls were coming in, one signaling another with long cries, and a clatter of crows rose like the sounds of a barroom brawl. As the noise died away except for a few isolated croaks, he heard the ten-horse outboard that Rafe used for running around the harbor. He was heading for the island in his big lapstrake skiff.

"Oh, goddam," Finn said aloud. It had been a fine morning until now. Dolly was working in Fremont, and he liked being alone on the island, eating his breakfast in silence with the door open, standing with his mug of coffee to watch the day lighten over the water and the islands. Only a narrow strip of water separated the island from the mainland, but the house faced the sea, and you did not become aware of the buildings on the Point until you went down to the wharf. Even then, you had an island feeling. It had to do with the sound of your own boots and no others on the path, the chickadees going along with you in a noisy friendly crowd through the alders, your own fishhouse standing alone in the frosty stillness, and the birds staying with you as you went back and forth. They were as used to you as if you were a deer, no menace to them; not exactly one of them, but understandable and an islander too.

Swearing again mildly, he walked along the edge of the wharf and hooked on another bait bucket and started its swing into space. Rafe cut off his engine and the skiff glided with a soft rippling rush toward the wharf. He put his hand on the stern of the bigger boat and stopped the motion. His face was flushed and he stared glassily up at Finn.

"I take it you're going to haul."

"You take it correctly," said Finn.

"You forgot what's going on today?"

"Nope. Watch out that don't take you side the head. I'm kind of reckless."

Grudgingly Rafe put out a hand and guided the bucket to the stern of *Foam-Flower* and unhooked it. "Thanks," said Finn. "I guess that's it." He hauled up the big hook, coiled the line and hung it on a cleat on the side of the hoisting mast, tucked his dinner box under his arm, and went down the ladder. As he stepped onto his boat he said cheerfully, "Weather report says not much wind today, and that's for me. Any chop at all, and she starts leaking again."

"I don't get you at all!" Rafe burst out. "What if Gardner shows up this morning?"

"What do you need me for? You'll do all the talking."

"How'll it look if we ain't all there? The whole family? That's the point of it, you damn dumb ox." The red in his face deepened. "What'd you say to the girl yesterday when you were nipping along the path with her, being Prince Charming?"

"Listen. What you say to your women is your business and what I say to mine is my business." He grinned. "Okay, Cap'n?"

"She's older than you are," Rafe said coldly. "Plenty older, I'd say. She's probably still laughing herself sick at the way you pranced around her like some brainless pup."

"If that's supposed to make me feel bad, it doesn't." He gave Rafe an exaggerated leer. "All women are crazy about brainless pups. Now I'm going to haul. I'm not one of the rich Judsons that can afford to sit on their arses on a day like this. I'm the poor relation." He moved swiftly along the washboard from bow to stern, loosening the lines, and then jumped into the cockpit and started his engine. "Gardner won't be over till late this afternoon."

"How'd you find that out?" Rafe said suspiciously.

"Never mind. I wouldn't tell you that much, only I feel kindly this morning. Want a tow back down the harbor?"

Rafe gave him a blank stare, started his own engine, and backed away from *Foam-Flower*. When he had gone down the harbor at full speed, Finn moved more slowly out into the channel, pulling on his oilpants. The boat went along in the shade of the island woods, the bow slicing through water like dark-green liquid glass. Across the harbor the Point was washed in sunlight, the damp roofs and wharves glistening, slopes newly bare of snow already beginning to green in the hollows. There was a cluster of boats around Gil's combination float and lobster car. Elmer and Larry were there, and several men from the lower harbor. They were getting their day's bait from the load of bream that has come down from Limerock last night. Finn glanced complacently at his own bait; he had no use for the trash from the redfish factory, and had bought enough herring in the fall to fill four hogsheads. He knit his own bags, and whenever he began to bait up he remembered Pa saying, "The smell of corned herring is one of the good smells of this earth." Finn took an expert's pride in the smell of his bait. He wouldn't insult the lobsters with something so old and rotten anyone could smell his boat a mile away, given the right wind.

The mouth of the long harbor was in sight and the island woods had ended, so that the sun hit Finn's face. There was warmth in it now, enough to be called spring heat; the touch excited him, and then for no reason the girl came into his mind, and the way she had stood and looked out over the harbor and the island as if she couldn't take in enough, as if she were soaking in peace like the weary geese that stopped in the island coves on their way north. He wondered what she would think of this polished morning.

He was just passing Cleon's anchorage, and was reaching forward to speed up the engine, when Cleon came out from under the sprayhood of the *Onni J.* and waved both arms violently. Finn groaned, wishing he'd seen Cleon's skiff in time to have gone up the other side of the harbor. Cleon sat on the washboards lighting his pipe as if he had time to spare; Finn shut of his engine and held the boats apart by his gaff.

"What you want?"

"Where you bound for this fine large morning?"

"Out to haul, if I ever get out of the harbor."

"Kind of foolish to be going alone, isn't it? Leaking the way you do."

"It's flat calm this morning. Or was, when I started. Now if Roy doesn't muckle onto me I might get out there before it breezes up. You want something special?"

"I just don't think you ought to be out there alone in case she starts leaking bad." He sounded worried and fatherly. "When are you going to do something about it? Trouble with you young squirts is you lallygag along from day to day till everything falls apart at once."

Finn said patiently, "I'm having her recaulked and renailed as soon as I can get a fistful of money to pay Spicer for the job. I got Spicer's promise that he'll do it. Besides, I'm not alone out there. Larry and Elmer haul within sight of me most of the time, and we're side by side down around the Seal Rocks where there's most likely to be a chug on."

Cleon snorted loudly through his nose. "Side by side! Right on top of ye is more like it. Every time one of those two gets a good haul I figger they've made a little mistake in whose traps they're hauling."

"You got anything more to say to me or can I go out and try to make a dollar?"

"Listen, Finn, you know I'm not riding you." Cleon's forehead was deeply creased, his heavy voice sad. "I know you're loyal to those two, and loyalty's a good thing. But it's even better when it works for your own family. You just think of that, boy, when you're out there.... Hey, what's that niece of Mag's like? I hear she's down here looking for a man."

Finn hadn't been really annoyed before, but now he was. "Where do you get your secret information, anyway? She's about sixty and she likes young boys. Younger than me. How's that for news? And that reminds me, I gave her a dollar from you and Onni for the cancer drive, on account of nobody was home at your house when she called there."

"Yesterday morning? Onni was home yesterday morning. Said she planned to wash. You sure she even went there?"

"She said she did, and there's a few people in the world ain't liars, though I don't know many of them." Finn held out his hand and Cleon managed to extract a dollar from his billfold, scowling the whole time. "Thanks," said Finn. "I'll talk to Rafe later. I might even get it from him if Hester don't know about it." He laid the gaff down on the washboard and started up the engine.

"If you see Gardner coming across the river you better come right along home!" Cleon yelled at him. "You'll know him, he's got a big Nova Scotia boat, calls it *The Gardner Girls*!"

Finn pretended he didn't hear, circled away, and headed out of the harbor at full speed. In the lower harbor Morry Spicer was at work on the boat he was building for a Pruitt's Harbor man. Bart Collins was just leaving his wharf with a load of traps. He and Finn waved and they went out of the harbor on parallel courses. Collins swung upriver, and Finn headed across the broad mirror sweep of the river mouth to the cluster of islets that led to open sea.

It was a good day. The winds were light so that the boat didn't have to take the pounding that always started her leaking. The lobsters were beginning to crawl; a few more days like this one and he could make a date with Spicer for getting *Foam-Flower* up on the railway. Down off the Seal Ledges, where he hauled in company with Larry and Elme, he could tell by the way Larry's grimace split his bony face and by the way Elmer shook hands with himself over his head that they were doing better than they'd expected. He was glad for them, and for himself, and when he turned home in the later afternoon he was tired and at peace. The heat of the sun striking through his wool shirt and sweatshirt was strong, and the distances had the hazy yet brilliant blue that promised summer. He didn't have a radio aboard his boat, but he didn't miss the voices calling back and forth, or the loud music some of the fishermen liked to get on the standard broadcast band. The sounds of ocean, wind, birds, and his work were enough for him; the wash at bow and stern, the splash of a trap sliding overboard, the steady pulse of the engine, the drone of the hauling gear when he flipped a wet warp around the brass winch. Sometimes he liked his own voice singing whatever came into his head, from "Shall We Gather at the River" to "The Foggy Foggy Dew."

After he had hauled the last trap on the way home, he did his cleaning chores, shaking out old bait bags, which collected a following crowd of gulls; sweeping up the sea urchins, starfish, and crabs that had fallen off traps, washing down the decks and floorboards with an old broom. Entering the harbor, he went slowly among the moorings. Elmer and Larry were already back and he could see them on their wharf. Another fisherman from the lower harbor, Tom Hunt, was putting gas in his tanks while Gil weighed his lobsters. At the car Finn sat on the engine box smoking, listening to the other men and thinking about what there was to do when he got home. He'd have a staving bowl of the clam chowder he'd made last night, and some of those mince turnovers Dolly had baked last time she was home. Then he had dishes to wash, and he'd neat up the place a bit before he went to get Lila tonight. If he left anything undone, like a stack of dishes or a row of smoky lamp chimneys or a rip in his shirt, Lila began acting as wifely as hell and wanted to spend the whole evening showing what a good housekeeper she was. He thought of Lila in bed and gazed with quiet pleasure at Rafe's wharf. Getting Lila onto the island under his brothers' noses was one of the major delights of life. . . . Better put on clean sheets, he reminded himself.

"Whose Novy boat is that coming in?" Tom Hunt said. He was a very thin man with sunken leathery cheeks and darting eyes. "I never see that one before. She's painted up too good for Ozzie Goodsell's."

Gil narrowed his pale blue eyes at the oncoming boat. "Must be that one from Ballard's Island," he said to Finn.

"Who's from Ballard's Island?" Tom asked with uninhibited

interest. Gil uttered the ambiguous growl that was his all-purpose comment whenever he didn't choose to make himself clear, and went back into the shed to finish his figuring. "You know what he's talking about, Finn?" asked Tom.

"No more than I know if that was a groan or a belch he made," said Finn. "Cryptic, that's what Gil is. His wife fell in love with him because he was so mysterious."

"Looks like Rafe knows that feller," said Tom. Rafe was down on the end of his wharf, beckoning to the broad-beamed boat. With a barely audible throbbing of her diesel engine she changed course and moved with slow grace toward the other wharf.

"By gorry, now," said Finn, "seems like Rafe does know him. Maybe he gave Rafe a Masonic signal or something." Hunt snickered. When Rafe joined the Masons most of the Point considered it a form of social climbing.

Cleon was halfway up the wharf, leaning against a pile of traps; he looked as if he had nothing on his mind. Up by Rafe's fishhouse door Roy stood with his hands in his pockets. His son Danny, who would some day be as big as Finn, sat on the chopping block.

Gil came out and handed Tom his slip. "Here, take this, if you ain't too entranced to care. What's going on over there? Looks like kind of a hard-boiled reception committee."

"Why, Gil, Rafe's just being friendly," said Finn with an innocent smile. "Besides, that big boat would kind of crowd things over here, with everybody coming home about now. Tell you what, Gil, I'll go over and find out what's going on and then I'll come back and tell ye."

"Well, I won't hold my breath till you show up. I got a stinking suspicion I know already what's going on. Here, get those lobsters over here."

Finn and Hunt slung the crate from the washboard to the scales. "Thanks, Tom, and I'll get my slip later, Gil," Finn said. Gil grunted something at the weights he was adjusting. Finn cast off and went across to Rafe's wharf, and tied up on the other side of the float. Beyond him the deep dent of the inlet was a lustrous green in the shadow of the spruces. A couple of Johnson and Curtis children were lying on their stomachs on the flat ledges, sailing boats in a tidewater pool. It was the same pool in which he had sailed chips loaded with periwinkles while his father helped Gil pack lobsters. *Pa'd rather tend out on somebody else than work on his own gear.* That was Cleon grumbling. Oh well, Finn thought, swinging his long legs over the side, Cleon was most likely right. What the hell does it matter now, anyway?

On the wharf Rafe and the stranger were introducing themselves and shaking hands. Gardner was a slim fox-colored man, and as neatly put together as a fox. His face with its pointed features had the same blend of wariness and unhostile curiosity that Finn had often observed in the foxes on the island.

"And this in my youngest brother, Finn Judson," Rafe said. Finn nodded, but kept his hands in his pockets, disapproving of Rafe's cordiality. The man was a crook, and it put the rest of them a dite on the crooked side to make him feel that he was being welcomed to Saltberry Point. Rafe was even touching his arm, smiling. "Come on and meet the rest of the clan," he said.

Cleon straightened up, wearing an expression of sleepy amiability. During the handshake he glanced past Gardner's ear at Finn, who winked; Cleon's benevolence blinked out like a dying flashlight and he gave Finn a brief cold stare and then ignored him. The procession toward the fishhouse resumed, Gardner now flanked by Rafe and Cleon, Finn behind with his hands in his pockets.

"This is sure a beautiful spot," Gardner was saying. "Not rugged, like what I'm used to. But this is something my wife's looking forward to. She says she's had enough of Alcatraz. That's what she calls Ballards. Born there too, she was." He laughed, and the others laughed with him. He said more seriously, "But she's been scared so many times out there I guess it ain't really funny. Not for a woman, anyway. You get a bad winter storm out there and that's just when somebody needs a doctor."

"That must be hellish hard," Cleon said with sympathy. Finn wished he'd been able to get home and eat. There was a roiling in his stomach that had to be hunger.

Roy gave Gardner a choppy nod without a smile. Rafe dropped a hand on Danny's big shoulder and said fondly, "The youngest of the clan, my nephew Danny."

"Gorry, there's a lot of him, ain't there?" Gardner was admiring. "Say, Danny, I've got a boy about your age. The younger kids are all excited about moving in here, but Kip was kind of worried about not knowing anybody. Would you give him the lay of the land, just till he gets to know his way around?"

"Well, sure." Danny blushed and slid a glance at his father, who gave him no help.

"Let's go inside a minute," Rafe suggested. The roiling in Finn's stomach and the quickening of his heartbeat infuriated him. He was acting like some nervous girl about to get rolled in the hay for the first time and not wanting to, but thinking she had to go along with it; not having the guts to say *I'm getting out of here*. There's no comparison, he argued with himself. This is something we have to do as a family, as Saltberry Pointers. He followed into the low building, and it seemed to him that Gardner's relief was as tangible as the fishhouse smell of paint and oak laths and the whiff of bait from the adjoining shed. Gardner had been nervous till he stepped ashore, and now he thought he had been accepted, and that the Judsons spoke for the whole Point. You could hear it in his voice. The words rushed.

"I know you don't make the money in here that they can make out there. But money isn't everything. Now that I'm leaving the place I don't mind saying there's as big a bunch of pirates out there as ever sailed the seas. It's worth giving up a couple of thousand a year to move into a law-abiding place where the kids don't have to grow up carrying the old folks' feuds on their backs."

"Danny," Roy said. 'You better get home and start on your lessons."

"Oh, let the boy stay," said Cleon. "He's one of the Judson men too, ain't he? Time he took his place in the family councils."

"I'll be the judge of that. Danny, *out*."

There was silence in the fishhouse as the boy went out, ducking his head in the low doorway as Finn always had to do. Finn hoisted himself up on the workbench and lit a cigarette. Rafe put more wood in the pot-bellied stove. Cleon said to Finn, "How'd you do today?"

"Can't complain," said Finn. Out of the corner of his eye he saw the first movements of uneasiness in Gardner.

"Well," the stranger said, "I guess if somebody'll point me toward Mrs. Abbott's, I'll be moving on. She's expecting me."

"No hurry, she won't be going anywhere," rumbled Cleon.

"Oh, for God's sake!" Roy snapped. "Get it over with!" He ripped open a fresh package of cigarettes, and thrust it toward Gardner. Gardner shook his head. His face tightened, becoming more vulpine than before. "What'd you want to say to me?" he asked Rafe.

"All we wanted to say to you, Gardner, is that we'll buy the place from you for a thousand more than you paid for it."

No one spoke or moved. Then a gull screeched from the low ridgepole over their heads, and ended the moment of trance. "I see," Gardner said slowly. "In other words I'm not wanted here."

"I didn't say that."

"You might just as well have. And I thought I was getting the glad hand all around. Joke's on me, huh?" His eyes were glistening as they moved from one to the other. Finn thought the glisten was tears, and that added to his queasiness until he realized with relief that the man was in a rage at the trick that had been played on him. The tight skin over his cheekbones was bright red. "Well, at least two of you had the guts to keep your hands in your pockets. I'd say you were a dite more honest than your brothers."

Cleon said, "No call to feel bitter about this, Gardner." He fondled his pipe and was all benevolence. Rafe had no expression at all, but the deep flush showed that he was excited behind his surface stolidity. Roy looked savage enough to tear Gardner apart with his bare hands, but if he hated the man at this moment it was for the same reason Finn did; for being their victim, for walking innocently into the trap and facing four of them, by his very aloneness turning them into bullies instead of the saviors of the Point.

"I don't have to sell," he said.

"Then you'll never haul a trap in these waters," said Rafe reasonably. "Set them, yes, but never haul them."

"Let's make this damn quick," Roy said. "Fact is, Gardner, we understand you're one of the biggest pirates of that Ballard's bunch, and we don't want a dishonest lobsterman in here. That's about the size of it."

"Thanks for being so blunt. We'd have saved time if your

brother'd told me that before I got off my boat, instead of shaking hands."

"I've got no use for this pussyfooting."

"Thanks, brother," said Rafe. "All right, Gardner, we'll buy you out, and you'll be a damn' sight luckier than if we'd let you move in here and set traps."

"You must be the one she told me always wanted the house." Gardner was quiet. He leaned against the doorframe and took out his cigarettes, watching Rafe. "She hates your guts and I wondered why. Now I'm commencing to see. Well, I know better than to move from one batch of cutthroats to another. But what if I won't sell the house and there it sits? You can't have it, and you'll never know when I may show up with a half-dozen relatives and we all set out till you're choked to death on traps."

"You wouldn't do that," said Cleon. "Now, would ye? You need the money. You can't leave six or seven thousand tied up in a place where you can't live. You need it for a house somewhere else because you can't go back to Ballard's. You been run out of there."

"Seems to me I've heard that story before. Simon-pure lies, of course, but they still don't do a man no good." Gardner's match burned steadily toward his fingers. He dropped it and stepped on it. "All right, I'll sell. I'll see Stark tomorrow morning. Call him about noon. The price is ten thousand."

He went out, slamming the door shut behind him as if to slam them into oblivion. It was as if he could not have stood there another moment without bursting into some violent act.

Roy continued to stare at the floor. Finn sat on the bench, his boots swinging. Cleon cuddled his pipe in his thick hand. Moving as soundlessly as a cat, Rafe went to the windows that looked out at the harbor, and watched. They could not see what he was watching, but they could hear the sibilant underbreath whistling of some little tune. Then they heard the diesel starting up and knew by Rafe's eyes when the boat backed away from the wharf and headed down the harbor.

Finn slid off the bench. "Maybe it is all lies," he said cheerfully. "Maybe we've condemned an innocent man. Maybe Stark will tell him he should sue us."

· 38 ·

"Oh, shut up," said Roy. He went out, slamming the door harder than Gardner had done; a can of copper paint on a shelf started to topple and Cleon caught it. He shook his head with infinite sadness, as if he stood by a coffin. "Ayuh, Roy's nerves ain't what they were. This trouble with Helen and all. Awful outlook for a man, no chance of getting shed of her while she's still locked up."

"Who says he wants to get shed of her?" asked Finn. "Did the idea ever come into your little pointed head that he looks like hell because he misses her, not because he can't figure how to break loose? Likely not. Your mind always was below your belt."

"What you so touchy about? You bleeding for Gardner? I notice you didn't have anything to say."

"There was enough being said. I was just supposed to be here to make it look good or something. Well, I'm going home and get my dinner."

·6·

Mag was stooped but fast, hurrying headlong about the high rooms like a hen plunging across the barnyard after a bug. Her features were small and round, of the type that are given charm only by the curls and moist freshness of youth and become non-descript when hair and skin fade. But in Mag's case she had passed from the insignificant appearance of her middle years to the distinction of age. Her thin hair, flyaway around her temples and twisted into a hard little bun at the back, was a pure glistening white. Her small eyes had never had any particular color, but they sparkled with greedy life among the many wrinkles that crosshatched her ancient skin. Whenever she did anything, whether it was baking a pie or turning out a closet, the surrounding area was charged with her energy. At eighty-five she was attacking the problem of moving with the same fire she had brought to everything. Giving up the place where she had been born and her father before her caused her no obvious pangs.

"Living in Williston'll be real exciting after being stuck in the middle of this field for eighty-five years," she said. "You can't even see the harbor from up here. Have to run upstairs to see out over the point to open water. I was always after Abbott to build down on the shore, had my heart set on that rise across the road from the fishhouse. I used to set there and dream of it. My lands!" she marveled. "The view! I thought the Prentisses—they lived in that house Larry Johnson lives in now, 'twas built by an own cousin of Father's—well, I thought Myra Prentiss had all the luck. You could see over the island and clear to Monhegan and beyond, and then you could look to the east'ard down the harbor, and when the woods was all cut off that end of the island you could see clear across the river to Port George, and see the sloops coming home to their moorings like gulls and then fold down their wings for the night."

The homecoming sloops sailed across Claire's vision and interfered with the letter she was trying to write to her mother-in-law. She was glad of the distraction. She would have liked to give herself up to Mag's memories, which sometimes had the serene, pastoral atmosphere given off by very old photographs, creating the illusion that all of life then had been as metrically peaceful and full of goodness and simple heartfelt delights as a poem by Whittier. One knew it couldn't have been but still one submitted gratefully to the deception.

With an effort she focused her eyes on the letter in the typewriter. Her brain seemed to lock itself up like a frozen brook whenever she attempted to communicate with David's mother. She knew that for Mrs. Carradine it was intolerable that Claire should have the right to take Nancy away from her and set her down in surroundings as wild, bleak, and alien to Mrs. Carradine as the terrain of the moon.

Claire was not resentful. Nancy was all that remained to David's mother of David the beloved, and she had half-convinced herself in her passion of grief that Nancy was her own child. Sometimes she had to recall Claire's existence with a visible effort, and then she would be clinging and dependent, saying that they shared a sorrow no one else could ever understand or alleviate. Poor soul, Claire thought now, feeling her own pain stirring awake under the carefully smoothed surface of day-to-day living. She was desperately guilty about being here with Nancy, even though she had known for a long time that she must get away for a while; Mag's letter had streaked out across the miles like a lifeline.

Her brother-in-law had approved, then urged when it looked as if his mother's distress would break Claire down. "Your duty right now is to help the old lady," he said. Privately he said, "Your duty is to yourself and Nancy. You need a change. You haven't been away from Mother since David died."

"Should I leave Nancy behind?" she had asked, oppressed and weakened by the atmosphere of his mother's hurt.

"No," he said, more sharply than she had ever heard him speak before. "She'll miss you too much, and she needs a chance to breathe, too. I'll keep Mother occupied. Maybe I can get her moving again. She's too young and healthy to retire from the world as she's done."

So they had come to Maine, reassured by Robert in spite of the lacerating farewells. But there was always this dreadful paralysis when it came to writing, as if she were afraid of making a fresh wound with each word she wrote. Oh, get to it! she told herself angrily now. But her fingers stumbled awkwardly over the keys, and she pushed the typewriter back and leaned her elbows on the table. Mag sat at the other end, going through the contents of some shoeboxes brought down from the attic.

"Why didn't Uncle Ralph want to build at the shore?" she asked, as if there had been no gap since Mag last spoke. "I didn't know a fisherman could stand being out of sight of the water."

Mag's chuckle was malicious. "He always said he never had the time to build, but I know the truth. He married the Oliver Salisbury house when he got me, and he didn't plan to give it up. *Him* move down to the harbor and be common like the rest? Not on your life!"

"I can sympathize with him," said Claire. "This house has so much dignity, and the proportions are perfect."

"Ayuh." Mag flipped complacently through a bundle of letters tied with red string. "Grandpa knew what he was about. My, the offers we've had for this place! Summer folks, you know, and people wanting to retire." She grimaced. "Me, I'd have grabbed at any of 'em. But not Abbott. He'd sooner sold me." She tossed the letters along the table. "Well, there's some kindling. Ought to get a good hot fire out of 'em. Love letters Uncle Theodore wrote to Aunt Gertrude when he was sailing in the China trade."

Claire put out a hand and then drew it back. "*Love* letters?"

"Take 'em if you want."

"Somebody else's letters, and so personal," Claire began, and then gave in. "Well, if you think Aunt Gertrude and Uncle Theodore wouldn't mind."

"Mind? Those two? Holding hands in public long after they'd had their fifth one? Had no shame, according to the family. Father cleared his throat to his dying day whenever they were mentioned. I used to think they'd done something real awful till I got the truth from Mother."

Claire laid the bundle next to her typewriter. She did not want to read anyone's love letters, knowing she would never receive any more. Yet she could not bear to see them turned into kindling after all this time, for they were part of a man's life, and therefore the man himself.

Mag pawed like a squirrel through her boxes. The Ansonia clock ticked loudly, sometimes drawing a hoarse breath which, after it had occurred, intensified the silence. Silence was absolute in much of the house, those rooms where the sunlight struck across faded carpets and those others that lay in shadow blue and cold as water; and in the gold-stippled old-wood-scented gloom up under the roof. Except for the clocks, a fly buzzing on a sash or a faint crepitation of wind, silence drowned this house, but it was not a dead silence. Sometimes Claire thought that if only she could immerse herself deeply enough in the silence she would arise from it all new.

Across the table two windows gave on three tall, thick old apple trees; a swing hung from one massive branch all gnarled arms and twisting groping fingers. Beyond the trees a yellow-brown slope curved against a sky whose spring blue was faintly fogged with a translucent nacreous sheen. A stone wall crossed the rise and disappeared over the brow like a long gray snake sunning itself. The scene was deceptively static; but now Claire knew that from the rise one beheld the point reaching out into the sea; a long thin triangle of alders, bay, juniper, and blueberries growing from its granite bones. What looked at first glance like a wall of woods was the spruce forest over on the island; if you stood on a whaleback of ledge you saw the stream between, broadly flowing and dimpled with contrary currents at high tide, at low tide a brook for herons and gulls. Trickling among the bluish-purple mussel beds, it began to widen and deepen off the island wharf and then become the harbor. But from the ledge the harbor didn't exist, just the wildness of rocks and ocean and whatever grew in this salt air.

Claire leaned across the table and looked up through glass, narrowed her eyes against the pale glow of the zenith, and saw the gulls up there as they always were, soaring in wide circles, so high that they were only flashing specks appearing and disappearing as the sun caught them. "Why do they do it?" she said aloud. "Those great arcs. Do they like it, or are they watching something?"

"Them cussid thieves," said Mag. "Just waiting for my blueberries to ripen, that's all. Well, never mind, Mag, somebody else can worry about the blueberries this summer. Gardner's got enough young ones to rake 'em, anyway. Last year Finn Judson helped me out. Dunno what I would have done if he hadn't come over and brought his nephew along." She said in a softer tone, "Here's Uncle Matthias, he died at Andersonville." She slid the stiff-backed photograph along the table to Claire who took it without seeing it. *Finn?* Her mind turned inward, doubtfully remembering the big hands hanging, black hair like coarse brush, and above the broad sunburnt cheekbones the eyes regarding her with innocent outgiving.

This was the day he was going to take her across to the island, but she did not expect him. Being young enough yet to act upon impulse without fearing commitments, being amiable, he had wanted to make a friendly gesture, but something else had come along that he wanted to do more. Or perhaps when he reflected upon it she had seemed too restrained and distant, and hadn't shown any real interest in his island.

"Wasn't he a handsome boy?" asked Aunt Mag.

"Not really handsome, but—" She caught herself. "Not handsome like a movie star, but very fine-looking," she pronounced of the boy in uniform posed by an artificial boulder.

"I was madly in love with him," said Mag. "Never knew him,

just that picture. I snuck it into my room. Used to cry myself to sleep thinking about him dying so far from home." Her voice was as dry as the rustle of leaves. "It *was* awful, when you come to think of it. And nowadays everybody acting like the Rebellion was a big family picnic, with fireworks." She said crossly, "If we were at the harbor, we could see that man Gardner coming. I'd like to know why he didn't come yesterday afternoon. Well, let him come when he's a mind to, I've got my money and that's all I care about." She closed her mouth with a triumphant snap.

"Some people would feel a little sad at pulling up roots and leaving the family home. I feel that way already about the house, and I've only known it for a week or so."

"Too bad Paul Gardner isn't a bachelor." Mag's grin was wicked. "Then you could marry him and stay here. I suppose I'd ought to leave the house to you, but 'twould be no kindness to a thin-skinned young one like you. You can prattle on about dignity and proportions and all that foolishness, but it's been full of ghosts ever since I can remember, and I've been wanting to leave it as long as that."

If I had it. . . . Longing made Claire slightly sick. *If I could say to them all, This is my house and here I stay. The ghosts and I.* She said, "Shouldn't you warn Paul Gardner about the ghosts, in case they go bump in the night?"

"They won't bother him," said Mag. "He doesn't know about them. Besides, that litter he's got will give the house a new start. It's really them I'm selling the house to. Once they get to whooping and hollering through the place it'll be like no Salisburys ever died in it shrieking in fear of the devil, or giving birth to some poor critter who'd hang himself in the barn twenty years later."

"Oh, Aunt Mag," Claire said, "every family has those things in its history! Why, you should have heard some of the things David told me about the Carradines, and they're so respected some people all but kneel when they say the name."

The old woman laughed, but she seemed tired all at once, as if her age had treacherously struck at her. "Oh, I know that, but when you grow up knowing the beam the rope was slung over, and every night you climb the back stairs Maria broke her neck on and nobody knew how, well, it makes a difference."

"Don't forget Uncle Theo and Aunt Gertrude. Doesn't their kind of love make a difference too? Doesn't that leave something behind in a house?" Claire got up. "Let me get lunch today. How about some coffee with it?"

"Don't coddle me as if I was in my dotage," said Mag crossly. "I know I am, but you don't have to show you've noticed." She pushed the boxes away with feeble anger. "No, a bunch of noisy young ones and dogs pounding through, and men coming home from fishing, that's what this house needs."

There was a knock at the back door.

"Sit still, I'll go." Claire went out into the ell shed, tying her apron as she went. She expected to meet Gardner's sharp sandy features. Instead there was a stocky, immaculate man whom at first she thought she knew, and then realized she had never seen before. The wisp of resemblance was gone as soon as he opened his mouth. His manner was civil, but he gazed at her with a bold concentration, as if secretly he had come just to get a look at her.

"Mag in? I'd like to talk to her. Tell her it's Rafe Judson."

"She doesn't need to tell me who it is!" Mag called from the kitchen. The tremor was gone. "I hear you. What do you want, Rafe Judson?"

"Come in," Claire said. He followed her into the kitchen, taking off his cap.

"Morning, Mag," he said. Her eyes went over him, small points of brilliance in her shrunken face. "If you've come to devil me about the place," she cried, "you can go home and tell your wife it's sold!"

He smiled. "I know it's sold, Mag. I bought it from Paul Gardner about an hour ago."

At first Claire was merely startled by Gardner's incredible conduct. Two days ago he had said he could hardly wait to move his family in. But when she turned to share Mag's astonishment, fright struck her chest like a fist. The old woman rose up in a frenzy, jabbing a shaky finger at Rafe. "*You!*" she screeched. "You—you——"

"What's the matter, Mag?" he asked genially. "You've got

your money. That's what you wanted. I got the place and that's what I wanted. Don't carry on till you have a stroke or something."

"It's you who'll get the stroke, from the hand of God, for your lying and your deceit. Now get out!"

"You can't order me out of my own house." He laughed softly as he said it. She flew around the table at him, her hands crooked before her like claws.

"Out, out, you evil man! It's my house still, and you'll never live in it, I'll burn it down first! I'll burn it down now, this minute!" She whirled away from him like a wild and passionate girl. Claire moved into her path, but Mag gave her a blind glare and darted past her into the next room. They heard a slamming door.

"You'd better go," Claire said to the man. "Please. Go at once." In her striving for poise she sounded bloodless and remote. She wanted to strike him in the face; the thin curling smile filled her with revulsion.

"All right, I'll go," he said agreeably. "But don't let her burn the house down, if you don't want her finishing out her days in an insane asylum." He turned toward the door. "So long as she behaves herself she can take her time moving out. All summer if she wants. I've got no plans for the place yet."

"I don't think, under the circumstances, that she'll want to linger," Claire said. He came back a few steps, giving her that bold intense stare again.

"What are you so toplofty about? Who the devil do you think you're looking down your nose at? You'll get your share of the money and that's what you came for, isn't it?"

She said gently, "I can see why my aunt would rather burn down the house than have you in it."

He laughed and then slammed the door on the sound, but she heard him laugh again outside, loudly as if for her benefit, and was exhilarated because she had stung him. Then she went through the house, prepared to find a lifeless little heap of old bones. Mag was in the parlor, sitting in a comb-back rocker by the empty fireplace, an afghan wrapped around her shoulders. She gave Claire a proud look.

"I was going for the poker to clout him with till my common sense got the better of me, darn it."

"I never did see how anybody could be hit hard enough with a poker," said Claire. "They must use a different kind for murder. . . . He warned me you might end up in the state hospital."

"In one of them padded cells, I s'pose. Must a warmed his heart up real good." Her laughter was a wisp of sanity, and Claire felt voluptuously light with relief. She sat down on a hassock by the cold hearth and looked around in pleasure. The pale April sunlight outside the windows was exquisite in its subtlety.

"You'll catch your death," said Mag.

"What about you? Come on out in the kitchen and let's have that coffee we were talking about before the troops arrived."

"I'm just getting my breath," said Mag. "I'm as tuckered out as if I'd split a cord of firewood." She put her head back and shut her eyes. She was so fervent in all she did that it always came as a shock to Claire when Mag showed signs of fatigue. Out in the hall the clock began to strike noon, and vibrations flowed through the house in wave after shimmering wave. When the last one had died away Mag opened her eyes and said strongly, "I'll tell you one thing, he's not having that clock."

"Why do you hate him so?"

Mag lifted her hands off the arms of the rocker and dropped them again. "I dunno. He's always set my teeth on edge. Maybe it's because he's been at me about the place so much, trying to sweet-talk me one time and bully the next. First his wife used to come." She made a face. "You met her?"

"On the cancer drive," said Claire dryly. "She doesn't approve of organized begging. Or the beggars. She has a—a rather bitter tongue. . . . She pronounces her *r*s very carefully."

"That's to make folks think she wasn't born just across the river and her father a paving cutter. Flattens out her *a*s too, so she sounds like an old sheep. Well, she acted like she'd die if she didn't get this place. Then somebody discovered their place, that used to be Joshua Clark's, was older'n this one. I could've told her that. Well, she stopped swarming around here and went to collecting antiques, or what she thinks is antiques." Mag put back her head and laughed with sudden youth. "She's got a glass pitcher up there, come from the attic, and she thinks it's some fancy kind of milk glass! Land of love, we all got one for free the year Lou Dunnet was selling Simmons Products from door to door. They was special with a two-dollar order, and they was worth about a quarter each."

Claire laughed. " 'Bout the time she gave up on this place," Mag went on, "she comes tippytoeing in here one day rolling them *r*s like a hive of bees, and tells me she just found out that Richard Salisbury had to leave the Cleaves Grant down Portland way because he was such a sinner they gave him his choice of getting out or being hanged. It gave her so much pleasure I didn't bother to tell her she was talking about the other Richard, third cousin or so, who got drowned in the harbor down here when he was full of rum one night, and never left any descendants. Legal ones, that is." She looked pensive. "Foolish, ain't it? Grown woman carrying on so. She'd give her eye teeth to belong to the DAR, but she's got the wrong ancestors. They came over too late." Mag rocked and watched a gull slant by small panes. "Did get herself into the garden club up in Williston, but it ain't the same. They'd take anybody in. They took her, didn't they?"

"*Devastating* is the word for Aunt Mag," Claire said, and smiled at the old woman's perplexity. "But you were going to tell me about Rafe. I met two of his brothers the other day and they seemed pleasant enough."

"I got nothing against them. I just can't tolerate that Rafe. His father was a good man, and his mother's honest, though she's no better than she should be. But that Rafe—" She pounded her fist on the rocker arm. "I don't want him in this house!"

"You said yourself you didn't care about the house."

'But he's won out, can't you see?" Mag cried. "Even when *she* let up, he kept after me, just like he couldn't stand having anybody set themselves against him, and if they did he'd hector 'em into their grave if he had to. That's all he wanted, to win out over me, and that's what he's done."

"Yes, I see," said Claire. She sat gazing at the old woman

with wonder and envy. What must it be like to have passion to spend at eighty-five? She was twenty-nine, and she had been extinguished for a long time. Suddenly she was aware of the chill of the room. She stood up. "Come on back to the kitchen, Aunt Mag. Please."

"Oh, well, I s'pose you think I'll have pneumonia next," Mag muttered. "Here, give me your arm, I feel a dite wivvery."

·7·

Mag's appetite was poor, she talked in feverish starts and then retreated into silences that seemed to take her far from the present. At the end of the meal she said, "Leave the dishes in the sink. I'm going to have a nap." This in itself was so unusual that Claire's anxiety increased. When Mag fell asleep on the dining-room couch, Claire fully expected her to drift away completely or, if she did wake up, to be irrational or speechless from a shock. She wondered nervously how to get in touch with Gil Murray or his wife without leaving the house or using the telephone. Gil was Mag's last surviving cousin and watched over her as well as he could without appearing to; she accepted his doing the man's chores about the place as his family duty, but objected stridently to any obvious surveillance. But today, Claire thought, she may not be able to object; she stared at the afghan covering Mag, her eyes smarting with the effort to see the gaudy wool lift. It did, at last. She was still breathing, but was such a light, soundless process a good sign or bad?

Her hands clammy, Claire put away her typewriter and the unfinished letter to Mrs. Carradine, tucked Uncle Theodore's letters into the case, and tried to read. Suddenly the solution came to her. When Nancy came home from school she could carry a message to Gil. Claire wrote the note furtively on her book, but Mag didn't wake. The shadow of the stone wall changed, and that of the nearest apple tree reached into the house and spread like a ghostly vine.

The noise of the elderly school bus turning around outside brought her to her feet. She went soundlessly through the house and out under the fanlight onto the front doorstep. The bus was chugging out of sight, Nancy, the last passenger, was across the driveway opening the mailbox. She frowned at each envelope as if reading the writing and conjecturing on the contents. Then she stood on tiptoe, shut the mailbox firmly, and came across the road. She was small for her age, with neat brown pigtails and straight bangs. Her narrow face was thoughtful as she concentrated on walking in the puddles, getting the full use of her red boots. In one of the deepest spots she stood still, as if to experience completely the sensation of water up to her ankles. She carried her blue lunchbox in one hand and the mail firmly gripped in the other. In the next puddle she splashed, watched with a scientific objectivity as the water settled, then tucked the mail under her arm and wiped her bare knees on her pleated skirt.

"I suppose you'll try standing on your head in the next one," Claire said. "Just give me the mail first."

"Hi, Mama!" Nancy came on like a pony. A smile transfigured her from a plain child to a charming one. The missing front teeth contributed to the total effect. Her eyes were her father's, a warm golden hazel, thickly lashed. If nothing else is beautiful about her but her eyes, Claire thought, she will still be lucky.

"You know *what*?" Nancy demanded. "Elmer pushed Bobby down because he wanted to sit beside me on the bus. And then Mr. Marsh made Elmer sit behind him, so Bobby sat beside me anyway." She giggled. "But I'm going to play with Elmer this afternoon."

"Come in and change, and then you can take a note to Mr. Murray for me, when you go to Elmer's. Be quiet now, Aunt Mag's asleep."

"All right," Nancy said in a loud whisper. She struggled out of her boots. Claire took them and the lunchbox and the mail, and the two tiptoed across the hall. Nancy went up the front stairs with exaggerated caution, eyebrows arched, tongue curled, feet lifted high. Claire, watching, marveled at the ease with which the child had taken to this life. She found nothing sparse, freakish, or strange in it; she was unabashed by Mag's lack of sentimentality toward her, ran errands for her around the house and even into the darkest corners of the attic, filled the woodbox and dried dishes, and conversed with Mag while they worked as if she were a junior of eighty to Mag's eighty-five.

At night she slept soundly in an old bed with a towering headboard, in a room hung with dark reproductions of Victorian engravings. She had named the noble dogs and rescued children, the anguished heroines and dying heroes, and constantly made up new stories about them. Back in Brookline her room had been exquisitely decorated just for her; Claire alone knew how many times Nancy hadn't known what to do in it because there was too much to choose from.

She was upstairs now, bursting into hearty song which she quickly throttled. She had become louder in this environment. What shall I write Mrs. Carradine about her? Claire questioned wryly. That she's a *femme fatale* on the school bus, and the rest of the time either a rowdy or Aunt Mag's crony?

Mag was gone from the couch. She was out in the kitchen building a fire. She looked refreshed and energetic. "My lands, what's that young one doing overhead?"

"Changing her clothes."

"Sounds like changing the guard to me, horses and all." Mag threw kerosene onto the kindling with a reckless swing. "Woke me up; about time too. I don't figger on sleeping the rest of my life away."

Claire crumpled up the note in her pocket, and Nancy ran down the back stairs in her jeans. "There's a man coming into the shed," she announced. "I saw him out the window. Can I go now? Elmer's walking up to meet me."

Someone tapped at the door from the shed and opened it. "Hi, Mag," Finn said. He quite filled the doorway.

"What do *you* want?" she asked crossly. "We already had one Judson here today, and that didn't set good with me at all."

"Aw, Mag, you aren't holding Rafe's actions against me, are ye?" He cocked his head at her, his smile tender and beguiling.

"I dunno," said Mag. "Claire, give Nancy a couple slices of that applesauce cake for her and her beau."

Claire went into the pantry and shut the heavy oak door. She was unpleasantly startled. She hadn't expected Finn to appear, and she wished that he hadn't; Rafe's visit had wiped away the possibility of her ever again being easy with the boy. She took her time cutting the cake, hoping that Mag would make short work of him. But when she went back into the kitchen Finn stood with one foot propped on the stove hearth, and Mag was in her chair with her knitting. Her attitude was not exactly grandmotherly, but it was not hostile. Nancy stood staring into Finn's face. He gave her a sidewise wink without a smile and went on speaking to Mag.

"Here, Nancy," said Claire, "one piece for you and one for Elmer. And come home at five."

"I don't know if I'll go now."

"You promised Elmer, and he's coming to meet you."

Nancy sighed. "Oh, all right."

"Don't go away mad," Finn said to her. Nancy giggled and gyrated back to him like a compass needle to the north; Claire took her by the shoulder and escorted her toward the back door. Outside, Elmer was to be discovered lurking around the wood-pile by the carriage house. When he saw Nancy and her mother he disappeared entirely. "Hey!" Nancy yelled at him and plunged off the doorstep. "Want some cake?"

When Claire returned to the kitchen Finn took his foot off the hearth shelf and tucked his thumbs in his belt. "You ready?"

"For what?" Mag's head swung from one to the other.

"I invited her over to the island today. Didn't she tell ye?"

"Not that one." Mag looked at Claire with appreciative surmise. "She's a sly besom."

"I could tell she was the wild kind," said Finn. "That's why I asked her over for my evil purposes."

"Well, I'm sorry your evil purposes must go to waste," said Claire, "but I don't think I'll go. Aunt Mag hasn't been feeling very well today."

"What you talking about? I never felt better! You get along with him now and stretch your legs."

Claire stood in a trance of indecision and embarrassment; the boy seemed infinitely older than she in his tolerant gaze, and Mag regarded her as she herself must have regarded Nancy a few minutes ago.

"All right," she said weakly, "but will you please not do anything strenuous?"

"I'm going to turn on the radio and listen to my programs, if I can have some peace around here."

"Is this what you wear?" Finn took Claire's old tweed topcoat from the hook behind the door. "Better wear boots too." As she was pulling them on he said to Mag, "So Rafe made one of them visitations, did he?"

"He did, and I like to killed him, only Claire got nervous and stopped me. Say, I might just set the house afire while you're gone. He's scared foolish thinking I'll do it."

"You better set it from the outside," Finn advised her, "so you won't get caught in it. I'd hate like hell to sift the ashes for your bones." They both laughed inordinately. Claire couldn't understand either of them, considering that Finn should have been deeply ashamed of his brother and that Mag had been dangerously upset by the encounter. When she and Finn were outside the house she said coldly, "I still don't think I ought to go. This morning I thought she was going to collapse."

"On account of Rafe, you mean?" He still didn't sound ashamed, only interested.

"Yes, on account of Rafe. Granted, he's bought the house and has the right to say so—"

"*They've* bought the house. Cleon and Roy were in on it too."

"He said *I*, the whole time. When he became impossible and she told him to get out, he said, 'You can't order me out of my own house.' "

"That's Rafe, all right." Finn shook his head, bemused. "That thing called tact—well, as far as Rafe's concerned it's something you hit with a hammer. Makes him awful popular around the Point."

"I can imagine," Claire said aridly. Her heel slid off a rolling pebbled and she lurched sidewise. Finn caught her by the elbow with a grip that sent a shock through her of homesickness for David's hand steadying her the same way. She almost stopped, ready to turn and run, not toward anything because there was nothing to run to any more, but *away*; however, she had been too well brought up to do the violent, the unexpected, the un-heard-of thing. Unconscious of the storm, Finn kept his fingers loosely around her arm, and they descended the path toward Abbott's wharf.

The air was cool from the traces of melting snow, but it smelled both earthy and grassy, and around the wharf there was a brininess that took her back to childhood summers on Cape Cod. Children's voices rang piercingly from beyond the ledgy rise covered with bay and juniper. She heard Nancy's shout soaring up like a bird toward the sky.

They went down four wooden steps built against the stone retaining wall between the wharf and the fishhouse. Finn helped her into the skiff with an easy courtliness that led her to think he had been handing girls in and out of boats for years. Rowing with quick short strokes, he took the skiff away from the wharves and the moorings and down a wide avenue of water that flowed in luminous blue curves between the wooded banks of the island and the high, shrubby shores of the Point. The very tip of the Point reached out toward a long rocky finger extending from the island and beyond this narrow gateway lay the azure plain of Saltberry Bay.

In this hour and this light it was a country in a dream. The velvet fields fell shoreward in soft and careless folds of bronze and antique gold; the spruce woods on the bank were a feathery darkness pierced mysteriously by the phantom gleam of white birches. Small seabirds fed and played in little coves, leaving sparkling wakes behind them on the shadowy water. Gulls paddled above their almost perfect reflections, turning their arrogant heads and cold eyes toward the skiff and away again, not flying. A little flock of fox sparrows flew across from the Abbott pasture to the island in a flurry of gentle cheepings. Claire watched the flight and it took her eyes to the house on the island, at the top of a sunlit field. Beyond the house the spruces were blued by the faint smokiness in the air to the color of Concord grapes.

"So Rafe was real nasty," Finn said.

She did not want to talk about Rafe now; she wanted only

to remain in this painless dimension between dream and reality. She dragged her gaze from the approaching island. Finn's eyes were almost the same blue as the woods. "Yes, he was nasty," she said. "He came to gloat over a tired old woman. If he's always wanted the house, and she's opposed him for no very sensible reason, I suppose that could hurt his pride badly. But once he'd won out, couldn't that be enough for him?"

"It's hard telling about Rafe," he said. "He sure didn't need to do it that way. He could have let Roy or Cleon do it." He rested on the oars and gazed at her. "But he's Rafe, so he did it that way."

Apparently Finn saw no use in trying to explain his brother, or even to show indignation. Rafe was a fact for him, like bad weather or poor lobstering. It was a mature viewpoint, she supposed; or a very young one.

"*My* house," he said, grinning. "They'll like that. He talked them into it, all but begged them, and now he's taking all the credit."

"What do they want with it?"

"Well, Cleon or Roy would have told Mag something she could understand. Gardner's supposed to be a bad actor, a real reprobate. Been kicked off Ballard's Island, that's about twenty miles to the east'ard. We've never had a thieving lobsterman here, so the boys saw that he sold out before he ever moved in." He was amused by her expression of astonished distaste. "They didn't use force, if that's what you think. Nope, he gave up without a struggle. He got the message, you might say."

She felt a curious stirring of excitement, whether pleasant or unpleasant she couldn't tell. "Well, if you knew he was dishonest, if you were sure of it, I can see why you wouldn't want him. But to do it like that—meet him at the town line like a gang of vigilantes in a television western—I don't know, it just seems impossible." She had to laugh at her own bewilderment. "Don't misunderstand me! I'm not criticizing, I'm just trying to take it in."

The skiff glided along the spilings of his wharf. He shipped oars and reached out to take hold of the ladder. "Well, you see," he said equably, "It'll save a—a heck of a lot of trouble for everybody if Gardner never moves in. This way he doesn't lose any traps, and he's got his money back with another thousand. He's not exactly a fool, you know. He stopped being crazy about the place the minute he saw what was waiting for him. . . . Can you climb a ladder?"

"I'm not that much older than you," said Claire. "And we do use our legs in the city, more than you'd imagine." She felt an almost gay vanity about her balance and speed.

He came up beside her and tied the painter to a post. "Look," he said, "you tell Mag how it is, huh? Tell her Rafe's not going to live in the house. When she's through with it they'll sell it first chance they get, to summer people, not a fisherman. So you tell her." He gave her a smile of great sweetness. "Come on, I'll show you the sights."

·8·

When Finn was walking up to the Abbott place, he had a sudden fit of self-consciousness. Maybe she'd only been polite when she said she'd like to go to the island. People like her, who spoke in the way that was elegant without being fancy, could make the smallest word sound important. It was the difference between her and Hester; Hester worked till she was blue in the face trying to sound the way Claire sounded without trying, and Hester never came anywhere near. That's why Hester was so damn nasty to her, he thought; the minute Claire opened her mouth Hester could've killed her. And he grinned with pleasure at Hester's chagrin, and then bit his lip with bashfulness. A girl like that was used to being nice to everybody; even if she had been laughing at him behind that gentle look of hers, as Rafe said she was, she was too much of a lady ever to let him know. He felt as if he'd taken on a new tight varnish of sunburn, he was so hot suddenly, and he stopped on the road and wondered what in time he was wagging these damn boots up to Mag's for.

Then he went doggedly on. Hell, he'd go all the way and let her tell him she wasn't going. If she'd been brought up to be polite to everybody, she'd know how to get rid of him without being embarrassed. He wouldn't want to embarrass her, he thought earnestly. And he wouldn't get stuffy about it and think she was a stuck-up bitch. Anybody had the right to choose, didn't they?

But when he saw her there in the kitchen his picture of her became completely false. Just by dwelling on her voice he had made her something different. Now he saw her in slacks and shirt, her short hair ruffled as if she'd been running her hands through it, her cheekbones flushed, no make-up, so that she had an oddly kiddish, shiny look; and in her eyes was the same expression he'd seen in Gil's store when he and Roy met her, a not-knowing what to expect next or where it was coming from.

He stopped being self-conscious, and was again eager to show her the island, or at least the surface of things. "I'll just give you the twenty-five-cent tour today," he told her. "You have to go in training for the five-dollar one. That takes in the whole two hundred and fifty acres."

"Then I'll go into training tomorrow," she said. "Because I can't pass up the chance to get acquainted with an island."

He took her across the Neck, where the beach gravel and rockweed had been strewn over the path by breaking seas in the last storm. They skirted the edge of the woods and he pointed out the beginning of the old road he'd found and cleaned out to the very eastern tip of the island. "The place with the thrushes is on the way," he said.

"When do they come?"

"I'll tell you when they're here."

She gave him a serious nod as if to seal a bargain. In the fishhouse she looked around intelligently, and didn't wrinkle her nose at the smell of bait, at least not when he was looking at her. The chickadees discovered them when the path went through the alders and impudently accompanied them; he was pleased because they showed off so well, and made her smile.

Across the field behind the house he showed her where the woodcock was courting, flying up and up in the dusk and scaling down in a chittering, whistling descent until the instant when he plunged straight like a stone; to repeat his flight from twilight to dark, over and over, night after night, until his mate was won, and sitting on her eggs. And he would go on with it until the eggs were hatched.

"Keeps her entertained," said Finn. "Better than television. I've got a couple of pair now. Partridges in there too. They know I won't shoot 'em." He cleared his throat. "Of course I don't talk about it off the island."

"I won't either," she said.

He showed her fresh deer tracks, and the wild apple tree where he had once seen four does and their fawns in an October dawn. Then he took her around to the front of the house and down to the shore of the big cove. "Right here," he said, pointing to a spot in the overgrown field, "an old dog fox used to go mousing. Pounce just like a cat." He saw the rusty-yellow animal clearly and his mind went up over the hill with him to the unknown den, and was a little disturbed. "Come to think of it, I haven't seen him for a long time. . . . See that nice flat ledge there with the water washing easy around it? There's a seal flops up on there on good afternoons and suns himself. He looks like a gravy pitcher."

Claire laughed, and he was happy to have pleased her. On the beach he told her how he'd had his first traps out in the cove, and how he had gone fishing every afternoon, even in the rain, for pollock to bait his traps because his brothers wouldn't let him beg off them. "Why should they, anyway?" he said. "They paid for it, salted it. I learned early to get my own bait and take care of it. But my mother used to think they were awful mean to the baby." He went on talking about the cove and the life he had lived on or around it, and she listened with solemn attention, her eyes on his face except when they followed his explanatory gestures. Then, as if the island were an animate and loving child of his, wanting to make him proud of it, it managed to turn up a perfect flint knife at his boot toe. With a smile of satisfaction he felt its edge, and gave it to Claire.

"It hasn't been out of the ground for long. Feel that blade.

It'll still cut. Our hands are likely the first to touch it in three or four hundred years."

"*Really?*" She stared at the object on her palm; it was leaf-shaped, with a waxy green luster, and looked freshly worked.

"Yes. Some Indian lost it here and I'll bet he went around for days groaning and saying, 'You know that was the best damn knife I ever made me!'" He didn't know why it tickled him so when he could amuse her. "I took the scales off a mess of harbor pollock with a scraper I found. It really worked, and I told my brothers."

"What did they say?"

"Oh, they think I'm not all there and that just proved it, they said."

She said, "People said the same of Thoreau, but his words are still being read."

"Who's he?"

"A man who wanted to live in a hut by a lake and fish, and raise beans, and have time to think."

"And he wrote about it, huh?" said Finn. "I suppose the people who read it are the ones who wish they could do it, but they don't."

"Sometimes they can't," said Claire, "and sometimes they don't dare to. Or they haven't found a place. There aren't many left." She looked up at the thick grove of blue spruces climbing the hill, at the wild field, the smoke bank of alders behind the house; she kept turning, taking in the wild apple trees, the jumbled rocks of the shore, the big cove; then her eyes came back to the Indian knife in her hand. "All this is becoming as rare and strange as if it were on another planet. I never knew what it would be like. I never dreamed." Suddenly she shivered; her face looked pinched, her eyes too big. He hadn't planned to take her into the house, not expecting she'd do it anyway without his mother there—he knew that much about the proper thing—but now he felt concern for her and said, "Come on up to the house and warm up, and I'll make some tea."

"All right," she said in a natural way. He liked that; she didn't behave as if he were making a pass at her, or working up to it. In the house she looked around, not caring if he saw her curiosity. "I love lamps," she said, "but I suppose they're a nuisance to you. Do you mind my asking how you manage to get those soap-bubble chimneys so clean?"

"You ought to see how many I've busted. Nope, I have to admit my mother's the reason it looks so good around here," he said. "She's home once a week and scrubs the place up, and I kind of neat it up in between."

"That tea kettle's a work of art, it's so shiny," Claire said as he set it over the flames.

"Ayuh." He kept his face straight, and went hastily into the pantry to get cookies out of the crock. The tea kettle had been one thing he'd overlooked when he was getting ready for Lila, and she'd spend an hour scouring it and had sent him to the well twice. He'd expected to have to drag her upstairs by force, lugging her over his shoulder like those women being toted off by the soldiers in the old books.

There were a few cups and saucers left of the old set sprigged with fine brown flowers that had been left in the house when Dolly's folks moved into it. He got out two of Dolly's good napkins and the flowered pot Roy had sent from Japan at the end of the war. Claire sat in his knitting rocker at the end of the stove. It was a funny thing that she didn't make him nervous, gazing around at the crazy collection of odds and ends on the mantel and the window sashes and then at him, all with the same thorough attention.

"I guess you've never been in such a place," he said, digging a tablespoon into the can of loose tea.

"I guess you've never made much tea in a pot."

"Huh?"

"A teaspoon's better." She had a little quirky smile. "One for each cup and one for the pot."

"Guess I'd have come up with a good sheep dip or something fit to tan leather in. Why don't you make it?

"All right." She moved easily around the old wood stove, as if it were all natural to her. She warmed the pot with boiling water first, and then turned it economically into the wash basin; he thanked God piously that he'd scrubbed out the black sink. "What a lovely pantry," she called out to him. "And with a lilac outside the window."

"White one," he answered back. "Double. Smells some pretty."
All at once he could see Pa sitting in this very chair, nursing
his old corncob pipe in his big hand, and he could hear Pa's
voice so plain it was startling. "A lady bred and born. . . ."
He must have been talking about someone they knew, but it
could have been said about Claire.

"I think by the time we set the table the tea will be ready to
pour," she said. He jumped up and they carried the dishes out
to the sun porch. "You like milk in yours?" he asked her.

"I like it without anything, when it's good tea like this." She
lifted the pot and poured the tea. Everything she touched, the
old cups and saucers and the faded oilcloth, became something
different from what it had been. Elegance, he gloated. Pure
elegance, like a racing sloop.

"How come you never visited Mag before?" he asked her.

"Aunt Mag was just a name to me for years. We're not really
related, you know. She was my step-grandmother's cousin, and
all I ever knew of her was what Stella told me in casual conversation. And Stella always had so many other things to talk about
there wasn't much time for Mag." She lifted her cup and
sipped. "You have a beautiful view here everywhere you look."
She kept her eyes on the view and went on. "When my
husband died there was a card signed Mag Abbott, and a
message written on the back of it. I don't know if you've ever
seen it, but she has the strongest, most jagged, blackest writing
I've seen. Its vitality fairly shouted at me in that sickening
hush. She told me that if I ever needed to get where I could
breathe, she had room for me."

"So you came."

"Not for a year. Then she wrote and asked me to help her get
ready to move. And she was right, this is the place to breathe
in. I'm sorry for all the years when I didn't know what it
was like."

"So am I," said Finn. "Maybe you'd have married one of
my brothers."

"Rafe?" she suggested, and they both laughed. Then Finn
said, "Heck, that's not so far-fetched. If you had, he might be
halfway human by now." She was looking down at her cup,
her narrow face emptied, and he was ashamed without know-

ing why. "I guess I shouldn't joke that way," he said. "Even if you'd come here a lot you'd never have married a Pointer. It'd have to be someone in your own class."

She looked up at him from gray eyes that were watery-bright, but her smile was amused. "And just what is my class? No, I like your jokes, Finn. And Mag's. I like to laugh, I always did."

"I guess you haven't had much to laugh about, though."

"More tea?" She lifted the pot and he pushed his cup across to her. "Not recently, no. David died of cancer. We had a long time to prepare for it. So long that I'm in danger of forgetting there was anything else to our marriage but that. She handed the cup back. "And then there's this terrible sense of injustice one has to fight off before it corrupts what's left of life. I've done better here. . . . And I've been talking and not giving my full attention to the view. What's the name of that big island over there?"

"Hollowell." Finn folded his arms on the table edge and studied her. He felt a new awe in her presence. Those calm eyes watching a fish hawk hovering over the cove had watched her husband die. *Cancer.* The word twisted in his guts. They could give the man things to kill the pain, but they couldn't give her anything. She had to find it in herself, and she had found it, so she could sit opposite him now, straight in her chair, looking out at the cove and sipping tea from an old cup as if she were in one of those fancy hotels in London or Paris.

This was the woman Hester tried to insult, the one Rafe called a stuck-up bitch. He felt hot, his hands made into fists under the table. What bastards they all were! He wanted badly to give her something, and he remembered the day they'd told him about Pa, and how on his way back from the woods he'd picked some violets for Dolly, wanting to give her something because she was unhappy.

He got up abruptly and went to the door and opened it "You see that cove? A man from across the river took fifty thousand bushels of herring out of there right under my nose last summer. Another man took plenty more out of the harbor here. Well, if anybody's going to get herring around this island it ought to be me. So this is the year I'm getting in on it, but I haven't told anybody yet. Anybody but you, that is. I want Larry and Elmer with me, but I'm not saying anything till I get the twine."

"I won't mention it even to Mag. Scout's honor." She held up her hand. "What do you mean by *twine?*"

"The nets, the seine. It's expensive as hell." He was so excited that when he heard the word he couldn't go back to pick it up. The idea had simply been puddling around in the back of his mind, never clear, never really possible, until now, and he couldn't tell why it had suddenly become something he could touch, handle, *do,* with no more waiting. "What you do is get one of the factories to fit you out, and you pay for your gear as you go along. Or you go to some big seiner like Harvey Eastman over at Port George and see if he'll outfit you. It means you're really working for him but you're still on your own, because all he wants is for you to come up with herring. My boat's all right, or she will be as soon as I get her fixed up."

"It sounds awfully good to me," said Claire.

"It *is* good. You have to work around the clock sometimes, and pull your guts out—excuse me—dragging on that seine, but when you know you've got fish it's like nothing else in the world." He struck one fist into the other palm. "Like nothing else. . . . Oh, gorry, I'll have to have a radio on my boat now so I can call the carriers." He was deflated. He dropped into a chair and thrust out his legs and stared at his boots. A radio meant three hundred dollars more than what he'd saved to pay Spicer for the work on the boat. He pulled at his lower lip; despondency rushed in, a wet icy flood to replace the exhilarating belief that everything was possible. Oh goddam, why had he burst out with it like some little kid? Made a fool of himself in front of her. He pulled himself up with an effort and grinned at her. "You must think the Judsons are crazy as coots."

"What's the trouble, the radio?" she asked.

"How'd you know?"

"Because the same thing's happened to me; I've had just enough to do something and then needed more, and it had taken me so long to get the *first* amount that—well——" She shrugged. "Result, total desolation. Or so I thought at the time."

"You weren't ever that hard up, were ye?"

"I worked for a living before I was married. I intend to work again. Look, isn't there somebody'd who'd help you get the radio-telephone? One of your brothers?"

"Oh, I'll figure out something. Maybe Harve will stake me to a telephone along with the twine." Immediately he felt that this would actually happen. The talk about the herring had been his gift to Claire, like the violets to Dolly, but in some curious way it had turned out to be a gift to himself too. He felt like kicking off his boots and turning cartwheels across the lawn. He had to do something quick. He jumped up, almost knocking over his chair, and went into the sitting room to fetch the *Dolly J.* off the mantel. He set the model down before Claire. "Look, my father whittled her out, made the sails, anchor, blocks, the whole thing. She's a salter. And you should see her go. I'll take you and Nancy out to sail her some day in the cove."

"She's a handsome vessel and we'd both love it," said Claire. She sighed. "Time to go back. Look how far the tide's gone."

"Now you can show me how well you go down a ladder."

"You'll be astonished. Going down a ladder is only one of my many talents."

"Maybe you should have been a fireman,"

"What do you think my job was?"

They talked foolishness going along the path, but when they reached the wharf she said, "I'm the first person you've talked to about going for herring. Well, Finn, you're the first person I've talked to about David. I know it wasn't much, but for me it was a great deal. So thank you."

"I thank you too," he said stiffly. He couldn't tell her that it wasn't just for getting him going about herring; if he told her it was for gracing his house, for pouring tea at his table, she might think he meant something else and she would be embarrassed and the whole thing would fall apart like a pine-boarded skiff caught in the surf on a galeswept ledge.

·9·

The warm spell gave way to cold and wind, spatters of freezing rain, and a miserable gray-and-white chop in which it was hard to find the buoys. *Foam-Flower* began to leak at the Seal Ledges. Finn looked around and saw only one of his brothers in sight, Roy was pitching in the heavy seas off Mackerel Shoal; he would be having all he could do keeping his balance and finding his pots. Rafe wasn't out. Finn's relief that Cleon couldn't see him tempered slightly his wrath at having to give up a day's hauling when he needed the money so much. He headed home, bow into the short deep northeast chop. Larry and Elmer were hauling near each other out by the can buoy, bouncing around like a pair of sea ducks. Their boats might be small, but they were tight. Blast the need for recaulking and renailing. He hunched his shoulders under his oilcoat and watched bleakly as Tom Hunt disappeared past the end of Hollowell, and Bart Collins vanished into the mist of spray and showers to the west'ard. Almost everybody was out today and everybody would do staving, and where in hell was all his ambition about the herring? Oh, it had been fine yesterday in the sunshine, showing off like a kid walking the barn ridgepole in front of a girl. Showing off was all it was, if a cold wind and a leaky boat could kill it off that quick. God, but he was cold.

He was crossing the broad mouth of the big cove and he could see his house serene and yet watchful as he went by. A vision of the warm kitchen made him colder; the snug disorder, the teakettle droning away like bees in the catnip, the creak of his chair as he knit a traphead, his book on the table handy to be read while he ate. He had half the length of the island to go, straight into the wind, before he could make the turn into the harbor.

Water streamed constantly down his windshield. Off the easterly point of the cove there was a tide rip that threw him all ways for Sunday. By the time he'd got her over the shoal and into deeper water Cleon was abreast of him, engine wide open so that his bow was slicing the waves through before he dropped too deeply into the troughs. Cleon signaled frantically past the sprayhood and Finn tried to become invisible between oiljacket and sou'wester brim, at least to make Cleon think he hadn't seen him yet. He swore loudly and stared ahead through the streaming glass. But out of the corner of his eye he could see *Onni J.* forging closer and closer.

They were traveling close to the shore, and a little point with tall trees on it made a sort of windbreak. Finn slowed down and went into neutral as Cleon came alongside, his gaff in his hand.

"What's the matter?" he yelled.

"I'm going back for a clean hanky," Finn shouted back. "And I forgot to go to the bathroom too!"

Cleon was not amused. "Leaking bad?"

"Bad enough," said Finn. "But I'm not kicking. I got plenty I can do ashore. Go on back to work."

"Listen, you going to be a numbhead all your life? They've got just the boat for you at Johansen's in Williston. I saw it when I was taking a look at Rafe's new boat the other day, but every time I see you you're in a goddam hurry."

"I'm in one now," said Finn. "I got a feeling the water'll be coming through the floorboards any minute."

"Ain't you interested in that boat?"

"No sense being interested in something I can't afford."

"Who says you can't afford it? You got a family, haven't ye?" Cleon was red-faced under the sou'wester brim.

"Ayuh, I got a family but I'm a stiff-necked son of a bitch too!" Finn yelled back at him. "You told me that yourself. Remember?" He grinned at Cleon, who unhooked his gaff and slammed it down on his washboard, gunned his engine and swung out. *Foam-Flower* rolled in the backwash.

Finn allowed himself one tormenting vision of the boat hauled out at the shop in Williston. Rafe and Cleon had likely been all over her, so Cleon knew what he was talking about. What would it be like to step into a boat that needn't be babied? Having *Foam-Flower* overhauled wasn't any guarantee that she'd be good as new; she was too old for that, she'd been old when he got her four years ago.

Suddenly she lurched under him and his mouth twitched. He patted the upright beside him. "Don't you worry, old girl. I'm not putting you up on the bank to die yet. By the time I'm ready, you'll be ready too."

There was more tide running hard at the harbor mouth and then, abruptly, silence and calm with the sea pigeons and old-squaws paddling around among the moorings where only skiffs were left. On the purple-mussel beds the gulls and crows were feeding amicably.

Finn came up to his mooring and gaffed his buoy with the leisurely expertise of experience. The tide was too low for him to take the boat to the wharf; he'd have to bring her in later and put his bait back in the pickle. He'd taken only fifteen lobsters so far, and no use getting Gil into his oilclothes for no more than that. He put them in a crate off the stern.

Once he was rowing down the harbor, the rain pattering on his oilclothes and Gil's woodsmoke perfuming the wet air, he felt more agreeable; the spell of fine weather had been a big help, and if he got a couple of balls of nylon knit up today that would put him well ahead on that chore.

He began to whistle; and then as he approached the wharf he saw Rafe's outboard skiff at the foot of the ladder. There was a bristling sensation at the back of his neck. So what? Rafe had a right to come over here, but why the hell did he always come when Finn was gone?

There was no sign of life around the fishhouse and nothing was disturbed, but as he went up through the alders, fresh smoke blew down from the kitchen chimney. "Makes himself right at home, don't he?" he growled. "Hasn't missed a corner from cellar to attic. Nosier than ten women."

He opened the door more violently than usual and tramped heavily into the porch.

"Well, here's my bouncing boy now!" Dolly announced. "Where'd you come from? When I hit the house you were going down by the can buoy toward the Seal Rocks."

"Leaking again?" Rafe had a smug grin. "I told you he'd be in, didn't I? He can't stand anything more than a five-mile breeze." He stood at the end of the stove with his foot on the hearth. Hester sat in Finn's knitting rocker. She gave him a careful smile so as not to disturb her lipstick. She was a big woman whose thighs swelled over the sides of his chair. Her fine regular features seemed to grow smaller each year as she put on weight. She wore an expensive tweed skirt and a wine-colored suede jacket, with a jaunty pointed cap of the same leather perched on her thick crown of braids.

"Hi, Hes," said Finn as he kicked off his oilpants. "Where's your bow and arrow?"

Hester managed an artificial titter. He knew at once that she was bound and determined to be pleasant, and that made him tired. Hester working to be nice was a lot harder to take than Hester being downright cussed. It was painful, that's what it was. He turned to his mother, who sat at the table with a cup of coffee and a cigarette. "What are *you* doing here?"

"What a welcome from the apple of my eye!" Dolly was short, plump, and loud; he hoped Hester was wincing as the vibrant tones bounced around the small kitchen. "I switched days off with Bess, that's all. And I got the worst of the deal, if you ask me. I should've stayed in town and gone to a movie."

"Well, why didn't you?" Finn got a mug out of the pantry and dumped instant coffee in it.

"Thought my youngest just might possibly need some cooking or cleaning done, but from the looks of the place he's had ten women looking after him."

"Well, one that we know of," drawled Hester.

Dolly put her arm around Finn's middle and squeezed. "Real lady's man, ain't he? Just like his pa." Dolly colored her hair a richer red-brown than it had ever been, and kept it relentlessly curled; but behind the lipstick and eyebrow pencil which she applied with a dashing disregard for precision, she kept the high-colored good looks, too vigorous to be called prettiness, that had worried her father. "What girl did such a good job on the stove and the teakettle, honey? Whoever she is, grab onto her."

"It couldn't have been the one he brought over here yesterday," said Hester gaily. "I'm sure *she* never blacked a stove in her life!"

"Maybe not," said Rafe, "but that don't keep her from thinking the place goes with Finn, and that makes him a pretty good catch for a widow with a kid. That is, if the place could be sold, afterward." He was smiling, to show it was a joke. Finn ignored him and took his coffee over to the kitchen table. There was a box of doughnuts open and he took one.

"Let's all sit down and be cozy," cried Dolly. "Listen to it rain now! Tell me about the widow, Finn. Where'd you meet her? Is she pretty?"

"She's about ten years older than he is, that's all," said Rafe, sitting down at the table. Hester sipped from her cup and smiled into it. "Staying with Mag. When I went up there to tell Mag about the place, *this* critter—well, when I saw her with Finn yesterday afternoon I thought God help my kid brother if she's got her claws into him."

"That's a little strong, Rafe," Hester said. "After all, Finn wasn't born yesterday. He must know *something* about predatory females."

Finn gave her a look from under his eyebrows and went on stirring his coffee.

"He'll land on his feet," Dolly said. "Don't keep trying to bring him up, Rafe. He's all brought up."

"He'll be brought up with a round turn one of these days when that boat sinks under him."

Finn laid down his spoon and his doughnut and stared at Rafe. "Did you come over to bring Dolly," he inquired, "or to needle me?"

"Oh, don't be so touchy. Anybody'd think you had a guilty conscience. Sure, I brought Ma over, and then I figured I might get her to talk a little sense into your thick head. Cleon told you yet about that boat up at Johansen's?"

"Talk about a thick head. He comes all the way across from Hollowell when he sees me going home, to ask me *if* I'm going home, *if* I'm leaking, and then to tell me all about this boat as if it's flat-arse calm in the middle of June."

"That's old Bumblefoot," said Rafe. "I don't know how he stays out of his own way. But if he told you that's the boat for you, he's right. She's thirty feet long, only eight years old, practically a new Chrysler in her, been all renailed. You could step in her today and bring her home."

"Who wanted to get rid of her and why?"

"I don't know him, but he had a heart attack and had to stop lobstering. Look, Finn—" Rafe leaned across the table, his eyes taking on the familiar blue shine. "We'll get her for you. We're ready to, the minute you say the word."

"Oh, Finn honey!" Dolly bounced like a girl. "I'm glad I came home after all, to get in on this. Let's drive up and take a look at her."

Finn looked fixedly into Rafe's eyes. "What's the deal?"

"What do you mean, deal?" Rafe was soft, not affronted.

"What do *you* want out of it?"

"Not even interest!" Rafe tipped his chair back, tucked his thumbs in his belt, and waited.

"Oh, you should have heard the two of them after they'd seen the boat," Hester murmured to Dolly, chuckling intimately as if she really liked her mother-in-law instead of considering her a disgrace. "They were like two doting uncles planning to surprise their nephew with an electric train. They were so excited. Rafe even wanted to buy it right away and bring it downriver and tie it up at the wharf here."

"Is that a fact, Rafe?" Finn asked solemnly. "Were you all tickled at the thought?"

"Well, I wasn't quite that hysterical about it. Just hated to see one of us lose out on a good thing, like the Abbott place. You have to grab those things while they're available."

"Come on, Daddy," said Finn, "tell me more about how you bought up all the railroads, and cornered all the gold that time."

Dolly giggled. "Look, are we going up to take a look at her or not? Who minds the rain? We're all good Baptists here. Except Hes." She threw a twinkle in her daughter-in-law's direction. "I keep forgetting she's practically a Catholic."

"Episcopalian," Hester said in the dead tone of one who has said it a hundred times and expects to go on saying it for a lifetime. Dolly's laugh, the sparkling young spray of sound that had won Jud, made even Rafe's mouth twitch; carefully he disregarded his wife. "Come on, Finn," he said. "What are you scared of?"

"You don't want to ask me that right out or I might tell ye." He took his mug over to the stove and poured more hot water in it. "Look, I'll say what I told Cleon. I'm a stiff-necked son of a bitch. I thank you for your offer, but I'll have me a new boat when I can pay for it cash on the barrelhead, and then I'll be beholden to nobody."

"I told you, Rafe. I *told* you." Hester's voice climbed, shedding its gentility.

"Shut up," said Rafe. "You won't be beholden to us, you ape. No interest, pay as you go—"

And for the rest of my life, Finn said, but to himself. If he said it aloud the battle would be on, and if he ever intended to speak that bluntly to Rafe he didn't want Hester around. He said amiably, "It ain't that I don't appreciate your interest. It's just that I got my own way of doing things, same as you have."

Rafe stood up. "You're a stupid jackass," he said tightly. "You always were. Come on, Hester." She got up from the rocker with surprising agility for one so big. She took her raincoat and hat from behind the stove and went out into the porch to put them on, staring woodenly at the sodden day as if she couldn't bear to look at Finn or his mother another moment.

"It was real nice of you to come along with Rafe, Hes," Finn said to her back.

"I thought it was," said Dolly chattily. "We don't see enough of Hes over here on the island."

Finn reached out and took another doughnut and Rafe finished fastening up his oiljacket. The typical flush of his anger stayed.

"Thanks for coming out in the wet to bring me over, son," Dolly said.

He grunted something and went out. Hester gave them a sidewise dart of her dark eyes and followed him. "Open that door again," Finn called to his mother, "and let's get some fresh air in here."

She obeyed and stood in the doorway for a few moments. "Hester walked right along good when we came up to the house," she observed. "Now she's acting like she's walking through a solid mess of cowflaps. I'll bet she won't go down the ladder and he'll have to take her off the rocks. I don't know who she thinks she's fooling, after all this time." She came back into the kitchen, looking contrite. "I hadn't ought to be mean about poor Hes. At least she's striving ever upward, like they say we should."

She sat down opposite Finn and lit a cigarette. "Well, now that the Four Hundred's gone I'll say it's good to see you," said Finn. "Met any new bus drivers lately?"

"You're a disgraceful pup. Who told you about bus drivers?" But the twinkle was there, irrepressible, and a girlish dimple appeared in her florid cheek.

"You can't keep anything like that quiet. Drinking coffee and eating pie at one in the morning in a public place with these dashing young guys on their way to Bangor or some such romantic spot. You've been seen, Ma, you've been seen. Who's the red-headed one? Is it the uniform that gets you, Ma? Same as Pa's uniform got you?"

"No harm in a little foolish talk and joking, is there?" Dolly sighed. "They know I'm old enough to be their mother, that's why they kid with me. They know I won't take it serious and make trouble for them, especially the married ones." She turned her wedding ring on her finger and said absently, "Trouble is, I don't *feel* old enough to be their mother. I only know it when I look in the mirror." Then the inextinguishable female rose again. "Of course I don't mind working nights on account of being able to take my coffee break when I do. Kind of peps me up for the rest of the night, warms up that miserable time toward dawn when we're likely to lose one." She pointed a finger at him and cried, "How'd you know about that red-head? You been driving up around Fremont in the middle of the night, spying on your old mother?"

"By gorry, that's an idea now! I'll come in and catch ye in the act and sing 'Mother, dear Mother, come home with me now'...." He was laughing so hard his eyes filled, and she began to gasp and dab at her own eyes.

"You young devil, you."

"It was Lila's brother saw you. Oh, he wasn't spiteful, Dolly. He thinks you're a fine figure of a woman."

"That's that fresh Ronnie." But she looked complacent. "Speaking of Lila, I found one of her bobby pins in your room. Now Finn, I know you're over twenty-one and this is your home, but I hope you aren't leading that girl on. And suppose one of your brothers found that bobby pin, instead of me?"

"They'd screech," said Finn, "like they'd lived in a monastery till they got married, instead of being the biggest whoremasters that ever were. No, I'm not leading Lila on." He was surprised to find he was blushing. How'd he overlook that damn bobby pin? Your mother might suspect you were carrying on, but just so long as she didn't know anything more about you than you did about her, it was all right; something was preserved. To get over his embarrassment he said, "Suppose Rafe and Hes saw you through that lunchroom window?"

She rolled her eyes to the ceiling. "*Screech* would be no word for it. Rafe never did approve of me and Hes thinks I'm a loose woman to begin with. She's scared to death somebody might connect me with her . . . Poor Hes." She always said that as if she meant it. She looked at him seriously. "Finn, honey, what did you want to be so stuffy about the boat for? My God, if Rafe wants to do something for you, you ought to grab onto it!"

"Like grabbing hold of a nice sharp steel trap," said Finn. "Look, Ma, you ought to know well enough by now that when Cleon and Rafe do anything for anybody they expect a hell of a lot back."

"Now what do they want? Just tell me that. What could Cleon want from you?" she persisted. "He only wants to help you. He fusses over you all the time like a mother hen."

"Then he ought to've hatched out some eggs of his own. If Onni had some kids maybe she'd keep out of mischief. Ma, if he helped me get a boat it'd never be my boat. And nothing I ever did in it would be my own business. He'd think he had a leash on me for fair."

"He tries to make up for you losing your father. He told me so."

"Ayuh," Finn mumbled. He went over to his rocker and began to work on the half-finished traphead hanging from the hook in the window sill. "But he don't need to. He wasn't responsible."

"What does Rafe want, then? If he's getting brotherly feelings, seems to me you'd ought to help them along."

Finn laughed. "Mebbe he wants me to use my influence with you."

"What influence?" She was suspicious at once. "Finn, has he been henning around again about me working? Ain't he got enough to do with running people out of here and buying property but he's got to get going on *me?* Won't he be content till he's got me shut up over here like one of those girls in the fairy tales?" She wiped her forehead. "There, I knew it, brought on a hot flash. What are you snickering about, you brat?"

"If Rafe's getting sonly feelings seems to me you'd ought to help them along."

She gave him a virulent look. "Well, is that it? Me working?"

"Ma, he's never mentioned it since the last time," he soothed her. "All I meant was that whenever Rafe does a favor he wants something back, and there's nothing I've got that he could possibly want unless it's your ear. That's what they all think, and you know that as well as I do."

"If it's not to stop me working, what is it then?"

"You own the island, Ma." They looked at each other for a moment, and then she sat down at the table and lit another cigarette.

"What do you think, Finn?"

"Same as I aways did." He began to knit again, keeping his eyes on the flat wooden shuttle darting in and out of the green nylon mesh. "But hell, it's your island. You could sell it tomorrow and go to California with the cash and none of us could say a word."

"I'd *have* to go to California," she said wryly. "Or to the moon. You'd be after me with a shotgun."

"I dunno as I'd go that far, but I wouldn't send you any more Mother's Day cards."

"You're a corker, Finn. That's what your father said first time he saw you. 'By gorry now, he's a corker!'" She ground out her cigarette. "I better go put on some potatoes. I wish you'd brought home a couple lobsters. I've been thinking of lobster for a week."

He jumped up, dropping the shuttle to dangle from the hook. "I didn't have enough to sell, so I put 'em in the crate. You just put on some water to boil. I'll have your lobsters here in a jiffy."

In the late afternoon the day cleared off to a dry crisp brilliance. Finn rowed Dolly across the harbor at five o'clock.

"It's some handsome out now," she said pensively, "but I'm glad I'm going back to Fremont."

"And the bus drivers," said Finn. "The Point can't offer anything like that. 'Course you might try for the gink that drives the bait truck."

"The way you talk anybody'd think I was man-crazy," Dolly protested. "I'm a respectable widow. I can't help it if men like *me*."

"I'm glad they do, darlin' mine. Just so long as you and that red-head don't elope to Mexico in his bus."

Dolly's laugh rang in the hush. Elmer and Larry, loading Elmer's boat with traps to set the next day, shouted a greeting at her from their wharf, and she went up the ramp with a springiness and a tilt to her head that made her younger than her daughters-in-law. Her old Chevrolet was parked near Gil's store. She had to sit on a cushion, and starting the engine took a great deal of energetic bouncing up and down in the seat as she tramped on the pedals. "Don't know how I'd ever get used to a car I didn't have to kick to get going," she said. "Well, I'll stop off and see Roy and Danny and leave the things I took last week to mend. Roy won't chew at me about you, he's got too much on his mind, poor young one." She looked worried and motherly for a moment, then she leaned out and kissed him. "So long, darlin'. Did I ever tell you you're the most like your father?"

He watched till she left the dirt road and was going up by Rafe's, and then he went down to where Larry and Elmer were working. He joined in the job without speaking. What had begun when he saw Rafe's skiff at the ladder in the morning had stayed all day, behind the joking with his mother; an icy resolution that was new to him. His brain worried at it, nosed it around, turned it over, struggled to give it a comprehensive shape and name. He did not like it and yet suddenly it had become a part of him he could not do without. The morning when he gazed yawning from Rafe's fishhouse and thought *It's April* seemed an impossibly long time ago.

Someone spoke to him. "What?" he said absently.

"Ain't it time you took your boat down to Spicer?" Larry said.

"I'm going to talk to him right off. Hey, Elmer, can I rent your dory and outboard while she's laid up?"

"Sure." They finished loading the traps, all the squat broad boat would hold on her stern, and Elmer checked the lines fore and aft. "I guess she'll keep for another half-hour before I put her back on the mooring. Come on up to the house and have a mug-up. My supper's down in my left foot somewhere."

"Wait a minute," said Finn. "Can I take the dory now to go over to Port?" He hadn't planned it that way; it was this new cold drive in him that wouldn't let him be, even to sit in Elmer's kitchen plaguing Josie and trotting the baby on his boot. *This is the way the gentleman rides, Galop-a-trot, galop-a-trot . . .* Pa's voice, Pa's way. But he wasn't Pa, for all Dolly called him the one most like.

"What's over there, a new line of goodies?" Larry was shamelessly greedy. "My God, I'm only a year older than him and got three kids, and a wife that ropes and ties me if I so much as wave at a girl on a fancy speedboat in the summer time."

"Oh, stop drooling," said Elmer. "They'll catch him sometime. Ten years from now he'll have a *pot* on him and six kids and a worried stare. Sure, Finn, take the dory. The outboard's in the fishhouse and the tank's full."

Finn carried the engine down the ramp to the dory and the other two came behind him, Elmer carrying the tank and Larry mourning, "Oh, for a bachelor existence! Entertaining pretty ladies in your own snug little house. Got one kind for nights and another for daytime." He whistled a bar of "I Wish I Was Single Again." "I'd go with ye tonight, except I'd cramp your style. Women like us short fellers, you know that?"

"Brings out the mother in 'em, I shouldn't wonder," said Elmer.

"When I come back I'll tell you what I found over there," Finn said. "If I find anything real enticing, that is."

"What's the good of telling us if we can't have any?"

"Well, you could be glad for *me*, couldn't you?" asked Finn piously. He started the outboard and headed for the lower harbor. He stood in the stern, his hands in his pockets and his big shoulders hunched against the cold flow of air around his ears. Wet rocks flashed and gleamed as the late sun struck them. Reflections writhed in serpentine patterns that broke and reformed constantly; a yellow light lay over everything. Spicers' children were out rowing in a skiff, and they waved and shouted at Finn, who returned their greetings with the expected enthusiasm. He went slowly past them across the floating green-bronze rockweed that dragged at the dory's bottom.

Morry stood on his wharf and watched the approach, his hands in his pockets and a cigar in his mouth. He was a stout man, growing bald, wearing glasses with heavy black bows. He waved the cigar at Finn. "Great evening."

"Finest kind. You see your way clear? I've got the money."

Spicer waved the cigar again as if in blessing. "Bring her down tomorrow morning and we'll get her up on the high water." He pointed the cigar at the children in the skiff. "Warn't for them I'd give more credit."

"Listen, I don't blame you," said Finn. "I'd do the same thing myself. See you tomorrow." He backed away across the gently pulling weed and made a wide slow circle around the children.

It took him fifteen minutes to cross the river to Port George. After the rain squalls and the racing gray and white chop, the water now moved in long gentle swells. Over the open sea the sky was clear and bright except for a freighter's trail of smoke, distinct as an ink scribble. To the north the water moved in a slow broad tide between the banks toward Williston; beyond the visible end of this avenue of light the Fremont hills were washed in with delicate clarity against a pale sky.

Finn came around a long wooded point and entered the harbor of Port George. It was a big harbor, crowded with lobster boats, seiners, small draggers, and a few yachts still snugged down for the winter. The Port George Packing Company was at the far end, and one of the big carriers, *Thetis*, was tied up at the factory

Eastman's *Nerita*. This is your day, old son, Finn told himself, dock. A forty-five-foot boat was made fast beside her; Harve unless he's uptown getting drunk.

The seaplane from which Junior Eastman spotted herring was anchored in the lee of the dock and Otter Hill, looking like an exotic red-and-silver bird blown off course in a storm and resting now on alien waters. Finn admired it as he passed. When he shut off his engine and came along side *Nerita* he could near the radio crackling aboard *Thetis*, and the skipper's answering drawl. "Ayuh, ayuh, Chick. Well, I'll tell ye, we're taking off for Cape Porpoise in another hour, Chick, so it looks like we won't be able to take out your fish till tomorrow night. How many you think you got anyway, Chick? Ovah." The distant voice began again. Finn climbed aboard *Nerita* and knocked on the canopy roof.: "Anybody home?" he shouted.

"Hi, there. Somebody want me?" Harve Eastman came out of *Thetis'* wheelhouse, squinting in the sunset glare. "Who's that?"

"Can I talk to you a minute, Cap'n?"

"Guess you can if you ain't serving some kind of papers, land me in jail." He was rawboned and hawk-nosed, moving his angular body with deceptive ease as he came down over the side and landed in his own cockpit. "Well, it's one of the Judson boys. Finn, ain't it? Hello!" They shook hands. Finn felt the warning tremors of excitement and his mouth was drying. Goddam a fool, he thought, you aren't proposing marriage, just a business deal.

"I took a chance you might be here," Finn said. "I didn't want to go up to your house and bother your wife for nothing."

"God, deah, nothing bothers her. If it did, she wouldn't have stayed married to a seiner all these years. Come on below, away from that radio. Clint's talking with everybody from Isles of Shoals to Machias."

In the cabin he turned on the gas stove and set the coffee pot over the flame. "Now," he said, "sit down and tell me what I can do for ye."

"Well, I guess there's no way to lead up to it gradual," said Finn. "I want to go seining for you. I've got a boat, and I can get the crew."

Harve's eyes had a glint like the frozen river under a winter moon. "That's all there is to it, huh? And you'll make your fortune and mine too. How do I know you won't turn the twine back to me in a week all tore to hell and say that's the end of it, you ain't a herring man after all?"

"You don't know," said Finn reasonably. He wanted to wet his mouth, but not while Harve was watching him. He hadn't known, talking to Claire, that he'd feel like this; it was worse than proposing marriage could ever be. He said, "All you know is I want to do it, and I'm pretty sure I can."

"Ayuh, I know." Eastman poured bubbling black coffee into mugs, pushed one toward Finn, and a can of evaporated milk. "One thing I hate is drinking alone."

Finn was glad of the coffee to moisten his throat, and give his hands something to do. He added milk and sugar and stirred vigorously. He wondered if he should say more, but there was nothing more than what he had just said. Finally Harve had his coffee fixed the way he wanted it. He took a long noisy sip and said, "God, deah, the best cup I've had all day." He smacked his lips and set the mug down. "Well, I'll tell ye, boy. You're a Judson, and from what I've seen of the rest they're a hard-headed crew who'd never let anything stand in the way of making a dollar. I hear that Rafe Judson would sign a contract with the devil himself if he could make anything on the deal. So if the cut of your jib is anything like the rest of 'em, I'm inclined to be partial to ye." He took another drink of coffee and smacked his lips again. "Dammit, I dunno how I got that just right. . . . Tell you what, you line up your crew and then come back and talk to me a couple a days from now. Any of your brothers ever gone seining?"

"My brother Roy went seining for five years with Darby Dunton. He took charge all one summer when Darby was laid up, and they made plenty that year."

"I remember that summer well. Darby's gang skunked us all. Well, sounds as if you got one man who ain't green. Come back— let's see—" He stared at the calendar, which was decorated by an extremely nude girl. "We're going down east but I got to be back by Sunday. Junior's having his boy sprinkled and none of the womenfolk'll speak to me again if I ain't there. You know fishing ain't what it was in the old days," he said plaintively. "Imagine telling a man he's got to be back by Sunday. It's a god's wonder I ever make a dime."

"Well, it's not every day you have a grandson christened," Finn said. "When shall I come?"

"Oh, Monday morning." He shrugged. "I'll be here or home.... Did you happen to see how much sugar I put in this brew?"

"Gorry, I didn't," Finn apologized. Harve shook his head.

"Once in fifty cups I get just the right blend and I can't remember how I did it."

"Hey, Harve!" someone shouted from the carrier.

"Whoever it is, come aboard and bring your dory!" Harve shouted back. There was a noisy thudding of boots and a burst of swearing and laughter. Finn said good night and left.

Outside the harbor dusk was blotting out the distances and hurrying toward him over the sea. The water rushing past him had a satiny shimmer but no color; the dory plunged smoothly headlong, and he stood up so he could watch out for the lobster buoys that showed like seals' heads. The island and the mainland blended into one long black mass, but as he approached it the harbor opened to him, broad and glimmering with the last stolen light from the sky.

The Johnson-Curtis fishhouse was lighted, and he thundered with his fists on the sliding door. "Open up, it's the law!"

"We ain't got no bad wimmen in here, nor whiskey either," Larry whined. Finn went in, blinking against the light. They were knitting trapheads. "Gawd, you're back quick," said Elmer. "Couldn't you make no time with her?"

"Well, no wonder, going courting in rubber boots," said Larry.

"Ayuh, I've been courting all right," Finn hoisted himself onto the bench. "And the rubber boots didn't make a particle of difference. How'd you smart alecs like to go for herring this year and catch some of that money that's swimming around?"

Larry's small bony face twisted into a monkey-grimace. Elmer looked stupidly blank. "What do you mean about herring?"

"Just that. Something I've been thinking about for a long time. Well, tonight I put things in motion. I went over to see Harve Eastman, and it's as simple as that."

Larry's voice squeaked. "He's going to fit you out?"

"I'm almost positive. He just about talks anybody to death, but I got that much clear. He's inclined to it, he says."

"Did he say, 'God, deah, you're hired'?" asked Elmer. They all laughed wildly, like overexhilarated children.

"I'm supposed to line up my crew and see him Monday morning," Finn said. "So now I'm lining up my crew. I had you guys in mind from the first, so if you don't want to go that's the end of it."

"Jeez, I'll go," said Larry reverently. "I'll go tomorrow. Take up my traps first," he added more practically. They both looked at Elmer.

"Well," he said. He made two more knots on a traphead. "I suppose all those new traps'll fish just as good next winter as this summer."

"Now look, Elmer, you don't have to decide tonight. I ain't twisting anybody's arm. Maybe you want to talk it over with Josie first."

"I don't have to talk it over with Josie! Don't tell me I can think it over, not with you two watching me like I was a cod-head and you a couple of blackback gulls. All right. I guess we got as much right as anybody to get some of that money."

Larry's rebel yell ricocheted from wall to wall. He was already rich; that was the way with Larry. Finn himself didn't want to yell, he was suddenly confronted by the responsibility of his acts. He glanced toward Elmer as if for reassurance and saw that Elmer was smiling into space with quiet pleasure, seeing God knew what, but something good anyway. A new car, a bathroom, some rooms on the house.

"Listen," Finn said. "It's not certain yet. So don't start wearing your thumb out counting your greenbacks. And then we might not make much. Get a chance at it, that's all. Could be a bad year for herring. Or there could be so much fish around that the price goes way down."

They gave him kindly looks, as if to soothe his youthful doubts. "Sure, we know," Larry said. "Don't worry, Finn." Then he whooped again. Elmer groped under the bench and came up with three cans of beer.

Finn drank thirstily, then set down the can and wiped his

mouth. "One more thing. How'd you feel about Roy going with us?"

"Is he in on this?" The giddiness was wiped off Larry's face.

"Not yet," said Finn. "To tell the truth, I never thought of Roy till Harve asked me if any of my brothers knew something about seining. Well, Roy does."

"Would he go cap'n?" Elmer squinted at the label on the beer can.

"Not on my boat." Finn waited. Then Larry said grudgingly, "Well, he ain't like the other two. Don't have much to say one way or the other." He looked sidewise at Elmer. Finn said, "Want me to go out so you can talk it over?"

"Damn it, no," Elmer snapped. "You're giving us a good chance here and if you want one of your brothers along we'd be showing a hell of a lot of gratitude to say 'We don't want that bastard aboard.' Besides, as far as I know Roy's all right."

"I'll see him tomorrow then," said Finn. He picked up his beer can and lifted it toward them. "Here's to us."

·II·

After the school bus went up the road Claire stood listening to the birds. The banks of alder, wild cherry, and birch were full of them; their small talk was tossed like petals on the light northwest breeze.

The letter to Mrs. Carradine was in the mailbox. She had been able to finish it at last, the day after her visit to the island. The phrases had come so quickly that she was afraid she was being too glib, but it had been a good letter finally. At least Mrs. Carradine wouldn't be able to complain that Claire sent her no news of Nancy. So that Robert would know she was getting out into the air, she included a brief description of her visit to the island with a friendly boy who was one of Mag's neighbors.

Still thinking of Finn, she broke off an alder twig and a thin red wand of wild cherry and went back toward the house. It had been easy to speak to him about David, and why? She had puzzled over it that night, holding the Indian knife and studying its work. Perhaps it was because David was only a name to him and she was little more, so that his sympathy could be impersonal.

As if her brain had conjured him, he appeared around the bend in the road. A flock of grackles rose up from the field as he passed by, and wheeled in a shower of shiny black spangles behind his head. He came up to her, pushing his cap back, smiling down on her with that benevolence which always took her by surprise, it seemed so elderly.

"What are you doing with those twigs? You a water witch?"

"A water witch sounds rather nice," she said. "Is it?"

"Finest kind. They locate water."

She held off the twigs to look at them. "I was going to take them inside to watch them leaf out, but now I feel as if I should be muttering spells and incantations with them."

"Oh gorry, we got enough of that going on around here without you adding to it. Times when the air's blue. How about a ride across the river to Port George? My boat's on the bank, but I've got the prettiest little dory you ever set foot in."

"I'd love it," she said. She felt excited and adventurous, like Nancy getting off the school bus with a glorious afternoon of play before her. "And Aunt Mag's set for the day, Mrs. Gi drove her to Williston to see some old friend." She ran in to get her jacket and kerchief. Catching sight of her face in her mirror, she had to laugh aloud. She was probably being ridiculous, rushing around like this; but how long had it been, she wondered, since she'd done anything so youthful and spontaneous? Not since that long lifetime ago when she was first married to David. And to set off like this under the blue sky of spring seemed in some way a gemlike gift from the past.

The dory felt like a clamshell, one frail layer of wood between Claire's feet and the water pushing upward. It seemed as if a breath would roll her over. But once she was in motion, she became as secure and strong as a gull, flying across the water with only the flashing bow wave to prove that she touched it.

Finn slowed the dory at the end of the harbor to point to his boat hauled up on the shore. There was a man standing by the stern, who waved his arm with a slow pontifical gesture, as if from a balcony in Rome. The boat's name was *Foam-Flower*. Claire thought,

> *And the sea moving saw before it move*
> *One moon-flower making all the foam-flowers fair.*

In the instant of the quotation she seemed suddenly to be waking from a dream and did not know where she was or why she was there. Or else she had dropped into a dream and would waken shortly in Mrs. Carradine's house to the warm and oppressive silence; or waken even further back in time from the nightmare catnaps in a chair in David's room.

"Seals!" a man's voice called, and dazedly she followed the pointing hand and saw the round shining heads coming out of the water, and the round curious eyes gazing back at her. The moment of disorientation was gone.

The ocean in the path of the sun gave off the watery fire of diamonds, and by the time they reached Port George she had retrieved the memory of what used to be a voracious part of her; an avid ingathering of impressions, a soaking up of scents and sounds, colors and textures. Inside the big harbor Finn slowed the outboard down to where he could talk without raising his voice.

"I guess I should tell you, since you're kind of responsible for this," he said diffidently. "I've already been over and talked to Harve Eastman about going seining and he told me to come back today. It's almost a sure thing, though." He grinned. "You'll get a kick out of him. He calls everybody 'dear,' even men, so don't think he's being sassy."

"I won't. I'm glad for you, Finn. Can you get the other two to go with you?"

"Oh, sure, and they're so excited they're likely to bust right out of their skins. There he is, right on his mooring."

They eased up to the big boat named *Nerita*, and a gaunt man with a lean prow of a nose came out of the cabin. "Mrs. Carradine, Cap'n Eastman," said Finn. He stood in the dory with his big hands holding to the side of the boat, and Claire found herself smiling because he was; how wonderful, she thought without resentment, to be the owner of a fresh and unmarked life that had only begun to realize its capacity for being overjoyed.

"I've got my crew," Finn said. "All but my brother Roy. I went to see him Saturday night and he doesn't want to tie himself up, because his wife may be coming home from the hospital any day. But he told me about somebody he knows, a good man, he says, and has experience."

Eastman looked amiable but solemn. He nodded slowly. "You new around here, deah?" he asked Claire.

"I'm visiting Mrs. Abbott at Saltberry Point."

"Margaret Abbott," he said. "My father used to take me there when I was a tyke."

"Margaret," Claire repeated. "Margaret. I suppose that's her name, but I never heard her called that."

"My father always called her Margaret," he said softly. "In a kind of special way. I never knew why." He sat down on the washboard and nodded at Finn. "I'm sorry, deah, but it's all off."

"What?" said Finn. He was still smiling, but the color rushed up his throat and into his face, and then the muscles slowly gave up the smile. Claire was angry at the bony man with his soft voice and his *deahs*; she wanted to snap at him, Why did you let this boy think one thing when you meant another?

As if he were answering her he said, "The other night I didn't see why it wouldn't work. What I knew of your folks and all. But since then. . . ." He shrugged and reached into a shirt pocket for his cigarettes, held them toward Claire and then toward Finn. Claire shook her head and Finn ignored them.

"I've got to have an explanation," he said. "You've got a reason, and I want to know what it is. I think I have a right to know."

"All right. Mebbe it is your right. Your brothers came to my house last night. Not Roy; the middle two."

Finn's big fist came down on the railing. "I might have known. My nephew heard me talking to Roy last night and he wanted to come in with me, and Roy said no. The kid went out mad, and must have run right over to tell Rafe and Cleon. What'd they say to you?"

"Nothing bad, deah, believe me. Said you was young and kind of impetuous, but likely to run out of enthusiasm after a while. Eyes bigger than your belly, so to speak. Another thing—" he studied his cigarette—"and mebbe you'd better think about this. If you come to me some time with a different crew, I might think you're a better risk. I don't know these boys personally, but your brothers being responsible citizens, kind of settled down, they ought to know. Said it's just a question of time before the community over there runs those lads out."

Finn was no longer flushed. "Anything more?" he said. His lips barely moved.

"Now if you were to get together with your brothers and make up a crew, there'd be no question."

"Thanks," said Finn with neither anger nor sarcasm. He pushed away from *Nerita*.

"Pleasure to meet you, deah," Eastman said to Claire. "Remember me to Margaret." She nodded stiffly. The engine started up and as Finn shoved the speed lever to full ahead, the dory leaped forward like a savagely roweled pony. Claire kept her face turned to one side so as not to look at Finn. She attempted to keep from expressing or even feeling the kind of pity she hated; she would not humiliate him with so much as a glance, and she wished she had not been a witness to the scene. He would hate her for it and she couldn't blame him.

They rushed through the harbor, pitching and rolling through the wakes of bigger boats, and she kept her hands pushed up in her sleeves so she wouldn't be tempted to grip the gunnels. When they were out of the harbor and the river mouth lay before them like a broad blue floor, the boat swerved violently toward the high island, Hollowell.

The open horizon had an aquamarine glaze, and the cold deep-sea scent agreeably prickled her nostrils. At least it would have been agreeable under different circumstances. Two lobster boats were working in a shimmering lagoon of calm water behind Hollowell, and the dory was heading in that direction.

She turned around in the bow seat, ready to give him any excuse for taking her back and getting free of her. He was standing up, his hands in his pockets, his head back. Against the sky his dark face was a mask of passionless resolution; the calm eyes expressed nothing but sight. The effect of maturity made her realize that in thinking of him as a wounded and humiliated boy she had been guilty of pity after all, and of self-deception.

Without looking at her he leaned down and took hold of the steering lever. Turning more gently this time, they were headed back across the river toward the Point. He sat down then and lit a cigarette. When they reached the Abbott wharf she was both relieved and let down. She thought, He is too proud to want to see me again after this.

At the ladder she stood up carefully. "Thank you for thinking of me this morning, Finn," she said. "I enjoyed the sail very much, at least until we got to Port George." He nodded, patient and noncommittal. The echo of her voice and words stayed in her head. Good Lord, how prim and formal! She put out her hand and he took it automatically. "Finn, I'm so sorry," she said.

Instantly his hand tightened hard around hers. "Thanks," he said, and not as he had said it to Eastman. He kept on holding her hand so firmly she could not have pulled it away. "Sit down again," he said. She obeyed. They were alone in the harbor except for the voices of the young children and a dog barking at the lower harbor.

"Thanks for something else too." Finn said. "My brothers were out behind Hollowell. I set out to go after them, and then I thought better of it. It was no place for you."

"What would you have said to them?"

"Everything I could think of, and it wouldn't have done a damn bit of good. They could afford to listen to me, because they'd won out, and it would have rolled off them like water off a duck. And I'd have come away sick of myself."

"Maybe they really do think the project's too much for you. The older ones in a family are sometimes inclined to worry too much over a younger one, don't you think?"

"*Worry*." His smile broadened. "Depends on how you mean that word."

"Maybe they want you all to go together, a family group."

"Four Judsons on one boat? Who'd be captain?" He laughed outright then, and it sounded so genuine she smiled.

"What are you going to do now, Finn?"

"First thing is to give young Danny a piece of my mind. He

didn't run and tell on purpose, most likely; he was mad at his father and me and he was looking for sympathy, so he made a beeline across the yard to good old Uncle Cleon. Ayuh, I know how it happened. But that doesn't mean he isn't going to hear about it."

"Second thing?"

"Tell Larry and Elmer it's off. That's the worst of it." The rage showed in his hands. "They were like kids when I told them. Larry was whooping all over the place and Elmer didn't have much to say, but he just beamed. I warned them it wasn't final, but I was pretty sure, myself. This is going to be worse than when I got it in the guts from old Eastman."

"What did he mean about the community running them off? I think that was what he said." She leaned forward indignantly. "Finn, will they treat those two the way they did Paul Gardner?"

"They'd like to," he said bitterly. "By God, they'd like to. But they can't. Larry and Elmer are already settled here and they're decent. That's probably something Cleon threw in to convince Harve I pick my friends among the lower classes."

"Does this mean that you won't be able to go seining at all? Is Harve Eastman so powerful?"

"Gorry, anybody can go that has the twine and the men. But it's getting the twine, you see. That's a couple of thousand dollars right there."

"Isn't there anybody else? Didn't you mention the factory?"

"Harve's in pretty thick there. He'd tell them I was a poor risk. Oh, he's got no ax to grind, he honestly believes we're a bunch of—" He hurled his cigarette as far as he could and stared after it as the current bore it swiftly on.

"But you're going to see them anyway, aren't you?"

"Oh, sure, I'll see them." He grinned at her. "I ought to take you along to talk for me. You know, I don't see how anybody could say *no* to you."

"If I've taken too much on myself I'm sorry—"

"God, deah, don't start apologizing. Well, I've got to get my bait aboard and go to haul. I'll take my lobsters in to Port George and sell, and go over to the factory then. Time enough to talk to the boys after that."

She stood up and reached for the ladder. "I still don't know if I talked too much, Finn."

"If I didn't want you to say anything back, I wouldn't have spoken in the first place. But I guess I had to talk about it out loud before I went up like one of those rockets, and you're the safest one to be listening to me because you aren't involved." He shook his head in amazement. "I was some mad over there. I don't know when I've ever been so mad. You know that kind when you feel cold as ice and you could plan out a murder and commit it without even blinking an eyelash?" Then he smiled and shook his head. "No, you wouldn't know. Not you."

"How can you be so sure? Yes, I've felt that kind. Afterwards I was ashamed, but while it was going on I was beyond shame."

"Well, I'm not ashamed. I'm just glad I didn't get a chance to cut anybody's throat so I'd have to go to prison. None of them are worth it."

Claire said with mild wonder, "If anybody ever told me six months ago that on a day in April I'd be standing in a dory holding this conversation with a fisherman, I'd say they were having hallucinations."

She waited on the wharf and watched until he had reached the island. There was a small chattering over her head and a tree swallow shot by, back and mask gleaming like dark blue silk. He flew very high, over to the island. Another one followed. She stood still, breathing in the warmth and the scents, listening to the quiet, but conscious of the malice and mischief that worked under this generous sky amid such beauty. At the same time she had a new sense of well-being that was apart from everything else, and she decided it was because Finn had talked freely with her. Perhaps he would have talked to someone else if she hadn't been there; Gil Murray, or the man who was fixing his boat. But she was the one who was there, and the fact that he had confided in her showed that she was still a part of the human race, she could communicate, give something, receive.

"I am alive," she said aloud. Waking in the nights before she came to the Point she used to say it aloud, also, and try to convince herself she was speaking the truth. Sometimes it hadn't worked. This time she believed it.

·12·

"Hi, Claire!" It was Nell Johnson on the rise among the bay bushes. "I heard Finn's engine start up so I thought it was safe. I've been waiting to ask you in for a cup of coffee with me and Josie."

From her long habit of withdrawal Claire started to refuse, then said, "A cup of coffee is just what I need. I didn't have my second one this morning."

"I guess Finn was after you real early. School bus hadn't any more than gone up, had it?" Her dark eyes were merry behind her glasses. It was impossible to be offended by her. "Come on," she said. "I've been frying doughnuts. We want 'em while they're hot." She led the way along the narrow path. Her bottom was no more than a young boy's in the tight jeans, her shoulder blades peaked under a shrunken sweater that showed an inch of bare flesh at the waist. Her ponytail bobbed up and down like the genuine article.

"Oh, and something else too," she said over her shoulder. "Somebody kept ringing Mag, so Josie finally answered and said nobody was home. It was long distance, for you."

Claire felt a little sick, then thought, Nancy's safe in school and it won't be about David now.

"And you're to ask for Operator 54," Nell went on. "You can call from here if you want." They reached her yard, with the inevitable washing strung out between the spruces and the children playing joyously in the mud. "We'll all git out of the way so you can talk private."

"Well, I don't know what it could be," said Claire. "Nobody has to get out. Hello," she said to the children. "Isn't it about time I got you straight?"

"You can pick out the two Johnsons, they're mousy-brown like me," said Nell. "Cindy and Marshall. The other two are Bonnie and Betsy Curtis."

"Marshall's kind of outnumbered by females," said Josie from the kitchen door. "But he's just like Larry, so it don't faze him a bit. The more women the better."

Nell giggled. "Larry always said he could manage a harem real good, if anybody'd give him a chance. That's my Timmy in the carriage."

Josie Curtis was a fair placid girl, tall, largely pregnant but not ungainly. "You tell her about the phone, Nell?"

"Ayuh. Come on in, Claire, and get your call over with while we get the coffee ready." She hustled Claire through the cluttered kitchen, pleasantly odorous with the scent of new doughnuts. "Phone's in the sitting room, go right in and make yourself comfortable.... You kids stay out!" she commanded. "Josie, give 'em all another doughnut, and Cindy, don't you drop that one in the mud. Why don't you go up on the ledge and eat? Go on, go over on the ledge where it's dry."

"Betsy, you go and the others will follow," Josie's more temperate voice joined in. Claire took down the telephone and rang one long peal for the operator. Out in the kitchen the girls were whispering loudly and trying not to make a noise with the dishes.

Claire asked for Operator 54 and waited. She was not afraid, because she had no one left that was a part of her but Nancy, but she was apprehensive just the same.

"Claire, dear!" The high sweet voice took her by surprise, and she jumped.

"Hello, Mother!" Her own voice sounded impossibly bright and chirpy. Artificial. "How are you? Is anything wrong? Are you well?"

"As well as I can be, in my body. The spirit is another matter. How are *you*, Claire darling?"

"Oh, I'm—" Not *fine*, that would be unfortunate. "I'm sleeping better than I was. It must be the salt air." She knew she was rushing, but couldn't stop. "I mailed a nice long letter to you this morning, telling you all about Nancy. You'll get it tomorrow."

"Claire, I've been going over some things." Her voice changed, it became lower, suffused with emotion, watery and quaking. With a wrenching pain at the pit of her stomach, Claire knew she was going to speak of David. "Robert seems to think I should be giving them away. Tennis rackets, hockey equipment, records

—oh, everything that David had. I don't need to tell you it's been pure agony for me. But Robert and Dora insist—" Claire heard her swallow. "What do you think, dear, about giving his things away?"

The pain wrenched harder and tighter. Poor Mother, she kept thinking. Why does Robert do this to her? She tried to think what to say but felt as if she had no voice in her dry throat.

"Are you still there, Claire? I hope you don't resent my calling you like this. But even so far away from home you can't want to put David out of mind—"

Guilt was worse than the visceral cramping. Crossing the river this morning she had not thought once of David. "I never could put him out of mind, Mother," she said. "How could I?" She does this to me because she is in such torment herself, she thought. She's so absorbed by her own pain she doesn't know what she's doing.

"You're the only one who can ever begin to understand, dear," Mrs. Carradine said. "You're a mother too. Pray God you'll never have to lose a child. How is my darling?"

"Oh, she's fine, Mother. If you called after supper some night you could talk to her. Or we'll call you."

"Oh, it would break my heart to hear her little voice coming over the miles and know I couldn't touch her. Claire, when are you coming home?"

Don't gabble, Claire told herself. Don't sound guilty even if you're drowning in guilt. "It won't be till Aunt Mag's moved and settled, anyway. You know she's an old lady, and—and even Robert thought I should stay as long as necessary."

"I know very well what Robert thinks." Mrs. Carradine was unexpectedly crisp. "Robert may be my son, but he is lacking in a great deal of common humanity. He would place almost any-one ahead of his own family."

"Mother, you can't say that after all he did when David was sick."

"Need you mention that time of horror?"

"But Robert is thinking of your good and mine." She was glad of the need to defend him; it pulled her up out of the swamp of old despair. "And he's not being cruel about giving David's things away. Some boys would be very grateful to have them, and I don't believe David would want them simply to rot."

"I can't bear to think of anyone else wearing his skates! I can see him on the ice every time I look at them—like a bird—and laughing in triumph, you know that wonderful laugh of his—"

Sweat stood on Claire's face and neck. David, David, she cried silently, but it wasn't for a laughing boy on skates, but for a wasted, speechless, dying man. "Then don't give them away, Mother." She was tired enough to weep. "Don't give anything away."

"Claire, you sound changed. What has happened to you? I thought it would help me to call because I feel so absolutely alone here, no one else shares what you and I do, but I have the strangest feeling that you are not the same."

"Mother, I *am* the same, believe me. But I'm talking in someone else's house, and I—" she was relieved to hear a clicking on the line—"and somebody else wants to use the phone. Mother, I think you should do exactly as you please about David's things, and not let anyone else dictate to you."

"Thank you, dear!" The voice was round and warm. "I knew you'd feel like that. I only wanted to be sure of your support. Come home quickly, dear. I need you. Maybe you can find someone to help the old lady."

"I'll let you know. And now we must really give up the telephone. Good-by, and remember me to Aunt Dora and Robert." She hung up, and instantly someone rang in, furiously hard and long to express indignation. Claire sat back in her chair, shaky and sick, struggling for the composure to get her out of the house and into privacy somewhere. Outside the window the harbor twinkled and shimmered under catspaws of wind. A family of sea pigeons paddled in a satiny pool of calm. She watched them and gradually the storm died down in her.

"Coffee's ready!" Josie called.

"I'm coming." She still felt unsteady, but she went out to the kitchen smiling. "My mother-in-law apparently thinks we're on the edge of the Arctic Circle. She worries, and has to be reassured."

"Nice she thinks that much of you," said Nell. "Mine would

like nothing better than for Larry to drop me overboard and take the kids to her to bring up."

"Well, I don't have any complaints," said Josie. "Elmer's mother's real good to me."

The coffee filled Claire's stomach with comforting heat, and she began to feel better. She was able to eat a doughnut as if she were not imagining Mrs. Carradine crumpled and weeping beside the telephone in Brookline.

"Claire, why don't you stay around here after Mag moves?" Nell asked her. "They're going to build a big new bank in Lime-rock, and you could get a job there easy, I bet. You'd look real natural in a bank. You ever noticed how girls who work in a bank look different from the others?"

"Oh, I always thought that," said Josie airily. They studied Claire with kindly young eyes, and she was grateful to them and wished their husbands were not going to be disappointed about the herring.

·I3·

Because he was late starting out, Finn didn't catch up with Larry or Elmer all day, and he was glad of that. He cursed himself for ever having mentioned herring to them before he was sure of Eastman. Let it run out of you like gruel out of a goose, you goldarn chowderhead, he told himself bitterly. How old are you anyway? Maybe they're right, you're too young to make sense. Six foot four and not dry behind the ears yet. *He's young but he's daily agrowing*, Pa used to sing. Agrowing more stupid by the hour, Finn revised it.

He had scarce hopes of getting any help at the factory. They wanted to be sure before they put two or three thousand bucks' worth of gear into your hands. That wasn't to say he wouldn't try. If he didn't go to the factory he couldn't face the other two, or Claire either.

As he hauled through his string, getting the traps up hand over hand, he tried to get riled with Claire for interfering, but he could not. Instead he could see her sitting on the bow seat where his dinner box was now, giving him that solemn attention as if she were concentrating on his words so hard that no other part of her existed. It was a curious thing about her. Everybody else, including Lila, was always in such a damn hurry to get their five cents' worth in, you wondered if they'd even heard you in the first place. Maybe people only heard what was strained and filtered through layers of what *they* wanted, what *they* thought, what *they* expected. With Claire it was as if she'd given up wanting or expecting anything, and so she saw and heard him as no one else ever had. It was the difference between water fetched up from a spring in a cup, and water going through yards of pipes to come from a faucet. The only similarity was that they were both wet.

Such thinking calmed him. He remembered how today, even when rage was eating away at his guts so it was almost a pain you could touch, he had noticed that her hair grew down in a little point in the middle of her forehead, and her brown eyebrows had the sweeping curve of a fish hawk's wings. He hoisted a trap to the gunnel and looked around him while his hands brushed off the starfish and sea urchins. He was in a little blue lake of calm among the islands beyond Hollowell. The treeless ones looked like the moss-covered humps of ledge found in the woods; where there were spruce woods, there was also their scent lying heavy on the warm quiet air, and ripples of light shimmered endlessly over the green walls of close-woven boughs. He shook out an old baitbag, and the dark arrowy shapes of pollock shot through the liquid emerald below the dory. He thought of bringing Claire and the kid here to fish on a day like this. They could go ashore and build a fire and fry the small sweet pollock for their dinner.

He saw her smiling, relaxed, taking in the sun like a buttercup. Nature heals, Pa used to say. Out here is where you meet yourself.

He knew that was so; he was free and his own man only while he was out here. When he got among people they crowded him, impeded him the way water in gasoline bothered an engine. Not contented with that, they chipped little hunks off him here and there, just for the hell of it. I don't wish them any harm, he thought more in bewilderment than in anger. So why can't they leave me alone even if I don't want them buying me a boat? Is independence an insult, for God's sake?

When he left the sheltered spot the wind had shifted and was coming in southerly puffs. He hauled with the dory dancing under him, and as the puffs grew longer and harder there were times when the dory rolled down so far to meet the upcoming trap she seemed to be trying to pitch him out.

"Tittlish is no word for you, my lady," he told her. "Mean and perverse is more like it. One more like that and I'll christen ye Hester."

The distances had taken on the silvery haze of the smoky sou'wester, and surf was beginning to explode over some of the ledges where Finn had traps. Reluctantly he started for home, leaving these unhauled.

Following seas swept him on. It was so late in the afternoon that he thought everyone else had gone in so he was surprised when he looked astern and saw beyond a rising green comber a flash of red that was the jigger sail on Roy's boat. The thirty-eight-foot *Helen* overtook him easily and slowed down just ahead of him. "You wanna tow or are you too proud?" Roy yelled between his hands.

"This dory'd take the pride out of anybody!" Finn shouted back. He caught up with Roy, climbed aboard and tied the dory astern. "What you out so late for?"

"I had to make a telephone call, so it made me late starting. Fun hauling in that clamshell?"

"It beats swimming from trap to trap and carrying your bait in your teeth."

The big boat plunged softly forward and the dory rode high on the following seas. "What's the reason you're turning up your nose at that boat at Johansen's?" Roy asked.

"I can't afford it," said Finn. "You said yourself every time Rafe worked up some family feeling it cost somebody money. If it's not money in my case it'll be the best years of my life. Hell, Morry won't be too long on my boat. He knows he'll get paid." They passed the black can buoy in the channel off Hollowell, and toward Port George the water was like boiling lead in the sun.

"I was going into Port to sell today," Finn said.

"You mad at Gil?"

"Nope. Should I be?"

"Cleon's been mumbling around about Gil not going up on the price as quick as he should, not getting enough bait, stuff like that."

"I've got no kick about Gil. Do you think Cleon'd put fourteen, eighteen hours a day down on that wharf like Gil does?" He grinned. "I wouldn't know about the bait. I salt my own and don't expect Gil to hold back on what he gets till the Royal Family's helped themselves."

"Oh, Cleon's always got a beef. If he can't think up one, Rafe'll put him onto one. It was a big day for Cleon when Rafe was born."

Finn's anger revived unexpectedly, knocking against his ribs. Bastards. Mad because he wouldn't put himself in hock to them. His lips moved: *Rule or ruin.*

"You say something?" Roy asked.

"Nothing but my prayers."

"If you've got an urgent reason to go to Port, I'll take you over. I don't mean a girl."

Finn shook his head. "It'll keep another day." He didn't want anybody along to know his business.

"When you going over to talk to Eastman?" Roy asked.

"I've been. This morning. He's changed his mind."

Roy squinted at him. "Give any reason?"

"Just changed his mind, that's all."

"Some notional, ain't he?"

"Too damn notional for me. Maybe I'm better off without him and Junior."

Helen headed toward the harbor end of Saltberry Island, She felt solid underfoot and slid through the tumbling water with the greased smoothness of a whale. This is a boat, Finn thought. She had cost close to thirteen thousand before she was launched from Johansen's, because for once Roy was going to have everything perfect. Finn saw Helen blinking tears above the armful of red roses. Helen, she's supposed to be launched with champagne, not salt water, he said to her. She'll have enough of that once she's overboard. But what if I can't break that blasted bottle on the first try? she whispered back at him. Will it jinx her?

It was so sharp it was agonizing. He could see the specks of light in her eyes and the freckles across her nose and cheekbones, and hear that hoarse voice of hers saying with no effort fast funny things that could rock you with laughter. The agonizing part was in trying to realize that the voice was worn away with grief, and the specks of light in her eyes had been washed out by the stare of someone lost even to herself.

He felt a thickness in his throat, half fright, half grief. He turned quickly to Roy and the words jetted out over the rush and hiss of water. "You said last night Helen might come home."

"That's what the telephone call was about," Roy said. His dark face was impassive as he watched for lobster buoys half-drowned in the green and white water. "Last week when I was up there they told me. She's been coming along good for long enough now so I guess I can mention it." There was a twitching in the lid toward Finn and in the corner of his mouth, as if he were trying to keep something from breaking out. "She's had so goddam many ups and downs. . . . But it seems like spring's been getting to her, even up there, and she's been speaking about it to them. More and more. The doctor wanted to talk to me today, so I went up to Williston and called from the booth."

"Gorry," said Finn. "You mean she's got better all at once? Like somebody coming out of the fog?"

"Something like that, only she's got a way to travel yet. But she's homesick as hell, and she wants to be at Danny's graduation, especially where he's got an honor part."

Moisture stood in the corners of Roy's eyes. Finn was suddenly reminded of Roy in his greens being hugged by Dolly while she wept for Pa; there'd been that wet glisten in Roy's eyes then, too. He had thought then, and for a long time, that it was a queer thing for a man to cry, until the night over a year ago when Roy and Dolly had taken Helen to Augusta. Alone on the island he had kept seeing Helen struck by the killing frost, and he had been appalled and outraged and then he had wept; it was as if for the first time he had glimpsed life as an abyss in which fathers were blown to bits and dear friends went insane.

He'd been all right the next morning and after a while he'd got used to Helen's being gone even if he didn't like to think about it. But when he heard about Claire's husband he'd been attacked again by the terrible and irreversible fact that living was like walking a tight rope over the abyss of disaster.

"It'll be a couple of weeks," Roy was saying. "They want to build her up some, and get her used to looking after herself and mixing with people more. Keep it to yourself, huh? I don't want to hear any comments on it."

"I won't say anything," said Finn. "I'm glad she's coming home. I've missed her like hell. And if there's anything I can do for her you let me know."

"You just come around and see her," said Roy. "And don't come in on tippytoes with your cap against your chest like you was approaching a coffin."

"I won't," said Finn solemnly. "I'll come lugging her the best slack-salted codfish I can find."

They were both laughing when they came up to the mooring. Finn ran up on the bow to gaff the buoy. Two boats away Rafe stopped washing down his decks to watch them.

When Finn stopped at Gil's wharf to sell his lobsters, Elmer's car was gone from his driveway, and there was no sign of Larry either. He hoped they hadn't gone uptown to order a new living room set or a freezer on the strength of their expectations.

"Girl called up and asked was you dead," Gil said, writing out Finn's slip. "I told her if that warn't you I'd been seeing it was a pretty solid ghost. She thought I was being flighty." He handed Finn the slip. "She said that if that son of a bitch don't call her before tomorrow she'll call him and he won't like it one bit. She sounded real earnest."

"She always does," said Finn. "What'd you say to her?"

Gil put his pencil carefully behind his ear. "I told her I'd deliver the message only if you put in an appearance at this car. I ain't no cupid."

"You *ain't?*" said Finn in falsetto. "Why, Gil, you'd look some cunning flitting around here in nothing but a little pair of wings."

By the time he had taken care of his leftover bait, and washed down the dory and put her on the haul-off, it was suppertime. He heated up a kettle of rain water from the barrel by the back door, and shaved and took a bath before he ate .The day before, he had freshened one of the big pollock he'd caught and dried last fall, and made a Sunday dinner of it with pork scraps and boiled potatoes and mashed squash, the whole laced together with Dolly's green tomato piccalilli. Tonight his supper was a hash made of the leftovers and fried to crusty gold in the oversize iron skillet without which he wouldn't have been able to keep house. He brought up from the cellar a jar of last year's dandelion greens, and the smell of them was pure spring.

He set the table out on the porch and fetched his book from his room; he was reading *The Spiral Road*, which he'd borrowed from Roy's bookshelves last night. Helen's name was on the flyleaf and he thought of her return with a steady warmth tempered only by the fear that she mightn't ever be the way she was before Mark died. I don't care, I'll keep going there, he thought. That ought to count for something.

He was putting a tea bag in a thick mug while he considered Helen, and suddenly he realized what he was doing. He went into the sitting room and got the Japanese teapot out of the hutch cupboard, and a brown-flowered cup and saucer. He measured tea into the pot as Claire had done. After he turned in the boiling water he remembered he should have warmed the pot first.

Finally he sat down to his supper and ate it with enjoyment, reading part of the time, and sometimes looking out over the familiar contours of field, forest, and shore. He planned his evening as he ate and looked. Not in detail, because the minute you did that you began finding excuses not to do what had to be done. You simply said, This and that has to be done before I go to bed tonight. Then you did it.

Elmer puckered up his mouth and chewed at the inside of his cheek, gazed at nothing for an instant, and then said, "Hell, you did your best, Finn. He as much as told ye it was a sure thing . . . didn't he?"

"Why else do you think I told you about it?" Finn said. "He all but said it straight out."

"I hear he's kind of unpredictable," Elmer was always moderate. "Anyway, he's not the last word, and try never was beat, they say." He was so eager to show Finn he didn't blame him that it made Finn feel worse.

Larry's eyes were wild in his bony face. He swore in a high stream, he kicked into a pile of buoys and sent them clattering and rolling, pounded his fist on the bench and set everything jumping. Finally he hefted a hammer in his hand and stared at a window as if he hated it. Elmer reached past him and took the hammer.

"Now you've had your tantrum, sonny, suppose you start acting like a grown man and the father of a family."

"We coulda got everything squared away and paid up! I been counting on it. So's Nell!"

"So's Josie and me," said Elmer. "So's Finn. But we still got our traps, and we haven't starved yet around here. And like I said to Finn, Harve don't say who can and who can't catch fish. We'll get our twine somewhere else, that's all."

"I'm going to the factory," said Finn. "They might turn us down too, if Harve tells them we're a bunch of fool kids with big ideas same as he told me. Well, just as Roy and I were coming up to the mooring he spoke of Waisenen, up at Pruitt's Harbor."

"And I heard yesterday there was some big new outfit from New York opening up in Rockport," said Elmer. "Gemini Seafoods. They're going to buy everything, so mebbe they'll have their own herring plant."

"Worth inquiring into," said Finn. They both turned to Larry. He was slumped against the workbench, stirring a sardine can of tacks with his forefinger. He returned their inquiring looks with a brightening one. "Well, if they haven't thought of it maybe we can put the idea in their heads," he said. "We'll be the first vessel in their herring fleet. How's that sound?"

"A hell of a lot better than being tail pig to Junior Eastman," said Finn. Larry was perking up again, and nothing under God's heaven could keep him from soaring like a kid's lost balloon.

"I'll try to keep him pinned down," Elmer said to Finn.

"For Pete's sake, Larry, don't go around acting like it's a sure thing," Finn pleaded. "Just keep on tending your traps and possess your soul in patience, as the feller says. I've got to get moving now."

"Be good to her," Elmer called after him.

"I've been too good to her, that's the trouble," Finn said. As he slid the door into place he heard Larry's voice begin, jumpy and piercing with excitement. He shook his head.

The dusk was mild and still, and the peepfrogs were singing from the alders along the black road. When he reached his car he stood quiet, listening. From the time he was a small child the peepfrogs' piping had filled him with a pleasant uneasiness, a conviction that something was waiting for him, something wonderful if he only knew what to do. He felt it now, and grinned at himself. Big oaf, standing here in the dark like a young beagle wanting to run in the woods all night, even with no rabbits to chase; just to run for the joy of running. He didn't want, actually, to *run;* but he expected more from the spring night than Lila, and that caused him vague sensations of guilt, because Lila had been good enough for him up till now.

I'm just sore because she called up Gil and swore like a proper slut, he thought. So what? I've heard her swear before. I've laughed because it tickled me to hear her cussing in that twang of hers.... He got angrily into the car and started it without the usual concern he showed for its elderly gears.

·14·

Lila lived with a married sister ten miles up the road, just this side of the town line. Her parents lived across the river in Port George, where her father was a respectable and industrious lobsterman, but Lila had moved out following a fight about her staying out all night after a dance. She was a neat girl with a long Yankee face and a high-bridged nose of which she was very proud because it was pure Rankin, and a Rankin had been one of the first settlers on the Port George peninsula. Lila was a good waitress, tidy, quick, and willing, and she had worked in almost every place in Limerock and Fremont that hired waitresses; the cocktail bars in the hotels, the diners, the one-arm lunches, the five-and-tens, and the restaurants where families went to eat and businessmen congregated at noon. She always made a pleasant impression with her soap-and-water polish, her pure Rankin nose, and her friendly manner toward elderly people and children. But she was lustful, and men knew it. Finn knew when he asked this girl for a date that they both understood, without words, that it wasn't simply an engagement to go dancing or to a movie.

Lila was adventurous, and she liked variety. She wasn't a prostitute, and if she decided to withhold herself she did so; at times she backed up her decision with the gift of a bloody nose or an expert knee to the groin. If she decided the other way, it was with a cheerful air of good fellowship. Going to bed with someone was a simple matter for Lila, if she liked the man, and he was clean. To offer to pay her would have been an insult. She was a good housekeeper and loved children. When she married, as these girls always did, she would be a faithful wife and a strict mother, and live her new life as completely and enjoyably as she had lived the old one.

Finn had met her at a Grange Hall dance in the fall, and as far as he knew she hadn't slept with anyone else since. "Who'd want to?" she said once when he asked her, and he thought that he knew what she meant. After all, she wasn't like some of these women you read about who were crazy for it; she liked it, that's all. It was a friendly thing with her, like getting drunk together, a hell of a lot of fun and no fussing about it afterwards.

But tonight he called himself worse than a chowderhead for not seeing something else in her words. *Who'd want to go to bed with somebody else after they'd been there with you?* He should have known then that's what she meant, and called it off quick. But no, you were having too damn much fun, he told himself. An easy lay and a willing one. You didn't have to think you were ruining some kid who was crazy about you. Didn't it ever get through that solid cement head of yours that when she was being so wifely it wasn't just because she thought it was time she grabbed onto a husband, but because she wanted *you* Finn Judson?

"Oh, God," he groaned aloud, and his back was wet under his clean shirt. The car hit a hump raised by the frost, and lurched toward the ditch and the alders. He righted it, swearing.

When he swung into the driveway the brother-in-law's car was gone. Well, maybe Gladys would be there, he thought hopefully. But when he walked into the kitchen and heard only the low-tuned television from the sitting room, he knew grimly that Lila was alone, baby-sitting. The dog stood in the doorway, his hair on end. Finn said, "Hello, Bruno," and the big mongrel came happily to meet him, putting his paws on Finn's chest and trying to lick his chin. Past the dog's ears Finn greeted Lila.

"Hello. What you doing?"

"What's it look like?" She went back into the sitting room and sat down again, picking up her cigarette. Finn shed his jacket and took Ed's easy chair, sprawling back as if he were more comfortable than he felt. The dog settled down beside him. "What's this show?" Finn asked.

She shrugged. She was staring so hard at the screen her greenish eyes were bulging. He watched her, tapping his fingers on the arm of the chair. He felt nothing for her but an uneasy conscience. But I never made her any promises, he thought. It was all just a good time, no strings. He got abruptly to his feet, took two steps to reach the television set, and turned it off.

She gasped as if he'd struck her, "What did you do that for?" she cried indignantly. "I was watching!"

"The hell you were. You never saw a thing. Now what's the matter?"

"What do you mean, what's the matter?" As she took out a fresh cigarette, her hands were trembling.

"Calling up Gil and swearing over the line like that. Haven't you got any pride?"

"If I had, I wouldn't a been calling you up!" she snapped back.

"Gawd, that Gil's some stupid. It's a wonder he told you."

"Well, he did," said Finn. "What'd you want?"

"I wanted to know where you've been this week."

"I've been busy if it's any of your business." He sounded more gentle than he felt. "I'm not in the habit of accounting for my time to anybody."

"That all I am—just anybody?" She laughed, deliberately raucous. "So now I know just where I fit. Maybe I'm not even anybody. Mebbe I'm nobody."

"Stop that, Lila," he said. "You know you're a friend of mine, same as you always were. But I never made you any promises."

"Oh, no, you were some old careful, weren't you? Never say anything, just take what you could get. Good old Lila, she's good-hearted like all the whores, she's—"

"*Shut up!*" He stood over her. "I never thought of you as a whore. But I never thought of this as anything that was going on and on either. We had a hell of a good time together, and now we're getting real cantankerous toward each other, so it's time to quit."

She ground her cigarette out in the ashtray and then leaned her head against the back of the chair and stared up at him coldly.

"Just like that."

"Just like that," Finn agreed. He felt lighter already, and the uneasy conscience quieted. "Look, as long as it never bothered either of us it was all right. But now I'm getting you riled up, and you're getting me riled up, and first thing you know we'll be fighting like Kilkenny cats. We're fighting now."

She kept on staring at him, her long face like a mask, the greenish eyes bright as stones surf-washed on the beach. "Funny it never happened until something new come on the scene," she said.

"What do you mean?" He was honestly puzzled.

"Oh, I've heard about the merry widow. Didn't take you long to wrassle her over to the island and into bed, did it? So the other old place don't look so good any more—" She flinched suddenly and shrank back, and he realized he had swung his arm back, poised for a slap that would have knocked her across the room. He was shocked, but still felt she deserved it. He drove his hands hard into his pockets. He thought of a dozen things to say but they all died behind his teeth; besides, it was indecent even to defend Claire because in some crazy way that would set her and Lila side by side and reduce their differences to the one basic fact: one did and the other didn't.

"I never thought of you as a whore," he said again, "but now you're talking like one. They think every other woman is, or would be if she had the chance."

He picked up his jacket from the sofa and slung it over his shoulder and walked out through the kitchen. "I notice you ain't troubling to deny what I said!" she screamed after him. "She any good? Was she crazy for it? Was she——"

He slammed the door on her words and ran toward the car.

The night was velvety dark, and there was a salt smell of low tide. The peepfrogs bothered him now, picking at his nerves, rubbing his anger like a shoe against a blistered heel. *Bitch, bitch, bitch!* he said softly. He was glad he hadn't slapped her because he might have broken her neck; not that she didn't deserve to have it snapped, but he wouldn't let her make him a murderer.

·15·

Mag and Claire had been going through trunks in the attic ever since Nancy left for school in the morning. Now they emerged blinking in the blaze of early afternoon. "Couple of bears coming out of hibernation," said Mag. "Skinny ones. Been living off their fat for years, from the looks of 'em." She turned her small bony face to the sun. "My lands, I'd almost forgotten we had so much sky. And smell that wind! There's May in it."

Claire sniffed. " 'And the arch of the leaves was hollow,' " she said, " 'and the meaning of May was clear.' "

"Don't make much sense, but's it's kind of pretty," said Mag. "You go see what mail we've got. I'm going to look for my daffodils and pineys." She disappeared around the corner. Already Claire had learned not to expect disaster from that reckless headlong gait; what worried her more was the fear that going over old things was confusing Mag between past and future. Occasionally she became steely-eyed and said she wouldn't leave this or that for Rafe, but all this morning she had talked of her flowers as if she didn't intend ever to depart from them.

The mailbox held Mag's *Limerock Patriot* and *New England Homestead*; Nancy's monthly magazine, and the usual envelopes addressed to Box-Holder. There was nothing for Claire, and she realized with suddenly slackening muscles how tight she had been with anticipation. But Mrs. Carradine would write, wanting a follow-up to her telephone call; she was too obsessed with her sorrow to be patient. In a way it would be a relief to get the arrival of the letter over with.

She went around the corner of the house to the apple trees. Mag was down on her knees poking in the dirt along the foundation of the house, where the new spears were thrusts of emerald. She was talking to herself. "Scilla's up. Be a barrel of daffodils this year. . . . Sweet William didn't winterkill." Her head came up as Claire sat down on the bench against the warm clapboards. "I get anything?"

"Just your magazine and your paper."

Mag's eyes were jewel-bright. "Anything in the headlines about Rafe Judson getting arrested for rape or murder?"

"I'm sorry to disappoint you. There's a school-board fight in Putnam, and a bad accident up in Fremont, and the governor's coming to speak in Limerock, otherwise things are pretty quiet."

"Oh, well, if I ever got rid of Rafe I'd have to deal with that besom Hester, and I dunno but what that might even be worse." Her fingers worked at the soil. "You know, I wouldn't be surprised but what she's had her eye on my plants all this time. She'll likely have 'em all dug out of here before I get up the road. . . . Well, she won't have the chance. I'll give them all away before, that's what I'll do." Her head jerked up again. "*You* get a letter?"

"No," said Claire. Safe today, she thought. This whole afternoon is free.

Mag made a small sound of contempt. "Funny folks. Funny-peculiar. Act like you dropped off the edge of the world somewhere. They think we got no post office in this wilderness?"

"Mrs. Carradine called me the other day, remember, and found out we're well. Robert never writes letters if he can help it. He'd rather talk face to face." She tilted her head back against the clapboards and shut her eyes to the beneficence of sunshine on her cheeks. "He's one of the nicest people I've ever known. After David, of course. When David was sick Robert and I did just about everything for him . . . Robert was going through great agony because he and David had been inseparable as boys, but of all the family he seemed to be the only one who ever thought of me during that time." She opened her eyes slightly;

rainbows flashed in her lashes. "Robert is gentle where David was bold. You get the impression that he has no life of his own except where the business and the family are concerned, because they call on him for everything. Even David used to do it sometimes, and I would be a little ashamed, but David would say, 'Oh, he likes to do it.'" She stopped. She heard the small sounds of Mag's fingers digging the warm earth around the bulbs, a far-off engine, a fish hawk piping over the harbor. She opened her eyes wider and sought for the gulls and found them. She followed the sweeping circles and heard her voice going on like running water.

"Did you ever know a person who lets himself be imposed upon so much that you could despise him for it? To me, at first, there was almost something unmasculine about Robert. But when David was sick, and when he could still talk enough to beg us not to have nurses, then Robert became"—she hesitated—"splendid." She added without expression, "Robert was the only one I'd let see me cry. I'm afraid a whole bevy of relatives think I'm a very cold woman."

Mag suggested tersely what they could do in their bonnets. She got up, creaking and grunting but wanting no help, and sat on the bench, her dirty hands laid palm upward on her knees. "Feel that sun," she said. "I got to get out in it more. I feel as white and soggy as those Indian pipes in the woods. When I move to town I shall take a walk uptown every blessed day."

Robert was only thirty-five, but some of the family called him with patronizing affection the Old Bachelor. Robert was born grown-up, his mother said. Didn't anyone ever let Robert be young? Claire asked David once, and he laughed and said, "Sweetheart, Robert likes the way he is! Don't try to make him into a psychological puzzle, for Pete's sake."

Mag slapped her hands down on her knees. "I been thinking. There's no call for you to go back to those folks, they're not your kin. And the way you and the young one have bloomed since you come here, anybody'd think you'd been living under a rock. Now if you get yourself a job and a decent rent after I get moved, I'll load up your place for you with the clock and the Hitchcock chairs, and the ironstone set, and that deck bureau—" She stopped to haul in a breath. "You get a place with a yard, you can have everything you can dig out of this one. Land of love, what it'll be to have you and the young one dropping in! 'Course I've got along till now, and would again, but a body don't mind a few extra frills to living."

"Well, you've added quite a few to living for Nancy and me," said Claire.

"*Me?*" Mag squawked. "Old bag of bones been cheating the undertaker for too long? I can't stand any more of this. Next thing we'll be handing out the compliments, and praise to the face is open disgrace, so I was brought up." She bounded up with surprising agility and went scooting back around the corner of the house. Claire felt a prickling in her eyes and nose and sat winking tears back, until a shriek from Mag brought her to her feet.

Finn and Mag stood by the shed door. Mag turned an elf face to Claire. "Seeing a good-looking man on my doorstep was such a shock I like to went out of my skin with joy."

"You must have been a pure hellion when you were young, Mag," Finn said with respect.

"Oh, I was! Father was some glad to marry me off to Ralph Abbott, I can tell you. Well, I'll leave you two to yourselves because it's certain-sure this boy ain't up here calling on *me*." Her laughter floated behind her as she went in.

Finn took Claire's elbow very lightly in his fingers. "Walk along a bit with me." He steered her across the road and past the mailbox.

"Have you been to the factory?" she asked eagerly.

"Can you smell the alders?" he said. "The catkins are all opened up out here in the lee." The long tassels formed of minute blossoms hung golden from violet-brown boughs in a Japanese pattern against the tumbling wind clouds.

"They're exquisite," she said, "and so fragrant. What do they make me think of? What do they smell like?"

"Alders?" suggested Finn.

Claire smiled and began walking again. The wind stirred a gilt dust from the tassels and the sweetness blew in warm puffs around her face. "I asked if you'd been to the factory," she said.

"I was over there today." He was neither solemn nor ex-hilarated. "Come on up here and sit down on a rock." He took her hand and led her off the road to the left, through the fine growth of alders and young birches, and along a narrow footpath up over ledges and between spruces; they came out into the pasture of the Murray homestead. North of them the barn hid the house. South and west of them lay the community of the Point, the harbor, Saltberry Island, the actual geographic point, and Saltberry Bay, and beyond all these the line of open sea.

They sat down on a shelf of warm granite with another ledge behind it like a backrest. "Well, is it good news or bad about the factory?" Claire asked. "How long are you going to keep me in suspense?"

"Oh, that." He looked almost sleepy in the heat. "They turned me down. They said they didn't need us, they get plenty of herring up and down the coast without fitting out new-comers."

She said angrily. "Are you sure Eastman didn't have some-thing to do with it?"

"It made sense, and it was what I expected, anyway." He sprawled back against the ledge and lit a cigarette. "Leaving Harve out of it, why should they take a chance on somebody they don't know from a hole in the ground? . . . The skipper of the *Thetis* told me to go up and see a man at Pruitt's Harbor. Roy told me about him too."

"Are you going to?"

"Ayuh," he said drowsily. "The boys and I are driving around there tomorrow. He's out to Matinicus today." His eyes were shut, and his face turned blankly up to the sky told her nothing; he could have been as empty and unthinking as a young lion sprawling in the sun, and if he opened his eyes they would blink with empty brilliance. Blue, though, not tawny. . . . Oh, what is it, what is it! she demanded of herself. What do you *care*? Why must you be always trying to decode people? Why must they always be for you something more than they seem? Why isn't the *seeming* good enough for you? Be satisfied.

"If this man turns you down, Finn, what then?" she asked.

"It won't kill me," he said. "If that's it, that's it. If I had any way of raising the money to buy the gear outright, I'd do it.

As it is, I can pray for good lobstering and put away every cent I can."

"There's no way at all you can get a loan?"

He opened one eye and looked at her. "I've got nothing to get a loan on. The island belongs to Dolly. The others are scared foolish I can talk her into mortgaging it and giving me the cash to play with." He grinned. "Gives 'em nightmares, but I don't even daydream about it."

"She wouldn't do it, then?"

"I wouldn't ask her. See, the island's not just a valuable hunk of real estate." He pushed himself up on his elbows. "I mean it's not something to take chances on. I don't know if I can make it clear without sounding like I was soft in the head." The eyes were not empty, after all. She said, "You've made it clear, Finn."

"If this does fall through, I'll wish like the devil I hadn't got the boys into it. I've got time, but they've got families, and that shortens time up something fierce. But I had to be sure of a crew before I started looking for twine. Know something, Claire? Times when people bother me. They're either pushing you around or you find out you're pushing them around. Or you're responsible for 'em in some way, or they think you owe them something . . . and sometimes they're right, and you hate them for it." He said it not with indignant surprise but as if it were something he'd always known. She looked off toward the summer-blue open water.

"What are you thinking about?" Finn asked.

She answered without looking at him, "About what you just said. You're right. Sometimes a life is choked almost to suffocation with people, and yet we need some of them. If they didn't feel a duty toward us—certain ones, that is—we'd soon feel the cold. And because we don't get anything for nothing in this world, as we learn young, we have a duty toward certain others." She glanced around then, smiling timidly. "Do you follow me, or do I travel alone?"

"I follow. Of course it's round and round and over and under, but I'm a good tracker."

"I sounded awfully self-important just then." She played bashfully with a handful of moss, feeling very adolescent.

"No, you didn't."

But still she was relieved to hear the distinctive sound made by tires on the black road hidden by the alders. "I'd better get home before the school bus comes," she said hurriedly.

"Oh, you'll hear it making the turn clear back by the cranberry bog, roaring like a dinosaur, and I'll take you under my arm and crash on a straight line through the alders."

"I'm sure that scene would make my daughter's day, to say nothing of what it would do for the driver."

"Mag would tear out and give three cheers, most likely. Come on to the movies with me tonight, Claire." Her startled reaction amused him. "What's the matter, did I say something dirty?"

"I haven't even thought of movies for so long, and I used to love to go."

"Well, they've got two theatres in Limerock, and one goes in for monsters from outer space. When the lights come on afterward you can see plenty of them in the audience. The upper classes, I mean mentally, go mostly to the other one. I don't know what they've got on tonight, but it's bound to be an improvement on our state of mind right now."

She spread her hand to cover the yellow pattern of a lichen on the rock and studied it. Suddenly she wanted, more than anything else she had wanted for a long time, to start off in the spring dusk like a normal young woman free and unburdened.

"It won't compromise you," Finn said dryly. "Girls have been known to go out with men around here and not find themselves engaged the next day. Of course some folks might call us a little too progressive, but we've found it works out real well and we like it."

"Is that awful clashing and roaring the school bus?"

"By God, it is! Sounds like she's abeating her way around the reef at Norman's Woe, don't she?" said Finn. "Probably Nancy's lashed to the mast." He got up and held out a hand to her.

"Maybe we'd better not take your short cut. I'd be too marked up to go out tonight." She took a parting look back. Light flashed from two cars half-hidden by the bay and juniper that fringed the homestead's dooryard. Finn saw them, too. "I wonder what they're doing in there."

"Maybe Gil's going to have some work done on the old place."

"Maybe. Well, come on, we'll have to get started if you don't figger to let me do it my way."

They had reached the mailbox by the time the bus appeared, and the driver gave them an expansive wave as he let Nancy out.

"We've made him happy," said Finn, as they both waved in return. "He's a kind of romantic soul."

"Good-by, Mr. Marsh!" Nancy shouted. She watched the bus go and then approached her mother at a gallop. "Hi, Mama! You know what Gwen said about me today? It's awful, can I say it?"

"You'd better before you burst."

"She said to Elmer, 'Don't go near that old bitchy-bones!' " Nancy gasped with dramatic horror at her own utterance.

"That wasn't very nice, was it?" said Claire with studied calm.

"Well, now," said Finn, "you can't claim it's not colorful. If you applied it in the right places it might be real effective."

"Maybe you'd better go home before *you* burst," said Claire.

"Mama, can I tell Aunt Mag?"

"You may tell her and that's to be the end of it. I don't want to hear it again."

"Okay! So long, Finn!" Nancy ran into the house, shouting, "Hey, Aunt Mag! Wait till you hear this!"

Finn began to laugh. "So long, Claire. I'll pick you up around half-past six."

Mag was delighted that Claire was going to the movies with Finn. "It's about time you started acting your age instead of like some settled old woman. I suppose it'd give your fancy in-laws the high fantods to see you going out with a fisherman, but Finn's a good boy and a gentleman. He won't take advantage. At least," she added thoughtfully, "I don't think he will. 'Course he's full-blooded and all man."

"Aunt Mag, you sound positively lustful." said Claire severely, and Mag cackled.

Nancy was exhilarated by the wonder and novelty of it all; she had never known her mother to go out in the evening with anybody but Grandmother Carradine or Uncle Robert. She wanted to help Claire dress for the occasion, and was disappointed in the sweater and skirt Claire laid out. Claire finally sent her downstairs, where Mag was going to teach her to play solitaire. Nancy went grumbling and Claire thought, I hope she's not going to be one of those *managing* children, or I shall never have another moment's peace.

She washed in the warm water brought upstairs in the rose-garlanded jug, and dressed in the outfit of which Nancy disapproved, a wood-violet cardigan and a matching skirt of fine tweed, and a soft pink blouse that cast a flattering reflection onto her face. As a concession to Nancy—or was it? she skeptically questioned herself—she put small pink stars on her ears, and used sparingly the cologne Nancy had given her for Christmas. Mrs. Carradine had picked it out, of course, and it was expensive and very good. Not one of the more exotic brands that David used to bring home because, he said, the ads were so sexy. Don't wear this around where Mother can get a whiff of it, he'd warn her. And I don't want old Robert inflamed, it would probably kill him. Besides, nobody but me is supposed to know what a passionate wench you are under that demure shell.

The familiar ache came drearily into her throat, and she felt so tired and drained of life that she sank down onto the bed. What was she doing, getting dressed to go out when all she wanted was to turn her mind into a thick and brainless dark? Finn was a stranger seen at a great distance, through the wrong end of a spyglass. Crouching on the bed she heard a door shut far off in the house and then Nancy's running feet and her exultant hail from the foot of the stairs. If she didn't answer at once, Nancy would be up here.

She got up and opened the door and called down, and then quickly put out her light without another glance in the mirror, as if she were afraid to see. She picked up the coat that matched her skirt, her scarf and gloves and bag, and went downstairs. The enforced movements strengthened her limbs so that by the time she was crossing the darkened dining room toward the lights and voices in the kitchen, the bad moment was receding. As she appeared in the doorway, Mag cried triumphantly, "There!"

"Mama, you look pretty!" Nancy exclaimed. Finn had been leaning over the back of her chair telling her what card to play. He straightened up, holding to the back of it, and gave Claire a smile of the purest pleasure.

"Well," he said. "Well."

"I could say the same thing," she said. "Look at you."

"I bet you expected him to come in rubber boots," said Mag. "I could have told you those Judsons like to dress. Sightly critter, isn't he?"

"Oh, shucks, Mag, you'll have me blushing," said Finn. He wore a white shirt and a blue tie which picked up the color of his eyes, always a surprise in such a brown face. His tweed jacket was a rough mixture of blues and grays, his dark gray slacks an obviously good grade, his loafers not new but well taken care of. She had seen some of David's friends less scrubbed, less well turned out. "They get it from their pa," Mag was saying. "Not that Dolly don't always look neat, but my, how slick that man did look when he wanted to. I remember him first time he ever come around here, younger than Finn is now, and a sailor, he was—"

"Mama, he smells wonderful," said Nancy.

"So does Mama," said Finn, taking Claire's coat. "Once when Dolly was getting ready to go to a dance with my father I said, 'Gorry, you stink pretty,' and she never got over it."

Nancy gurgled. "You stink pretty," she repeated. "You stink pretty. Mama, you stink pretty, you know it?"

"I'm sorry I told it now," said Finn.

"Okay," said Nancy. "I'll say it just once more, like bitchy-bones."

"We'd better go before I'm tempted to cause an incident," Claire leaned down and kissed Nancy. "Be a good girl and start for bed when Grandpa strikes seven."

"Oh, she will, and I'll be right behind her," said Mag. "We'll holler back and forth across the hall at each other, won't we?"

"Mmm," said Nancy rapturously.

"Brookline never had such charms," Claire said.

"Don't you rush straight home the minute the picture's over," Mag's voice followed them through the shed. "You're over twenty-one and I trust ye!" She laughed and Nancy joined her without knowing why.

"What a pair," said Finn. "Think the movies'll offer anything better? What did you mean, Brookline never had such charms?"

"Oh, such charms as Aunt Mag and solitaire, and hollering back and forth across the hall after you've gone to bed, and peepfrogs to sing you to sleep, and the Manana light to see from your window, and the smell of the sea to breathe all night." They walked to the car in the pure pale blue-green light that followed sunset; it was an instant of such clarity and silence that she almost hated to leave it.

"Over on the island the woodcocks are starting their evening performance," said Finn. "And if you listen real hard you can hear gulls that have spotted herring out by Hollowell. I'm thinking of training me a few to work for me. They're a heck of a lot smarter than Junior Eastman. . . . I've got Roy's car tonight so we ought to get there with some kind of decorum."

"Have you talked to your nephew yet?" she asked him.

"Danny?" He grinned. "He's avoiding me. So I'll let him suffer for a while. Besides, it may turn out he's done me a good turn."

The picture was one which she had seen favorably reviewed during the winter in some of the more bitterly discriminating columns. It depended more on ideas than on physical action, the characters were unveiled through dialogue that required close attention; to Claire this was always an exciting sort of film, but she was made uneasy by worrying whether or not Finn was enjoying it. He was absolutely quiet beside her; sometimes she glanced at his face, but in the light from the screen it was as stoic as stone, and she wondered if in his boredom he had simply retreated within his thoughts.

When the picture was over and they had come out into the chilly evening, he said, "Let's go get something to eat."

"All right," she answered. She knew she sounded dull, but she couldn't help being depressed. The sidewalks were crowded with people leaving the early showing at both theatres. They all seemed to know one another. Finn had nothing to say as they walked along, except when he saw someone he knew. She felt lonely and guilty, as if the evening which had started out with such promise in the clear green light had been a failure, and somehow it was her fault.

Finn stopped her with a hand on her arm. They had come to a corner restaurant with ship models in the windows and beyond them the roseate glow of lamps on waxed wood paneling.

"Oh, this looks nice," she said with mechanical eagerness. He reached for the door and then stepped back.

"I guess we won't," he said. He was gazing over her head into the restaurant, and she followed his eyes to Rafe Judson, sitting at a round table with two other men and a high-colored woman with her hair wound in a crown of dark braids. As she tilted her head back to laugh, showing a strong thick throat, her earrings danced and sparkled. "That's Hester," Claire said in astonishment, "but she looks different. Happy and almost handsome."

"Oh, she's feeling fine right now. Limerock's not much, but it's devilish wild compared to Saltberry Point." He cocked his head thoughtfully. "Rafe looks good too, doesn't he?"

"Elegant and positively benign. Santa Claus couldn't do better."

"That's because he's feeling like one of those big-time operators. He's probably trying to sell Limerock Harbor to those city slickers."

The other two, by their dark suits, bow ties, their sort of clean pallor, their haircuts, by their way of holding themselves as they smiled and talked, were not local men. They were what Claire called them now, spontaneously, *deep city*. They had a stereotyped urban polish about them, they were the identical siblings of millions of other young men who all wore the same clothes and spoke with accents no longer regional, but all squeezed out of the same composite cookie press. Sitting there in the restaurant with Rafe they had for Claire the dapper artificiality of well-made mannequins.

"Maybe they're trying to sell Rafe something," she said.

"Could be, but I don't suppose we'll ever know unless he starts digging a swimming pool in his dooryard. Say, do you mind going into a place that serves drinks?" he asked. "Because if you don't, the next best place to eat is at the Oceanside Hotel, but they've got a bar there."

"I've seen bars before. This may come as a surprise to you, but I've even sat at a bar once or twice in my life."

"I just thought I'd ask." He took her elbow and turned her around.

The narrow bar and grille was pleasantly decorated and not so crowded as the restaurant. Away from the bar it opened up into a sort of gallery that would have had in daylight a superb view of the harbor. Their window reflected the warm lights and the sparkle of glassware, and themselves; but there was a sense of dark salt-scented emptiness outside the glass which she enjoyed. It was like being on the very tip of a promontory over the ocean.

They ordered coffee and apple pie. When the waitress had gone Claire said, "Tell me something, Finn, and tell me the truth, Did you like that movie?"

"Didn't you?"

"Yes, I did, but I want to know if you would have chosen that one for yourself instead of what they have at the other theatre."

He folded his arms on the edge of the table. "You see one of those blood-and-guts pictures, you've seen them all. Cossacks, Greeks, Turks, Arabians, no matter what it's about, it always turns out to be another western. You know, I could write the dialogue myself I can say it right along with the hero."

"Don't change the subject," she said. "What about the picture we saw tonight?"

"Yep. You know when I read the book I couldn't figure out how they'd ever make a movie of it. What's the matter?"

"Did you *like* the book?"

"Ayuh. Helen had it come in her book club. Of course my brow was what you might call furrowed most of the time, and I had to go back over some of the pages to see if I'd missed anything. . . . Don't you think some of these fellers try so damn' hard to be subtle they lose themselves in their own fog?"

She took a drink of water on the word *subtle*. "I guess that's why I couldn't get anywhere with the book. The author was lost in his fog and I was lost in mine."

"Well, I thought the movie was an improvement. They must have got somebody to tell the author what he was driving at. Probably was quite a surprise to him." They were quiet while the waitress set their coffee and pie in front of them. You're quite a surprise to me, Finn, she thought, and you manage to do it every time.

Finn ate like a hungry boy, his manners good but vigorous, giving all his attention to his food at first. Then he sat back and said, "You know, Helen and I, we'd read the same books and then talk about 'em. It would nearly drive Roy crazy when we got going on about these characters as if they were real people, arguing why they did this or didn't do that. But she's been gone for a year, and so I haven't had any of that kind of talk. We were all great readers when we were kids, over on the island. When you haven't got television, you'll take a stab at almost anything. If you want to stand the winter better, you want to work your way through some of those Russians. Those Siberian winters make the Maine kind feel tropical."

She leaned back, laughing, and he said "What's the matter?" But he showed his pleasure at pleasing her.

"Tell me what else you like, Finn," she said, wiping her eyes. "I haven't talked books with anybody for a long time, either, and I guess I've missed it."

"Gorry, I dunno where to begin. I've read all of Kenneth Roberts; I used to think I'd made that march with them in *Northwest Passage*. Dug through most of Dickens—I guess *Great Expectations* is the one I like best, because I always had great expectations . . ." He ate more, distant with concentration. "*The Old Man and the Sea*. Hemingway's great except when he gets going on bullfights." His eyes focused on her with brilliant attention. "I'm against bullfights. Spain's supposed to be a big Christian country, isn't it? Well, how can they allow it? That animal's innocent when he's shoved out into that ring—" He subsided. "Well, it always makes me mad to think about it."

"Me too," said Claire. "I'd probably be the only tourist who went to Spain and left it without seeing a bullfight. Go on talking, Finn." She felt happy and young; loneliness was held somewhere at bay, she was not Claire the ravaged and forlorn, but a young woman out with a young man, enjoying innocent good companionship. *Innocent*. The bull was innocent, Finn had said. A strange word for him to use. She wondered if there would ever be an end to his surprises, or if he were really no more than what he had appeared to be on their first meeting. Perhaps she was seeing him as something more complex because he was the first person she had actually looked at after the long anesthetized year.

Suddenly he whispered, "Oh, *Je*—what are they all doing uptown tonight?" He was staring toward the bar. A woman had had just come in and was looking for an empty booth. Her long yellow bob shone like a fluorescent wig, and she was made up like a showgirl. Heavy costume jewelry flashed around her neck and in her ears.

"About put your eye out, wouldn't she?" said Finn. "They ought to stand her up somewhere for a lighthouse. Or to scare the gulls off in blueberry time." He leaned forward uneasily as several men came in at once. "Cleon must be parking the car. I wish we could get out of here."

"Is that Cleon's wife?" Claire tried not to sound incredulous.

"Yep, that's Onni. She goes for everything shiny the way a crow does." A broad red-headed man with a rolling walk pushed through the doors and went to Onni's booth. He slid into the opposite seat and was hidden from them.

"I've got a nasty feeling that Cleon's not going to show up," said Finn. "He's likely down on the Point thinking his wife's gone to a hen party somewhere."

"Does she make a habit of this?"

"I'm afraid of it. We've all got our suspicions but Cleon, and nobody wants to tell him. She's not a bad girl, and she was brought up strict. Darned good cook and housekeeper too, just got too much time and money to spend. Should have a bunch of kids," he said grouchily. He looked much older now than when he had been discussing books. "I don't want to run into her. They've got a back door here for quick getaways, thank God." He signaled the waitress, and paid for their food. The back door was hidden behind an ornamental screen and let them out into a short badly lighted lane between dark buildings. The harbor scent surrounded them strongly; the pungence of wharves and green-slimed spilings, mud flats, and the seafood plants.

"That waitress thinks either your husband just came in," said Finn, "or my wife." They both burst into spasms of adolescent laughter, hurrying on around corners and behind closed stores like children on Hallowe'en. "I shouldn't have laughed," Claire gasped when they reached the car. "It wasn't funny."

"Might as well laugh as cry. But I'm sorry we had to run into that, spoil a nice evening."

"It couldn't spoil it, Finn. So can't we just forget seeing Cleon's wife there, and never mention it again?"

"We will forget it," he said strongly. "All right."

·17·

Finn was disappointed to wake to fog. He had plenty of things
to do when the weather kept him ashore, but today he was
too restless. He remembered the way Claire had looked when
they said good night in Mag's kitchen, softened, younger than
himself, her eyes full of dark light. When they shook hands he
had to be careful to hold hers only a moment, and he had thought
all at once of the husband and wondered how it had been to be
in love with her and know time was short. This he recollected
in the morning, prowling restlessly around the foglit rooms with
his mug of coffee. And he was jabbed at odd moments by the
way Lila had shouted after him the other night. It wasn't what
she said, but the near-bawling in her voice. She'd always prided
herself on being tough as a man in picking them up and letting
them go, so he didn't have to be uncomfortable about her,
but today he was, damnit, and it was all mixed up with Onni.

"Well, for cripes' sake, I don't have to feel any responsibility
for *her!*" he said loudly in the kitchen. "Nor for Cleon either
if he's that half-arsed he doesn't know what his wife's up to!"

He put on his rubber boots and went down to the fishhouse.
Birds fluttered and challenged around him in the fog. The cat-
bird was back and the barn swallows tried to get into the
fishhouse with him. He lit a cigarette and leaned on the bench
staring at nothing, and wondered what Claire thought when
she woke up this morning. That he was a proper gaum, going
on about books as if he knew something? Or that she'd got
herself mixed into something kind of smelly and nasty by having
to sneak out of the place last night?

He left the fishhouse and rowed across the harbor, solitary
in a wet white cloud. On the Point all outside activity was
cancelled by the fog, and when he walked up the boys' wharf
the thud of his boots seemed loud enough to be heard down
to the lower harbor. Cleon hailed him from the door of Gil's
store, smiling and rubbing his hands. "Well, how you been?

Long time no see!" He said it as if he had just thought it up.

"I'm busy," said Finn. "I got my way to make in the world." He waited stolidly for Cleon to reach him. "You want something?"

"Just to tell ye there's no hard feelings about the boat. Like I was saying to Rafe, mebbe it's a good thing you're independent as a hog on ice. Mebbe we ought to be proud of ye instead of mad." He slapped Finn's shoulder. "You're the biggest in the family now, we ought to tread easy." Cleon was monotonous in his tactics; if the worried or stern father approach didn't work he was full of bumptious good fellowship. It was either one or the other, always. "Rafe's got the coffeepot on in his shop. Come on over. It won't kill ye. It's for the good of the family."

"When you say that, smile," said Finn. He'd been on his way to Elmer's for a second breakfast in a roomful of kids; that always gave him a big heft back to life.

"Roy's over there," Cleon said.

"Well, I suppose he'll take the curse off it," said Finn. "Mebbe I ought to go, just to see what else Rafe's got on the fire beside the coffeepot."

"I'm kind of wondering that myself," said Cleon blandly.

"I love a liar, but you suit me too well. Good God, neither of you two can break wind without telling the other."

Cleon decided to be amused, and slapped Finn's shoulder again. At the fishhouse Rafe greeted him with a broad smile and a mug of coffee. "How much you charging?" Finn asked him.

"That's right," said Roy, "you want to be suspicious. You could go out here without anything left to your name."

"I'm safe enough then. I've got nothing to lose but my expectations." He caught the flash between Rafe and Cleon. *Expectations* to them meant the island, and they were always nervous about that. Then Rafe laughed. "I don't know why you fellers are so suspicious. We got the Abbott place easy, didn't we?"

"I dunno if Gardner would've cost us that much in the long run," Roy said.

"Look, we'll get plenty for that house some day," said Rafe. "Anyway, that's water over the dam. I've got something more to talk about, something so good I have a hard time believing it myself. You've heard about Gemini Seafoods, haven't you?"

Cleon barged in eagerly on cue. "That big place that's making such a splash up to Rockport? Sure. They say there's a million dollars behind it."

"How far behind it?" Roy asked. He and Finn laughed. Rafe waited indulgently, then went on. "I dunno if it's a million, but it's quite an operation. Well, last night Hes and I went to Limerock, had dinner at the hotel with—uh—oh, that's no account," he said modestly. "Just somebody I know in the Masons —well, as a matter of fact it was George Washburn, the investment broker. We're thinking of starting an investment program. After I get the new boat paid for, of course."

"Nice to know you're human like the rest of us and have to think about paying bills," said Finn. "If you're having a hard time getting into your story mebbe I can help out. You met two ginks from this By-Jiminy outfit and went for a cup of coffee with them in the Crow's Nest. I saw you in there. And either you sold them, or they sold you, the idea of having a place down here."

"Aint you the mean son of a bitch, taking the wind out of his sails like that," said Roy.

"Look, all we have to have is the land for their buildings, and some shore with deep water for them to build their wharf. They'll pay plenty. Once they get squared away, they'll be hauling fishermen in from all around here, putting every other dealer out of business."

"They're paying ten cents a pound extra," said Cleon. "They'll rake in every lobsterman on the coast before they get through."

"I've heard that ten-cent business before," said Roy. "Sounds fine at first, till they start making excuses. Price goes down, Nova Scotia lobsters coming in and glutting the market—"

"That's beside the point," said Rafe. "The point is, they'll pay a damned big price for a couple of acres of land and a decent shorefront. And it won't be just lobsters they'll be handling, but scallops, clams, mackerel, herring, any kind of seafood they can get. It'll be a big thing for us. Real big."

"Damn sight bigger than podding around with Gil," Cleon said. "Trouble with him he's running his business, if you can call it that, the way his father did. Times have changed."

"They sure have," said Finn. Rafe gave him a sharp glance.

"Another thing," he said, "we can run the thing for them at one whopper of a guaranteed salary. They want to use local men if they can find any smart enough. Finn, if you get yourself that boat you're so set on finding all by yourself, you could go smacking for us."

"*Us?*" said Roy. "Sounds like a sure thing."

"It is, as soon as we can show 'em some land," said Cleon, rubbing his hands.

"You planning to sell the Abbott shore front?" asked Roy. "Better be sure they see it at high tide."

"Go ahead and grin like a Chessy cat," said Rafe. "You'll grin even more when you find out what I'm willing to drop in your lap and only ask for a small percentage for making the deal. You got the land and you got the shore, Roy. You and Cleon also have between you a good road for those trailer trucks to come in on."

Roy sat staring up at Rafe, the coffee mug halfway to his lips. "Helen's field?" he asked. "You want Helen's field?"

Rafe bit at the inside of his cheek. It was plain he hadn't expected this reaction. Cleon went blundering in. "Well, gorry, Roy, we all know how much store she set by that field and the strawberries in it, and the view, but it's not like she's home to see the difference."

Roy banged the mug down on the bench and stood up. "Don't you bastards think she's ever coming home again? You think she's locked away up there for good? You think I've wiped her out of my life?"

"Now, Roy," Cleon said nervously. Rafe still chewed at his cheek, looking glassily at nothing. He's not taken aback, Finn thought; he's mad because Roy's putting up a fight. He said mildly, "Hey Rafe. What about your land going down to the inlet there? That'd make a good pound, I always thought, and they could run their dock off the mouth of it. Plenty of water there at low tide."

"It's not fit and you know it."

"Because Hester's planning out her garden there?"

"That's got nothing to do with it! Don't you think I'd sell

it in a minute instead of trying to put the business in Roy's way?" His cheeks had a shiny purple bloom. "Roy's got the best place of the whole harbor on account of that field where they can put up buildings, and have room for the trucks to park, and he's getting sentimental about a handful of strawberries. *Jesus!*"

"Ayuh, damn fool, isn't he?" said Finn. "His wife's where she can't say anything. Different in your case. Hes can yell bloody murder about cold storage sheds and trailer trucks blocking off her view."

"Goddam you, you leave my wife out of this!" Rafe shouted, coming at him. Cleon's arm fell between them.

"Can't we ever get together without a fight?" he asked plaintively.

"'I dunno. Ask Rafe."

Rafe was sweating, the veins thick in his forehead. "All right, all right! . . . Where are *you* going?" he yelled at Roy.

"I'm leaving. Any objection?"

"Maybe I shouldn't have thought of you. Maybe I shouldn't have had some fool idea I was doing something pretty good for one of my brothers. It's like wanting to get the boat for this lunkhead here. You act like I was insulting you, for God's sake! We've had the Abbott place two weeks and you still act like you were trapped." His breath sounded thick and his color was still violent. "All right. But those men are ready to move in here when we say the word, and if we miss the boat we'll be sorry for the rest of our lives. You want to keep fubbing around with a few traps when you can sit ashore and make money? You want to give up a chance to belong to something big, bossing fishermen from Port George to Bristol and beyond?"

"You mean you'll be doing the bossing," said Roy.

"There's something for each one of us, I told you."

"This is a big business and we'd never have the capital to start it with, never in a million years," said Cleon. "Sounds so good I couldn't believe it myself for a while." He shook his head reverently and folded his thick hands over his chest as if he were at a funeral.

"Well, you guys go ahead and sell yourselves and have fun," said Roy. "I've done all right up to now fubbing around, as you call it, and I never figured big business was very soothing to the nerves."

"I guess I'll be going too," said Finn. "I dunno why you think I'd be any more reliable smacking lobsters than seining."

"You halfwit, we only wanted to keep you free of those two over there," said Cleon with his most guileless grin. "This'd be something entirely different. A family business. Just what Pa would approve of."

"Leave him out of it, why don't ye?" said Finn.

Cleon looked hurt, but Rafe spoke first. "Listen, you two, before you skin out of here like it was a leper colony. Best place in the harbor of all is Gil's right next door. Why don't we buy him out?"

"I can see him selling," said Roy.

"Listen, anybody'll sell if the offer's good enough," Cleon protested. "And Gil's getting on, he can't tend to business the way he should. Back bothers him. Besides, he can use some extra cash."

Finn was suddenly tired of the whole business. If I had the sense God gave a louse I'd walk out of here right now, he thought. He said idly, "Oh, Gil may have a pretty good little nest egg pretty soon. He had somebody up at the home place yesterday."

The results were entirely satisfactory. Cleon and Rafe both sucked wind, and Roy said, "Who was it? Summer people? Retired? Or a fisherman?"

Finn shrugged. "I couldn't see. I was too far away. Just saw Gil's car outside and another one. Might not be anything at all, of course. But gorry, I wouldn't blame Gil, the place just standing there empty all this time." He meandered on, vacant and innocent. "He could give him wharf privileges for his traps. . . . If it's a fisherman, I mean."

When he stopped, nobody said anything for a moment, and then Roy said, "Ayuh. Well, good-by, all."

"Wait a minute!" Rafe said.

"That's all he's been saying today," said Finn to Roy. "Either 'Wait a minute,' or 'Listen.' Somebody ought to teach that parakeet some new words."

"He's just as liable to sell that place to a fisherman," Rafe said. "Or maybe sell the whole thing, wharf and all. We've *got* to get it first! Do you realize," he whispered hoarsely, "that if we could get his place we could turn around and sell it to Gemini for *twice* what we paid?"

"If Gil don't get wind of Gemini and sell it to them first," said Roy. "But somehow I can't see him selling to anybody."

Cleon said, "I can, if we can offer him enough money to make his eyes pop. Remember, he's getting tired. Hit him all of a sudden with such a good offer it'll knock the wind out of him."

"Where do you plan on getting the money to offer him?" Finn asked. "Ask Dolly to mortgage the island?"

"In any sane normal family that'd work," said Rafe. "In any sane normal family the island would belong to the sons so they could go and mortgage it themselves. But us being the Judsons, Dolly's holding onto the island as a kind of private park for her pet, and if *he* don't want to buy out Gil *she* won't mortgage the island. So that's that. But there's three more of us here."

"Two," said Roy. "I went in with you on the Abbott place. But I'm not going in with you on this. I got other uses for my money. If you can talk Gil into selling, if you get this other company in here and turn into the lobster king or whatever it is you see yourself as—and Cleon here, I suppose he'll be the prime minister—well, good luck to ye. And you won't have to share anything."

He went out. Finn said cheerfully to the others, "So long," and followed him. Prudently they walked out on Rafe's wharf before they spoke. Roy shook his head. "What next?" he said in a tone of weary wonder. "That boy's out of place here. He ought to be in one of those big fancy offices with twelve telephones on the desk in front of him and all of them ringing at once."

"He wants to be important, all right."

"Too bad he was too young for the war. He'd have had enough importance then to last him the rest of his life. Well, I'm going home and do some painting."

"News still the same about Helen?"

"Ayuh." Roy's eyes glinted, as if that were the nearest to a smile he allowed himself. "God, they made me some mad in there, talking about the field. Even if I didn't think she was ever coming home I'd never let that field go."

"Couple of jackasses, the two of 'em. Or worse."

"Never heard you sound that peeved before," Roy said. "I thought you could take 'em or leave 'em alone."

"Mebbe old age's creeping up on me and turning me sour."

"Hey, what was that about Eastman?"

"Oh, they were the ones who crapped on that deal," said Finn. "Got wind of it somehow and rushed right over to tell him I had a crew of desperadoes lined up, or something."

He turned to leave the wharf and Roy said, "Wait a minute." He sounded reluctant, almost timid. "Mebbe you hadn't better stick so fast to Larry and Elmer."

"Oh, don't give me that, for God's sake," Finn snapped. "I've had enough dictating from Fidel and Raul in there."

"I'm not dictating. I'm just telling you what you ought to know, that Rafe's got it in his head to run this place and get everybody out of it that's not a Judson or a Judson arse-wiper, and as long as you hang to those two he'll stay up nights thinking up ways to break you apart. If I was you I'd drop the herring idea right now, and mebbe he'll be so busy with his big operations he'll leave all three of you alone for awhile."

"The hell he will," said Finn. "Look, while I got breath and blood in me, and while there's a chance I might get the island, he won't leave me alone, nor Cleon either. Now I got as much right to run my own business as he's got." He heard the hard clang in his voice and tried to soften it. "Might be you're talking sense, probably are, but I never been noted for having much sense."

Roy flapped his hand at him. "Well, go ahead and find out for yourself. I'm going back to my painting."

"You need any help?"

"Nope, Danny's working on it with me at night. I got Dolly to choose some new paper. . . . Wait a minute." He walked back toward Finn. "How'd they know about the Eastman deal? Danny tore out of the house mad as a wet hen that night because I stepped on him—"

Finn nodded. "Most likely Danny, but not meaning any harm. I planned on having a word with him myself."

"Well, I will," said Roy flatly. "One thing I can't stand is a kid running from one house to another telling all he knows."

"Don't be too hard on him. We may be better off not working for Harve."

Roy grunted and went down the wharf. Finn turned toward the land. He heard a low mutter of voices as he passed Rafe's fiishhouse, drowned out by the rattle of the bait truck as it turned off the black road. Gil came out of his back door and cut across the lawn toward his wharf, making it just before the truck did. A wind stirred the fog and blew it in steamy billows that gathered up scents from everything they passed; the harbor, the rockweed, the flats, the sodden woods, wet earth, and new grass.

·18·

They talked with Waisenen on the end of his wharf at Pruitt's Harbor. He was a short, white-blond man with a flat nose and pale blue eyes. "Sure," he said. "I ain't like Harve, the Herring King. I can afford to take a chance. Besides, one of my crews is breaking up. Two of 'em got piles." His lips turned up in a chilly grin. "And one's got to keep his eye on his wife. That's the skipper. You got another man yet?

"There's one I was going after, when I had something sure to tell him," said Finn.

"If you ain't said anything to him yet, how about taking this feller that's left? Good man, not much to say."

"One man's as good as another to me, and where you're fitting us out you got something to say. But if I'd already talked to this other guy," he said warningly, "he'd be the one."

Waisenen nodded without expression. "When can you start in?"

"As soon as my boat's overboard and that ought to be in a week. It would be ready now except that Morry's been laid up with a cold."

"Make it two weeks," said Waisanen. "I'll turn the gear over to you then. Twine, pocket, purse seine, anchors, kegs, dories, whole works." He gave them a short nod and put out his hand. They each shook hands with him silently, and then he went down the ladder to his boat. They went back up the wharf to the truck.

"Jeez, that was some easy," said Larry wonderingly.

"At least he didn't talk us into a coma," said Finn. "That Harve's so damn gabby I should have mistrusted him from the first."

They had little to say as they drove out of town, crammed into the cab of Elmer's old pick-up. It was a sobering condition to be seiners at last, instead of just dreaming about it. Up till now your big worry was whether you'd get the chance or not. But when you got it, you were lost in a whole mess of little worries like a blind cod in a school of herring; the chief one was whether you'd get enough to pay your expenses and have anything left over to take home and pay toward the gear too. For himself, Finn would just as lief put everything into buying the outfit, but the others would want something else. They had the women to pacify, and kids growing out of shoes while you looked at them.

"Well, next thing's a radio-telephone," he said aloud. It was the first time anyone had spoken in ten miles and they were just entering Williston. "Can we ante up three hundred dollars amongst us?"

"Are you kidding?" Larry squealed. "Can't you talk to some of your rich brothers?"

"Are *you* kidding?" said Finn. "Hey, wait a minute. I've got an insurance policy I can cash in. Ought to be worth something."

When they came by Rafe's place he and Hester were just getting out of their car, and they looked toward the old pick-up with frozen faces as it rattled by.

"Look at the dudes," Elmer said admiringly. "Any kin of yours, Finn?"

That's the high-class branch of the family."

"Well, they say the higher up a monkey goes the more he shows his rump," said Larry. "They ought to be feeling the draft pretty soon."

"Look, son," said Elmer, "if Finn wants to make talk about them, he can, because they're his relatives. But hadn't you better keep that jaw of yourn from flapping quite so fast?"

Finn laughed. "That's all right, Larry. Long as you don't go making them little dolls and then start sticking pins in 'em, I reckon talk won't hurt a bit." Been up to Limerock, he thought. Now what? Rafe doesn't want Gemini to find out about Gil's place and make Gil an offer direct, but on the other hand he's not got much to offer himself, even with Cleon. Been to the bank? Loan and Building?

He turned down invitations to a mug-up and struck off over the path across the ledges toward Abbott's road. When he reached the door into the kitchen he waited a moment; he could hear voices on the other side, Claire's soft and so clear without her even trying, the way a violet or a rose is perfect without thinking. Nancy's was chirpy and energetic like the chickadees. "Show me again how to make those petals curls, Mama," she commanded, and Finn knew they were making Maybaskets; his fingertips itched with the remembered feel of paste, and the bits of colored paper sticking to them while his mouth dried from the heavy tougue-pointed breathing. Claire laughed at something and though he had heard her laugh before, he'd never heard this low, loving sound with a selfishness about it. Not consciously selfish, but right now it was just her and the kid; she didn't know if anybody else existed and she didn't give a damn.

"Mama," Nancy said, "if you hang Finn a Maybasket will he chase you and kiss you?"

"You bet he would," Mag shrieked. "Dunno but I'd hang him a Maybasket if I thought he'd chase me!"

Finn knocked on the door and followed his knock in. He leaned over Mag's rocker and gave her a loud smack on the cheek. "That's for making me feel like Casanova, Mag."

They all began to laugh at once. Nancy slid off her stool and threw her arms around Finn and clung with a wiry strength. He picked her up and past her cheek he said to Claire, "Waisanen's setting us up."

"I'm glad, Finn," she said. "I hope it'll work out just the way you want it."

"Of course that's on the laps of the gods, you might as well say." He put Nancy down and she still tried to hang on to him.

"Come back and sit down, Nancy," her mother said. "Leave Finn alone."

"I don't mind her."

"Children can overdo a thing and become tiresome." She began cutting yellow paper scallops, her face thinned and older. Finn tried to get the other mood back. "Is that one for me, Nancy?" he asked.

"Land sakes, you don't suppose she'd let you see it aforetime, do you?" asked Mag.

"Gorry, Mag, you sound like Nancy and me was getting married," he protested, and Nancy clapped her hands over her face, stifling unsuccessfully her giggles and peeking through her fingers at him. He winked at her, but it was no good. What had been in the kitchen when they'd all laughed after he kissed Mag was gone, and he was feeling the draft.

"Well, time I got home and started baiting up for tomorrow," he lied; he was already baited up. When he got out he was sweating and angry. He didn't know why, he wanted to shake his head and stamp like a bull plagued all out of reason by black flies.

He was eating his supper at the porch table when Danny appeared out of the fog. He still had his skinniness but in the oilclothes he was a young giant, all Judson in that build and the wiry black hair, but with something of his mother in the freckled cheekbones, and the light quick eyes. His big mouth was still a child's above the strong jaw.

He began shedding his wet oilclothes with reckless gestures. "Outdoors with them," Finn ordered. "What are you, a goddam water spaniel?"

"Sure, sure, Nunk." Danny shook the oilclothes outside, then hung jacket and sou'wester on a hook beside Finn's and banged his boot into a chair before he managed to sit in it. Finn steadied the table until Danny was settled, or as settled as he was likely to be. You never knew when he was going to heave up again. Was I ever like that? Finn wondered.

"Get yourself some grub, Danny," he said. "No, don't. Stay put. I'll get it."

"I just ate. We had supper over at Uncle Cleon's. Boy, can that Onni cook when she puts her mind on it! Then Uncle Rafe and Aunt Hes came over, so I left." He squirmed as if a quart of spruce spills had been dropped down his neck. "Anyway, I'm over here with a message for you, and Uncle Rafe wanted you to have it so bad he's trusted me with his outboard. Now that's confidence for you."

"It's something," said Finn. "What's his message?"

"We're all driving down east tomorrow to see Uncle Rafe. My great-uncle. Dad told me to tell you he's going and you might as well come along and get a look at the doings."

"Oh, I might, huh? What's the idea?"

"Confidentially, I think Rafe's going to put the bite on him for some money. See, he wants to hit Gil with a really big offer right out of the blue, and he can't raise enough in the family, with Dad saying, No, no, a thousand times no. Anybody he talked to in Limerock wanted to come down and see the whole set-up first and that would spoil the surprise element, see? It would tip Gil off that something was in the wind."

"You mean," said Finn in sardonic astonishment, "that they talked this all over in front of *you?*"

"I know, I know." His color deepened and he grew visibly hot. "Dad's already taken me apart and put me together again. But honest, Finn, I wasn't carrying anything, at least I didn't mean to. I was just grousing because I wanted to go seining so bad this summer, and they were sympathetic." He spread out his big hands and shrugged. "I was sorry as hell I messed things up."

"All right. I know you didn't mean it, but watch your tongue, and you'd better start scraping the hells and damns out of your conversation before your mother gets home. It's all right for us reprobates and ignoramuses but you're the one who'll bring some fame and honor to the family—we hope."

Danny looked at his hands. "I'd rather be a fisherman." He lifted his head and gazed at Finn, who with an unpleasant wrench under his breastbone recognized Helen's eyes when the woe had begun to get into her like a killing frost. "Because of Mark I have to be something different. I have to make myself over, and it looks like a damn' long life ahead of me to do it in. And I can't even put up a fight. She's coming home to see me be valedictorian. She wants to see me in Orono next fall. Then she'll be sure I'm not going to be drowned hauling traps, and she'll be cured. If I said one thing"—the icy passivity of his voice began to crack—"just *one* thing wrong, I could put her right back in that hospital for good."

Finn was moved and ashamed. He wanted to say the right thing, but there wasn't any right thing. "Gorry, it might not be like that, Danny," he began. "Sometimes after someone's been through what your mother's been through, they're stronger afterward than they were before, stronger than a lot of people around them."

Danny said patiently, "Look, I *know*."

"Well, you don't know everything yet. For instance, you don't know what you'll find out if you get away from this place. What are you, eighteen? Sure, you want to be a fisherman because you never knew anything different. But there must be things you like about school or you wouldn't have done so good. Gorry, you can't have been gritting your teeth and fighting your way through *all* the time."

A small smile flicked Danny's mouth. "Sure, I like school all right. But does that mean I shouldn't want to be a fisherman?"

"Nope, but it means you've got quite a lot in your head besides boats and traps. You like chemistry, physics, math—hard stuff like that. So it might be that when you think you're humoring your folks you're really giving yourself a chance." Danny gazed sullenly out at the fog. "For Pete's sake," Finn said, "how do you know they wouldn't have insisted on this even without Mark drowning? Just so you'd find out what you really want? If you're no good at anything but fishing you'll find out that soon enough, too."

He pushed back his chair and began to clear the table. If I'd had his chances at eighteen, he thought, and somebody to boot me into taking them.... He was no longer sorry for Danny, except for the boy's fear of sending his mother off the deep end again. "So we're going up and see Uncle Rafe, huh?" he said. "He know about the visitation?"

"Rafe's called up. He's expecting us." Danny came behind him carrying the butter and the flowered teapot. "Hey, I never saw this before."

"Be careful with it." Finn took it from him. "What time they leaving?"

"Eight on the dot, from Uncle Cleon's. Dressed up so as to look sharp. We're going in the new Olds." Light really seemed to shine from behind his eyes, it was a way taken from his mother. "I may get to drive it, if Uncle Cleon's feeling just right."

"Well, I'll be there."

When Danny had gone Finn felt empty, which was worse than being mad or disappointed or plain lonely. He found himself walking around aimlessly touching things, and that drove him outdoors. In the dusk it was slowly clearing; the alders were a band of shadow beyond the field, and from them he heard a woodcock's nasal *beep* and then after a few moments the sound of the soaring flight. "Well, you're a happy little son of a bitch," he said sourly. Suddenly he wished he could go and get Lila and bring her back here and keep her all night, love her up, get up and eat, go back to bed again, love her up again till they were both half-dead, and then sleep till morning like a drunk, with her hugged in his arms like the teddy bear he'd dragged out of the closet when Pa died and started taking to bed with him again.

·19·

It looked like a fine large morning to go and take a look at an uncle you'd never seen before and who, so far as Finn knew, had never shown any sign of interest in his nephews. "In fact," he said aloud as they were going through Belfast, "how do we know that Uncle Rafe ever existed? Maybe Pa made him up, so's to give us a nice cozy feeling about a rich uncle."

Rafe gave him an irritated look over his shoulder. "I talked to him yesterday." Danny snickered and Rafe said, "Oh, funny, huh?"

Cleon, who was driving, gave him a sidewise grin. "Kind of nice to have some comedians along. Like a traveling floor show.

If they had more room back there they'd probably give us a real hot buck and wing."

"God, don't suggest it," said Roy. "Or else let me out. With these two long-legged gandyguts just sitting quiet back here I feel like that guy wrestling with the snakes."

Everybody laughed. They all felt good this morning, whatever their private theories about the mission. The countryside as they headed east was bare and yet springlike under a warming sun, rocky pastures were greening, there was even a softer look about the shadows cast by the spruce woods. Whenever they came in sight of salt water it was bluer than the last time.

As they left Ellsworth Roy said, "What did he sound like on the telephone? Glad to hear from you? Real eager to lay eyes on his kid brother's boys?"

"I told him who I was," said Rafe, "and he said, 'Ayuh'. I said we'd like to see him and he said 'Ayuh'. Then I said could we come today and he said something else."

"What?" asked Finn.

"He said, 'Lavven-thutty.' So help me, 'Lavven-thutty.' Sounded just like old Abbott." They all laughed. "If I didn't know for a fact that he's the big blueberry man up there and practically owns the Stiles Paper Company, I'd think he was some old character left over from the year nineteen-hundred."

"That's probably his act," said Cleon. "Makes people think he's homespun as hell."

"Rafe, how'd you find out about the blueberries and the paper company?" Finn asked. "That's not just something you remember from what Pa said, is it? Because things could have changed a lot since them."

"Nope, he's still right there raking it in. I had Hes investigate," Rafe said smugly. "She's good at that. Knows just what kind of letters to write, and who write 'em to. I've had this up my sleeve about Uncle Rafe for a long time. Had a hunch the old bird would come in handy."

Finn glanced sidewise at Roy, who dropped one eyelid slightly. It would be kind of mean to ask Rafe why he was so sure Uncle Rafe would want to come in handy. Besides, you never could tell; Rafe was a slick talker and he might just tickle the old man and bring it off.

"Everything's working out like clockwork," Cleon said. It was too bad he was driving so he couldn't rub his hands. "There's no chance of the Gemini fellers going down and taking a look at the Point while we're gone, and mebbe approaching Gil on their own, because they've gone back to New York for some kind of a conference."

Rafe was looking for landmarks along the road that wound narrowly through woodlot and pasture, with here and there a little cluster of houses. "I did get the directions out of him, such as they were," he muttered. "He has his office at home. Yellow house on the right after you pass a road that says Sands Point."

"There it is!" yelped Danny. He plunged forward to push his head between Cleon's and Rafe's. "There's the sign. And I can see something yellow through those trees."

"And we'll arrive there stone-deaf in at least one ear," said Cleon. "Will you just set back, boy, and try to preserve a little decorum?"

Danny sank back halfway. "Do you think he's going to feed us? I don't know about you guys, but it sounds like a dogfight in my stomach and that'll probably drown out the negotiations."

"Next time we'll bring along some dog biscuits for you," said his father. The car went around a bend past a plantation of big pines seething and glistening in the freshening wind. At the top of a long gentle rise beyond the pines stood a large yellow building, a conglomeration of ells and wings, mansards and steep gables, roofed in red. Outbuildings all in the same aggressive yellow clustered like chicks around a huge red hen of a barn. Trucks and machinery glittered in the barnyard. There were no shade trees; just the monstrous collection of buildings on the barren rise.

The name *Rafe Judson* was on the mailbox in neat black letters. "Well, what do you know?" said Finn. "We have got kinfolk up here after all. In a yellow house too, just like he said."

"That's sure yellow," said Roy. "Knock your eye out."

"Well kept up," Rafe sounded tense. "Lot of money there." He was flushed, staring hard ahead.

The good humor Finn had felt on the road deserted him. He looked glumly out at the field. He felt a kind of shabbiness even though he wasn't the one who wanted the money. They'd never had so much as a Christmas card from this man; he was just a name with no voice, no face, no little ways like Old Abbott's snuff-taking and Harve Eastman's *deah* and Gil's one-sided trot down the wharf. He thought, I don't want to lay eyes on the old skinflint and if I had any guts I'd get out now and start walking back toward Ellsworth. They could pick me up when they come away with a million dollars or a swift kick in the rear, whichever they get.

The car took the final curve and stopped at the front door. Nobody said anything. Then Rafe said angrily, "What are you waiting for?" They all followed him out. No one looked especially pleased except Danny, who was probably still hoping they'd be fed. "The office is back in the ell we passed," he said helpfully. "There was a sign over the door."

"Hell, we're relatives," said Rafe. "We go in the front door." He strode up the brick walk and seized the knocker. After the second clang the door was opened and a stout woman, with shiny black hair that looked painted on, stared out at them; she had the biggest bosom Finn had ever seen, covered with a flow- ered apron. She didn't say a word. Rafe smiled. The old silk was back in his voice. "Good morning. Mr. Judson's expecting us."

"Ayuh," she said, unmoved."Office's back there. You can see the sign."

If Rafe was disappointed you'd never know it. "Thank you," he said with a little bow. Real courtly, Finn thought. The woman was impressed enough to say "You're welcome" before she closed the door.

They went back along the drive to the office ell. There was no fancy knocker here, but the door was opened before Rafe's knuckles touched it. A bald rangy man with a paunch looked out at them from eyes so like their own it was a little chilling. The eyes went over them all in turn, carefully. They returned to Finn twice. Rafe, surefooted as ever, pushed out his hand and said, "Uncle Rafe, I'm Rafe Judson and these are my brothers."

"Joseph and his brethren, is that it?" The voice was cracked and twangy, too old for the man. The gaunt face smiled and the teeth were long, bright, and false. He shook hands with each of them and repeated the name and then said, "Well come in, come on. Sit down."

The office wasn't big and they crowded it; if you moved an elbow wrong you were likely to scrape a calendar off the wall or bump into the rolltop desk. The desk itself had so much stuff on it Finn wondered what happened if a sneeze ever took Uncle Rafe by surprise. Then he decided that nothing ever took this man by surprise, not even a sneeze. Uncle Rafe rocked back in the old leather-padded swivel chair and put his fingertips together and said, "So you came up to take a look at the old man, did you?"

Cleon, looking about as natural as a bear on a bicycle, boomed, "We thought it was about time." Rafe sat at his ease and gave Uncle Rafe the famous smile. "There's a time comes when you want to know your family. You can go along for years thinking it doesn't matter, you don't care, you've got along fine so far; and then one day it hits you. Who are you, anyway? Where'd you come from? What kind of people are responsible for you being here?"

Uncle Rafe cocked his head as if to say, *That so?* The others looked at Rafe with surprise and something like respect. It sounded so damn sincere, and when you came to think of it, it was the best reason in the world. Cleon was nodding violently. "Pa told us a lot about you and we always liked to hear it," he assured Uncle Rafe. "He was always talking about taking a trip down east to see you. Then he—" Cleon looked at the floor and shook his head as if he couldn't go on. Rafe picked up the melody, his eyes fixed on that bony and noncommittal face behind the fingertips.

"After we lost Pa we were so damned busy scratching for a living and looking out for our mother and the youngest here that we never could take the time to go traveling."

Uncle Rafe's eyes rolled toward Danny. "This being the youngest?"

Danny grinned. "Nope, he's talking about Finn." Finn felt more of a fool than he had at the door. He said bluntly, "My mother worked too." And Rafe never so much as bought me a pair of shoes, he wanted to add, except that it wasn't worth throwing Rafe off his stride when he was starting out so good.

"Ayuh," Uncle Rafe said dryly. "I reckon she was always entergetic. Your father used to brag on it in his letters. Well, from the looks of you your work's paid off. All of you fishermen?"

"All but Danny here," said Rafe. "He's the family scholar, you might say. Going to the University of Maine this fall."

Uncle Rafe appraised Danny, his long head slowly going up and down. "Well, now. What are you good in?"

"Math and chemistry."

"If you want to stay in Maine after you graduate, let me know. I hope you want to stay, young feller. We can't afford to keep losing blood."

"I want to stay," said Danny. The gaunt chin chopped down swiftly with approval, and Uncle Rafe looked back at the others. "Well, now you've got a look at the old man, you satisfied?"

"In one way," said Rafe. He settled back and hooked one arm over the back of his chair. "You're what Pa told us you were, but you're a lot more too. See, he saw you as his brother. He couldn't see you any other way because he'd grown up with you. But we don't know you so we see you as something else."

"And what's that? . . . Don't the rest of you ever say anything? You struck with Spanish mildew?"

"He does it so much better," said Finn, "we wouldn't even attempt it." His uncle's eyes narrowed, and he put a heavy hand over his mouth and then stroked his jaw with it. Rafe waited with a patient smile.

"All right, what do you see me as? Tightfisted old Yankee horse-trader who's made a fortune out of cheating widows and orphans?"

"No," said Rafe softly. "As one of the smartest business men in the state of Maine. If we had more like you, Maine would be way out in front. You know something, Uncle Rafe? I used to listen to Pa talk about you and I thought I was something special because I'd been named for you. And I used to think, if I'm this proud because he's my uncle, how'd I feel if he was my father?"

"That's so," Cleon put in eagerly. "Once he was all set to run away from home and hitchhike up here."

"Good thing he never made it. I'd have shipped him straight back again," said Uncle Rafe. The swivel chair creaked as he sank far back, fingers made a church again before his face. "That all of it?"

"Not quite," said Rafe. "It didn't need what you just said to Danny for us to figger you know a good thing when you see it. You want to keep the brains in the state and bring some in from outside, if you can find the right kind."

"That so? And what's the right kind?"

Rafe's eyes had taken on the mystic shine. His voice was superbly self-assured in the cluttered room. "The kind that'll beef up the state's economy, put plenty of money into Maine pockets, not just set up a plant here because the taxes are low and move in their talent from outside. What do you say to an outfit that'll set up the rig and put local men in to run it? An operation that thinks in millions instead of thousands?"

"You got a finger in such a pie?"

"I could have." Then, as if he remembered the promise in the fishhouse, Rafe added quickly, "We all could have. There's a job in this outfit for each of us brothers, and it'll make us rich, or so close to it you can't tell the difference. Besides that, it'll warm the pockets of every fisherman on the coast when it really gets going."

"Sounds world-shaking," remarked Uncle Rafe. "What's the name of it, or hasn't it got out of your head and down on paper yet?"

"Oh, it's a going concern, Uncle Rafe. It's going high, wide, and handsome. Gemini Seafoods. They come from New York. You must have heard of them. They've got a branch up at Machias. I want to bring 'em down to Saltberry Point."

"Then ask 'em, ask 'em." Uncle Rafe waved his hands. "Goddlemighty, you don't have to pay 'em to move in, do ye?"

"No, but we have to have land for them to buy," said Rafe. Uncle Rafe sat up. Damned if he isn't interested, Finn thought. He glanced sidewise and saw the sharpening in Roy's face. Danny might have been watching a good show on television, but Cleon was grinning as if he'd known all along that Rafe could do it. He caught Finn's eye and winked happily.

"You got no land down there? What about that island?"

"That belongs to my mother, and besides, it won't do. There'll be trailer trucks coming and going and so forth. No, none of us owns anything that's fit, but there's one perfect spot if we can make a big enough offer for it. Then we turn around and make that much again from Gemini."

"And run the business for 'em into the bargain."

"That's the story. We'll be buying everything in the way of seafood, selling supplies back to the fishermen, bait, gas, rope, trap stock, and so forth. We'll freeze some stuff right there, so we'll be hiring some women for the processing plant. Of course we'll be shipping lobsters live along the East Coast, and flying them to Europe."

It sounded good the way he put it. The only thing was you couldn't see Saltberry Point at all, just an extension of Limerock Harbor.... Oh hell, I'm not the only one down there and I live on the island, Finn thought. Maybe the rest'll all be crazy about it. Besides, we'll be seining most of the time ... if that pans out—

"And what do you want me to do about this?" Uncle Rafe was saying in that fussy cracked voice of his.

"You lend us the money to get the land to offer Gemini, and charge whatever interest you see fit. You'll get it all back, I guarantee it, within three months."

"You're a slick talker, I'll say that for ye, and I've heard a lot of 'em in this office. If words was pennies I'd be a millionaire three times over.... What else do I get out of this besides interest?"

"You get a chance to help the Judsons take over their part of Maine the way you've taken over your part. The trade name'll be just that, a name." He leaned forward. "Everybody'll know it's the Judsons running the business. It'll be our business. Your nephews' business."

When he stopped it was as if he'd flung a net and caught them all; even Finn, wanting nothing to do with it, thought, He makes it sound possible. He moved his eyes furtively toward the others, trying to see who was believing it, who was staring bug-eyed into Rafe's future. Their uncle laced his hands behind his neck and rocked slowly back and forth.

"Sounds fine," he said nasally. "Sounds like pretty music to me. Mebbe I ought to be glad to do it just for the interest and the family name, seeing as my own boy never saw fit to cast any glory on it. But I don't know anything under God's heaven

· 143 ·

about you boys except that you're Jud's kids. I couldn't deny that if I wanted to." His gaze moved over them one at a time, coming to Finn at the last and staying there. It stayed there long enough for the silence to get oppressive. Finn could hear Danny's stomach sort of yowl. Then somebody shifted a heavy foot and Uncle Rafe tilted his head toward the sound with a tired annoyance. "You're all got fine clothes on, but that's no sign of anything. You come in a new car—hell, every woodchopper's got a good car nowadays, whether it's paid for or not. I see television aerials on tarpaper shacks where they haven't even got a decent privy. You boys could be nothing at all, you see? Nothing except a bunch of dreamers—I won't call you scoundrels. At least one of you can talk to beat the cars, but one of the best talkers in town here is an unprincipled reprobate who—" He shot a look at Danny from under his eyebrows and cleared his throat. "And you come in here asking me for—how much?"

Rafe said it in a loud clear voice. "Ten thousand. We'll get twenty thousand easy from Gemini Seafoods."

Finn felt shock like an elbow in the belly and saw Roy's eyelids quiver; Danny started to whistle and choked it, blushing. Even Cleon hadn't known what Rafe proposed to offer Gil, you could tell by that foolish grin. Only Uncle Rafe was unmoved.

"On what collateral?" he asked.

"My God, Uncle Rafe," Rafe exclaimed, "you can look up Gemini yourself! They're no fly-by-night outfit! And they want to get in at the Point!" He emphasized each word with a wag of his head; his eyes were glassy now with excitement, his color blooming, the vein in his forehead swelling. "Uncle Rafe, charge ten per cent interest if you want—you'll get it, all right. We aren't a bunch of dreamers! We may be your brother's kids but we aren't like him, if that's what you're afraid of. We know what he was! I was ashamed of him before I was ten." He leaned forward, wetting his lips. "We aren't like him!"

Cleon mumbled something but Rafe ignored him. Finn stood up. "I'm getting the hell out of here," he said. "I'll walk back." He elbowed his way blindly through, banging into a chair, and was at the door when his uncle's voice, not raised, called him back. "*You*. Finn, is it? Wait."

He waited, his head bent, staring at his hand on the knob. "So you aren't like your father," their uncle said. "And you know what he was. What was he, eh? A fool? He was that, not to have drowned you at birth. And if he could hear you now, he'd forgive you. Yes, a fool all right. If he hadn't been fool enough to marry your mother you wouldn't be standing here today passing judgment on him. Ever think of that, eh?" The words cracked. "Sh'd think that'd make him quite a monument of a man in your eyes, thinking he'd fathered the fine specimen you think you are.... And the rest of ye, does this one speak for you? Not him at the door there, I know, but you, Roy—you and your fool of a father went to war together. You had to, but he didn't have to, so that makes him a gaumless idiot, I reckon. Ayuh, I called him a few names at the time, but I knew he had courage and a feeling for his country most of us never get, and I'll tell you one thing, I *envied* him his foolishness."

"What I felt about Pa's my own business," said Roy. "Rafe's not speaking for me."

"Pa was good in a lot of ways," Cleon began thickly.

"I want to tell you something about your father. He was a *good* human being. You numbheads know what that means? You ever meet one? He was also my brother. What he did and what I did are two different stories, but that never changed the facts any. He was still my brother." He stopped and Finn, still not looking around, could hear his breathing and the squeak of the old chair in a crazy kind of rhythm. He was sweating down his back and his eyes felt itchy. His hand had tightened so on the knob it was cramped.

"I'll tell you something else too. I ain't had the learning this boy here's got, and going to have. But I had some, back in the days when school was school, and here's something I remember, and the next time your pa's memory sticks in your craw you remember it too." He stood up and when he spoke again the sweat on Finn's back dried cold. " 'Beat not the bones of the dead; while he lived he was a man.' I may be a word or two out, but if they can say that about any of you, or about me either, we'll be lucky. Now git."

Finn was out first and walking fast away from the house and down the side of the drive. He had to have silence, for a few minutes anyway; he felt as if his skin had been peeled off, leaving his bloody and raw, and another word would be more than he could bear. Shame was mixed up in him with hatred, of what or whom he wasn't sure; but the worst was the sour thickness of grief that kept rising in his throat, so hard to keep back there would have been a degrading relief in giving in to it. It was as if the six-year-old child had known all along what this sorrow was, but had realized he was too small to hold it, and that the meeting would come later, like this, with crushing weight in a strange place.

Gradually the hands kept asserting themselves over the tumble in his head. The hands. On the arms of the chair, clasped around a knee, pointing a finger, making a church, stroking a jaw. Big, thick-palmed, knuckly, the black hair on the backs of them. *Pa's hands.*

He was on the road, walking in the cold resinous shadow of the pines, when the car stopped to pick him up. Nobody had anything at all to say.

· 20 ·

The thick silence held all the way back. Danny didn't mention food. Each was withdrawn into himself, the faces variously sullen, preoccupied, or blank. When they were going past Limerock Rafe suddenly spoke in a brisk and ordinary voice. "Well, that takes care of the tight-fisted old son of a bitch. Okay. So we go ahead without him and serves him right. This is what we do. Now I'm ready to borrow on my place, and—"

""Hey, don't you think we ought to let this string of pots set at least overnight?" said Cleon.

"You ought to get rid of some of that pork," said Rafe jovially. "You wheeze like an old accordion. You think letting things set overnight gets you anywhere? We're not waiting for lobsters to crawl, chummy. As I was saying," he went on, "I'm ready to borrow all I can get on my place, and it ought to be plenty, and

Cleon can do the same on his, and Roy, and we'll be all set to hit Gil hard amidships."

Cleon revived, loyally. "'Course it'll be tight-arse and pull-up for a while, but in the end it'll be clear 'tater, kids, clear 'tater."

"Well, it's like I said the other day." Roy settled deeper into the seat. "If you fellers want to peddle your hide, go to it. I want nothing to do with it. Nothing."

Rafe stared straight ahead. Cleon sputtered, "Of all the self-centered, narrow-minded—" The car swerved toward the center line and Rafe said, "Tend your wheel." Still without moving his head, as if his blushing neck had gone rigid, he said, "Finn, how about talking Dolly into borrowing on the island?"

"I dunno where you get the idea I can talk her into anything. She's no more foolish over me than she is about the rest of ye. Go ask her yourself."

Cleon took the car rocking and tire-squealing around a curve into Williston, and Rafe said, "Drop me off at Johansen's. I'll get a ride down later with somebody." He left them at the yard without speaking. They crossed the bridge over the river and when they were on the home road Roy said, "Gone in to take comfort from his new boat. She's bigger than anybody's."

"He wouldn't be this ugly if you hadn't frigged things up!" Cleon exploded. "You watch it, brother mine. Just watch it. He won't get over this in a hurry."

"Oh, shut up," said Roy, and Cleon for once didn't bother to answer.

When they were getting out of the car in Cleon's dooryard, Onni came out, wearing an apron over skin-tight slacks and jersey. "You and Danny want to eat supper with us?" she asked Roy. "No use asking *you*," she said haughtily to Finn. "You wouldn't drink a cup of coffee with us if you thought it'd please Cleon."

Finn shrugged and walked away.

"From the looks of you all," Onni said, "you must have got there just in time to bury the old buzzard."

Cleon said with strained gentleness, "Onni, would you mind shutting your goddam mouth? Hey, Finn!"

Finn didn't want to wait, but he walked slower until Cleon caught up with him. He put his hand on Finn's shoulder and kept it there. "Why don't you just have a little talk with Dolly, eh?" he said confidentially. "Sure, you like to play you're not the favorite, being a kind of modest gink, but you know what the score is."

"Ayuh, I know what it is." Finn looked him hard and long in the eyes. "And seeing you and Rafe been so much help to me, I ought to be panting and blowing to help you, hadn't I?"

Cleon removed his hand. "You ain't even going to try, are ye? Cutting off your own nose to spite your face." His voice shook. "Sometimes I think Onni's right when she says you only like yourself, and I've cussed her out for saying it. Can't you ever get it through your thick head it's time you took stock of yourself and got squared away for your future? You can't keep fubbing along like you was playing at life."

They had reached the top of the ladder where Finn's skiff was tied. "Listen," he said kindly, "you need some advice too. Why don't you stop trying to be my old man and pay a lot more attention to Onni? After all, you got a legal right to that." He went down the ladder fast, but Cleon was already tramping up the wharf, and never looked back.

After that Finn was left alone, and it suited him. He baited up and hauled, and tried to wipe out the taste of the down-east trip by playing cards with Larry and Elmer, endlessly talking herring, trying to teach them to mend twine, and running down leads for secondhand radio-telephones. The boat was ready and he brought her back up the harbor and ebbed her out on the wide stretch of flat ledge on the harbor side of the island, across the Neck. He coppered her bottom on one tide, and on the next he gave her a fresh coat of white. May had come in on a warm wind from the south, full of birds, and behind him the spruces and birches were alive with wood warblers. Somewhere up in the grove a nestful of young crows bawled in their quavery infant voices, and close to Finn the adult crows walked about searching for food, and gulls dropped mussels near him. When they came down to eat the orange meats from the broken blue shells they ignored him as if by treaty.

The boat was afloat by ten that night. There was a southerly breeze ruffling up light surf on the outer shore, but the harbor was quiet. He rowed from his wharf to where *Foam-Flower* lay, a pale shape moving lightly under the black loom of the woods. As he began towing her out to her mooring across the calm black water, the last light on the Point went out, and at once he was visited by the old sensation of peaceful solitude. He hadn't had it for a long time, and he sighed, unconsciously.

He should have been feeling good, he knew; they'd located a radio-telephone, and he could remember when getting one of those was about the biggest thing he could think of. Now he was glad they'd have it, but it didn't put clouds in his boots, any more than the thought of going seining did. Must be spring fever, he thought glumly, the kind that makes you not give a good goddam for anything.

Standing up in the skiff, he made *Foam-Flower* secure for the night. She smelled of fresh paint and she was tight and dry. Another thing to be glad of. He wondered what Claire would think of this night silence and the air warm and easy around your face, and the feeling that time had stopped. Suddenly he knew that he did want something intensely after all, and that was Claire in the skiff with him right now, watching and listening. They wouldn't need to talk. I will go to see her tomorrow, he decided, eager now to get back to bed and sleep and bring tomorrow quickly. All at once the seining and the radio-telephone became exciting and important again, but only because in some perfectly logical way they were involved with Claire.

·21·

Finn walked into the kitchen on Saturday morning, while Claire was ironing Nancy's school dresses, and invited her to go to haul with him. "I left a few over from yesterday, on purpose," he said. "Enough to give you an idea of what it's like. Kind of tiresome to go through the whole string, and with the bait and all you might get a little squarmish in your stomach."

"Wear something warm," Mag said. "Leave the ironing, it'll keep."

"Can I go, Finn?" Nancy launched herself at him.

"I wouldn't have it any other way.... Don't look for them too soon, Mag. We may go ashore somewhere and cook us a few lobsters."

"I hope you do. Getting out of the house is making her look more human all the time. When she got here you'd think she'd been living under glass."

Finn at the wheel of *Foam-Flower* had a new kind of authority. Mechanical dexterity was no sign of maturity, but this was a man going about his work, thoroughly at home in his environment, as if the sea were his element as well as the air. Watching him haul, empty, and bait a trap, explaining to Nancy as he did so, giving a casual glance toward the nearest ledge and a touch to the wheel like a direction to a sensible horse, she was impressed. Competence always impressed her; David used to tease her about that. "I'm afraid of losing you to a traffic cop, or a man who runs a bulldozer, or to somebody who can read Greek as if it were English, or to Robert if you ever catch on how well he runs the business."

Coming back to the wheel, Finn said, "You look happy."

"I was thinking of something happy." She got up from the dry lobster crate Finn had placed for her seat and went to stand beside him. "It must be the blue ocean, or so much sky, or . . . I don't know what. But sometimes now I think of things in the past that amuse me all over again. Not in the same way, but at least they don't make me feel like crying."

He nodded and she wondered if he really knew what she meant. They were in the shade of Hollowell, the boat rolling gently near the black can buoy on which a gull stood, watching them. Other boats were at work, up in the river or down toward the open horizon, appearing between islands or from behind ledges where the gulls circled with warning cries and beating wings. Claire let herself go with them, with the motion of the boat. Mrs. Carradine and Robert were dim images on the periphery of existence and growing dimmer. All physical, she told herself. It's like hypnosis . . . Nancy's voice piping above the engine, Finn's answer, a pink-brown starfish curved over wet laths, a spiny sea urchin, a lobster lacquer-green in the sun, the baitbag stabbed out of the barrel and into the trap, Finn's hands in white cotton gloves, the neat fillip of the baitline around the button, the splash of the trap, the leap forward of the boat. . . . Sun on buff deck paint, rubber boots on the splashed floorboards and the gaudy yellow of oilpants. A whiff of bait, gone again as the boat swung around nose into the wind. Another boat heading toward them, how fast, how beautiful the high bow and the pure curve of the bow wave forever reforming itself in crystal curl. The men's faces brown under the duckbills, the arm swung in greeting. . . .

The hypnosis was abruptly broken. The oncoming boat didn't pass but slowed down, and so did Finn's. They rocked gently toward each other, and the man who reached out with a gaff was Rafe. The other was a boy who made her think of Finn; he grinned and said, "Hi, Finn," and tried not to look at her, but it was hard, his gaze kept sliding toward her until she smiled and nodded. Then he could pay attention to the men. Rafe had no difficulty ignoring her.

"You hauled down around the Seal Ledges this morning?" he said curtly.

"Not yet, why?"

"Save yourself the effort. They've been hauled."

Finn didn't show astonishment. "How do you know?" he said.

"You sure you want to discuss it in public?"

"You started it in public. Go ahead." Claire stood up to go toward the cuddy door, but Finn gestured her back to the crate. She drew Nancy down beside her.

"Danny'll bear me out on this," Rafe said. "He's lending me a hand today. Tell him what we saw, Danny."

Danny nodded and became solemn. "I saw it, Finn. I'm sorry, but I did. We came out between *Dollar* and *Cutlass* and Larry was in among that gang of traps at the Seal Ledges, and I guess we appeared kind of sudden and took him by surprise. . . ." His speech slowed down. His hands fidgeted. "Anyway, he had one of your buoys on his washboard and one of your traps hanging over the side. He let it go and threw the buoy over after it. I guess he was just going to pull it aboard. Then he saw us and scooted out of there."

His voice faded away. Rafe, who had shown no expression throughout, said, "That's the way it was. If I was alone and saw it you'd call me a GD liar . . . I went over and took a look at your traps. Five of 'em hauled, clean as a whistle."

"Ayuh," said Finn. "Where's your father today, Danny?"

"Gone to Augusta," Danny said defensively.

Finn's smile was cold. "Went early, didn't he?"

"He had to get the car greased first—"

"You running Roy's house for him while he's gone?" Rafe interrupted. "Danny'll get his chores done, if that's any of your business. Meanwhile I'm giving the kid a chance to earn a few extra dollars. That's not what I came out of my way to tell you."

"Well, you got the message over." Finn gave him a choppy nod and started up his engine. The boat started forward so fast that the gaff was almost pulled out of Rafe's hands. Claire felt an odd trembling in her hands and calves. Without knowing it she had squeezed Nancy too hard, and the child was squirming like a puppy. Claire let up her grip, but said, "Sit here for a minute. Finn's busy."

"No he isn't, he's just steering—"

"*Nancy*." The child subsided, pressing her lips in tightly with exasperation.

From where she was sitting she couldn't see Finn's face, but she could tell that he was searching for something. If it was Larry's boat she hoped cravenly that he wouldn't find it. She couldn't yet recognize the Point boats herself, but she found herself straining to pick out one after another, trying to guess if Finn were heading for this one or that one. They passed two of his buoys and Nancy jumped up and pulled at his sleeve, and pointed at them already swimming astern. He shook his head.

They swung around the southern tip of Hollowell, were saluted by a man from the lower harbor who was peacefully hauling there, and followed a wide sky-blue avenue through a cluster of velvety-green islets, startling sea birds and seals. They went through an opening between two long natural barriers of rock, down past a long high island crested with spruce, and out to open water at the other end, with Saltberry Island far astern of them and a new panorama of the western mainland opening up in fold after fold of varying blues. It would have been enchanting except for the almost intolerable tension emanating from the faceless figure at the wheel.

Suddenly he spun the wheel hard and brought the boat around to head back the way they had come, past the long wooded island to the gemlike spatter of little ones. They took a different way into the cluster and a small white beach opened up before them. A steep rise behind it hid the view toward the mainland, and three big spruces, their darkness sharp as a cry in the design of blue and white and green, stood in cold pools of shadow. Finn slowed the boat and took her gently in to the ruins of a wharf at one side of the beach.

He stopped the engine and turned around. There was no anger in him that Claire could see. "Here we are," he said.

He had brought bread and butter and coffee. There was a spring on the island, a brown pool in mossy rocks barely out of reach of the tide. Nancy drank again and again from the tin mug Finn provided. "It's so good," she said, gasping for breath, her upper lip wet, her eyes and skin all the same gold. When they had eaten the lobsters, Finn and Claire stayed in the shade under the spruces, drinking their coffee while Nancy played in the water. Her voice came to them in the stillness as she sang or talked to herself.

Finn was lying on his back, one arm under his head, smoking and looking up through the dark branches. He'd taken off his rubber boots and heavy socks and his bare feet extended into the sunlight, the strong long toes wiggling now and then as if with a private rapture of their own.

He said drowsily, "The way that kid muckled on to a lobster. . . . She didn't need any help opening it, no sir, not with all the rocks around. Tomalli flew to hell and gone, I think she had it in her ears."

"She's never even tasted lobster before, let alone tackle a whole one hot out of the kettle."

"Well, she knows about 'em now. Put me in mind of kittens when they get their first taste. You'd think they'd been waiting their whole lives for just that minute."

Did he lie like this, dreamily smoking, with one of his girls beside him, she wondered. Or was he different with them in every way? She imagined a coarse vigorous intimacy based on a camaraderie of the flesh, no subtleties, no sentimental gestures, just a lusty mutual enjoyment of each other. She put her hands to her face, and he said, "You've got quite a windburn."

"Yes."

"It looks good."

"Thank you," she said primly. Claire sat like an Indian and held onto her crossed ankles. "About Larry. Can I mention it or don't you want me to? You can be honest and tell me."

"Go ahead. You heard the whole thing."

"He's awfully fond of you, and you're going seining together—"

"That doesn't make any difference. I've heard of men hauling their own fathers and acting like real devoted sons when they're ashore. Kids like Danny making a good living off their uncles."

"Rafe doesn't like Larry or Elmer."

"You heard what he saw. Danny wasn't lying, he's not that good at it."

She looked obstinately at him and he grinned. "Stubborn little cuss. You look like your daughter when she's outnumbered but still fighting."

"It's none of my business, but aren't you going to talk to Larry before you make up your mind?"

"Naturally." He raised up on one elbow and stubbed out his cigarette and carefully buried the butt. "But for now, let's go and see what there is to be found along the shore."

"The perfect squelch," said Claire wryly.

He lifted his eyebrows and she said, "I know I shouldn't have even mentioned it in the first place. I'm sorry."

"What for? You had a right." His smile was disarming. "I make you a present of it, here and now."

"Sir, I thank you," she said gravely. They ducked out from under the trees.

He hauled more traps on the way back, including those he'd ignored earlier. Then he swung across the river into Port George, where they bought ice-cream cones at a store on one of the wharves, and watched the arrival of an early-cruising schooner and her settling-in for the night. It was midafternoon when they returned to Saltberry Point. Nancy sagged against her mother, a warm heavy lump drunk with fresh air and the pure minute-to-minute ecstasy of living. Claire was newly sunburned, the flush spangled with salt where spray had caught her in the face; in the afternoon the usual fresh breeze had sprung up and *Foam-Flower* had taken a few sharp ones on her quarter crossing the river.

Claire's eyes were heavy from the blaze of color that had burned in them all day. She yawned until she wept and Finn caught her at it. "Be too bad if I'd planned on asking you to a dance tonight, wouldn't it? The shape you're in."

"You weren't going to, were you?" she said. "Because I feel like Raggedy Ann."

"Well, you're a dite better looking. . . . Nope, when I ask you I'll make sure you have plenty of time to rest up for it."

She got up and stood beside him as they approached the wharf. "You'd better. Oh, it's been a wonderful day. I can't tell you how wonderful. To be so relaxed and carefree."

"Well, I liked it too . . . I'll have to take you in to Gil's, Abbott's is out at low tide."

There were no boats around the car; they were all back on their moorings. Gil was getting lobsters for a man who stood holding a cardboard carton, while two women stood up on the wharf hugging themselves against the wind. Fishhouse doors were open to the sun as men worked on their gear. Dogs were running madly across Gil's lawn in some mysterious game. Cars were driving in or out, children on bicycles had come from up the road to see if the flounders were biting yet off Gil's car; men rowed slowly in from their moorings, leisurely because the wind had lost the fire that could burn through heavy clothes and sear the insides of nostrils and throats. The houses, even the small old ones that needed paint, sat in the sun like cats with their forepaws turned in and their eyes blinking amiability toward all.

I love it, Claire thought with fierce tenderness. No matter what, this will always be the place that set me free to think about David and to know that we were married and in love and it was not always darkness and the death-hour rounding it. . . . Who said that?

Foam-Flower idled in to the car, and Finn swung a crate of lobsters onto the washboard.

"I don't want to forget all my stuff." Nancy was fussy with tiredness. "All my shells, and that boat I found, and the ball and everything. Mama, what can I carry them in?"

"Hello, Claire," someone said from up on the wharf. She heard it, she even recognized it, and yet it was so out of place that she ignored it. "Now you hold your horses, young lady," Finn was saying. "I've got a box here for your clutch, if you wait till I dump it out."

"Hello, Claire," the voice said again. "Hello, Nancy."

They both looked up then, and blinked at the people dark against the sky. Slowly one man became clear among them, thinning fair hair blowing in the wind, the light flashing off his dark-bowed glasses. Claire experienced a blow of disorientation; all at once she stood in neither one world nor the other. But Nancy, pressing to her chest a dismasted sailboat, suffered no shock. In her world these things happened and needed no explanation.

"Hello, Uncle Robert!" she shouted.

"If that's your uncle, you hurry up and see him," Finn said. "I'll bring up your gear." He took her under the arms and swung her over the side onto the car. She went up the steep ramp like a cat, and Robert met her at the top and drew her into his arms. She hugged him, talking fast. For Claire, events swung back into focus. He could be here only for one reason; Mrs. Carradine was physically sick with loneliness, and he had been forced to come and fetch Claire and Nancy back.

She said to Finn in what seemed a normal way, "It's David's brother, come to see how we're getting along, I suppose. Thank you again, Finn. I'll never forget this day."

"Well, don't sound as if it's the last one." His eyes were astonished and angry, and she wondered how she looked. She wanted to say, It may have been the last one.

Robert was thin but putting on weight; he would have a middle-aged figure before he was forty. His eyes were the color of Nancy's behind the glasses. He held Claire's hands hard when he kissed her. "I've missed you," he said. "I knew I was punishing myself, but I didn't realize how much."

"I've missed you too, Robert," she said huskily. Finn was towering behind them and she moved to one side, smiling nervously. "Robert, this is Finn Judson, he's just given Nancy and me the most wonderful day on the water. Finn, Robert Carradine, my favorite brother-in-law."

"She has to say that because I'm the only one," said Robert. They shook hands. Finn was polite but distant. "Here, Mouse-knuckles," he said to Nancy. "Here's your loot."

"Thank you, Finn." She gave him an adoring gaze. "Look, Uncle Robert, I got all this on *one* island! And they wouldn't let me bring home everything I found." She called after Finn as he went down the ramp. "Thank you for the ride and the lobsters and the ice cream, and being on the island and everything!"

He waved his hand at her and began talking with Gil and Tom Hunt by the scales. Claire felt a faint sense of desertion. "Well, Robert, suppose we get out of this wind," she said crisply. "I've got to tidy up before I can even begin to talk."

"I think you look marvelous as you are," said Robert. "Nancy too." They walked up the wharf, Nancy holding her uncle's hand and talking. Though a few days ago she had been braced to go back if Mrs. Carradine needed her, now Claire felt like a drowning swimmer being swept out to sea and watching familiar marks disappear one by one—Nell and Josie crossing the lawn, Larry in the fishhouse doorway, young Elmer looking for clams.

"Elmer's my boy friend," Nancy said. "We sit together on the bus. Gwen gets some mad. You know what she said to me one day?"

"Nancy, we've heard the last of that, remember?" said Claire. Robert's car was parked beside Finn's. She saw Rafe and Cleon in the doorway of Rafe's fishhouse, but neither looked in her direction. She might have already disappeared from the Point for good.

She had a bad minute before they took the turn into the dooryard, wondering if Mag would choose to be outrageous, vague, or a frail and tired old woman. But the ironing had been completed, and a warm spicy fragrance hung alluringly about the kitchen. Mag was cheerful, dignified, and hospitable. When Claire came downstairs from tidying up, Robert and Mag were having coffee and fresh molasses cake at the table, while at the other end Nancy mulled over her treasures.

"I've found my spiritual home, Claire," said Robert. "I know now what nectar and ambrosia mean."

Mag laughed with crackling pleasure. "He's a corker. One of those quiet ones you have to watch. He's just hiding behind them eyeglasses."

"I think that's a compliment," said Robert. "It makes me feel devilish. Are you having coffee with us?"

"I'd rather have it after we talk a few minutes." Claire stood by the door that opened toward the field, and Robert got up. "Will you excuse us, Mrs. Abbott?"

"Good Lord, I know you can't wait to be alone with her. Nancy, you stay here. Push over your glass, and I'll put a little coffee in your milk."

Robert and Claire went across the grass past the apple tree. Robert saw the swing and said, "Nancy might always have been here. She's perfectly at home. I mustn't tell Mother that," he added wryly.

"Did you come to take us back?" she asked, suddenly unable to wait any longer. They had reached the beginning of the field, and they stopped and turned toward each other.

"Why. Do you want to go back?"

"I've been expecting something ever since I talked to your mother the other day. She was desperate."

"She shouldn't have called you. I told her so."

Claire began to walk toward the wall and he followed. "No, I came to counteract that call of hers. Aunt Dora told me how she wept and pleaded over the telephone. I knew what that would do to you, so I came as soon as I could get away. She doesn't know I'm here, she thinks I'm in Augusta."

"She must also think you're very cruel. There's a special, terrible loneliness that she and I know about, but at least I have Nancy." She sat down tiredly on the wall and wished there were some magic way for the ancient strength of the stones to become a part of her.

"I know about loneliness," said Robert. "I lost him too, you know. And my mother has me, though the fact seems to have escaped her." He sat down beside Claire and looked off across the point. The slopes were illuminated by a green-gold light intensified by hollows of velvety shadow. "This may sound pretty callous, Claire, but without you to encourage her and feed her self-pity she might begin to come alive again. You've already started to revive; I knew in the first glimpse today that I'd been right to send you away from us." His manner was not as self-satisfied as his words, and he didn't look at her but at some distant object. She felt a twinge of warning. "You were a different woman," he said. "Tanned, healthy, smiling. I hardly knew you. It was like calling to a stranger."

Had he been watching while the boat idled toward the wharf and she talked and laughed with Finn? But I was thinking of David! she wanted to protest, yet remained silent.

"Who is this young man, anyway?" Robert asked.

"A nice boy, a neighbor. I'm grateful to him for a chance to get out on the water. The same one I mentioned in a letter to Mother." She wanted to go on and tell him more about Finn, but his ironic expression stopped her.

"He didn't seem too pleased to see me."

"Oh, Robert!" She was both exasperated and amused. "You're imagining things! Finn has no reason to—to—" She fumbled for the words she wanted, and Robert went on.

"Mrs. Abbott told me he took you to the movies. I'm glad that you can do these things, Claire; you're young and it's right. It's just that the change is so complete it appalls me to think what we were doing to you, locking you up in that museum dedicated to David's memory."

"Do you think I forget for a moment? Do you think I've stopped loving him? Shall I go back to Brookline with you to prove it?"

Go back. The words had a chill clang. And she was shouting

at Robert. It was incredible; she bit her lip and stared at him, and the moment of suspense passed. She said weakly, "You're just hiding behind them eyeglasses."

His laughter broke from him like breath held too long. She laughed with him, but she felt shaky, and pressed her hands hard against the stones of the wall.

"Did you think I was accusing you of disloyalty?" he asked. "You'd never have to excuse yourself to me, whatever you did—least of all make apologies for looking well. That's what I wanted, for heaven's sake! That's why I drove you away in spite of Mother's floods of tears."

"The way you mentioned Finn, I thought *you* thought I was being foolish about a handsome young fisherman—"

"Nothing of the sort!" Robert interrumpted, flushing so that he looked suddenly young. "It was just—oh, a feeling of your having started a different life and left us behind."

"As if that could ever happen," she protested. Her eyes filled with tears. They reached for each other's hands, and he blinked behind his glasses. "Blood brothers," he said with a dry laugh. "Until death." They squeezed each other's fingers, and she felt a great surge of love for him. After a moment he said, "If I asked you to come back, would you want to? Be absolutely honest, now. This is old Robert, remember? So don't fob me off with any slick little fictions."

"No, I wouldn't want to go back right now, and leave Aunt Mag. She's come to depend on me to see her through this business. And I wouldn't want to go back because it's marvelous for Nancy and me to be on the seacoast in spring, and I've felt better and slept better. But if you and Mother needed and wanted me—"

"Oh, we want you, all right." His smile ridiculed something. "We want you. But I'd want you like Claire in Maine, and that Claire would be an affront to Mother."

"Now *you* are cruel."

"No, objective. You fall in with Mother, you know. You go right along with her, helping her to believe that David's mother's grief is so much more important than even his wife's could be. You wouldn't even laugh aloud in her presence, a year after David's death, would you?"

"It's a sadist behind those glasses, and I never guessed."

"Perhaps I am a little nasty, in a juvenile way, because I can't believe that Mother would still be so broken up a year after my death." He was quiet a moment and then said thoughtfully, "Not that David didn't deserve everything good he got out of life. *Everything*," he repeated. "There was never anything that I begrudged him."

She didn't know why, but she was glad to see Nancy come out of the house and stand looking around with her hand shading her eyes. "Out here!" she called, and Nancy came at the gallop.

·23·

After Claire had gone away with her brother-in-law, Finn left the boat at the car and went up onto the wharf again. Larry was leaning in his fishhouse doorway, his hands in his pockets, and he saluted Finn with an upward jerk of his bony jaw. Elmer was down on the shore looking for a leak in a skiff. The sight of them both reminded Finn of the hauled traps, but the effect was dulled. He knew his insides should be all roiled up about it, but instead he was craning his neck for a strange car and not seeing it. Claire and Nancy had disappeared so fast it almost made the whole past day a dream.

Gink couldn't wait to flap 'em out of here, he thought furiously. Probably thought the smell of Gil's bait wasn't fit to breathe. Probably thought they were being contaminated by this bunch of savages, chiefly me.

Then he was ashamed of himself. The man had a good handshake and a steady eye. Kind of guy you'd like, ordinarily; no la-di-da stuff, trying to be one of the boys with the peasants. The only trouble was that when he kissed Claire and whisked her off like that it was as if she'd gone for good, and that was a little too sudden. Dammit, his stomach was roily after all. He turned into the store for a bottle of soda, and wished he hadn't; Cleon was there, drumming his fingers on the showcase and brooding on the harbor scene beyond the windows.

"Looks like her boy friend came for her," he said. "Probably heard she was carrying on with a lobsterman."

"I wouldn't be surprised," said Finn. "We're a hard lot. Anything else on your mind?"

"Larry's been watching for you. Wanted to see how you looked, I guess."

"Then he knows I look the same as I did this morning, except I'm half a day older. That all you wanted to say?" The thought of soda made his stomach feel worse. He went behind the counter and picked out a candy bar.

Cleon talked as if he were afraid of waking a baby upstairs. "Too bad it had to come to this. I hated like hell for you to find out, but it had to happen sometime. God, that was some brazen, bothering you with us right around."

Finn put the money in the saucer on the case. "You there?"

"I'd just gone by. I was beyond the Hourglass when Rafe come down and told me. And that ain't all. Elmer was hauling in Indian Cove, and I knew you had traps down there, so I moseyed down and took a look." He blew hard. "Same story. They'd been hauled clip'n'-clean."

Finn sounded vacantly bewildered. "Funny, huh? All at once like that?"

"All at once?" He stabbed at Finn's chest with his finger. "Listen, boy, they might not a been doing it every day, might only been doing it once a week or so, but I bet every time you thought the lobsters weren't crawling for ye they'd crawled right into those two robbers' crates."

"Ay-up," said Finn, wagging his head. "They sure have covered up some good, didn't they? I'd never have known. What a pair of experts! When you think of all the meals I've had with 'em, too."

"And you were going to take 'em seining. Listen, son, I'm glad we sent that little plan to bottom. I bet you won't bare your teeth at us now when we want to give those two the word."

"I dunno what a man'd do without brothers. I can't hardly feature it. Sometimes I try, though."

Cleon cocked his head as if to catch a faint sound, then slapped Finn on the shoulder. "You come around to the house. We'll make up for the meals you'll miss."

"Yep," said Finn. He went out and across the short steep bank of grass to the other wharf. He knew Cleon was watching him; he could imagine the satisfied smile as Cleon waited for action. From down on the rocks Elmer held up his hand in greeting like a Roman soldier in a super-movie. "Listen," Larry said, "I been wanting to ask ye. How come you took the kid along? She insist on it? Scared to be alone with you, or playing hard to get?"

"Around here everybody's mind is below his belt," said Finn. "Come on in the fishhouse, you two. I want to talk. Privately," he added.

Elmer climbed up and they went into the fishhouse and slid the door across. "I want to tell you something first," said Larry. "Some of your traps was all fouled up with mine this morning and I'd like to know how in hell it happened. They weren't *that* close, and it ain't been rough. Anyway, I had to haul yours up to get 'em clear. I didn't want to cut yours and be damned if I'd cut my own."

"You see Rafe?"

"No, why? He's got no traps near there."

"He saw you. Claims you took one horrified look and shot out of there like you were leaving a launching pad."

"Jeez, I never saw him." The meaning began to come through, with a queer motion of the eyelids and the pinched pasty look he got when he was upset. "He says he caught me hauling your traps?"

Finn held up his hand. "Don't wet yourself. I'm not through yet." He looked over at Elmer, who was gazing at him in pained surprise.

"You see Cleon?"

"Yep, I saw him fooling around out there and then he took off around the tip of the island like a scairt cat."

"See him near Indian Cove before or after you hauled there?"

Elmer slowly rubbed his hand in circles on the back of his crewcut, his eyes glazed. "After?" he droned. "No—before.

Because I looked down from the can buoy and saw his boat just going in past the ledges there, and I wondered what in Tophet he was doing, if he'd gone and plastered us with pots when we warn't looking. When I got down there there was just yours and mine, so I figgered he must've seen something on the beach and gone in close to have a look."

"Jeez, what *is* this?" Larry whispered.

"What's it sound like?" asked Finn. "Elmer, when'd you see Cleon take off around the end of the island?"

"I was hauling over by Two Bit a little while after I'd left the cove, and the boat swung around, and I saw him. Wouldn't have give a second look except that he was going like he was trying to outrun the Judgment Day."

"Mebbe he was," said Finn. "You see me anywhere around then?"

"You were heading in between Hollowell and Dollar. You went out of sight."

"Ayuh." There was a knot in Finn's stomach. The rope that tied it must have been kept in a deep freeze beforehand because it has a sickening chill to it. "I was looking for Cleon," he said, examining the palm of one hand with a scientific detachment. He had to be detached because of that freezing Turk's-head in his belly. "That's where he should have been hauling. But he got an early start this morning. Went out and hauled a few traps by the Seal Ledges and fouled them up so a kid like Danny could swear you had one of my traps aboard, Larry. Went down and hauled a few more traps in Indian Cove, then went down there again as soon as you left there, so he could discover my traps had been bothered. Then had some bloody urgent business in Putnam soon as he knew Rafe had muckled on to me. Ain't got much faith in himself as a crook, has he?"

"Well, I'll be buggered," Elmer said.

"I know I'm a stupid jackass," said Larry, "but I don't get it. You taking our word against theirs, Finn, that we never touched your traps?"

"I didn't have to ask you. I just wanted the details." He stopped and listened to his own words. They were true all right. He hadn't doubted the boys even when Claire took his silence for doubt. He knew it was possible for them to do it and still act matey to him on land, but he still knew they hadn't done it, and they wouldn't unless he did them a dirty rotten trick first.

The other two were silent, as if they knew he had to think. He lit a cigarette and looked out at the harbor. *Brothers*, he thought. The words charged into his brain that Helen had said one time when they were all together on a holiday, all good fellows then. *We happy few, we band of brothers.*

"Well," he said, watching a gull bank down to the mud flats, "I got work to do."

"Who hasn't?" said Larry. "Standing around like this won't buy shoes for the baby or pay for the ones he's wearing." He sounded shaky. Elmer said nothing at all, and Finn went out. He wondered what they would say when he was out of earshot; it was as if somebody had suddenly put up a wall between them and him, thicker than the fishhouse door. If it was anybody else trying to frame them, we'd all yell and curse about it together, he thought, but it's my brothers so they won't cuss to my face, they'll just start guessing how far they should trust *me*.

Cleon had left Gil's and Finn walked over to Rafe's fishhouse, but that was locked. There was a short cut from here to Rafe's house, a narrow track starting from under the big oaks and going down a slope through spiny wild rose bushes and tawny winter-flattened ferns, with here and there the new ones standing in short downy pale-green curls. At the lowest part, where the inlet came in, the track led among big spruces with broad, down-sweeping boughs that used to shelter playhouses, before Mrs. Rafe took over. Upward the path went into the old Clark orchard planted on a slope toward the sun, and led under the ancient greenings and astrakhans into Rafe's dooryard.

Cleon's car was beside Rafe's. They glittered elegantly in the same windy sunlight that fell through the apple boughs onto Finn. He went into the kitchen; they were all there and they greeted him as if they loved him most in all the world. "Here's the boy!" cried Rafe. "Get him some of that pie, Hester, he can use it."

"Sure, he's all hollow, always was," said Cleon. "Come on and sit down." He pulled out one of the captain's chairs from the waxed trestle table. "Move along a little, Onni." Onni moved along. She stared enigmatically into her cigarette smoke. It was something odd to see her in Hester's kitchen, they didn't hitch horses at all.

"You mean you let common folks eat off that?" Finn asked.

"Now Finn, don't be difficult!" Hester laughed heartily, as if she's just said something witty. "Sit down and give your order. Custard or cherry? And maybe you'll be more of a gentleman than your brothers and spare me the obvious joke."

"Why, is there one about custard pies?" asked Finn. Hester patted his shoulder. "See, he *is* a gentleman. I always said he was!"

"Never mind the pie, Hes," Finn said mildly. "I didn't come to eat. This is business." There was no stove hearth in Hester's modern kitchen to prop his foot on, so he stood against the door. "I don't suppose you women know what's going on. The boys probably figure the fewer that know about it the better. But I don't see it like that. I think everybody ought to know about some things."

Rafe's good humor soured. Cleon's eyes glinted under drooped lids. Something reached Onni in her sulk so that she looked around at Finn. Hester said acidly, "We know those two thieves have been hauling your traps and at last they've been caught in the act."

"Have they?" asked Finn mildly. "They been actually *seen* opening up my traps and taking the lobsters out?"

"What is this?" Rafe came up out of his chair. "You heard what happened this morning, what I saw and what Cleon saw. We caught 'em as near in the act as don't make any difference."

"Well, I heard what you had to say, and then I heard what my friends had to say. It all adds up. It fits together, neat as a gnat's ear."

"You sound," said Cleon in his most grandfatherly rumble, "as if you believed your—uh—so-called friends."

"You know something funny? I do. Because they got no ax to grind. They're not trying to drive somebody off the Point, they're not trying to take me over body and soul, they're just interested in feeding their kids, and somehow that takes up an awful lot of their attention."

"You think your brothers are lying then," Onni said, "when they say they found your traps hauled?"

"Oh, no, I won't go that far." Finn grinned at her. "Sure they found them hauled. But who hauled them? Huh, Onni? Bet you don't know, do ye?"

"Do *you*?" Arrogantly Hester shot the question at him.

"Sure. At least, like Rafe says, sure enough as don't make any difference. Rafe and Cleon hauled those traps."

"Now wait a minute!" Cleon was up. "That's a pretty serious charge! You standing there with that foolish grin on your mug and telling us you'd take the word of that—that—"

"Poor white trash," Finn supplied. "Like me. We got nothing and we aren't supposed to have anything. You want to get rid of them so as to cut me down to not even having a friend. Then what? Do I turn tame overnight? Sell you my soul and my hide for the little pats and the loans and the new boat and all the advice I can swallow without puking? Do everything I can to get Dolly to turn the island over to you to sell? Is that the story?"

Rafe came forward, dangerously dark. "You're out of your mind. Lemme get one thing straight. Did those little bastards tell you they *saw* either one of us hauling your traps?"

"No, they didn't. Get that straight. They didn't even know what I was driving at till I told them. They couldn't get over it. Kind of knocked the wind out of them. Funny, huh?" He laughed. "Anybody being so blasted dumb, they couldn't imagine somebody pulling a trick like that on 'em. But they know now. It took those smart, upstanding, honest Judson boys to teach 'em."

He reached behind him for the knob. "I just thought I'd let you know, in case you had anything more up your sleeve. Remember that case up the coast where the state proved criminal conspiracy?"

It was a good line to make an exit on, but Cleon moved fast for his bulk and grabbed Finn's arm. "You listen here," he hissed. "You just listen. Who the hell do you think you are, coming in here and reading the riot act to us on the word of those two little pissabeds? You've been acting like something on a stick for quite a while now. All at once you're too good for us, and I want to know the reason why."

Finn twisted his arm out of Cleon's grip. "I bruise easy," he said.

"I'll tell you why he's acting the way he is," said Rafe. "It's that stuck-up bitch over at Mag's. She's taken him up in a big way and he thinks she's got class. Oh, she's so damn refined . . . but she knows what a dollar sign is, and that island's got them plastered all over it."

"Not only that," Hester said, "but she's filling his head with all sorts of ideas that'll only harm him in the long run. When she's gone, and he hasn't a friend left, and he's turned all his family against him, she won't care. And once she finds out he's got nothing she *will* be gone. I know about women like that."

Finn cocked an eyebrow at Onni. "You got anything to add to this clambake to make it real tasty? You might as well." If she says one word, he thought, I'll let her have it about her red-headed friend. She shrugged one shoulder very high, arched her eyebrows to match, and put another cigarette in her holder; she said nothing. Finn left.

·24·

Dolly walked in on Finn on Sunday. She'd rowed over in one of Roy's skiffs and was going back there at night to stay for a few days and do some cleaning. "I'll take your wash along and do it over there," she said. "You can come in there and eat too, you know it's all right with Roy."

"Thanks," he said morosely.

It was a queer kind of Sunday. He couldn't settle down to anything, and there was plenty that needed doing. When Dolly asked him what was going on he had to leave out the latest, because he'd never tattled on his brothers; but they thought he did, and were probably even now wrecking a good

Sunday for themselves with wondering what he was telling Dolly. Rafe and Hess drove seventeen miles to Limerock to the Episcopal church, and Finn could imagine Hes dipping her knees and crossing herself, if they did that, and sniffing the incense with a real holy expression while she was thinking murder. It was even weirder to imagine Rafe doing it, because he'd been brought up a Baptist in the old meeting house here in town. But of course you never met anybody important in it, like bankers and investment brokers and all the rest whom Rafe considered Big Time Operators.

Finn did tell Dolly about the trip to visit Uncle Rafe, leaving out what Rafe had said about Pa; but he included what their uncle had said, and Dolly said at the end in a stifled voice, "Yes, he was that, I guess you could say. He was a man, I never doubted it. I've never seen one since that I wanted to keep. Well, now! I heard Gil's sold the home place."

"Ayuh, but I don't know who to. They're having a worm in case it's a fisherman."

"I suppose nobody thought of asking him straight out. They're scared of what he'll *think* if they show an interest. Well, it takes one of Gil's old girls to turn the trick. He was on the car when I rowed by, and nobody was around, so I stopped to pass the time of day. I asked him."

"Who is it, then?"

"Summer people. New York state. May retire here if they think they can stand the neighbors. I hear you've got a new girl."

"Gil tell you that too?"

She was too casual with her shrugs. "Why should he?"

"Well, I've got no girl. That's one of my worries." He smiled at his mother. "You ever know any men you liked talking to without wanting to take 'em to bed?"

"My life is full of them," said Dolly. "Nothing I like better than some good lively conversation with a male of practically any age. Look at me, all set up after running on with Gil. He liked it too. But, Finn, it's different with you. You're twenty-four years old, and I don't want you to start thinking like a bachelor, because first thing you know you'll be one of those plain old aginners."

"You want me to get married, you must want something from it. What?"

"More grandchildren," said Dolly. "There's just Danny now, and it seems a shame when Jud brought four boys into the world they can't do any better for his name."

He held up his hand. "Ma, I solemnly promise you I'll do the best I can. Just don't rush me, I'll work cheaper. But whatever they're saying about Claire, it's not true. If anybody ever stopped to think about what she's been through, they'd know you don't get right up from something like that and say, 'Well, that's over, now for the next one.'"

Dolly gave him a perceptive look. "You really like her, don't you?"

"Sure I do! But I'm not in love with her, if that's what you're trying to find out!"

"Well, don't shout, darlin' mine, I'm not deaf."

"I dunno but what I'll rent one of those islands out there and go live where you can sneeze without every horse's arse making a comment on it. Besides, she's maybe gone back home by now so they won't have her to talk about anymore." He was suddenly overwhelmed with a sad sullen rage, and went abruptly out of the house.

By late afternoon he was tired of everybody, tired even of his life, as if all the struggling didn't amount to Hannah Cook. It was like wearing clothes with grass seed or loose hairs caught in the fabric, making you itch, scratching at your temper till you wanted to shuck the whole thing and dive overboard and come up somewhere new. Life before the wars had been better, he thought, longing for an existence of which he'd read and heard, but had never experienced except in yearning imagination. You took off on the road for the west or Alaska, you went on a ship, you worked your way around the world doing anything you could turn a hand to and trying a hell of a lot of things you'd never tried before. What am I doing *here*? he thought in panic as he walked between house and fishhouse. Fubbing around with lobster traps, dying to catch a few herring, and thinking it's living.

He stood looking out at the open line of horizon to the south.

He wondered if his father had ever stood here and looked too, and wished to be gone. Doubt clamped him in iron hoops. . . . Was that why Pa went off to fight when he didn't have to? Was it at least a part of it, besides the blur in your eyes when the flags went by and a kind of love for your land that was as strong as your love of your woman and your kids? I wish I knew, he thought, I wish I knew if it ever got too much around here for him so he wanted to be up and gone, and the war was his chance.

The next day after he hauled he took the boat to Port George to have the radio telephone installed. When he got back to the Point in the late afternoon he went to the boys' wharf so they could fool around with the rig. "Well, it's out," Larry told him. "They all know we're going seining. Gil asked me about it today." He was fairly bouncing. "At first I thought it was the kids, but we've been careful never to say anything they could lug. Nope, it come from across the river, from that guy we're supposed to take with us. He told somebody he expected we'd keep this harbor stopped off all summer long, so that's how it got out."

"Well, no harm done, I guess," said Finn. "I was hoping to keep it quiet till we came in with a dory full of twine."

"Bart Collins told me we ought to do real good if we was of a mind to work," said Elmer. "And Gil, he seemed kind of taken with the idea too. He plans on buying bait off us when the bream's scarce."

"Well, come on, let's see what we can haul in on this thing, or if Finn got cheated," Larry said impatiently.

Finn stayed with them a little while, but he felt edgy, as if something were prowling at the edge of safety like a tiger kept at bay by a campfire. It wasn't the fact that their plans had got out; that could have happened at any time, and he doubted that his brothers would try the same trick with Waisanen that they'd tried with Eastman. Nell's screeching at the kids scraped at his nerves instead of making him laugh; Larry's enthusiasm was wearing and he found himself thinking, Won't he ever grow up? . . . He left them abruptly and went up to the store.

He heard Josie's placid voice before he saw her, magnificently large and proud, surrounded by several children all messily eating Tootsie Rolls. "You don't want to come in here unless you bring a basket," Gil said to him. "I keep trying to start her for home because I ain't no midwife."

"You're just afraid Elmer'll make you keep it," said Josie.

"Aren't you two ashamed to be talking like that in front of all us young kids?" said Finn. A child launched herself at him, grabbing his big hand with two sticky ones; just as he recognized the golden eyes someone moved out from behind Josie's bulk, and it was Claire.

"Hello," she said.

Finn had been so sure since yesterday that she had gone that now he could only stand there, Nancy holding his hand and a couple of smaller ones pressing jealously against his legs, and look at her.

"What's the matter?" Josie was laughing at him.

"I thought you'd gone back to Boston with your family," he said past her to Claire.

"Oh, Robert just came down to see for himself how we were. He says we're disgustingly healthy."

·25·

Mag read in the paper that Rafe's new boat *Princess* was to be launched on Thursday at the Johansen yard in Williston. "There!" she said. "That's something you ought to see, Claire, a la'nching. Never mind if the boat belongs to that unholy pair, we'll have to go."

"Don't you have to be invited?" asked Claire.

"Invited, fiddlesticks," said Mag. "Besides, Andy Johansen's father-in-law is a second cousin to me and Gil's father, and it was his yard first." She went over to the telephone, got Mrs. Tom Hunt off it with a series of grinding rings that should have been just cause to report her to the telephone company, and called her second cousin. She came away with an invitation to the launching. "Guests of the Yard," she said triumphantly. "I *told* you. Now we'll get Gil to take us."

Claire turned a hem on a dress of Nancy's and listened to Mag's side of the next conversation, which was punctuated by angry exclamations as Mrs. Tom Hunt tried to get the line again. At the finish Mag announced that Gil couldn't go, but that Mrs. Gil could take them.

"I hope she doesn't mind," Claire said dubiously. "She might have something else planned."

"Oh, she'll be glad enough to go," said Mag. "She's always looking for a chance to be on the road."

Mrs. Gil was a stout woman with curly gray hair and humorous eyes behind thick glasses. She had been a schoolteacher and now substituted occasionally in the village school.

"I'm glad you thought of this, Mag," she said when she came in on Thursday. "I haven't been to a launching since Adam was a kitten, and I never expected an invitation to this one."

Mag preened. "Cousin Billy would never refuse me a favor. He was real sweet on me once, but Father was set against cousins courting." She wore her spring coat over a giddy nylon print, and her straw sailor was heavy with artificial flowers. Excitement rejuvenated her; she had done a week's work in the two days since the date for the launching was made. "Just think, if Father hadn't been so set, I'd be living in that big house on Water Street now, overlooking the yard and the river. And I'd never have let Billy retire so early and turn the yard over to the young ones."

"He didn't retire till he had that stroke," Mrs. Gil said.

"Well, *I'd* have seen that he didn't have a stroke."

They were to watch the launching from Cousin Billy's lawn. The house was across the road from the yard and above it, an unpretentious and dignified white house built in the days when the yard turned out sailing vessels. Cousin Billy was a slight, lame, swarthy man with thick white mustaches. When he greeted Mag his dark eyes lighted up, and he began to tease her as if it were a joke continued from yesterday; the two of them dropped years. His housekeeper was either a distant relative or a lifetime acquaintance, because she and Mrs. Gil were instantly involved in an exchange of news and names that meant nothing to Claire. She didn't mind. She sat in a little vacuum, smelling the flowery yet salty breeze that ruffled the new leaves overhead, watching the alternate glitter and darkening of the river as the clouds sailed over it. A robin sang with piercing enthusiasm from one of the maples. Cousin Billy's black-and-white cats rubbed against ankles or lay decoratively among the jonquils and Red Emperor tulips. Neighbors walked down the road to watch the launching, calling up greetings to Cousin Billy. This is one of those perfect little moments suspended in time, Claire thought.

Rafe and Hester were across the road with the Johansens, moving into sight now and then among the sheds and past half-finished hulls, gaily talking with their guests. There was no one from the Point except Cleon, who, however, seemed more comfortable with the workmen.

The actual launching was a quick affair. Hester, carrying an armful of red roses, called out the right words and successfully broke the bottle, and *Princess* slid down the ways and into the water with hardly a splash. It was unexpectdly moving. Claire found herself clapping hard with the others on the lawn. "Even if it's *his* boat," Mag grumbled, sniffing, "she's real pretty. . . . I always cry at la'nchings same as some folks cry at weddings."

"You and your son-in-law must be very proud every time you launch a boat," Claire said to Cousin Billy.

"Oh, she's a beauty all right. Kind of a pocket Venus when you look back on what we used to turn out here. But then they're all beauties when they take to the water for the first time." He blew his nose. "Look at her there. He's really got himself something fine."

"I'd better go in and get ready," the housekeeper said.

"Can I help, Robbie?" Mrs. Gil said.

"No, the table's all set, I just have to mix the punch." She whispered loudly behind her hand, "The silver bowl will have the Launching Punch same as always, but the teetotal kind will be in the cut-glass one."

"Thanks for telling me, Robbie. I'd hate to go home drunk. . . . The Launching Punch is a tradition," Mrs. Gil explained to Claire. "The first batch was concocted by one of the captains with rum he'd brought back from the West Indies. Wouldn't you like to see Robbie turning in the rum? Disapproving of every drop. She's WCTU, but loyal to tradition at the same time."

Claire laughed, but she was not comfortable. The launching party was coming across the road now, and Hester's voice carried gaily above the others. There was a tiny interlude of freezing shock when Hester came up from the street and saw her on the lawn.

"Oh, you must be Aunt Mag's grandniece," said Mrs. Johansen. "We're glad to have you here today." This seemed to make up Hester's mind for her.

"Oh, hello, there! Did you enjoy the launching?" Her smile was dazzlingly artificial.

"Oh, yes. It was my first one, so it was all new. The boat is a beauty."

"Isn't she? I think Rafe's more in love with her than he ever was with me!" They all laughed. She introduced the other women, who were polite and friendly, greeted Mrs. Gil effusively, and swept down on Cousin Billy and Mag. "Captain Salisbury, what an absolutely handsome boat they've turned out! She's far too beautiful to mess up with bait. How nice to see you, Mrs. Abbott, I'm so glad you got a chance to come."

"Ayuh," said Mag dryly. Claire turned from watching them and met Rafe. He said amiably, "This is a surprise."

"I want to congratulate you," she said. "That is, if you do congratulate people at a launching the way you do at a wedding."

"It's somewhat the same, isn't it?" said Johansen, the builder. "Except that he's taken unto himself a boat instead of a bride."

"And such a beautiful one," said Claire. Rafe was smiling as he listened; his eyes swept over Claire with a peculiar softness as if today she existed only to praise the boat and was doing it well. The smile had a faint resemblance to Finn's.

"Thank you," he said. "Thank you very much. Do you—uh—know these people?" He introduced the men, whose pleasure gave Claire's vanity a stimulating lift. "You didn't tell us you had anything like this at the Point, Rafe," one of them said.

"Well, we like to keep some things to ourselves," said Rafe. "We don't want the place overrun by tourists." He nodded at Claire, and went on to the group around Cousin Billy, taking the men with him. The talk and laughter of a successful party rose in the warm air like smoke. Cleon was the last one she met; he turned from telling a joke to the workmen, with the broad laughter still on his face, and saw her.

"Hello," Claire said. "This is quite an occasion, isn't it?"

He said bluntly, "Where'd you come from?"

She resisted an impulse to say "Out of the everywhere into the here," and answered, "Oh, Captain Salisbury invited us. He's a cousin of Aunt Mag's, you know, and a step-cousin of mine."

Cleon went on without speaking.

In the house they circulated through the rooms, forming groups, separating, forming new groups; it was like the action of rockweed in the pools as the tide starts to move. Hester, exhilarated by her performance and several cups of Launching Punch, was heard most often above the rest, thrilling with excitement and exaggerated *r*s. Stopping to look at some figurines on a mantel, Claire saw Hester's high-colored face reflected in the mirror from behind her. "Dresden, aren't they?"

"I don't know," said Claire. "But they're enchanting, aren't they?"

"Enchanting." Hester tasted the word. She smiled at Claire in the mirror; they might never have met before. Claire marveled at the ease with which Hester ignored the earlier encounter. She had a big mouth and fine teeth. The better to eat you with, my dear, Claire thought.

"Are you enjoying your stay at the Point?" Hester asked.

"Oh, yes," said Claire, gazing into the reflected eyes, which were brilliant and watchful above the great smile. "I love the place. Who could help it?"

"Oh, I know! Truthfully, *I* couldn't imagine what I'd do to entertain myself in such an isolated spot, but it was Rafe's home, and so—" She shrugged with simple gallantry. "But now I couldn't bear to live anywhere else! . . . I see Finn is doing a good deal to make your stay even more pleasant. He's a likeable boy."

"I agree," said Claire. "I like him very much."

"But a boy is just what he is," said Hester with a sigh. "Perhaps someday he'll grow up. Heaven knows we all *hope* so. In the meantime he's such a worry to his brothers. They never know what he'll get into next."

"The youngest is always at a disadvantage, I think. Just as the oldest is."

"But Finn has no sense of responsibility. No concern whatever about his future. He has *nothing* to his name, you know, except that old boat and a handful of traps. And he only seems to care about associating with the worst element, and chasing women. And such women! Oh, dear!" She shut her eyes and rocked her head from side to side. "The brothers never know from week to week that will come of it. And women chase him, too! Oh, how they chase him!" She dropped her voice to a loud whisper. "They think the island goes with him, you know, and they know the price of a property like that today. They drop off fast enough when they find out the truth."

Well, you're clever in a way, Claire conceded, because almost any answer I make will give you some satisfaction. She knew that she looked composed to the point of being colorless, but she was very angry with Hester for her pretense and her greed and her vulgarity. She thought, What a voracious woman. I'm almost sorry for Rafe; some day she will eat him alive.

She turned her head to face Hester directly and said with a gentle smile, "Oh, but he's such a happy person, and isn't that the sign of real success in this world? I'm afraid that when we fuss at people like that for their way of life we're really committing the sin of envy."

The triumph went out of Hester's face, leaving it agape and stupid with surprise. Claire turned away and slipped through a doorway into the dining room.

The tide had gone far down in the cold-misted silver bowl, and some of the guests were rather flushed and bright eyed. Voices were louder, laughter more uninhibited. Cleon was out by the front stairs giving the carpenters another good story. The housekeeper was anxiously watching Cousin Billy as he narrated a portion of the yard's history; the snapping swoops of his cane kept his listeners flinching and dodging.

"His blood pressure," the housekeeper whispered to Claire. "I can *see* it climbing. I guess it's time I said something to Mr. Johansen."

Aunt Mag was sitting on a window seat looking tired and confused, as if wondering where her bed was. Claire sat down beside her, and Mrs. Gil came to them from another room. "Mrs. Washburn and I went to Gorham together but we haven't seen each other for years. We had quite a reunion. Ready to go home, Mag?"

"Yes, I am," said Mag emphatically. "This high life'll do me in, if it don't get Billy first. He's carrying on like a ten-year-old at a barn raisin'. When the wine's in, the wit's out."

"Don't worry, Mr. Johansen's about to end the party," said Claire.

As they drove away from the house, Mag said, "My, that was a dull one, taking it all in all. Why, most la'nchings Father went to, there was always someone falling-down drunk."

"You sound disappointed," said Mrs. Gil.

"Not at all," she protested, but she fell into a long silence from which she suddenly roused, halfway home, and announced, "Well, we showed that besom. How'd it set with her, I wonder, you getting off so well with that Mrs. Washburn? I could see her watching and trying not to. . . . Of course it near knocked her off her pins to see us set out on Billy's lawn. That Rafe was so tickled with the boat he acted almost human for once. . . . Say, don't that Cleon look like a drinking man to you? He started buttering me up and I asked him where his wife was. I says, 'Ain't she got enough tone to mix with the Four Hundreds?'"

"Aunt Mag, you didn't," said Claire.

"Yes, I did. Teach him to come around me rubbing his hands and saying, 'You're looking mighty fine today, Mrs. Abbott.' As if I didn't know I look like something set out last year to keep the crows out of the corn."

"If you get them all mad they may make you get out of the house sooner than you planned," Mrs. Gil warned.

"I'd like to see them try."

"I wish I had some of that Salisbury blood in me," Claire said. "I'd feel immortal."

"So would I," said Mrs. Gil with a sigh.

When the thanks and good-bys had been said, and Mrs. Gil had turned her car around and left, Claire walked across to the mailbox. There was a letter from Mrs. Carradine.

She dreaded reading it but knew that, unopened, it would oppress her even more. She read it there by the mailbox. The barn swallows swooped noisily toward her head and shot up again, and the cries of the gulls came as small specks of sound borne on unseen currents.

"My dearest Claire," Mrs. Carradine wrote. Her hand was that of a healthy woman in her sixties, but Claire could hear her voice, tremulous with emotion as if she were very old and had been broken by life. "A year and a month ago our beloved left us. I thought I could never again endure the month of May, which was his favorite, and this May is as intolerable as I had expected. And to have you and David's baby away from me at this time only adds to the torture. Birds sing and flowers bloom; I loathe them for living when David is dead. *David is dead.* Can you believe it?"

Yes, Claire thought drearily, I can believe it because I watched him die. And I prayed while I watched for him to be beyond his pain, because there was nothing left for him but that. Now he *is* beyond it, and what service is it to him to keep going over and over it? The letter trembled in her hands and she wanted to stop reading, but she could not.

"Robert says you look well. You must be making a superb effort to hide your grief from those strangers, because I can't believe that you are able to live through this ghastly spring with any real peace of mind. You are the only person who can even imagine what I am going through." David's mother's grief is so important, Robert had said, and she had called him cruel, but now the words he had spoken on the wall that day ran like a discordant counterpoint to the words she read.

"My sister keeps imploring me to look out and not in, to remember my faith. Faith! What sort of God could wrench my son from me? And Robert is so cold. I believe now he has always been envious of his brother's special gifts, and urged you to leave me not truly for your good or mine, as he insists, but to deprive us of each other's comfort and support. You and I and David's dear child—'little David'—belong together. Don't let Robert separate us for much longer." She signed it, "Your loving Mother."

"That's not so about Robert!" Claire exclaimed aloud, crumpling the letter into a hard ball. "How can she—after all he's done—" Her voice stabbed the green and sunny stillness; her anger was therapeutic, it kept the other things in the letter from flaying her. She thrust the paper ball into her pocket and went down the road to the Johnsons', where Nancy had gone straight from the school bus, and didn't think of it again until Mag and Nancy had gone to bed.

At least she didn't consciously think of it, but it was there, and when she walked up to the stone wall in the amethystine light resounding with robins, fatigue and despair attacked her. In the lee of the wall were some early strawberry blossoms that would probably blight in a May frost. They had been premature, like the euphoria she had felt once today as she sat on Cousin Billy's lawn and played with a bewitchingly friendly cat. Than it had seemed perfectly probable that she could find a job and go on living in Maine, in a house furnished with Aunt Mag's things and decorated by a kitten from Cousin Billy's house. Now, because of the letter, she felt herself crippled again by the weight of tragedy, and shamed by forgetfulness.

But I have not forgotten, she fought back, any more than Robert is cold and envious! Perhaps he's always wished he were more like David, but to begrudge David anything—no, that's not so. Why can't she really *look* at Robert and take what he wants so much to give?

The house on the island showed chalk-white in the fading light between the dark bank of alders and the black hill of spruce woods. She wondered if Finn were there, or if he was with his friends. The thought of him was oddly soothing, but then she imagined Mrs. Carradine wandering comfortless through her house in the warm spring dusk, and that made her get up off the wall and walk restlessly. Compassion wrenched at her, an ugly intestinal thing unrelated to sweetly sad sentiment; but she couldn't tell whether it was for Mrs. Carradine, Robert, or herself.

·26·

The next afternoon when Finn came in from hauling he looked up toward Roy's as he always did, and saw something familiar moving against the sunlit clapboards. It was Helen. The light struck a fiery gleam from her hair as she leaned down to the dog, and he was relieved; he was afraid she might have turned completely gray up there. The dog's tail was waving slowly back and forth without stopping. Finn's mother came out of the front and together the two women inspected the long bed of perennials under the sitting-room windows. They didn't see Finn. He went along past the moorings to the lobster car, smiling to himself. Seeing Helen at home and the flame still in her hair was like a good-luck omen.

The secret had been well kept. Nobody thought anything of Dolly's taking a week off to clean house for Roy, and even Danny had managed not to let it out.

Finn had left home in the morning before the sun was really up, and everything had been silvered with a cold mist. Now when he walked up through the alders the whole place seemed to dance and shimmer in a green light. The thrushes were really going it from the woods, the notes dropped into the green reflections with a wait to see how the rings grew and spread, and then a new shower. Sunday he was taking Claire for that walk in the woods, and he had already chosen the spot where they would sit down and listen.

It came to him that when he started seining, before the next week was out if Waisanen kept his word, he would not see her very often. When you went seining you lived and died for herring, you worked all night and slept in the days except when you got one of those john-rogers big strikes and worked for twenty hours at a stretch. You set out at sunset with your dories when lobstermen were yawning and wondering if they'd stay awake through *Rawhide*. You were a gull, a seal, a porpoise —something that thought only of fish and where they might be.

He was glad to be going. Wasn't it what he'd been wanting? Claire was an accident, and she'd be leaving the Point anyway as soon as Mag was ready. Hell, she wasn't his girl even if everybody was chewing about it one way or another. It was even kind of funny when you thought about it, everybody thinking it just had to be a goddam love affair, when it was the last thing either of them was thinking of. Couldn't anybody believe in pure honest-to-God *friendship*?

He grew very angry, very hot, and he decided suddenly to go to see Helen. He wanted to take her something, but he didn't know what and found himself swearing in a monotonous mumble. Finally he took a spear point he'd found on the beach at Indian Cove in the winter; it was shiny black, satiny under his thumb, and so lately washed out of the bank that the edges were still keen and the tip unbroken. When he was ten or so, and boarding with Helen and Roy while Dolly was working away from home, he and Helen used to come over to the island to dig dandelion greens, and they always worked in some beach-combing and what she called Indian-hunting.

Roy was loading traps on his boat when Finn rowed up to the float. He couldn't keep from grinning. "Come on up and have a cup of coffee with Dolly and me," he invited.

"You sly dog, you've got a red-headed woman up there," said Finn. "I saw her."

"Oh, hell, nobody can live in sin around here with any privacy," said Roy. They walked up to the house together. Roy hadn't much else to say, he just kept smiling to himself. The dog came to meet them and he caught the big head in his hands and said, "I guess you're satisfied now, old boy, huh?"

Just outside the door Finn had a bad feeling he was going

to put a foot wrong no matter what. She'd look different to him, and he'd show it; he'd fumble his words, act like a gaum, blush or go tongue-tied. . . . "Is that Finn out there?" somebody called. "Is that my little brother Finn?" He heard Dolly laugh. The screen door flew open, and Helen put her arms around his neck. He hugged her hard, rocking her back and forth. He felt a prickling in his nose and eyes.

"My God, look at this," Roy said to Dolly. "I got grounds right here and you can be my witness."

Helen held Finn off by the shoulders. "Now I know I'm home. Aren't you magnificent!"

"I've always been magnificent. You never noticed, seeing me all the time. You look pretty good yourself." He'd expected to see her bones sharp as a skull's, her eyes in blue hollows, her hair without life even if it hadn't grayed. She was thin but she always had been; she had always been pale, but the ashy look was gone. Her hair was short, and he liked the way it sprang brightly back from her temples and tumbled over her forehead.

"I should look good," she said. "Roy and I went on a shopping spree in Augusta last week. I never had so many new clothes all at once in my life and such nice ones. He was like a wild man. I said, Are you sure this isn't Danny's whole college education you're blowing? And he just grinned. Look at him now." She herself looked, and the kitchen became quiet. She said after a moment, "He has a right to grin. He's earned it. Come on and have some coffee, Finn. Roy, you want a fresh cup, don't you? Onni came in with one of those gorgeous Finnish coffee breads and welcomed me home and then she was off in a cloud of dust."

"Dressed to the teeth," said Dolly. "Earrings to *here*, in the middle of the day, mind you. And green eyeshadow. That must be some card party she was going to, if they're all dressed up like that. Anybody'd have to wear dark glasses."

"Onni's childhood must have been unspeakably drab," Helen said. "She told me once they never had a curtain to the windows or a bit of new wallpaper. If the kids brought home things they'd made in school—you know, Christmas and Valentine cutouts—they went into the stove. So after a while they never took anything home. Well, come on, boys."

"Don't pour any for me yet," said Roy. "I want to put the boat out on the mooring before the tide goes any more."

"I guess I'll take those sheets in before they get damp," Dolly said. The two went out together. Helen sat opposite Finn and the dog flopped down beside her with a thump and a sigh. "My old hero," she murmured, rubbing his head. "Now, Finn, tell me about you."

"Tell you what?"

"Oh, that Judson look! That glaze of innocence. I want to know about Claire."

The name said in her funny hoarse voice almost made Finn jump, and she laughed. "Finn, sweetheart, I haven't been in one of those convents where you never hear of anything in the world and you see people through a lattice. At least not for the last month or so, and when Roy sets himself to entertain he entertains like mad. You never heard such a talker."

"What'd he say?"

"That she's a nice girl, ladylike, and quite a change from—who's the last one?"

"For God's sake, Helen, she's older than I am, and a widow."

"You don't sound very convinced. What are you blushing for?"

"I am not!" But he was, and the back of his neck was damp; he only hoped to God that neither Roy nor Dolly walked in right now.

"How much older is she than you? Twenty years? Is her daughter Danny's age?" She went on teasing him and it was all blessedly familiar. One side of him was delighted and the other side wriggling and angry. "When are you going to bring her to see me?"

He could agree, with relief, to that. "Any time. I didn't know if you'd want to meet strangers right away."

"I've been living with strangers for a year. What have you told her about me?"

"That you had a breakdown. She understood because I guess she was almost ready for one when she came here. Her husband died of cancer. Did Roy tell you that? I don't know if he knows it."

"No, he didn't tell me that," she said thoughtfully. "How—I was going to say *awful* but I don't mean that. Maybe I should say how *human*. I don't know if anything horrifies me any more, but I get a great deal more pleasure out of any good thing than I ever did before."

"You mean it's human to suffer, so nothing should ever surprise us?"

She smiled. "I mean that when you go through your little hell and come out on the other side of it you've joined a club that's not a bit exclusive. Everybody joins it sooner or later and then we look at life with a different eye. . . . You will bring her?"

"Yes, I will."

From the end of the lane they heard the familiar clashing of the school bus's gears and Helen's face became radiant. "I think I'll walk down to meet Danny," she said. "He's been expecting me, but not today." As they walked toward the door, Finn suddenly remembered the spear point and handed it to her.

"What a perfect beauty! Where'd you find it?"

"Down in Indian Cove."

"Do you think there's anything else there?"

"There ought to be, after what the winter's done to the beach. Getting on for greening time, too."

"I'll be over, Finn, I'll be over."

On Sunday Claire rowed across alone about two o'clock. He had expected Nancy to be along, but he couldn't help being glad she wasn't. "She's gone with the Curtises to visit somebody who has a farm up on Appleton Ridge, wherever that is," she said.

"Oh, that's Josie's sister. Ayuh, Nancy'll have a high old time up there. What's Mag doing?"

"The Murrays are taking her to see a distant relative across the river. She wants to iron out some fine point of genealogy, and also give her a chamber set this woman always fancied."

Her eyes were tired. "Been losing sleep lately?" he asked her.

"Why? Do I look it?"

"A little. I didn't know but what the birds and the sun were getting you up early."

"They are, and so is my daughter. She's so excited with spring. And then I read too late at night. That's all." She sounded as if she expected him to challenge her, so he changed the subject. They were crossing the Neck, and he said, "See there?" Goose-tongue greens. I'll have to cut a mess for Mag as soon as they're big enough."

"What do they taste like?"

"Grass, unless you cook 'em with salt pork, and then they taste like grass with salt pork." He stood back to let her enter the path where it began in the alders and birches. She exclaimed in pleasure as it opened before them through the trembling gold-green light, over moist ground stippled with flakes of gold. Warblers flashed through the birches and at the base of their trunks the ferns were greening. He let her go ahead without preparing her for the wild apple tree that always blossomed early in this spot of nearly windless heat, and when he reached her she was looking up into the dense cloud of bloom. Bees and fragrance hung about it. She turned to Finn with tears in her eyes.

"It's enough to break your heart," she said. He had the feeling that something else had overwhelmed her, not the apple tree, and his hands went out before he knew it. "It's supposed to make you happy," he said.

She moved back before he touched her, and wiped at her eyes with the back of her hand. "It does," she said, half-laughing. "That's the trouble. It's just too much. A whole orchard of them couldn't have the effect that this one does."

"I guess I'd better not let anything else take you by surprise. You'll be all melted by the time we reach the end of the island."

"You ought to know how women are," she said. "They come all unglued about babies, puppies, and solitary apple trees."

The path now entered the warm winy dusk of the spruce woods and their footsteps struck silently on the path. "These are fairy-tale woods," she said. "Not the bright pretty Walt Disney kind, but something very ancient. You expect to find a charcoal-burner's hut, or a tower all wound around with briers and ivy."

"You know I used to think I'd find something like that in these woods if I looked long enough and hard enough? ... A deer's been through here just before us."

"A stag who is really a prince," she said in a mysterious voice. "Listen, he's getting messages. The thrushes are telling him where and who we are." They listened to the song from the dark interwoven ceiling of spruce boughs. Another one answered. Claire and Finn sat for a while on a log without speaking, hearing the thrushes, and her eyes gleamed like water in the shadow under the trees. It was just as he had hoped it would be.

At last they came out through the twinkling light of a birch grove onto the high easterly end of the island. They walked among the wax bells of blueberry blossoms and the flat silvery-green rosettes of juniper down to where the rock began its descent in serpentine folds toward the water. They were up above the harbor here, and opposite the houses and moorings of the lower harbor. Finn told her who lived where, and who the children were rowing or playing along the shore. The young Hunt boys were creeping .and crawling over the chain of bar-nacled and pointed rocks that lay off their beach. They'd left their skiff hauled up on a fairly level spot.

"What can they be looking for there?" Claire asked. "It's nothing but rock."

"Known as the String of Pearls," said Finn. "Somebody felt like a poet, I guess. No, there's nothing there but ledge and mussel shells, but they're probably out in the middle of the Pacific exploring a desert island."

"Wouldn't you like to be ten again? What a wonderful world it is, in spite of all the worries children can have." She sounded far-off somehow, and sad, and she turned half-away, looking across the broad blue river toward the horizon.

"Somebody's got herring to the west'ard," he said. "That's *Thetis* going down."

"They'll be coming for your herring soon, won't they?"

"If we get any." He flopped over on his stomach and examined the turf at close range.

"That's not a very positive attitude."

"You mean lying on my belly like this?"

She laughed. "No, I mean saying *if* we get any."

"That's what's known as not spitting in the face of Provi-dence."

"Oh, I see. Well, that's a form of wisdom that I have yet to learn. I must have spent my life spitting in the face of Provi-dence."

"What's wrong?" He turned his head on his folded arms and

watched her. She gave him a slight youthful smile, one-sided. "Nothing, except all this beauty is making me melancholy instead of gay. I keep thinking of sad things like 'Look thy last on all things lovely,' and 'Brightness falls from the air, queens have died young and fair.' " She jumped up. "Oh, I'm impossible, quoting away like a show-off, trying to impress myself with the sound of my own voice because I know darn well I'm not impressing you. Finn, I'm wrecking your Sunday. I should go home."

He rolled over on his back and folded his hands behind his neck. He liked her against the sky, the way her blouse and slacks fitted, and the long line of her throat as she turned her face away from his eyes, the light falling on her cheekbone and on the blowing tips of her hair. "Sit down again," he said. "Look at the scenery and remember how long it's been here. Makes you feel less important and that's kind of a relief sometimes. I may be lying on a hunk of three-million-year-old rock. See those sails coming down the river? That sloop may be fiberglass and the sails nylon, but that guy's got to go by the wind and the tide, the way men have been sailing since the first one got up enough courage to put to sea. You know the navigators in those big trans-atlantic jets take a fix by the stars?"

"And we call some stars by names Persian astronomers gave them several thousand years ago." She sat down beside him and hugged her knees. "You're right and I'm a self-centered ant. Look, there's a real beauty coming down the river."

"Rafe bringing his new boat down, I guess. They've been putting the engine in the last couple of days. I hear you were at the launching."

"Mag worked it through Cousin Billy Salisbury. I guess Rafe and Hester were surprised to see us, but they were nice enough.... You know, there was something about the moment when the boat touched the water, she looked so fresh and new, in a way so *young* ..." She laughed as if she were embarrassed. "Do I sound silly?"

"Nope."

"Anyway, I almost liked Rafe that day, because of the way he looked at his boat."

"She's a big thing in his life," Finn said. He was impressed by her honesty. She had no reason at all to have any kindly feelings for Rafe. But she understood that the launching of a man's boat could be as important to him as his wedding, and that a beautiful boat could stir and move a man as much as a woman could, especially if she were his own.

"Yes, it's Rafe," Claire said. "Oh, she's lovely in motion. I never used to think anything with an engine could be beautiful, but I'm getting awfully boat-minded." Finn sat up. They watched *Princess* make a long flowing turn around the mainland point opposite them. Now she was just off the island, and heading into the harbor. Hester and another woman sat in canvas chairs in the stern, Rafe and a man stood up under the canopy by the wheel. The boat shone with coat after coat of paint rubbed to a porcelain gloss; her lines were as functionally perfect and flowing as a gull's; the Diesel engine's sound was a soft music scarcely heard through the light splash on the shore. She was virgin, she was handsome, and she was Rafe's. Finn hauled in his breath hard as if to squeeze out of existence the pain under his ribs; not a pain you could touch, but a longing and a rage so blended together as to affect his body like the shock of passion.

Eyes drying from his long stare, he watched the boat's passage around the humped point of the island and past the String of Pearls. The children stopped playing, and at Spicer's the men stood and looked. Finn got up to watch her into the harbor proper, past Roy's wharf and Cleon's, past the inlet and thence to her own wharf. He didn't realize until then that he hadn't breathed naturally since that first long hard breath back there.

"Well," he said, fumbling for his cigarettes. "Quite a craft. She's a big one, might be he and Hes plan to do some cruising in her. Take another couple and go out to Monhegan, down to Boothbay, up to Mt. Desert. . . . I hope he's checked that ground line on his mooring before he puts all that extra weight on."

"What's a ground line? And what would happen if he hasn't checked it?"

He could turn to her naturally then, and he explained the principle of a mooring, the ground line, anchors, and pennants. "There's just himself and Cleon on that mooring. Roy and Cleon put it down, but Roy sold out his share to Rafe, and put down one of his own, farther up this way, after he got his new boat. There's space for three boats on the mooring, and if somebody comes in to lay overnight here they can use the spare one."

"What happens if the ground line isn't checked?"

"Nothing, most likely. Rafe being Rafe, he probably knows just what shape that ground line is in. If it was up to Cleon now, I wouldn't be surprised at anything. He's inclined to let things go that he doesn't see. But a chafed or frayed ground line could give way with the boats pulling on it in a long hard wind, and then they're whipping back and forth on the end of the mooring chain with enough scope to ride down on whatever's to leeward of them. And the weight of the boat pulling so hard on the mooring line could make that part, too."

She said, "But nothing very bad ever happens here, does it?" She hugged her arms across her chest, as if she had seen his explanation too vividly and felt cold. "I hate to think that any violence could touch this harbor."

"Oh, we have a hard time now and then, have to stay up all night and watch the boats. Bart Collins' wharf got carried away last year, and in a no'theasterly last winter Larry's boat drove 'er down the harbor and went up on my fish house point. You cold?"

"The wind's blowing harder. Look, it's making a little surf on the String of Pearls."

"It's freshening as the tide turns. We'll go back along the harbor shore, it'll be in the lee and the sun all the way." The tiredness was around her eyes again and when she wasn't speaking or listening to him there was a set around her mouth that disturbed him; he hadn't seen it before. She looked smaller than usual, too, in some curious way, and something about her shoulders made him want to take hold of them. In fact he wanted to so much that he put his hands in his pockets, and began to talk just to fill up the kind of silence that had hardly ever come between them. She followed where he led and let him talk, and that disturbed him too, because it was as if she were too preoccupied to respond, too burdened even to try to think of answers.

·27·

Claire refused to stay for a mug-up. She said she had letters to write while the house was quiet. He wanted to ask her again what was wrong, but it wasn't his business. Maybe she just didn't feel well. Sometimes you could get depressed with a headache or a squeamish stomach, or it could be a womanly thing. He watched from the fishhouse doorway till she had tied up at the boys' wharf and gone out of sight. Then he went up to the house and got the gasoline mower out of the shed and began to cut the lawn.

The wind kept freshening, and it didn't drop off at sunset; by dusk there was a steady thumping and booming all along the shore below the house. A strong ocean smell mixed with that of newmown grass, and the surf shone ghostly in the twilight. It was not unusual. The wind blew southerly or sou'westerly almost every afternoon, and sometimes it decided to blow that way for a much longer spell. He went to sleep hoping it would flatten out enough tomorrow for him to bring in a load of traps. If everything went the way it should, they'd be looking for herring on the next dark of the moon.

He supposed his excitement would come back with the first good strike. He hoped so. He went to sleep thinking of the silver boil of herring in the purse seine, and the clean acrid scent of them in his nostrils. When he got up at daylight, breakers were still crashing ashore, and the sea was streaked and smeared with white, the islands almost out of sight. But as the sun rose through the mist, and the water began to turn blue, the smears became fewer, the chop smoothed out, and the roar grew less. It would be a good day after all, and if he kept at it he could get the rest of his traps in and stacked on the wharf to dry.

He thought of Claire as he went down through the alders. He wanted to do something with her before they started seining.

Maybe they could have a picnic down on the southerly end of the island. You could hear the rote from there this morning, the dulled yet powerful voice of the breakers coming in from open sea, to hurl themselves over the eroded black volcanic rock and the bleached granite.

Bemused with the thought of a fine day spent down there with Claire, he was rowing down the harbor when Elmer whistled at him from his wharf. He and Larry were standing together in the pale early sunlight. He swerved over toward them, rowing stern-to so he could face them. "I thought you two'd be out there and halfway home with a load by now," he said.

"Jeez, ain't you *seen* it yet?" Larry pointed. "Look at my hand shake! Jeez, what a sight to get up to. I was sick enough to heave. Still am." Finn turned the skiff around, not knowing what to expect. Instantly he saw what in his preoccupation he had missed; he hadn't even looked at the harbor when he went out onto the wharf and down the ladder to his skiff. *Foam-Flower* was submerged almost to her washboards.

He couldn't speak. He was sick, but not like Larry; there was nothing to heave, there was nothing at all. He sat in the skiff, his hands on the oars, and he was only a shell shaped like a man. After a moment something began working in his brain. All that money, and she's not tight. It's to be done over again, and Waisanen's waiting for us, and Morry's got men already waiting their turns. And then she'll sink on us again because she's old, she's frail, she can't do the work.... "But, my God," he exclaimed aloud, "she was tight yesterday! She's been tight ever since I got her back. How could she fill up at the mooring in one night?"

He began to row toward her. Larry and Elmer came behind him, Larry talking in frantic jerks while Elmer rowed. "We'll have to take down the engine ... clean out the gas tanks ... Jeez, the radio! ... Jeez, what'd that guy caulk her with, Kleenex?"

Finn circled the boat. It was more than everything going wrong, it was seeing the boat like this, like something dying, an old horse or dog you'd thought would go on forever.

"*Finn*." Elmer's whisper cracked like a snapping branch. He was on the other side of her, where the hauling winch was. "Come over here." Finn paddled around the bow and looked where

Elmer was pointing, at the deep wound in the planking. "She's been rammed, Finn," he whispered. "Rammed good." He looked over his shoulder, his eyes ranging over the other wharves and boats. But the light was misty, and the shadows deceptive.

Larry stared at the hole, his face blank with wonder. "Now who could have done that?" he asked almost reverently.

Finn shrugged. "Hard telling, this time of year seiners go through here on the high water. That was two, three o'clock. Could be some outfit from way to hell and gone that don't expect to go through here again, so they aren't hanging around to find out who they rammed." He smiled coldly. "Let's hope he's got a goddam big hole in his boat too and he sank before he got where he was heading for. No, I guess I don't hope that, unless they had a chance to get aboard one of their dories first. At least they didn't drown me along with my boat. Mebbe I should thank 'em for that."

He sat looking at his hands for a moment. The other two watched him in respectful silence. Again he felt the suffocating weight of responsibility. "First thing is to call Waisanen," he said finally. "We can't do anything with her till high water, then we'll get her ashore and see just what's to be done. From here it looks as if they did a real thorough job on her, with her age and all, but let's not hold the funeral yet."

"Jeez, no," breathed Larry. His color was coming back, as if Finn's decision had restored him. "Come on back ashore to my place and call from there," Elmer said. "We'll have Josie brew us up a fresh pot of coffee. Good and strong."

"We need more than coffee," Larry said. "I got something in the cupboard. Nell always squawks when I touch it like I was heading for a drunkard's grave, but she won't yip this time."

Rowing back across the harbor Finn looked down toward his brothers' moorings. Roy was just going out past the Pearls, Cleon had his boat ashore this morning. Rafe's two boats, the old looking almost as trim as the new, lay side by side on their moorings, bows pointing into the wind. Rafe ran down the ramp to his float with an eagerness that Finn could not only sense, but taste, and his envy was as corrosive as battery acid. *Oh, Christ!* he cried silently. Why couldn't it have been one of *his* boats they rammed?

"Somebody going through the harbor in the night rammed my boat," he told Waisanen. "She's full to the washboards. Looks like a long job if it's worth doing at all." His bleakness was wearing thin; it was like the reaction after an accident, when you go through it all over again and begin to sweat. It was *his* boat he was talking about. He said loudly into the telephone, "I'm going to try to get another boat. I can let you know for sure later today."

Waisanen had no comments. "You call me tomorrow night. I'm busy till then."

Nell had come across the yard with Larry. She and Josie went into the sitting room and talked low, as if there'd been a death. They kept the children in there, quieting them with sharp hisses. The men sat at the kitchen table and drank the smoking coffee laced with whiskey. Then they went out again; Finn got his dinner box from his skiff and went in Elmer's boat. The sea was flattening fast and they worked as a team hauling traps, taking out the lobsters, coiling and tying warps and stowing them and the buoys inside the traps, stacking the traps on the stern. When they had all they could safely carry they took that load ashore, landed the pots on either Elmer's or Finn's wharf, depending on whose traps they were, and went out again.

In midafternoon they came in with the last load. Larry had finished earlier; he had the smaller boat, but only his own traps to lug. The tide was brimming-high and the three set out to get *Foam-Flower* onto the island ledges where she'd just been painted and coppered. Danny was home from school and rowed down in his dory to help.

"My gosh, Finn, what happened?"

"Must have been one of those Cuban-based missiles," said Finn.

"Didn't anybody hear anything? You can't make that big a hole without making a noise."

"The wind was blowing too hard," Elmer said.

"Uncle Cleon got up on the high water and took his boat in to paint to day, but he didn't see or hear anything, either." Danny whistled. "Hey, good thing it didn't happen to Uncle Rafe's new boat."

"Thanks," said Finn dryly. "You helping or you just sitting there to whistle and stare like you're watching a striptease?"

"Sure I came to help!"

"Then you get astern of her there and just keep nudging, gentle but steady, see? Keep pushing easy, you're not rowing for Harvard."

Moving slowly and carefully around her in their skiffs and the dory, they got her from the mooring and over to the ledge. She grounded out before she would have if she'd been tight, and they had to leave her there until the tide went away from her and the water could pour out of her side. Then they would put a patch of canvas over the hole, and Finn would get up before the next high tide to haul her up as close as he could to the bank of alders.

When they had finished making her fast Larry wanted Finn to go home and eat with him, but Finn refused. "I've got business down the harbor."

"Coming to our place?" Danny asked, keeping the dory alongside the skiff. "Nobody's home. My mother and father went over to Aunt Sophie's in Putnam, and Gram's gone back to work."

"I have to see Rafe. And thanks for coming to the rescue. You were a big help."

"Honest?" The kid's grin was like the sun. "You had to bark at me a couple of times."

"I was barking at the world. No, you did fine. You've got boat sense, you knew just what to do once you got started. We needed another man and you were it."

"Thanks," Danny said solemnly. "Freshmen can't have cars at Orono, but I sure as hell wish there was a way I could get around the campus in this dory." Finn laughed, but Danny said, "I mean it. You realize what I'm going to be cut off from? It'll be so sudden I'll probably get some kind of pyschological bends."

"You'll survive," said Finn. He pulled in to Rafe's float and Danny rowed on by. Rafe was still out on his mooring, making *Princess* secure for the night. Finn walked up to the fishhouse and sat down on the chopping block outside the door. It was the first time he had been alone all day, and he didn't know if that was a good or a bad thing. Depression bowed his shoulders, and his cigarette tasted foul. I ought to stop smoking, he thought. Man in my position can't afford it anyway. Yesterday I had prospects and today I'm a pauper. He ground out the cigarette with his boot heel and watched for Rafe with his eyes squinted as if in unbearable light.

When Rafe came up the wharf he was springy in his rubber boots, and whistling. When he saw Finn he stopped short, then grinned. "You speaking or should I take a chance on it?"

"I'm speaking," said Finn. "Hi. Nice boat. How is she to work in?"

"Finest kind, but I sure hate to mess her up." Rafe looked back fondly. "She's a little lower-sided than the other one and that's easier on my back, I notice. And she purrs like a pussycat. You want to get an engine like that one, Finn. She's some smooth, I can tell you."

"Ayuh, I'll order one for my new boat," said Finn. "What are you doing about Gemini Seafoods these days?"

"Biding my time, chummy, biding my time." He kept watching the boat and smiling like a proud father. "Gil may be ready to give up any time and sell me the wharf at my price and be glad to get it."

"In the meanwhile Gemini could settle somewhere else."

"You needling me? Well, it won't take today. Besides there's a lot of land around the harbor yet and I'm working out my approach to the owners."

"Down to the lower harbor, huh? Could be. There's that field between Morry and Tom. But gorry, man, you're spending money like the government." He managed to sound nervously admiring.

"Oh well, live it up!" Rafe laughed. "You want to talk to me about anything special, Finn, or you just passing the time of day?"

"You see my boat over there?"

"I saw you fellers taking her ashore. She filled, didn't she? Did that Morry pull a fast one on you? What in hell do you ever give him any business for?"

It was quite a display of indignation. It didn't move Finn, at least not as it was intended to. It seemed to come a little too fast, a little too furious. He said tonelessly, "She was rammed in the night. I dunno if she'll ever be any good again."

"And you all set to go seining," said Rafe. "That's a damn

shame, Finn. You got no idea at all what bastard's to blame for it?"

"What good's an idea if you can't prove anything? Nobody saw anything, nobody heard anything. It was the middle of the night." He shrugged. "I might go around and talk to Cleon. I hear he was up on the high water. But that still won't give me my boat to work in right away. What I want now is to rent your old boat till I can do something about my own. That shouldn't be too long, with any luck." He hated asking. The words were stiff and cold, and that wasn't the right approach with Rafe.

"Oh, hell," Rafe said softly. "If this ain't the worst bind. I'd let you have her in a minute, Finn, and no rent but a good coat of paint at the end of the time, only—" Finn didn't want to look at him; he had known the instant Rafe spoke what it would be and how he would look, with the glaze of pity that a five-year-old could see through. *He's all blown up, Finn. Pa's all blown to bits. There's nothing left of him.*

But he had to look anyway, his rage salty and sick in his throat as if in another moment he'd vomit it into Rafe's face. "I've got her up for sale, see, and I've already had a lot of inquiries about her. Two men driving down this week to look at her, and more interested. I have to sell her, Finn. I can't afford to have two of 'em, when I can only work with one." He grinned. "Oh, you know how it is, dammit! I'm not made of money, I can use three thousand right off, fast. So I don't dare let her be out of the harbor when somebody comes, see, Finn?"

"Ayuh, I see." He looked steadily at his brother. "You're feeling real bad about this, I can tell. What do you know about what happened to my boat?"

"*Me?*"

"Forget it." With an effort Finn kept from slapping him aside, and went past him and down to the float. It was too late to take a look at Cleon's boat; he should have gone ashore there in the morning, the first thing. A day's work with wood putty, sandpaper, and paint would take care of any fresh scars around the bow. What are they trying to do to me, the cry went up in his head as he went down the ramp. They trying to break me down to nothing and drive me away? What do they hate me for? I never hated them! I never hated anybody!

He saw nothing as he untied his skiff and stepped in. Cleon's voice was as unexpected as a slap. He was sitting in his skiff on the other side of the float, holding onto a line.

"You look like you just heard bad news. Dolly all right? Helen ain't up and had another spell, has she?"

"No," said Finn. "None of that. But I've had bad news, all right." His words and Cleon's didn't seem to come from their mouths, they were floating around disconnected and without meaning. The sun was shining on the boats and the island trees, but it was a queer glare with neither warmth nor color.

"What kind of bad news? Hey, what happened to your boat? If I was you I'd fall on that Morry like—" He stopped as Finn rowed away, and then called after him, "Look, that offer still stands. Rafe isn't in it, if that's what you're scared of. Hey, wait! Do you want me to tell the whole harbor?"

"Go ahead," said Finn. "Blat your guts out all over the place. But don't speak to me again. Ever. That clear?" He rowed away. He saw Cleon holding his skiff motionless, growing smaller and smaller, staring after him, and he knew that if he saw his brother suddenly keel over dead in the skiff he wouldn't feel anything at all.

·28·

Writing to Mrs. Carradine had always been difficult. Now it looked to be impossible. To ignore her pleas and fill the letter with inconsequentials—and anything that didn't bear directly on David was inconsequential—would be brutal. To say that she felt as well as Robert said she looked would make her sound heartless. To defend Robert wouldn't help him, but would only drive his mother to find more fault with him. Then there was the aura around the letter itself. It was enough to make her shudder; it had surrounded her with an invisible wall filled with clammy silence through which the sun could not strike. She had to admit the truth, that each day away from Mrs. Carradine's house of mourn-ing made her dread all the more the return. David was lost to her there, but not here. Then conscience began harrying her, waking her in the night, and she questioned herself in the dark, Am I running away from that life like a fugitive, with relief stronger than guilt?

Yet she had to respond to Mrs. Carradine's anguished cry, and one afternoon she took paper and pen outside. Aunt Mag and Mrs. Gil were sorting a trunkful of linens, and Nancy had gone to the harbor to play. Claire sat on the doorstep that faced the carriage house, and while she tried to think what to write she watched the swallows go in and out of the loft window. Today there was the nervous and imperious communication between two fish hawks who swung through the sky in great unhurried arcs.

Mrs. Carradine used to like antiques, so Claire tried describing some of Aunt Mag's things. It was hard to sound natural, and she kept looking off, trying to plan her sentences. Finn came around the bend in the road. He was walking slowly, his head down; there was something odd about him, and a shiver passed over her. Without thinking she put down her paper and went to meet him. He looked at her with slow recognition.

"I didn't mean to come here. I must have done it without think-ing." He looked ten years older than he had the day before. "Gorry, I'm some absent-minded!"

"Finn, are you all right? Are you sick?" Her heart was jump-ing against her chest wall. She wanted to take hold of him and shake him into answering quickly.

He pushed back his cap and scratched his head. "I guess not."

"But it's something. You came here for a reason." She glanced around. There were only Mag and Mrs. Gil to look out at them, but she had an instinct to protect him from view. "Let's go into the carriage house," she said. He pushed the door ajar and they went inside. She sat down on the gunnel of one of the big dories, and put out her hand. He took it without looking at it, and she pulled gently. "Sit down beside me." He obeyed, still holding her hand as if he'd forgotten he had it, and gazing at the floor be-tween his feet.

"Now tell me," Claire said.

"My boat was rammed in the night. She filled right there at

the mooring. Cleon did it, and Rafe knows it. He won't let me use his old boat." He spread her hand out on his knee, carefully separating the fingers as if they were pebbles he was playing with. They both watched. "It's not the boat," he said thoughtfully. "Not *now*. That's what it was all day. It means we don't go seining, but we'll live. It's what just hit me." He gave her a sidewise flick of a smile. "Knocked out what sense I've got left, I guess. Look how I came to be on this road, not remembering how I got here."

"You wanted to talk to somebody, that's all," she assured him. "That's why you came straight along without thinking. Finn, if it isn't losing the boat, what is it?"

"All along I thought they wanted to team me around because I was the youngest and they were trying to boot me into showing some ambition instead of lallygagging along having a good time. I always irked Rafe by acting like such a numbhead, I knew that; and Cleon, he's got this picture of himself as a patriarch, and I'm all he's got to be a patriarch over. You see?" He picked up her hand again and kneaded it in his. "But it's nothing so simple, and damned if it hasn't shot everything out of focus. They hate me. I'm not saying that for pity," he explained. "I don't pity myself. I don't feel like a cat thrown into a snowdrift on a winter night. But there's a hell of a lot of difference between knowing you irk somebody and knowing they hate you. I mean you *feel* it!" He was incredulous. "You row down the harbor—you look in their direction, at their houses, at their boats—and it's there like a rotten stench, and it goes home with you and gets into your food and your book and your bed. And you wonder all the time, *Why?* Is it just because you were born in the first place?"

"That may be it," she said. "It wouldn't be so strange. Maybe they were all jealous of you. But—*hate*, Finn?"

"If you've never felt it coming at you, you're lucky." They sat quietly. The partly opened door let in a long blade of yellow light through which dust and small insects circled. Overhead there was the constant rush and flutter of wings and the tireless chattering. Finn's shoulders sagged forward as he stared at the floor. She wished she could put her hand on the back of his neck and knead the aching muscles there; it would be a gesture more to comfort herself than him. After a few minutes he turned his head and gave her a faint grin. "Gorry, I'd ought to give you your hand back, what there is left of it."

"That's all right. If it was any help you could have wrung it to shreds."

"I guess I should apologize for coming up here like this. It's not your affair, the crazy goings-on in the Judson family."

"I'm your friend, I hope, and sometimes the best thing a friend can do is just listen, and never mention it afterwards."

"Then I owe you a listen. Don't forget to take me up on it."

"I'll hold you to that," she said solemnly. "Look, you never mentioned Roy, and I know you do get along pretty well with him."

"Roy's different. He was too busy to pay me much notice when I was little, and then he went into the service before I was six. He got married right after the war, and when a man's got kids of his own he's too busy scratching for a living to wish his kid brother'd never been born."

"Well, then, you've still got Roy," Claire said, "and Helen too; she should count as real family by now, don't you think? Mrs. Gil told me she was home."

"Oh, gorry, yes." He smiled at that. "She's family all right."

"What are you going to do for a boat? Can *Foam-Flower* be repaired?"

"I doubt it." He was looking at the floor again. "That's the way they planned it. Cleon was right on hand to offer me a chance at a new boat. I was supposed to fall flat and moan with gratitude, and that's where I'm meant to stay. With his foot on my neck. They'll finish up what they've started with Larry and Elmer—or at least they'll try it—and when I've got no friends, no boat in my own name, no future, then maybe they'll stop hating me. You think I ought to help 'em save their immortal souls by giving in?"

"*No!*" she snapped, and they both laughed. Life came back into his skin and eyes. She felt a profound pride in her accomplishment. "Finn, why don't you ask Roy to sign a note for you, or to lend you the money outright for a new boat?"

For a minute he was blank, and she wondered how he would

take the suggestion. Then he said, "I never thought of Roy. I've never thought of ever asking anybody for help, to tell the truth. I—I'm kind of rigid that way."

"I know you are. But now, when you don't know which way to turn, it wouldn't be any disgrace to ask him, would it? He knows you've never expected any help before."

He tipped his head back as if he were listening to the swallows overhead. "He might do it. In fact, he probably would. Helen's so well, he's feeling real keen these days, and I never did ask him for anything.... It's just the *asking* that's hard."

"Is it so hard when you think of the alternatives?" she said.

He slapped his hands on his thighs and stood up. "All right then. Will you go with me?"

"For moral support? Your own brother?"

It was the smile she remembered from the first meeting, benign and ageless. "Just to show him I know how to choose good companions. Besides, Helen wants me to bring you to call."

"I haven't the face to refuse after all this inspirational talk I've been giving you. When do you want to go?"

"Well, today they went over to Putnam when Roy came in from hauling, to see an old aunt of Helen's. Let's go over tomorrow night after supper, make an evening call of it."

"I'd like that." She looked ahead as to a refuge that was in sight but still a painful distance away. She saw herself walking with Finn through the early evening light, leaving Nancy settled in her big bed and going to sleep to the cries of the far-off gulls; both of them safe, as long as she didn't think of Mrs. Carradine.

"Now, what's on *your* mind?" Finn was standing over her.

"Man's inhumanity to man," she answered lightly. She got up. "I wonder how much is intentional and how much comes from wanting something so much yourself that you can't even *see* anyone else except as an obstacle."

"I used to try to figure it out." Finn opened the door to the brilliant light. "It made life easier. If I couldn't see any sense in what somebody did, I just said, Well, that's life, or That's the way he is, and I walked away from it." He sounded neither bitter nor shaken now. "Know what? I'm going home and sleep now. All of a sudden I can hardly keep my eyes open."

"So he's taking you to call on Roy and Helen, is he?" Mag couldn't contain her delight. "You know what that looks like? It looks like you're walking out with him."

"Can't people be friends without courting?" She glanced out to be sure Nancy was still in the swing. "Look, Finn likes me because he's pretty sure I don't have any designs on him, and that's why I like him."

"You sure?" Mag said.

"You're disappointed."

"No, I'm not." Her eyes glittered with gleeful mischief. "I saw you two come out of the carriage house yesterday, and I saw the way he looked at you before he set off down the road, and the way you looked after him. Now let's go down cellar and get some of my wild strawberry jam for Helen Judson."

"Aunt Mag," Claire began, called upon to protest even though she knew it was useless. But Mag was already halfway down the cellar stairs talking very fast. "It won't be Mrs. Rafe who'll pick the strawberries this year," she said venomously. "She laces too tight to give herself that bust she's always pushing in everybody's face. Cleon's wife knows how to work, the way she was brought up, but she's thinking about more than picking berries these days, I hear." Her chuckle floated ghostly back to Claire. "I listened in on the telephone the other day. I dunno why some folks are so tarnation stupid and trusting."

Claire half-heard her; all day her mind had swung between Finn, his brothers' vendetta against him, and the inescapable atmosphere that had surrounded her and Finn as they sat on the gunnel of the dory in the carriage house; and there was nowhere to go from this unless it was to Mrs. Carradine. It made her uneasy, and she felt unreal, not herself, down in the cobwebby cellar among the dusty jars, with Mag muttering to herself like a witch making incantations.

"Mama, Finn's here!" Nancy shouted from upstairs.

She jumped and Mag said dryly, "Go on up, just don't break a leg on the way."

Claire had walked up the lane to Roy's and Cleon's from the black road when she was working on the cancer drive; but there had been traces of snow under the spruces and the puddles had been skimmed with ice. It felt so long ago that it could have been midwinter. The weeks seemed to have stretched into half a lifetime. Now the dooryards were green, the old fruit trees were in leaf and bud, and robins sang from them with loud and cheerful monotony. Cleon's barn doors were open and the car gone; a cat sat washing her face on the sill. Roy's dog got up from his back doorstep, with enthusiasm for Finn and a friendly curiosity for Claire. He was a big broad-headed shaggy animal like a Currier and Ives farm dog. "Nancy must meet him," she said, "their eyes are exactly the same color."

Finn opened the screen door and bowed Claire in. "Oh, thank you, sir," she said, feeling light-hearted. She looked expectantly around the big kitchen. No one was in it and for a moment there was no sound anywhere. Then there was a thump of feet and a deep mutter from another room, a broken-off exclamation. Someone ran up the front stairs, a door slammed, and a vibrating silence followed.

Claire's impulse was to leave. She turned to the door, but Finn was in the way. Without appearing to see her he put out his arm and held her back, and she thought, He doesn't want to be left alone with it, whatever it is; she waited, quiescent, almost against his chest.

There were light steps, and a thin red-headed woman appeared in the doorway from the hall. She stood there looking at them with a cool bright expression, her hands in the pockets of her tailored cotton dress. Or rather she *seemed* to look at them. Claire wondered if she really saw them.

"Helen, what's the matter?" Finn's voice had a dry scrape.

"I'd better go," Claire said. Helen shook her head, and the corners of her long mouth tilted upward.

"No need. You might as well get it direct. You're Claire Carradine, and I'm glad to meet you. I didn't plan on the—the surrounding circumstances."

Roy appeared behind her and said heavily, "Are you going to take one of those pills or aren't you?"

"No, I am not," she said. "I don't need one. Roy, I don't intend to go to pieces." Her composure had an odd lustre about it, as if she herself had burnished it. "Danny's *alive*, Roy. He's upstairs right now. Nobody came in here tonight to tell us they'd found his body. Now do you see why I don't need a pill?"

Roy came by her into the kitchen and Claire's stomach contracted at sight of his face. Ignoring her, he said to Finn, "Did you know about this girl over in Port George?"

Finn's head jerked slightly, as if he had been slapped. "What girl?"

"Her father called up tonight and says in a couple weeks they'll know if she's in the family way, and if she is, watch out."

"Oh, my God," said Finn. He dropped into a chair. "My God. Now listen, Roy, it can't—when did Danny ever have a *chance*, for Peter's sake?" He began to sound mad. "She's naming him because he's a decent kid whose folks are pretty well off. Somebody's put her up to it. Maybe her old man." He appealed to Helen. "You've got a lot to find out before you take this for gospel! What's Danny say?"

Roy sat down at the table and put his head in his hands. "Danny doesn't remember," Helen said quietly. She began to measure coffee into the pot. "Danny was drunk for the first time in his life. He remembers one girl more than the rest, but that's all. He doesn't even know how he got home."

"It was the Saturday I stayed up in Augusta all night," Roy said, gazing at the table. "Blast him, I can't find out anything. He swears he took the pick-up and went alone, but I'll be damned if he took himself around there, walked into a dance, and picked up a girl. And where'd he get the liquor? Somebody had to give it to him. When I find out who, I'll break his neck. Danny's first, though." He drew a long shuddering sigh. "Take him by the hand to a cliff and he don't know no better than to jump. He's that stupid. To hell with school, college, his mother, his brother, everything. *Valedictorian!* That lasted quick, didn't it? Wait till they hear the news up there!"

"You really don't want us here," Claire said to Helen. "If there was anything I could do by staying, I would, but—"

"Yes, get out," growled Roy. "No, I'm not saying it to be cussid. I mean for Finn to get out, for his own good, away from the Point. What they did to your boat was just a sample. . . . Sure, I heard Cleon bringing his boat ashore at high water, four in the morning, and he was working on her bow at daylight. They'll ride you till they kill you or drive you out of your mind. I'm getting it now because I laughed at Rafe's big ideas and wouldn't turn the field over to him. I know damn' well I'm getting it." He turned to Claire. "Make him forget that damned island. And you go too. They hate you now because they think you're making him stand up to them."

"Roy, Roy!" Helen cried softly. She stood behind him and put her hands on either side of his head.

"Can't you see it? They're trying to drive you back!"

"They can't," she said. "Nobody can, ever again." Claire turned and went out. Finn could come or not, as he pleased, but she had to get away. Her blurred sight confused her and she stood still outside the door, the dog companionably near her. Then the screen door slammed and Finn put his arm around her and walked her away from the house. She felt his hand splayed wide and hard over her ribs, its warmth going through her clothes, but nothing could alleviate the appalling loneliness that had over-taken her.

Finn stopped, holding her against his chest like a hostage, and a flashlight came toward them, bouncing to the rhythm of a man's stride. *"Finn?"* They could hear Cleon's loud breathing. "I heard it on the telephone tonight when I was trying to get the line. Listen, that bastard Rafe took him to the dance. I never knew about it till the next day, and he was laughing to himself fit to bust, about how comical the kid was with a few drinks in." His breath rattled alarmingly. "I was some disgusted, dirty way to get even with Roy, I thought. I never knew anything more about it till I heard that slimy bas—"

"Nobody's blaming you," said Finn.

"Christ, I know it, but . . . how's Helen?"

"Better than you are, believe it or not."

"That blasted Rafe. I'm through doing his dirty work for him. He's a nut, you know that? He thinks he's Castro. He'll be growing a beard next and carrying a revolver."

"Go back and mix yourself a good drink," said Finn. "Where's Onni?"

"I dunno. At her sister's, I guess." He didn't move. "Finn, I meant it about the boat. No strings at all. The old one wouldn't have lasted through a season of seining anyway."

"Good night," said Finn. They walked away and left Cleon there. When they reached the black road Claire said, "I think I could do better if you weren't squeezing my ribs."

"Sorry. That's what comes of letting your angry passions rise, as the feller says." He released her. "But you'd better take my arm. We're already compromised."

It could have been the middle of the night instead of just past dusk. The only sound beside their footfalls on the macadam was a quick furtive rustle in the underbrush and two owls hooting antiphonally from the spruce woods. The stars were thick, and the air was aromatic with earth and saltwater scents. She was glad of its coolness on her face. "You were awfully short with Cleon," she said. "He was really upset."

"It's good for him," said Finn cynically. "Though I dunno as I'd choose this way to shake him up. Hard on Roy and Helen."

"What do you think about this whole thing?"

"You've heard as much about it as I have. They don't have to let Danny marry the girl. I'm going to talk to them some more about it, if Helen ever gets Roy calmed down."

"She was wonderful. I hope it wasn't just a superhuman effort on her part to keep from breaking down."

"I don't guess so. Remember what she said? *Danny's alive.*" They reached Mag's mailbox, and the house was dark with silence and sleep. "You don't want to go in yet, do you?" he whispered. "You've never walked around the shore at night. The water's firing too. You haven't seen that." A little wind moved through the dark like a presence and was gone. The call of the owls, hollow and resonant, was infinitely mysterious. "Come on," Finn was whispering. His arm urged gently. "Come on."

She didn't answer, but began walking again. When they had

gone around the bend in the road away from the house she suddenly felt free and light. The road glimmered before them, and green and flowery scents rose from the verge. There was an intoxicating sense of being alone in a kindly world. The skiff floated pale by the steps of the wharf, and though the sea moved gently on the shore it made no sound.

The oar blades were rimmed in light, and liquid light dripped from them when Finn lifted them in the water. When he dipped them again luminous bubbles streamed up from their submerged and ghostly shapes. Pale fire rippled along the sides of the skiff and the wake gave off a greenish glow. Claire trailed her hand and lifted it to watch the bright drops run off.

On her first trip across to the island, the stream had been broad and blue, flowing on to a hazy distance, holding the promise of dreams. Tonight there was nothing to see but the black shapes of land and trees against the star-stippled sky; under the boat, moving stars of their own making, and the faint gleam of Finn's face if she looked up from light-scattering fingers.

At his wharf he shipped the oars and they drifted on the black water, watching for the shimmer of little fish. Once she wondered if they had been talking or not; she couldn't remember. She thought she had made some observation and he had answered, but she couldn't recall hearing their voices. Finally he said, "We've drifted halfway up the Gut. We'll be stranded on the mussel beds next." He stood up and poled the skiff back through a narrowing channel streaked with scurrying or darting things wearing jewels.

On the island they walked across the neck and onto the broad shelves of rock of the big cove. The serpentine folds of white in the ledges glowed up under their feet, as if with a peculiar light of their own. The water was barely whispering on the sand bar, but there was another sound if you held your breath, an infinitesimal scrabbling and hurrying. "What is it?" she said.

"Hermit crabs."

There was an agonized shriek and a convulsive flapping of wings almost under their feet. Claire's start was frantic and her cry involuntary; something was being hurt, preyed upon, caught, killed. And she wished she had not come. She should have obeyed that premonition of loneliness, for out here in the dark there was in microcosm the whole vicious scheme that terrified her, mystified Finn, tormented his brother Roy—

"Hey, where are you going?" Finn barred her way, laughing. "That was only a night heron taking off."

"No, something was caught in the dark—"

"I tell you it was just a night heron. He was fishing down there on the bar and we bothered him. He's over across the cove by now, likely fishing right below the house." He held her by the shoulders, shaking her gently. "Don't you believe me?" he said close to her ear. "Won't you take my word for it? Don't run. There's nothing to run from here." She was in his arms and she thought dazedly, He's very experienced. It had been a long time since she had been held and comforted, and she felt a guilty joy. She wanted to laugh out loud, but she was crying. Finn rubbed his cheek against her hair, holding her as if he would absorb her into him. "Claire," he was saying in a shaky whisper. "*Claire.*"

She put her hands on his face and held it away from her, and the intimacy of the warm taut flesh and hard bone under her palm sent a pang of tenderness through her. For the moment he was quiescent in her hands, humble and waiting. She saw the glint of his eyes and thought, They are blue, and he has a man's mouth, not a boy's. "Finn," she said, and reached up to his mouth.

It was neither a boy's kiss nor a boy's embrace. When they came apart he said as if in astonishment, "I love you."

"I'm afraid to say *love.*" She was sad that she had to say this. Without wanting to sacrifice any of David she wished this could be a first and utterly separate time.

"I know," he said. "It's too soon for you. You were crying, weren't you?"

He reached for her again. This time it was as if she knew his arms well, and the solid breadth of his chest with the terribly mortal pumping of the heart inside it, and in his neck, under her fingers, another priceless pulse.

"It was like the apple tree," she said. "A beauty I didn't expect."

"Come on over here." They sat down on a driftwood log wedged in between the rocks and she settled against him. He put his mouth on her temple, moving in small brushing kisses across her forehead, down onto her cheekbone. I don't know where he learned it, she thought, but it's pretty devastating. The question came from an earlier time; *Is he what he appears to be?* But she was not sure of what he appeared to be; whether he was a skillful boy or a man so deeply honest in his emotion that he could not make a wrong move. But she could be a victim of her own loneliness, her own youth. This was no way to find out. Get up and go home, she told herself, but she didn't move. The life of the sandbar resumed. The star reflections blurred in the black water, and a boat came between the islands from the east, or rather a phantom boat composed only of engine-sound and moving lights. "*Thetis* going somewhere to take out herring," Finn murmured.

"Would you be looking for herring tonight if your boat was all right?"

"I'd probably be stopping off this cove, and you'd be safe."

"Safe from what?"

"From me. But only till I got a chance at you." He took her jaw in his hand and turned her face to his. "I'm going to marry you, Claire. You don't have to agree, you don't even have to think about it yet. I'm just telling you what's going to happen."

"You're awfully sure of yourself."

"I am." He kissed her as if affixing a seal. "Claire, I *know*."

She leaned back from him, impelled to bring a breath of reality between them, however cold; it was for her own salvation more than his. "Finn, you know how it is for you, at least you think you know. It's fairly simple for you, but it isn't for me. I have to know why I—why I want to be where I am right now." She wished she could tell by his face whether or not he was listening to her or merely letting her talk until he kissed her again. As she struggled for the right words, there was a sharp coughing sound behind them, a drumming of feet and a wild thrashing in the bushes at the edge of the woods. She jumped and Finn pulled her against his chest. He was laughing again. "A deer came out and took one horrified look and beat it."

She squirmed free and said indignantly, "Finn, do you have these creatures *trained* to catapult girls into your arms?"

"I never told it before, but that's the true secret of my charm, you might say."

"I think I'd better go home." She stood up. She was cold

away from him, and depressed. "I have to think." She began to walk away from the log, and he came after her, taking her arm; their fingers linked naturally together. The warmth of his palm against hers and the grip of his fingers gave her a strong new sensation of joy. She allowed herself to enjoy it for a little while, until they reached the wharf and would have to break apart anyway. The tide was at its lowest and he brought the skiff in to the rocks and showed her the easy way down. When they reached the boat she said, "Finn, do you want something definite from me within a certain time?"

"No," he said. "You have to be as sure as I am, or else it's no damn good. Sweetheart, I can wait. But it won't be long. You'll see."

"Are you the patient waiter who's no loser?" She tried to laugh. "Finn, why are you so—so—"

"So what, darlin' mine?'

"If I say *good* you might be insulted."

"That depends on how you mean it," he said with a grin.

They didn't speak, rowing across; she watched the firing of the water, and the stars moving by the spruce peaks. They went up the road in silence, holding hands. At the shed door he took her by the shoulders and kissed her, went in through the shed with her and kissed her again outside the kitchen door. "Good night," he whispered. "Sweet dreams."

She laid her hand on his cheek as if to prolong the instant, and he took it and put it against his lips. Again she felt the strong wave of joy, and she knew it could drown her. She whispered quickly, "Good night," and went into the house.

Nancy and Mag slept the dream-filled sleep of the young and the aged, but Claire did not expect to sleep at all. In her robe she sat by the window brushing her hair. It seemed as if it had been night for a very long time.... If you looked out at a certain angle, you could see the roof and easterly gable of the house on the island, at least in moonlight or daylight. She gazed now toward the place where it was, feeling at once a straining eagerness for morning and a reluctance to see the night pass. Suddenly she saw a spark of light quite high up and knew that Finn must have passed an upstairs window with a lamp. She stopped brushing then, and went across the room to her bed.

And then the doubts began, bringing chills and rousing her to a sore wakefulness. She was astonished and dismayed because of what had happened and even now remembered Finn's embrace with a painful delight. David, David, she cried to him, is it missing you that did it to me? Or is Finn really—really—she knew what she meant but could not bring herself to put it into words. She lay shaking under extra bedclothes that couldn't warm her. No, David is still the one, she tried to convince herself. He has to be. It's missing him, that's all. I have to be careful.

·30·

When Finn woke up in the morning his first desire was to go straight across the harbor and see Claire. He knew he would not; she'd think he was a crazy galoot for sure. He lay in bed listening to the gulls over the cove and wondering how it would be to wake in this room with her. He could still remember the texture of her hair, the scent of her skin, the whole feel of her against him. When he began imagining her in this bed with him, lying on his arm with nothing between them, he thought he had better get up and go to work. He was in love, he was overboard, sunk, lost; and he had nothing to offer her. Last night it hadn't mattered, this morning he was shaken up by it.

And there was Nancy. From the playboy of Saltberry Point to a father in one magic step. He ran his hand frantically through his hair. Kids wore out a pair of shoes a month sometimes, and he had no boat, no property, no credit. Claire couldn't possibly be fool enough to want to marry him. Right now she was probably figuring out a way to let him down easy. Maybe she wouldn't say anything. She'd just pack up Nancy and go, today.

Sweat broke out on his forehead and his hand shook so that he spilled his coffee as he poured it. He wanted to go to her at once and promise her he would be able to buy Nancy all the shoes she needed; he would be the best father he knew how to be. He would be everything if only she wouldn't go. Oh, God, was life ever simple? Hadn't it been once, back when the snow was beginning to go and he rode with the wind from day to day, sparing himself grief and doubt, laughing at what he couldn't fathom instead of fighting it?

He got quickly out of the house and rowed across the harbor to the boys' wharf. They weren't there; while they were waiting to see what the score was they'd set a halibut trawl and had already gone to tend it. He went up into Gil's store and called Waisanen.

"Too bad," said the Finn. "If I had another boat I'd let you have it. You got nothing there at all you can use?"

"Nope, the others boys' boats are too small. No room in 'em at all for what we'd need."

"Well, that feller I asked you to take with you, he can get a crew up, he says."

"Good luck to him," Finn said heavily. "And thanks for offering us the chance, Mr. Waisanen."

"That's all right. I'm sorry you had bad luck. You come to me again."

"I will," Finn promised. "And thanks for that too."

He felt like a low-life going to hit Roy up about the boat, the way things were down there. But he had to live, and he had to make a living. *Jesus!* he thought, and it was a prayer, an entreaty. *Help me!* Claire was at once a fiery pain in him and a sweetness he almost couldn't stand.

Cleon and Rafe had gone out, but Roy's boat was still on the mooring. Up at the house he and Helen were sitting at the kitchen table; Roy didn't look up or speak. Helen had blue shadows under her eyes, but she smiled and said, "Hello, Brother!"

Finn took a cup of coffee to the table and sat down. "Where's Danny?"

"Off on the bus this morning with his books as if nothing's happened," Roy said. "He's either foolish or so damn' brazen it scares me."

"*He's* scared," said Helen. "I sent him to school. If any girl shows up with a claim, and she can prove it, she can wait at least till he graduates."

"Well, I'd do a lot of investigating before I signed anything," Finn said to Roy, or rather to the top of Roy's head. Roy wouldn't look at him. "When it comes to that, you don't have to sign him off anyway."

"I'm not going to. I've made up my mind." Roy lifted his head. The lines were seamed deep in his cheeks, and his voice was slow and hoarse with fatigue. "Anybody shows up here, let 'em whistle, or find somebody else to palm their daughter off on. Danny's going to walk the straight and narrow this summer, and he's going to college this fall, and he's going to stay in college, and then by God he'll get a job that'll take him so far away he'll forget what salt water smells like." He shoved his cup away, and Helen reached out and steadied it. "Know what he said to me last night? He says, 'If I did anything wrong, I'll marry her and go lobstering.'" Just like that. He's telling *us* what he's going to do, not us telling him. We can all go to hell."

"Roy, Danny was just trying to think of a way out," Helen said. "A manly way."

Roy pushed savagely away from the table, said something under his breath, and went out. Helen looked after him with wet glistening eyes. "My poor Roy," she murmured.

"I wanted to talk to him about something else this morning if he can stand to listen," Finn said uncomfortably. "He'll likely think I'm a hard-hearted character to bring it up, but I'm caught in a cleft stick myself, with my boat."

"After all, life goes on," Helen said. "Our life is going on too, though Roy's having a hard time believing it. Finn, Danny's *alive*! He's right up there in Williston High, and he'll be home this afternoon if the bus doesn't plunge into the river or explode. I want him away from here, I still don't want him to be a fisherman, but if he turns out to be one I don't think I'm going back to Augusta because of it." She looked out past Finn at the diamond sparkle of the harbor. "I was homesick for this view before I came home. Can you imagine it, after I kept the curtains drawn on the water side all the time? Roy asked me if I wanted us to move away, so I'd come back to a different house altogether, out of sight of the water. That's what I used to say I wanted, remember?" Finn nodded. "But how could I take him away from what he *is*? He belongs here, as much as a gull does.

If I dragged him away I'd be battening on his life like a female spider eating her mate. So—" She smiled at Finn. "We're here, and we're staying."

"The violets are coming along the path," he said.

"Are they?" The curious effect of light leaped up in her eyes. "I'll have to go out and see them. Finn, what did that poor girl think last night? She had such stricken eyes. I'll bet she's ready to leave the Point right now."

"Oh, gorry, I hope not!" It burst out.

"It's that way, is it?"

"I want to marry her," he said. "But I don't want anybody else to get their greasy paws on the fact. Besides, she's not sure yet. I am, but she isn't."

"I won't tell." She put her hands on his shoulders and kissed him. "I want you to be happy, Finn. You were always a happy little kid and I want you to be a happy man."

He felt choked with embarrassment and emotion. "And you know how I feel about you—gorry, sounds like we're getting ready to elope." He had the satisfaction of hearing her laugh as he went out.

Roy was coppering the bottom of a skiff set up on two saw-horses at the head of the wharf. It was Helen's own.

He glared at Finn. "What you doing down here? She shouldn't be alone." He started to put away his brush, and Finn said, "Oh, for Pete's sake, relax. She's a lot more able to be alone than you are. In fact she's more worried about you than she is about Danny right now."

Roy's tired eyes watered. "She's pretty good, you know that . . . I could kick that kid from here to Portland."

"I wouldn't mind handing him a few myself. Look here, no sense of beating around the bush, will you sign a note for me at the bank so I can get a boat?"

Roy straightened up and stared at him. "You die hard, don't ye? You want another boat out there for them to sink? You think you can stop off the big cove and have Rafe keep hands off? How long do you think you can hang on to Larry and Elmer? You want to spend the rest of your life fighting and *losing*?"

"I'll have to fight, sure, but I don't plan on losing."

"You're some smug," said Roy. "You think you can go on forever without getting your ears knocked off. This girl—"

"She's got nothing to do with it."

"That a fact?" Roy showed a gleam of wintry humor. "Well, take any girl you might want to marry. What kind of a life is it for her, you being the family punching bag? Listen, I'll help you get a new boat on one condition. That you get out of this place. Up the coast, down the coast, out on an island—somewhere away from here."

"Thanks, Roy," Finn said without sarcasm. "I know you mean well. But this is my home and I'm staying."

"All right, Roy said with finality. He went back to painting. "Call me a son of a bitch if you want to."

"Oh, hell, come off it. I'm not mad with you. You got enough on your mind."

"You look like I'd handed you one under the ribs."

"You look pretty peaked yourself. Well, I'll go back and get Elmer's dory and set out a few traps and see if I can make a dollar." He saw Helen coming down through the field. She was stopping to look at the violets.

"You can take my boat to set pots with," Roy said gruffly.

"Thanks! I'll get going before you decide it's against your principles." He waved at Helen and went down the wharf.

Roy's boat was big and beautiful under him, and as he went down the harbor to the island wharf he was divided between pure delight and ugly frustration. He was happy to have the use of her, just as he couldn't think of last night without happiness, but the thought of not possessing either Claire or a boat like this, after the smallest, most tormenting taste, darkened and embittered him. At the fishhouse he worked in stormy haste, loading traps onto the boat and then taking her out to his mooring before she could go aground at the foot of the ladder while he was baiting up. *Foam-Flower* lay keeled over under the fresh green alders; from this side you couldn't see the canvas patching. They'd have to hoist the engine out onto Gil's wharf at high water tonight. They had already taken out the radio telephone and put it in the boys' fishhouse.

He had a bad feeling about hauling the boat up somewhere

to die, and decided to knock her apart, saving everything he could use and burning the rest. From the time he was small, he had always seen something tragic in a boat rotting away on the bank.

Back at the fishhouse he baited up, and went to the house and made a lunch. Then he put his bait in the skiff and rowed across to Abbott's wharf.

Mag was kneeling by her flowerbeds, and Claire was hanging out sheets on lines strung between the house and the apple trees. She looked beautiful to him with her bare arms upraised, the wind blowing her dress against her hips and legs. He wanted to grab her then and there and bend her back in his arms, like one of those movie swashbucklers, and kiss her until she started fighting or stopped, depending on her mood. He could imagine Mag's shrieks, and his mouth twitched. He began to walk softly toward the clotheslines, and Mag saw him. "Land of love, you're stalking that girl like Gil's cat after a sparrow," she said.

"Ayuh, and I figger on eating her too."

"You ever hear about that feller was so much in love with this girl he could eat her, and after they'd been married a year he wished he had?"

"Oh, you two," said Claire. "I don't know who's worse."

"We're two of a kind," said Mag proudly. "Like calls to like, and the years between don't make any difference. If I was younger, girl, and that boy was standing there, he wouldn't be safe, I can tell you that."

"Gorry, Mag, why wasn't I born a lot sooner? Now I got to content myself with the younger generation. Claire, come on out with me while I set some traps. I've got Roy's boat."

"I think you'd better take Aunt Mag," said Claire. Her expression changed to one that locked him out. It was as if they had just met and he'd made an improper remark. He felt the exclusion like a dull blow in his chest. "No, I should finish this washing."

"Well," he said, clearing his throat and all at once not knowing what to do with his hands. They felt big as dogfish and brutally clumsy. He shoved them into his pockets.

"Thank you anyway," she added with a proper little smile.

"Oh, that's all right." He watched her pin a sheet, and tried to

imagine her in his arms; he knew, with that dull pain still in his
chest, that it wouldn't happen again. She'd taken a good look at
things in the light of day and had seen him for what he was,
a long-legged gandygut ignorant as sin and poor as Job's turkey.
To remember that he'd even dreamed of marrying her made him
burn with shame for his foolishness.

He spun around quickly and started away, wanting to get
out of her sight as far as possible. But he wasn't going to
be chopped off like a dead tree limb. Be damned if he would.
She'd have to say it right out; he'd force her to it. He turned and
went back.

"Can I see you tonight?" he asked gruffly.

She gave him a preoccupied nod, staring at him as if she'd
never seen him before. He nodded, and went away again.

·31·

Setting his traps he saw Rafe in the distance, and once passed
near Cleon. He pretended he didn't see him. When he headed
home it was early afternoon, and he decided to gas up and
take out another load to set. Once they were all overboard and
soaking, he could use Elmer's dory again and make a few dollars
while he tried to figure out what to do next with his life.

On the way home after setting the second load he saw a
strange boat in the big cove, not working but lying a little
way off the beach below the house. A skiff was pulled up
on the shingle. The boat was Nova-built and a stranger, yet
there was something about her that jogged his memory, and
kept jogging it all the way down the easterly side of the island
and around into the harbor. He had seen that boat somewhere;
she could have been tied up in Port George or Pruitt's Harbor,
or even in Limerock. He wasn't disturbed because a stranger had
gone ashore on the island, the sight of Rafe's or Cleon's skiff on
the beach would have riled him more. But right now nothing

much mattered. He was down as far as he could go, between losing *Foam-Flower* and knowing what he did about Claire. It seemed impossible that he had ever been happy in his life, that he hadn't always been moving and working in this kind of swamp mud that sucked and dragged at his heels.

He stopped at Gil's to ask him about using the hoist to take the engine out, and then at Elmer's to see if they'd got a halibut. Larry told him he'd set Dolly across about an hour ago.

He had forgotten the boat in the big cove, until he saw it again. When he reached the house, some of the porch windows were open and Dolly was talking. " . . . and of course when my husband was killed, there I was left with three young ones. The oldest boy was a man grown, he'd been in the service, too. In the Marines." Dolly had a new audience, male by the way she was sounding off, and who the devil could he be and what did he want? To buy some wharf logs, or get permission to put a weir out front?

"Here comes my youngest boy now," Dolly sang out in ear-splitting pride. "Image of my husband!"

Finn walked into the porch. The man who sat at the table drinking coffee with Dolly was slim and fox-colored. He searched Finn's face with narrowed eyes and said with deceptive mildness, "Ayuh, I met this one."

"Hello, Mr. Gardner. How are you?" He touched his mother's shoulder. "Don't have to ask how *you* are."

"No, your grandpa and your father always agreed anybody could tell about me by the strength of my lungs. If I couldn't make myself heard across the harbor in a southerly, I was a sick girl. Get yourself a mug-up, honey, and bring it out here. I want to talk to you."

He obeyed and sat down sideways to the table, his legs sprawled toward the open door. "Where'd you finally light, Mr. Gardner?"

"Oh, I'm still out at Ballard's. Nobody gunned me down yet or burned a fiery cross in my dooryard. But I still want to get onto the mainland, in just the right place, you understand. I need room for the kids, and for myself to do a little salt-water farming on the side." He ducked his head at Dolly. "So that's what washed me up on the doorstep here this afternoon."

"He wants to buy the island, Finn." You had to hand it to Dolly. She didn't blink. "He's offering fifteen thousand."

"Gorry," said Finn. If it didn't sound loud or impressed, it was because he didn't have much wind to do with.

"I'm not going to talk it over with the others," she said emphatically. "I'm leaving it all up to you, Finn. Maybe Roy hasn't hectored you, but I got no excuses for Rafe and Cleon. If I do sell, you'll get more than the others, enough to settle you anywhere you want to be, and buy you a decent boat besides. They don't need it."

"My gosh, Ma, you shouldn't throw anything like that at a man at the end of a hard day. I haven't got a wit in my head to think with."

"Now look, you don't have to decide now," said Gardner. "Take your time." He was pretty sure of himself, soft-voiced, all but patting them. He thought his fifteen thousand had scunnered them. "Just so I'm sure that if somebody else shows up this next week with the same offer or better, you'll give me first refusal."

"Why, is somebody likely to?" asked Finn. "They discovered a uranium mine on here or something?"

Gardner laughted heartily. "No, but you've got pulpwood and a good place for a weir, and whoever has that controls the lobstering in the cove. You've got cottage lots. You've got just about everything."

"You keep on and we'll be pushing the price up." Dolly slapped him roguishly on the arm. They both howled again. Finn watched them indulgently. Finally Gardner said, "Well, I've got to get moving. My sister over in Port George is expecting me to supper."

They shook hands all around and then he went. Crossing the lawn, he looked about him as if he already owned the place and was assessing the amount of pulpwood tied up in the woods. Nobody spoke until he disappeared down over the beach. Then Dolly said, "I like to shrieked my fool head off when he showed up on the doorstep. I thought I was all alone on the island and was going to have me a bath. That town water is something fierce on my skin." She giggled. "If he'd come five minutes later he'd have seen Venus on the hoof."

"Would you really sell the island, Ma?"

"Well, I'll tell you, Finn. Anybody has to be practical. As long as I have it, it's something for the boys to fight over. They keep chewing at me, and they get mad with you because you're on here, living in the house and all, and they think you've got the inside track." She blew smoke through her nostrils at the porch ceiling. "Well, you have, kind of. But they've done it themselves. I know some of the things been going on." She squinted an eye at him. "So when this one showed up today— say, he's a real ladies' man if I ever saw one, and practically a redhead—well, I thought I'd leave it up to you."

He was whittling lobster plugs from a sliver of pine. "What makes you think I want to leave the Point?"

"I sh'd think you'd want to!"

"Roy thinks so too. You and he must have talked it over."

"Well, he did say you get under their skin awful and they'll never let you be. They're jealous of you, that's all. Plain jealous, and I don't know why. Never did," she said pensively. She sighed, and for an instant her face sagged and aged. She traced a flower on the oilcloth as if she were really tracing something else, unseen to Finn. Then her head bobbled up and she said gaily, "But you could still live at the Point if you wanted to. The boys might sell some of the Abbott property, and Tom Hunt's got that land down at the lower harbor."

And look across at the island when it belongs to somebody else? he asked her in silence. On top of what was goweling him about Claire, it was almost too much. In a minute he'd start either swearing or bawling. "Let me sleep on it, Ma," he said finally. "Don't let's talk about it any more now. Let it mull. I've got to clean up. . . . You staying?"

"I've got till four tomorrow afternoon. This is Dorothy's time off, but she's got a chance to ride to New Hampshire on what would be my time, so I'm taking hers now and working on *mine*. Get it?"

"Nope," said Finn. He kept seeing the faces of the others when they heard she was ready to sell. It would be a damn fine payment for all their actions, and he could go to Claire with a new boat and a pocketful of money besides. That would make all the difference. He was not happy about it, but felt a bleak and wintery calm, like a person who at last submits to amputation in order to save his life.

At sunset Finn and Claire followed the ghostly track of the old ox road down over the point. The land was gold-washed in the afterglow, its new greens fiercely bright, and at the cellar hole of an early Salisbury house purple lilacs were in bud. "When they're out I'll move down here," said Claire. "I'll live in a house of lilacs as long as the flowers last." She was so friendly tonight after this morning's cold that he was weakened.

"Can I live in it with you?" he asked.

"Be my guest!" She laughed and began looking for an open blossom. His heart seemed actually to lunge ahead, and he put his hands on her waist and kissed the back of her neck. She stood quietly; frozen? he wondered. Just waiting for him to take his hands off her? "I want to talk to you about something," he said, louder than he'd intended. It sounded as if he was looking for a fight.

"Shall we keep on walking?" she asked without turning.

"No, I can talk better sitting down." There was enough of the old foundation to lean their backs against, and the short turf was still warm and dry. He put his hand over hers where it lay between them, and she left it there, giving him a bright and encouraging look. As if I was about Nancy's age, he thought bitterly. Going to be nice to me if it kills her.

"Dolly's had a big offer for the island," he said. "From Gardner. Remember him?"

"The man who bought Aunt Mag's place?" she asked incredulously. "He wants to buy the *island*?"

"Yep, and Dolly's left it all up to me."

"You've already said no."

"I said I'd sleep on it."

She stiffened as if she had suddenly found herself holding hands with a stranger. "You *can't* be considering it," she said in awe.

"Why not?" he demanded. "Look, what have I got now? That's what you've been thinking since last night, isn't it? Me talking marriage as if I had something to do with! You'd be the fool of the world to even give me a second look." She started to say something, looking distressed, but he wouldn't give her the chance. "No, you listen. I went to Roy about a boat this morning. Ayuh, he'll help me, on condition I get the hell out of here. And when I got home Dolly and Gardner hit me with this, the way Rafe was going to sock Gil. If the price is big enough you suck wind and then start thinking hard."

Her hand twisted in his, but he wouldn't let it go. The bright encouraging look was gone, she was angry and upset. "*What* have you been thinking hard about? It's not all money, I know that. It's—oh, *damn*, how can I make it clear?" She yanked her hand free and hugged her knees to her. "I can't believe I'm hearing correctly, not after the way I've heard you talk about the island. If you don't love it the way I thought you did, then I'm disappointed in you. That was one of the things that—" She broke off, and put her face down on her knees.

"One of the things that *what*?" he said ferociously. "Go on, say the rest of it. And if it's not money—me being not as well off as one of these sparrows—what else is wrong with me? I'm too young, is that it? No schooling to speak of? A bunch of reprobates for brothers?"

"Finn, it's nothing in you, it's all in me! Believe me, it's *my* ignorance and weakness that scares me, and a kind of poverty in me that doesn't have anything to do with money—" Water glimmered in her eyes. He reached for her and pulled her against his chest, rocking her gently.

"What is it then?" he whispered. "What is it?"

"I don't know." She didn't struggle but lay back looking up at him with the tears running out of the corners of her eyes. He felt a furious happiness at holding her. "I could take care of you, Claire," he said. "You wouldn't have to worry about those things, they'd take care of themselves. I do love the island, and I wouldn't give it up for anybody but you. If it does go I won't stay around here to see it in somebody else's hands. But there's this whole long coast, Claire, and plenty of sightly spots on it that would take your breath away. We don't have to stay here and breathe the same air as Rafe and Hes and Cleon." He hugged her tight to him and chuckled a little, as if now she were the child to be encouraged. "We could leave them here to be sick every time they look across at the island."

She struggled out of his arms and sat up. "I want the truth now, Finn. There's something else at the back of your mind about selling the island, isn't there?"

He told her then, because of them all she was the one who had to have the truth. If he lied now she would come to know it eventually, and despise him more for trying to cover it up than for honestly admitting here and now that he was a mean and vindictive son of a bitch.

"Look," he said. "They wake up one fine day soon, and stretch, and rub their bellies, and go down to the harbor, and the island's gone. I don't mean vanished. But it's gone out of the family and it's never coming back. Somebody else is selling off the pulpwood and the cottage lots, and carting the dollars off to the bank. Somebody else has got a weir in the cove and the right to tell 'em they can't set their traps within so many hundred feet of it—*their* cove, that they've fished all their lives. I'm gone too, so they don't have me to take it out on. And the rest of their days they've got to look across the harbor and know they never got rid of Gardner at all, and they've lost the island and to *him*. Now." He leaned back and folded his arms across his chest and grinned at her. "Don't you think that's one fine, magnificent, superb way to get even? And that faint sound coming on the wind is me laughing my fool head off."

She didn't speak and after a moment he said, "Well?"

She pulled up her knees again and wrapped her arms around them. "Will you be laughing?" she said.

"Wouldn't you be? Can't you see how perfect it is?"

"It's a perfect revenge, yes," she said thoughtfully. "But after you build up to the moment of shock, what then? Look what you've sacrificed to get that marvelous moment."

"It won't be a sacrifice if it gets us started off right, darlin' mine. Do you know what it is for a fisherman not to have a *boat?* And it'll pay for everything else to see them socked back on their heels."

"So you'd use the island that way? An instrument of revenge, that lovely place. Finn, it's not just the pulpwood and the cottage lots, even if the woodcock and the thrushes could go somewhere else. But it's your life up to now. It's twenty-four years of you. It's like your hands and feet." She moved closer to him, her hand pressing on his arm. "Look, if you're driven to sell it, let it be for anything else but revenge. That's an awful price to pay for getting even, and it's not only you that'll be paying it, but a lot of innocent wonderful things that you've loved. At least," she added dully, "I thought you loved them."

He turned and pulled her savagely into his arms. "God in heaven, why do you have to—listen, Claire, I never hated Rafe and Cleon until now. Whatever they did or said ran off me like water off a duck's back. Now I want to do something—do *any-thing* short of cutting their throats because I don't want to go to prison. I want to see them with the wind knocked out of 'em from a kick in the—belly."

"I know you do," she gasped. "Only let me breathe!" He loosened his arms a little and she didn't try to get away. She took his chin in her hand and held his head still. "My darling, don't you think I know what revenge is?" It's just that I don't want you to do something you'll regret afterwards. Finn, they can't keep it up forever, they've got to get tired some time. If you can just wait a little while . . . wait—"

He lowered his head over hers. He felt as if they were treading water among steep lustrous swells, lilac-colored like the dusk around them, and that if they stopped struggling they would go down, and he wanted to go down and carry her with him. It would not be death but the kind of drowning every man dreams about and seeks for his whole life.

"Wait, wait," she was saying, but it was not about selling the island. He let her go, not completely. He was dazed and angry. "We've got to talk," she said.

"Some day you'll forget to say that," he threatened her.

"Damn it, Finn, don't you think I *wanted* to let go?"

It made everything right again. He laughed in surprise and triumph, but didn't attempt to overwhelm her. "What did you want to talk about?"

"The island. If your mother trusts your judgment so she's leaving this decision up to you, and she's willing to give up the island anyway, would she put the place in your name? Then you could raise money on it for a new boat, because you'd have property."

She made it sound so simple. He'd been all round creation and half of Brighton, and there she sat with the solution in her hands. If it worked. You couldn't tell about Dolly. He said, "She always said we'd all four share it, or none of us would have it. So I don't know if she'd go for that or not. Of course she's pretty peeved with them right now." He pulled at his lower lip.

"You'll have to ask her straight out."

"*We'll* have to ask her. Come on." He got up and pulled her up beside him. "She's over there now. Probably reading paperbacks in bed. She likes that kind where the heroine's mistress of some king but she falls in love with the poor but gallant captain of the guard, after she's shacked up with about ten other guys in between. Dolly was born in the wrong century."

Claire was laughing. "But I can't go over there and let you pull your mother out of bed!"

"You've got to. It's your idea."

"She won't appreciate that—"

"Come *on*."

Dolly wasn't in bed. She was darning Finn's socks by lamplight and listening to the radio. She was wearing the warm flannel wrapper she kept at the island, and she had taken off her day's makeup; the round dark-rimmed glasses she wore for sewing gave her a prim, sweet grandmotherly look. Finn didn't know whether to be relieved or not. Sooner or later Claire was going to see Dolly in action. Maybe it had better be later. A lot later.

"Hello, dear," said Dolly, suiting her voice to her appearance. "Isn't this nice? I'll push the kettle over and make us some tea." Claire, looking about eighteen in her slacks and jacket, with her rumpled hair and warm cheeks, gave Finn a sidewise glance, as if she were comparing his description of Dolly with the facts and calling him a liar.

"I'm glad to meet you, Mrs. Judson," she said.

"I'm glad to meet *you*, dear. I keep hearing about you. Finn, honey, get out some cups. I made a cake tonight."

Finn felt suddenly like a big stupid lummox in a small room stuffed with women. He didn't know how it happened, but Dolly and Claire, without any words spoken beyond the first ones, were together. It was a hell of a good thing that they were for him and not against him, because otherwise he'd have lost before he could begin.

"We'd better talk before we drink any tea," he said, his voice bouncing off the walls and the lamp flame shivering.

"About what, Finn honey?" Dolly smiled over her glasses at Claire. Claire smiled back. Finn said what was on his mind, not too well, because he was sweating and when he came to the actual words about putting the island in his name, his tongue could hardly get around them. It was an enormous thing he was asking; he couldn't really believe he had come to the point of asking it.

When he had finished, he went out onto the porch and opened the door and stood looking into the dark, thinking he'd never cool off again. Behind him Dolly said in that tender grand-motherly voice, "You think that's a real good idea, Claire?"

"Yes, I do, Mrs. Judson," Claire answered. "Later, when Finn has the mortgage paid up, he could begin to pay you for the island because you shouldn't give up your rights in it for nothing."

"You don't think I ought to give it up to him free and clear?"

"You ought to know your own boy better than that, Mrs. Judson. He doesn't want something for nothing."

"Ayuh, I know him." The old vigor clanged in Dolly's voice. "And I've got a notion I'm getting to know you too. Well, I'll tell you, dear. If it was any other girl but you, I'd have no part of it. But you've got the class and intelligence, and you've got push too. That gentle look don't fool me a bit." She laughed to herself. "Blessed be, what a touse it'll raise in the family! But they deserve it."

Finn swung around and came back into the lamplight. "You going to do it, Ma?"

"You *sweating*?" She peered at him. "Lordie, you're some nervous. Well, I don't blame you. You're just asking for the world, and if it wasn't for her to anchor you, I wouldn't do it."

"I know that, Ma," he said humbly.

"I don't mind admitting I didn't want to see the island go to that man or any other stranger, but something had to be done, the way those boys have been carrying on. They need a shock.

Finn honey, this won't make 'em love you any more. Like I said, if it wasn't for Claire being behind you . . ." Her voice trailed off. She looked absently around the kitchen. "I'll have a little rent up in Limerock, close to the stores and the movies."

Claire looked embarrassed and unhappy. Finn saw her hands curl up into fists at her sides, and he felt a grim pity for her compounded with resentment; he was going to own the island but he couldn't enjoy what should have been almost the happiest moment of his life so far.

"Mrs. Judson," Claire said, "I have to tell you this, but please don't let it change your mind about putting the island in Finn's name. I don't know if I'm going to marry him or not."

"Don't you fret, dear," said Dolly placidly. "You'll marry him. You've loved a man once and you want to love another, and Finn's real determined. All my boys are. Now I'll make us some tea."

They rowed back after a while, with no words between them. At Mag's door he kissed her and she accepted it but didn't kiss him back. He held her for a few moments as if to comfort her as well as himself, fighting back a passion of rage against whatever was bedeviling her.

·32·

A verse from Claire's unfledged adolescence which had seemed to hint at unimaginable and dark delights came back to her now as a piece of cynical advice.

> Ah, take the season and have done,
>   Love well the hour and let it go;
>   Two souls may sleep and wake up one,
>   Or dream they wake and find it so,
> And then—you know.

In the late morning Finn called her from Limerock. "What we talked about last night is all taken care of," he said. She guessed at the emotion behind the colorless words, and thought, If nothing else happens maybe I've been responsible for one good thing at least. "I'm going to stay uptown and run down some leads," he went on. That meant he was looking for a boat.

"Well, good luck to you," she said. "How do you feel?"

"I don't know," he said. "I'll tell you later. I may not be home till late tonight, so I won't be over. Don't look for me till you see me."

When she came away from the phone Mag was watching her. "What was that all about?"

"Oh, Finn's trying to do something about a boat."

"He have to call you up about it?"

Claire couldn't think of an answer; her mind was so full of him that the simple noncommittal phrase had apparently left it forever. "*That* boy's courting," said Mag. "And he ain't being discouraged. I can tell."

I shouldn't have encouraged him, Claire thought miserably, avoiding Mag's expectant eyes. I know. I'm the criminal. And whatever you think, I'm not considering marriage, she wanted to say, but the lie stuck in her throat; she *was* considering it, fearfully and with a sickening astonishment. The desire to marry Finn swept over her like a drowning wave at unexpected moments, leaving her chilled to the spirit with irresolution and the now hideously familiar guilt.

The news about the property came out sooner than Dolly or Finn had expected. Mag found it in a list of realty transfers in the next day's *Patriot*, and screeched like a fish hawk. "Well, I must say his mother gave him a handsome wedding present! Oh, Sweet Beulah Land, won't they holler when they see this!"

Claire went upstairs to avoid conversation. She had promised to go fishing for flounders off Gil's car when the children got home from school; now an appearance at the harbor would be embarrassing, but she couldn't disappoint the children. It was late enough in the afternoon so that the men were all in and the boats back on their moorings; only Finn's anchorage was empty. A couple of boys from the lower harbor came up in their outboard skiff, and they were helpful and kind to the younger ones, whose lines kept getting caught down. This left Claire free to give in to her uneasiness. Even though nobody was around, at least in sight, she felt wretchedly self-conscious and vulnerable.

"Gorry, Nancy, you got a bite!" Elmer shouted, and everyone rallied to her side of the car while Nancy, pale and stiff with ecstasy, hauled in her line. An older boy stunned the flapping flounder while Nancy squeezed up face and shoulders and looked the other way. Everybody went back to fishing with renewed concentration, though Nancy refused to look at the fish in the bucket. Claire wished she knew where Finn was and what he was doing; his car was gone.

As soon as Elmer and Nancy each had two flounder she suggested they leave. She was driven by an instinct to get under cover somewhere, as if she could feel the resentment of Finn's brothers rolling down over the shore toward her in foul clouds. If she could get back to Mag's, or even up to Josie's kitchen, without meeting a Judson, she would consider it a kind of victory, or at least a small triumph to carry her over until the next day.

Larry was just coming out of the store as she and the children reached it. He pretended to steal Nancy's nose, and winked at Claire. Well, the news has made *him* happy, anyway, Claire thought. She went up to the road, glanced around to see why the children were dallying, and when she turned again she came face to face with Cleon and Rafe. "Hello," she said uncertainly. Their eyes looked emptily into hers and neither spoke. She reached behind her for Nancy's hand and started to cross the Curtis lawn. "There goes an interfering bitch," said Cleon.

"Who you referring to, Judson?" Larry's voice crackled. "Not to anybody in sight of us right now, I hope."

"Oh, get out of the way," Cleon growled.

The children dragged back, staring, open-mouthed. Claire put a hand between each pair of shoulder blades and pushed without mercy. "Go *along*," she said.

"What I always say is," said Larry, "there's bitches and bitches. Ask the man who owns one."

There was a scuffle and a shuddering thump. Not wanting too, Claire swung around as if by reflex action. Cleon had flattened

Larry against the wall of the store by a massive hand on Larry's chest. "You damn little squirt, you're walking around here ten feet off the ground because you think Finn'll fight for ye! Well, it'll take more than him to keep me from breaking every bone in your body!"

"I dunno but it'd be worth it, to see you behind bars." Larry was gray with rage, not fear. "You and that other highbinder there!"

Elmer escaped Claire's hand, and charged. "You leave him alone!" he shouted, and began kicking and pounding at Cleon. "I'll help you, Elmer," Nancy cried, but Claire was able to hold onto her. Rafe turned his head from a study of the harbor and looked long and hard at Claire, and she thought his lips moved. Gil appeared in the doorway, scratching his head, and said mildly, "Cleon, you want to manhandle anybody, you do it off my property. You want something in the store? You, Rafe?" Rafe shrugged slightly and followed him inside. Cleon let Larry go, wiped his hand ostentatiously on his pants, and went in.

"Come on home, Nancy," Claire said. "This is all none of our business."

Larry and Elmer caught up with them. Elmer's eyes were blazing, and he pranced around them in a primitive dance of battle and victory while Nancy admired. In his own way Larry was just as exhilarated. "Damned if he was going to talk like that about you or any other decent woman. They're so sick about Finn having something for a change they're foolish."

"Thank you for what you did, Larry," she said, giving him the proper smile for his championship. Josie, who had seen nothing, called to her to come up for a cup of tea, but she made some excuse about work. Nancy wanted to stay and play, so Claire went home alone.

She wasn't sickened by the exchange on the wharf; she didn't feel particularly besmirched. Curiously she almost granted the brothers a right to resent her. She didn't like them, but she could understand that they might see her as a threat. They would have nothing whatever to do with her decision.

Nancy came home with her flounder nicely cleaned, and they had them for supper. She told Mag there'd been a fight on the wharf, and Elmer had stopped it. "An argument about lobster traps, I think it was," Claire said. She waited helplessly for Nancy to ask, "What's a bitch?" But Nancy was too taken up with the charms of the basket Josie and Nell had been fixing for the baby.

Finn called after dark from Roy's. He was jubilant now, and didn't care who overheard. "I've got her! She's still up in Fremont harbor, but she's all mine and a sweetheart. Thirty-two feet—solid as a church, built to take it. She's only two years old, and the engine's practically brand-new."

"When are you going to bring her home?" Claire asked.

"Not till this storm is out of the way. It's off Maryland now. It may go out to sea before it gets here, but I'm not taking any chances on my ground line. She stays right where she is, all snug and cosy, till I can go over it. She's a lot heavier than my old girl."

Receivers were clicking on the line. "Well, Finn, I'm glad you've found something to satisfy you," she said formally.

"When I do bring her down I want you to come with me."

"I'd like that," she said; cool staid words to describe something quite different. My girl, you are in a state, she thought coldly after she had hung up. When Finn's away from you, you use common sense, or try to. Talk to him on the telephone and you become a fool.

She went from one thing to another as she lay in bed that night. She had no mercy on herself. Robert would be proud of my objectivity, she thought cynically. I'm being so objective that I'll probably pack up tomorrow and run, and spend the rest of my life trying not to remember the way a night heron squawks and that deer cough in alarm. . . . She almost lost her objectivity then and had to start all over again.

In the morning a flat sea glittered under the sun like aquamarine ice. There was not a sigh of wind, and everything, even a branch or a bird, shone with piercing clarity. Hollowell, seen over the neck, looked to be a part of the island. "Land's looming awful," Mag said. "We'll have an easterly out of this."

They dragged cartons of old woolen clothes out into the sun and spread them on the grass to air. "Rug rags," Mag gloated. "All God's legions of rug rags. Trouble is I haven't got all God's legions of room in that house in Williston. I suppose I'd ought to share," she said gloomily. "Helen Judson used to make real handsome rugs. She might like some." With the gusto of one greeting old friends she was identifying various garments, their seasons and owners, when Robert Carradine came around the corner of the house.

"*Hu*llo, Claire! *Hu*llo, Mrs. Abbott!" He kissed Claire's cheek. "I won't ask you if you're surprised, because you have that glazed expression. Pure shock. Is this a dirty trick or isn't it?"

She remembered what she had thought the other time he came, and felt a deep pain of suspense. "Is Mother all right?"

"Yes, though of course she doesn't think so. Incidentally, she doesn't know where I am. I started out at five this morning on the spur of the moment. I left word for Mother that I'd gone on impulse to check our distributors in Nashua, Concord, Portland, and so forth. Of course I wasn't lying; I intend to visit them all on the way home."

"She'll never believe you because you don't do things on impulse."

He looked hurt. "Surely at my age I can be allowed a few impulses. Besides, Aunt Dora will convince Mother that this is a better temptation for me to give in to than decamping to South America with the firm's funds."

"Take him in and give him some breakfast," Mag ordered. "He needs feeding. I'll mull over my rags a while longer and see what I can bear to part with."

"I ate somewhere along the road but I could stand something more," Robert said. When he and Claire were in the kitchen he said, "I admit I might not have taken off so recklessly if Aunt Dora hadn't been there. She has the most calming effect on Mother, just by listening to her and clucking in the right places. I argue, and that's bad." He took off his glasses to clean them. Without them he looked much older and more sophisticated. Whenever this happened Claire suspected that Robert had unknown depths. The suspicion always disappeared when he put his glasses on again. "Only two strips of bacon and one egg, dear. Cholesterol is always with us. Is that home-baked bread?"

"It is. Now tell me the truth; is your mother starting to show the improvement you hoped for?"

"I think she would if she'd let herself. But she has great resources of obstinacy, and I think she regards this whole thing as a contest between her and me."

Claire turned angrily from the stove. "Oh, it's a crime and a pity that the two of you are at swords' points like this! You both loved David, so why can't you unite in that? Instead you believe she's cherishing her grief to be cont'ry, as Mag would say, and *she* thinks you're jealous of her very tears—" She stopped herself, blushing with shame. "I'm sorry, I shouldn't have said that."

Robert was undisturbed. "It's all right, she's told me so herself. Maybe she's right. And by the same token I could be right about her. You know that, if you'd dare to let yourself think such uncharitable thoughts about David's mother. Are you burning my bacon?" He smiled, and she shook her head.

"The two of you!" she said again. "You could be so much to each other."

"And you could be free of us," he said without inflection.

"Oh, go and sit down, your egg's ready." She poured coffee for them both.

"To get back to the contest, if you'll accept the premise that it exists," said Robert, "you are the prize. And Mother is determined to come to you in person and beg you to go back with her. If I refuse to drive her, she'll hire someone. That's why I'm here, Claire, to warn you."

She set her cup in the saucer before her weakened hand could drop it. "Oh, *no!*" she moaned. "That's all I need right now, added to everything else."

"What else?"

"Oh, trying to find myself, trying to get back to life, as you told me to do." She thought she had neatly escaped Robert's pounce, but as he continued to watch her, smiling as if in tender amusement, she felt humiliated and confused. Oh, go back to Brookline and be smug there, she thought hatefully.

"You know," Robert began, "when I came around the corner of the house and saw you before you saw me, I noticed how well you looked, but there was something more. A glow, an aura . . . And all at once it hit me as if somebody had shouted at me. *She's in love.*"

"You're too romantic. I'd never have believed it of you."

"Let's not spar," said Robert. "Just tell me the truth. I won't accuse you, as Mother would, of being unfaithful to David."

"No one could ever make any difference between David and me. When I was a kid I used to be horrified when a widow married again. How *could* she! I was positive that you could only love once, and if you met somebody else later, that cancelled out the first. Well, it doesn't. It doesn't even touch the first."

"You've just confirmed my first blinding impression."

She was afire with embarrassment, her eyes stinging. "I shan't admit anything to you. I haven't even admitted anything to myself."

"You look so young when you blush." He leaned across the table and spoke softly and precisely. "I admit your right to fall in love, and to marry whomever you choose. I know you would never consciously harm Nancy. But I have a genuine concern and a sense of responsibility for you that has nothing to do with anybody else. Like it or not, Claire, I became your brother when you married David."

She reached out for his hand. "You make me so ashamed. I ought to be thankful for you instead of acting like a rebellious teen-ager. But Robert, I haven't admitted anything to myself because I don't *know* anything. Finn wants to marry me, but I don't know if what I feel for him is something for him alone —for the unique individual Finn Judson—or if it's loneliness, desire, the pains of coming back to life—" She gave him a difficult smile. "Oh, there's any amount of soul-searching going on around here. On the material side, Finn knows I don't have any money. He *doesn't* know that Nancy has enough for education and a few extras, and he's fully prepared to take her on and do his best for her in every way."

"A remarkable young man."

"You don't know how remarkable. He's younger than I am, and our backgrounds are far apart. But he's sensitive about other people, he has a good mind, and he's a very good person, Robert. I mean *good* in the sense of being sound and upright, and—oh, fitting into his life as if it were a second skin—" She stopped, puzzled by his expression. "What's the matter?"

"The aura is blinding."

Mag came in just then, calling lustily for coffee.

Later Claire walked Robert all over the point. Birds sang from every thicket of alder and bay; the first lilacs were open by the cellar hole, and bees hovered over the waxen bells of the blue-berry blossoms. The sea had the glaze of blue porcelain. "Good Lord, but it's beautiful," Robert exclaimed. "I never saw such light! You can all but taste it."

"Weather-breeder," said Claire professionally. "Robert, why don't you stay overnight?" She felt easier with him now that she had confessed, and grateful because he hadn't offered advice.

"I won't even make a token protest. Do you think I can meet Finn again?"

"He'll be up if he has time before dark. He's using the dory and outboard today, and hauling by hand. It makes a long day, and he has a lot to do when he comes in."

"You sound very knowledgeable about the business. But have you thought about the life of a lobsterman in winter, and what his wife has to endure?"

"You forget I've already learned to endure quite a bit."

"I'm sorry. I did forget. It must be this young new look of yours. It makes you seem hopeful but untried, if you know what I mean."

"That's a perfect description of a new boat taking to the water," she said. "Thanks, Robert, I've been trying to think of the right expression ever since I saw a launching last week. . . . Hopeful but untried. . . . Or should it be 'Untried but hopeful'?"

In the early afternoon a damp east wind began to blow and the distances dulled as if under a thin film of bluish smoke. Claire and Robert went down to the harbor to watch the boats come back from hauling.

Larry and Elmer were at their fishhouse, and she introduced Robert to them. They were friendly and talkative with Robert, answering in detail his questions about setting and tending their halibut trawl, marketing their catch, and so forth. It gave Claire a chance to concentrate all her attention on watching for Finn. He was the last man in; his oilclothes ran water, and the dory was wet inside as well as out because he had come home in the face of an increasing east wind and a bouncing chop. As she watched him and Gil heave a crate of lobsters out of the dory and onto the scales, she thought he moved and spoke as if he were tired. She wondered if he'd come face to face with either Cleon or Rafe since the news broke about the property. They had left the car, and their boats were back on their moorings, their bows pointing to the east. The splash and rush of water along their sides made them look as if they were driving ahead.

Finn left Gil's and brought the dory slowly to the other wharf. "What's this?" he called up. "You fellers starting a new political party? Who'd be the candidate?"

"We're thinking of Robert," said Claire. "He looks so trustworthy and respectable. We'll manage his campaign and then he'll give us all the big-money jobs."

"Then start me off with a sure-fire slogan," said Robert.

" 'To hell with poverty, throw the cat another herring,' " said Finn. They all laughed. "Hi, Robert," Finn said. "Nice to see you." He threw down his wet cotton gloves and reached inside his oil jacket for cigarettes. He looked thinner in the face than he had three days ago. "Well, I've got to get home and bag up before I can call it a day."

"You won't get out to haul tomorrow, chummy," Elmer said dolefully. "I can tell you just what's going to happen. It'll blow like a man, the power will go out, the telephone go out, and Josie'll start having pains. But there'll be a hell of a big hackmatack down across the road somewhere, so I'll end up delivering my own kid. I'm in a cold sweat already."

Larry whacked him on the back. "Oh, Jeez, think of the money you'll save!"

Claire moved apart from the others and sat on a crate by the edge of the wharf above the dory. "Hello," she said.

"Hello yourself." Finn's smile became subtly private. She realized that the others were going up the wharf and wondered whose idea it had been. "What's he doing here?" Finn asked. "Bothering you to go back to Massachusetts?"

"No, he was down this way on business so he stopped in. We're very fond of each other, and I don't have any other family left."

"Oh, sure, I know that," he said reassuringly. "I was just thinking about tonight, that's all."

"Come over anyway."

"No, I'm too tired to make company talk."

"Have you seen the others?"

"Roy doesn't care. He's got other things on his mind. Met Hes uptown yesterday and she gave me a look that should have turned me into a pillar of salt. Raul and Fidel have been giving me a wide berth."

"Are you unhappy about it?"

"Should I be?" He grinned. "Only one thing can make me that way now. See what you're to blame for?" He started up the motor and backed away from the wharf.

·33·

The storm was on them in the morning. The wind had shifted to southeasterly, and hit the roof at an angle that made the attic roar like a giant conch shell. The windows that looked over the point and toward the island were opaque with streaming rain. Nancy hoped there'd be no school so she could entertain Robert, but when the bus came she splashed out to meet it with her usual enthusiasm.

"I haven't felt so snug for years," Robert said. " 'The world forgotten, by the world forgot.' What can I do to help in this moving business?"

They spent the morning in the spare bedrooms, turning out chest and bureau drawers. Mag was tired of sorting the past, and told Claire to save anything she wanted and throw away the rest. "I've spent my life in a clutter and it never did me any good," she told Robert. "The trash anybody hangs onto just because Great-Aunt Sophie did! I tell you, I don't hold out any great hopes for the human race." Downstairs she cooked dinner and blissfully baked the first rhubarb pie of the season. Robert and Claire fingered tarnished jewelry and fabrics that fell apart at a touch; they pieced together the fragments of newspapers used to line drawers and read about the battle of Bull Run.

By noon the wind had shifted more westerly, and by the time dinner was over the sun was shining. Robert and Claire went out into warm strong buffets of wind scented with the odors of bruised earth and churned-up rockweed. "It wasn't much of a storm," Claire said. "But everybody has to get ready in case it's a bad one."

"I wonder if your friend's delivered his own baby yet," said Robert.

"If I know Josie, she took complete charge." They went out on the point and watched the seas run in from open sea past the island and across Saltberry Bay to break at their feet. While they were there, the wind kept shifting until it was north of west, and now the seas broke strong and deep across the bar between the point and the island. The wind freshened again, and whipped the crests off the waves like smoke. The bay glittered and boiled under a brightening sun, and the wind was cold now after the earlier warmth.

"Can we go around by the shore to the harbor?" Robert called to Claire. She nodded and led the way across the tip of the point and down over the banking to the Gut side. The wind still reached them in boisterous shoves, and the low thunder of seas rushing over the bar still filled the air, but there were sudden pockets of silence that made the ears ring.

"You can't really say the storm's over," Robert said. "The sun's out, but it's blowing just as hard this way as it did the other. It could do just as much damage."

"It'll probably flunk out when the tide turns," she said. "It's getting towards high tide, that's why it's so wild. What are you laughing at?"

"You sound so professional. You've really soaked this place in, haven't you?"

"Yes, and I know it can influence me," she said warningly.

"I'm not saying a word," he protested.

The shoreline curved suddenly outward almost opposite Finn's wharf. Nobody was in sight over there, and the dory wasn't on the haul-off. The wind drove at their backs and through their clothes with a dry knifelike cold. Crests raced away from them, up the harbor toward the moorings. A rushing cloud mass darkened the harbor to gunmetal, in which the boats and the smoking

crests shone unnaturally white. Brightness followed, all translucent greens and strong blues, then shadow again, and wind in a
steady pressure on the back of Claire's head, parting her hair and
blowing it past her ears, driving against the length of her spine
as if to throw her face down among the rocks and marsh rosemary.

She and Robert had given up trying to talk. They reached a
place where the dense alder growths ended and they could climb
up over the rocks beside the Abbott fishhouse.

Suddenly they were in a little room hot with strong sunlight
and no wind, walled on two sides with steep lichened ledges and
thick masses of shiny bay, and on the third side by the gray
shingled wall of the fishhouse. Below them on the forth side the
water flashed by the rocks, exploding in diamond bursts over the
goose tongue and marsh rosemary. Overhead gulls played on the
wind, and here in the lee the small birds fluttered and talked in
the alders. Robert cleaned spray off his glasses and Claire tried
to do something with her hair.

"It's magnificent," Robert said, "but exhausting for an effete
type like me. You love it, don't you?"

She sat on a granite seat and hugged her knees. "I do. I'm
primitive, I guess. But maybe it's because when you're out in it
you can't think of anything else."

"You're so at home here," he said, "that I'm beginning to
wonder what kind of fool I was to urge you to come. It's like
throwing a mermaid overboard, isn't it?"

She felt a prickle on her scalp. "What do you mean? So far
you've been very satisfied with the results of your act, haven't
you?"

"I was, until it began to look as if I'd cut my own throat. I
have a very chilly suspicion that it's going to be hard to get you
back to Brookline even without—" He nodded his head at the
island across from them. He did not look amused or affectionate
now. With his glasses in his hand he had again the appearance
of an older, sophisticated, and far more complex personality.
"Hell, for me, will consist of knowing that I did this all by my
clever little self, with my own clever little hatchet."

"Oh Robert, don't!" She tried to sound lovingly exasperated,
which was quite difficult when she was so apprehensive. "Weren't

we having a good time enjoying the storm together? Aren't we blood brothers? Why *this*, all at once?"

"Because it's not all at once. It's been happening. And I don't want to be your blood brother," he said angrily. "In fact I lied when I gave you that pretty little speech about being your brother. And I lied when I made the noble little speech about not begrudging David anything. Because I begrudged him you."

She wished he would put on his glasses again and become dear old Robert once more. But she knew with a stab in her belly that the glasses would never more perform that magic. She said, "I don't know what to say."

"Don't say anything." He lit a cigarette and she saw with distress that his hands were shaking. "Let me say it, and get it over with before it poisons me, which it's begun to do. I urged you to get away from Mother for your own good and hers too, but underneath it was for me. I wanted to get you back into the land of the living because I was so damned sure I'd have a chance with you then. We'd become acquainted all over again as two human beings, not wife and brother tending a sick man they both loved. You'd know me as nobody else has ever done. Nancy already loved me; she'd accept me. It looked perfect. How could I fail?"

She felt parched and sick, and wanted to wet her lips, but she couldn't move her tongue; she sat staring at the stranger and listening to the dry embittered voice. Behind him a yellowthroat kept singing in the bay bushes.

"I stayed away for a month, to give you plenty of breathing space. I could turn off all Mother's tears, reproaches, recriminations—they didn't really matter any more, because I was about to begin my life. So then I came, and saw you looking as I wanted you to look, tanned, healthy, lovely, and laughing into the eyes of—" He broke off as if the bitterness had risen in his throat and choked off his voice. He sat with his elbows on his knees, gazing at the turf between his feet. Furtively she moistened her lips, and swallowed. She wanted to go to him, but she knew she would never again go into Robert's arms and kiss him, and she felt resentful because he had done this to them both. Then she was ashamed of her self-pity. "I'm sorry, Robert," she said.

He behaved as if he hadn't heard her. "A nice boy and that's all, you assured me, so I tried to assure myself. But I think the knowledge was there all along, from that first glimpse. This time when I came back, I had only to mention him and your eyes changed, your mouth changed. All this for *him*." He lifted his head and gave her a sardonic look. "That's when I did the magnificent bit about being a brother. But it hasn't held up, you see. This wind you adore has battered me into a state of absolute truth."

"And now I'm battered by your absolute truth. What can I say, what can I *do?*"

"You can give me every chance, slight as they are," he said bleakly. "You were willing to go back to Brookline if I wanted it. Well, I don't want that, but I want you to wait—"

"I told you I hadn't made up my mind to anything."

"No, but you've never looked upon me as anything else but dear old Robert. You can begin to see me as something different. You can promise me you won't allow this young chap with his romantic background to rush you. You've known him a very short time. Take the whole summer, I'll deal with Mother and keep her away. Just remember that you're responsible for the futures of four people; you, Nancy, me, and Finn. And you and I have much more in common than you and a lobsterman could have."

"I don't intend to dispute you on that," she said, "and I don't intend to be rushed. By either Finn or you." She smiled at him. "I promise to do what you want, Robert. But damn it all," she burst out, "you're the one person in this world I've never had to feel guilty about, and now I do!"

"And you hate me for it." He didn't sound remorseful.

"I couldn't ever hate you. But why did you have to choose *me?* There are plenty of women who would treasure someone like you, if only they could have the chance to know you. Wasn't there ever anyone before me, or—" She stopped short, and leaned far over to pick a strawberry blossom. "Oh, well, never mind."

"You were going to say, did I choose you because David did? And that's why I want you now, because you were David's?" When she looked up he had his glasses on, and his slight mild smile was both familiar and unfamiliar. "I don't know. I shouldn't like to go into that, it might fatally wound my *amour-propre*." He stood up and held out his hand, and after a moment she took it and came to her feet. He held her hand tightly as they stood facing each other. "I have your promise. That's enough for now, it has to be enough. Now let's go along to the store. I need cigarettes."

They went around to the front of the fishhouse. The spruce woods were creaking and groaning up behind the houses and the children were being kept indoors; they rapped on the windows at Claire, who waved back to them. Larry and Elmer stood in their fishhouse doorway watching the boats. Theirs being smaller than the others, they came higher out of water on each leap, as if they had no weight to withstand the long gusts. When they dropped down again they were cruelly pummeled by the waves, and rolled as if in terror until they were forced into new upward lunges.

There was something about the plunging boats that filled Claire with dread. She couldn't put it into words, she knew it was primitive. She wondered where Finn was, and suddenly longed to have him appear within touch saying, "Oh, gorry, this is nothing at all."

He was not in the store, which seemed full of people and voices and cigarette smoke. Gil sat at his desk, and Spicer the boat-builder was sitting on a nail keg beside it; Cleon leaned his folded arms on the showcase and stared out at the wild and brilliant scene. He glanced around and then went on looking out the window. Rafe stood in the middle of the floor with his hands in his pockets. His eyes had a glaze of preoccupation, as if Claire didn't register, and she was glad of that. There were two other men in the store whom she didn't know, and they went on talking with Spicer about something that meant nothing to her.

Gil got up and waited on Robert, who seemed in no hurry to leave after that. He lit a cigarette and began talking with Gil about the wind; Spicer made an observation which Robert answered. Claire stood with her hands in her pockets, uneasily conscious of Cleon and Rafe even though they ignored her.

She looked out at what the brothers were watching. Their moorings began a little distance to the east of Gil's car, Rafe's old boat first, then *Princess*, then Cleon's *Onni J.* The three heavy boats pulled hard at their chains, bows rearing up as if in agonized battle against the drag of the heavily anchored ground line.

Water broke against them and exploded over them. She wondered if the men too felt this deep and wordless dread; if it was, after all, part of the fabric of their life.

All at once Finn came in, and when his brothers saw who it was they went on with their silent watching. He went to Claire, smiling and unself-conscious even with them there, and Robert. "Hi. Did you blow down from Mag's without even touching the ground?"

"Robert and I walked around from the tip of the point, after I nearly blew off it."

"Gorry, I'll have to keep a closer watch on you." It was his open declaration to the world; there were no denials left.

She wanted to be alone with him. "Let's go out," she said. "Robert, I'll be just outside." If he watched her go, she didn't know or care. It was heartless, but he had his promise; she could do no more.

Across the wharf from the store Gil had a small storage shed and they went into it. Finn put his arms around her. "Are you all right? You look kind of anxious around the eyes."

"I'm too worked up by all this wind. Finn, is everything all right in the harbor?"

"Oh, it's a dite wild, but I've seen it wilder."

"Larry and Elmer are worried, I can tell."

"There's always a chance. I've been down to Roy's helping him put an extra line on his boat. But this should flunk out soon, it's almost high water."

They heard someone's shrill voice in torn shreds on the wind, and looked out past the corner of the shed. Nell was out on the lawn, hugging herself against the wind, calling to Larry. The children crowded in the doorway.

"Josie's baby!" Claire exclaimed.

"Huh? No, look!"

She had seen it already, its shadow racing toward them like a tidal bore; a wall of blue-black cloud across the north-west and northern sky, growing blacker and higher as they watched. The day was darkening into an appalling night. *What is it, what is it?* Claire's mind cried, trying to be calm and not panic, but she imagined the school leveled into rubble, like something in a disaster photograph. Finn held her in his arms. "Don't panic," he said. "Hold tight. Come on inside here." But though she had to obey she couldn't drive away her terror, because she saw the awe in him as the shadow advanced coldly over them, and the new wind began; and it occurred to her, in spite of terror, that the world could end like this, in wind and a devouring night rolling over the world and leaving nothing behind.

They heard fragments of cries through the steady roar. Still holding her tightly, Finn put his head out the open door of the shed and looked down the wharf; his exclamation was ripped away from his mouth, and she crowded into the doorway with him. The water was the same blue-black as the sky, the crests nastily white, and the *Princess* was not where she had been before. She was sliding away from her mooring with a horrible speed; in the space it took to realize it, she went down past Cleon's boat. Rafe burst out of the store, his face a peculiar dark color. When he ran down the wharf, it was as if the wind were driving him to destruction at the edge of a cliff.

Claire was alone, because Finn had left her and was running too; Cleon went with an uncanny lightness for someone so heavy. Elmer passed the door of the shed, Larry after him. *Princess* was a long way down the harbor now. The cold gloom lay completely over them, like the shadow of a monstrous wing. The men had all disappeared down the ramp at the end of the wharf. She wanted to know what they were doing, what *Finn* was doing; to have him out of sight in the roaring unnatural twilight was terrifying. She slid out of the shed and the wind caught at her and drove her down the wharf too; Robert called to her from behind, and then caught up with her and grabbed her around the waist. They each hooked an arm around the hoisting mast and hung on.

The boom creaked, and they could feel the mast working like the strong trunk of a tree in the gale. Down below on the car the men struggled with Rafe, and he wrenched himself free, throwing them off like a lunatic and trying again to launch one of the skiffs that had been pulled up on the car. As he grabbed at the bow and shoved, they were on him again. She saw Larry flung backward across the car to crash against the scales. Cleon kept trying to get Rafe's arms, saying, "Now, now, now." Finn finally wrapped him from behind in an embrace like a strait jacket, and Rafe lunged and surged as the boats had done against their chains, yelling something that made no sense.

Princess had swept down past Roy's mooring now; she looked smaller than she really was, gay and foolish and alone. Beyond her the String of Pearls was a long chain of white explosions. As they watched, she reached them. Claire's stomach revolted and she turned her head away.

Rafe had stopped fighting. They walked him up the ramp, crowding around him in case he should make a sudden attempt to throw himself free. Claire hugged the hoisting mast until the wood pressed painfully into her breast. But Rafe didn't know she and Robert were there.

A yellow light shone from under the far edge of the cloud. The black wing was crossing the river now, and the brightness returned as swiftly as the dark had come, and the roar was dying away. Claire and Robert walked up the wharf behind the others and stood in the open door of the store. Rafe sat in a chair, looking straight ahead with shiny eyes and paid no attention to them. There were red blotches as if from blows on his face, and blood running down from one cheekbone.

Larry pushed out past Claire and Robert, and ran toward home, saying something about whiskey. The others stood around Rafe, breathing hard. Cleon touched the blood with a shaky finger. "Jesus, that's from my ring."

"He couldn't a saved her," Elmer kept saying. "The skiff would've turned over before he was halfway to the mooring."

Finn put his hand on Rafe's shoulder. "We didn't want to rough you up, but we had to," he said gently. He leaned over and looked into his brother's face. "You know that, don't you?"

Cleon braced his hands on the back of the chair. "We had to hold you back, Rafe. You all right? Huh, Rafe? Can't you say anything?" His heavy voice shook.

"It's having her just that little while," Finn said to Cleon over Rafe's head as if explaining. "And he felt different about this one."

Cleon wagged his head in agreement. Rafe kept on staring. Suddenly and shockingly he began to cry. His brothers leaned over him, awkwardly patting and muttering. The other men's faces were washed blank in their efforts not to show what they felt. "Let's get out of here," Robert said to Claire. But she stood still, watching Finn, her throat gripped by a fierce pain as if she too wanted to cry, not just for the boat but because of some richly dissolving emotion roused in her by the tenderness in Finn's face and big hands.

"Where's Rafe?" someone bawled from the doorway. They all turned and saw Hester there, her coat flapping like dark wings, staring at them with indignant contempt as if they were all responsible for the big wind. "Where's he gone off too? Does he know what's happened to his boat while he's been standing around here talking foolishness?" They regarded her impassively and she used her voice like a slap. "Didn't any of you see it? Are you all as stupid as you look?"

Nobody spoke, and in a lull in the wind they heard the sound of Rafe's retching sobs. Hester took a few steps into the store and saw him past Finn's arm. Her eyes protruded, and a fiery color swept up her throat. "*Well!*" she said as if confronted by some unimaginable scandal.

"He wanted to go after her, Hes, and we wouldn't let him," Finn said. "It broke him up some."

"Ayuh, I thought he was having a stroke there once," said Cleon. "Like to scared me to death."

Hester drove her hands into her pockets. The way she said Rafe's name cracked like shattering glass, but it made no difference, he didn't look up from where he sat doubled over, his head in his hands. "What a disgusting exhibition for a grown man!" she said to the back of his neck. "Haven't you any pride in front of these people? They'll laugh at you for the rest of your life!"

"Oh, leave him alone!" Claire cried at her. Robert pulled at her arm, murmuring, but she shook him off. "Are you such a fool," she asked Hester, "that you don't know when your man needs help? And if you can't help him for heaven's sake don't stand there kicking him."

Hester's face contorted. Her mouth moved and then the words began to come, but with the first one, choked out of her past life on the other side of the river, Finn straightened up. "Careful, Hes," he said gently. He reached out and moved Claire closer to him. There was a sudden noisy stirring back to life in the store, a throat loudly cleared, feet shifting, a chair moved. Only Rafe was oblivious, silent now, but still hunched over and shutting them all out. Hester laughed airily and looked around, appealing with deprecation to Gil, Robert, Spicer, anyone whose eye she could catch. "Well, really, there's no *need* of this going all to pieces! After all, the boat's insured."

Nobody answered; she shrugged. "Well, if he can't walk after this orgy of self-pity," she said to Cleon, "drive him home. I'm due at a meeting in Williston." She went out. Larry was just coming with the whiskey, he stood aside and then looked after her with bemused awe. "Mebbe she ought to have a shot of this," he said.

"Needs a shot all right," said Elmer. "I won't say where. Well, I'll go up and see if Josie's pulled a fast one on me yet."

Larry shoved the whiskey and a glass at Finn. "Here. I'll go with Elmer."

"Thanks for everything, both you guys," Finn said. He poured some liquor into the glass and leaned over Rafe. "Here's something to fortify you, son."

The telephone rang and the others looked toward the instrument with relief and expectancy. Gil answered, and handed it across the desk to Cleon.

"Of course we know it's been blowing," he said sourly into it. "And we've been having a hell of a time down here. Just look out at the Pearls if you want to see a real nasty sight—" He stopped and began to listen, gazing out at the bright racing waters. His features looked thick and wooden. Finally, without saying anything more, he hung up. Still looking out the window he said, "If you've got something else to do, Finn, I'll stick around and get Rafe home."

"Doesn't Onni want you?"

"*Her?*" His chuckle was as weird as Rafe's weeping had been. "No, she doesn't want me for anything, period. She just let me know she wasn't calling from home, and she won't be home when I get there. And she's not coming home tonight. So I've got nothing to do, see?"

The other men began talking all at once and moving toward the door, still marveling at the freak windstorm in overemphatic voices. Robert looked at Claire in embarrassed appeal, his lips shaping words. *"Shouldn't we—"*

Roy's pick-up stopped by the wharf in a shower of gravel. "Rafe in there?" he shouted.

"Ayuh," somebody answered. "Shook up some."

"Who wouldn't be?" Roy brushed through them and came into the store talking. "Bart and Tom are going out to get her off—" At sight of Rafe he stopped, then went on more quietly. "By God, you *are* all hawsed up, Rafe. I don't blame you. Like to heaved, myself. Hey, got any of that to spare, Finn?"

Cleon turned from the window. "I could do with a snort myself. You see when Onni drove out, Roy?"

"It was quite a while back." Roy saw Claire and nodded.

"She says it's for good, and I can't figure it out. What she want to go and do something like that for? She's had anything a woman could ask. I make a goddam good living, if I do say so." He was pathetic and ponderous, a bear beset by bees.

Claire went out then with Robert, who was obviously relieved. Finn followed them and slid his arm through Claire's. Without conversation they crossed the road and took the path by the Johnson and Curtis places. It was only lightly breezy now, the air dry and bright, the spruces moving against a blue sky; the grass was strewn with fresh green tips whipped from the boughs in the storm. The small children were out again, screaming excitedly at the passing adults.

As if they had been discussing it Finn said wearily, "No, Cleon can't figure out what he's done wrong, and nobody can tell him, not even Onni, because he won't listen. He's left her alone to chase after Rafe or team me around, wouldn't have kids—the idea's always scared him foolish. Nope, you heard him in there; plenty of money, that's all any woman needs to keep her happy. Well, he'll try to get her back and might be he'll make it, but it'll happen again."

"Poor Cleon," Claire said. "Poor Rafe too."

"Ayuh, poor Rafe. Seems like everything he plans goes to pieces. He's so busy scheming he forgets to check his mooring chain, and it gave way with all the strain on it." Finn sounded depressed. "He's been some crazy about that boat, ever since the keel was laid."

"I pity him more for the possession of his wife than for losing his boat," said Robert. "That was a breakdown we saw, and it must have been a long time coming. What will the future of their marriage be, I wonder?"

Nobody answered him. They crossed the rise amid strong scents of bruised bay and juniper steeping in the heat. Claire looked over to the island and to the dark blue cove beyond the neck, and the dull silver churning of the tide that rushed past Hollowell to flood the river. She wanted to stand now and be carried out there by her eyes as strongly as the gulls were carried on their winds, and thus leave the ugly last hour behind. But they kept on walking until they reached the Abbott fish house, where Robert stopped.

"By the way, Claire," he said in a dusty, indifferent tone, "I'm breaking that contract. Or rather releasing the other party."

She looked at him doubtfully, a tightening in her chest. "The one we were discussing before the big wind," he said. "I've decided that the whole project is a waste of time. The result is foreordained, anyhow."

She glanced at Finn but he was back to them, trying to make a lee with his shoulders in which to light a cigarette. "But if the other party understands your position," she said almost pleadingly, "and is willing to give you the benefit of the doubt—"

"What doubt?" He grinned at her, and was for the moment so much the other Robert—or rather the image they all had of him— that she felt the giddy relief one feels in dreams at discovering someone long lost. He took her arm and walked her a little way off from Finn. "You'll never be any more certain than you were back in the store. I used to see your eyes like that when you looked at David. You may think you haven't made up your mind, but you have." She started to speak, but he went on. "Oh, I still want you to take the summer, but you won't have me to consider at the end of it."

"I'll always have you to consider, Robert," she said. Her voice wavered. "You make me almost sorry that—"

"Spoken prettily. I shall cherish it. . . . It wouldn't have worked, you know. Mother would never have accepted it. How could she? It would mean the repudiation of the entire meaning of her life. David's wife married to David's brother? It's almost obscene. Believe me, she'd be happier to see you married to a complete stranger than to me."

"I wouldn't want to stop seeing her, and Nancy must keep on knowing and loving her grandmother, and you."

"Oh, you're not rid of me. And her rage at what she'll certainly call your betrayal will probably put her back in the world again. But I'll keep her off your neck this summer if I have to take her to Europe. Perhaps I shall," he said thoughfully. "I'll get her doctor to prescribe it.... Finn is watching us as if he were at least ninety and had achieved a vast loving kindness toward all humanity."

Claire looked back, and Finn got up from where he'd been sitting on his heels against the fishhouse wall. He grinned at her. She said, "Robert, there's a lot more to be said—"

"Not now." He walked back to Finn, holding out his hand. "Claire's just given me the news," he said. "May I be the first to congratulate you, as they say in books?" The men shook hands, and Finn's mouth quirked at one corner.

"Is this what you'd call a blessing?"

"You might call it that. And now I'm going back to the house and call home. They may have had the big wind, and our elms are always a threat." He left them, walking briskly up the rising curve, and Claire watched until he had gone out of sight past the alders. Then she turned to Finn and he took her into his arms and leaned his cheek on her head. She felt a long deep sigh begin to rise under his ribs.

"Gorry, that business back there was more tiring than hauling two hundred traps by hand," he said. "When are you going to marry me?"

"Not before you go seining, that's for sure. When does the season usually end?"

"Oh, October, somewhere around there."

"October then. I can have Aunt Mag all settled by then. Is it as beautiful on the island in October as it is in May?"

"This year it'll be more so, I promise you. Mag got anything to eat up there?"

She wanted to laugh, with no reason, but she did not. "A rhubarb pie," she said solemnly. "It's out of this world." They began to walk up the road as if they had all time to spare, their fingers interlaced, and all at once she remembered something from long ago. "Tonight I'm going to read Uncle Theo's letters," she said.

"*Whose?*"

But she only smiled mysteriously.